PENGUIN BOOKS

Just Another Missing Person

Just Another Missing Person

GILLIAN McALLISTER

PENGUIN BOOKS

PENGUIN BOOKS

UK | USA | Canada | Ireland | Australia
India | New Zealand | South Africa

Penguin Books is part of the Penguin Random House group of companies
whose addresses can be found at global.penguinrandomhouse.com

First published by Penguin Michael Joseph 2023
Published in Penguin Books 2024

001

Copyright © Gillian McAllister, 2023

The moral right of the author has been asserted

Printed and bound in Great Britain by Clays Ltd, Elcograf S.p.A.

The authorized representative in the EEA is Penguin Random House Ireland,
Morrison Chambers, 32 Nassau Street, Dublin D02 YH68

A CIP catalogue record for this book is available from the British Library

ISBN: 978–1–405–94986–6

www.greenpenguin.co.uk

MIX
Paper | Supporting
responsible forestry
FSC
www.fsc.org   FSC® C018179

Penguin Random House is committed to a
sustainable future for our business, our readers
and our planet. This book is made from Forest
Stewardship Council® certified paper.

For Neil Greenough, because every author needs
a helpful and full-of-ideas (and non-corrupt)
former police officer to help them.

Prologue

Julia knew from the way Genevieve rushed towards her that something was wrong. She burst through the door of the multistorey car park, let it swing behind her, a hasty, chaotic slam that pounded the walls. Julia shouldn't have let her go alone: that was her first thought. She had taken a work call, and Genevieve went to pay for their ticket by herself. And now . . .

'Mum?' Genevieve shouted, crossing quickly towards her. She looked haunted, white under the strip lights, eyeliner smudged. Eyes panicked, her gaze darting back over her shoulder. Dread began to churn in Julia's stomach. She could feel her pulse everywhere: in her hands, her legs, her shoulders; her body's siren call. *Something's wrong. Something's wrong*, thudded her heartbeat.

And then Genevieve indicated with a blood-stained hand behind her. 'You need to come.'

PART I

OLIVIA

First Day Missing

I

Julia

Julia is trying to work out if the man at the table next but one is somebody she has arrested before. He's ordering a caramel cheesecake, out with a wife and two children, and she's pretty sure she once charged him with murder. The lighting is low; she just can't tell.

She is trying not to let her husband and daughter know what she's seen, eyes down on the menu.

'Nando's is cringe these days, isn't it?' Genevieve says. Julia smiles at her arch only child.

'In what way?' Art says, bristling. Art, after Art Garfunkel, her husband. An English teacher, a pedant, a ditherer, the last man still using semicolons in text messages. And, until recently, the love of Julia's life.

The cheesecake arrives at the maybe-murderer's table. Julia watches him as he looks up. He has two phones, both face down on the table in front of him. A dead giveaway of a criminal. She's pretty sure it's him. Something about the brow . . .

'Oh, just – you know. Cheeky Nando's and all that. Like, give it a rest,' Genevieve says. She picks up a menu. She's in a black halter-neck tucked into high-waisted jeans. Large gold hoop earrings. She looks amazing, but she wouldn't care if she didn't. That's Genevieve all over: she does whatever the hell she likes. Sometimes, Julia is pleased to have raised a strong woman like this. Sometimes, less so.

It's seven o'clock in the evening, and Julia can't quite believe that she's here. That nothing came up, that she made it.

'They do nice chicken,' Art says mildly, perhaps slightly wounded: it was his choice of restaurant.

The cheesecake is almost finished. John. Julia thinks he's called John. She glances at him again and slips her phone out. 'John murder Portishead,' she types into Google. She's sure he shouldn't be out yet. It was a stabbing in the town centre, brutal. He got life, and not that long ago.

The Google search is too wide; too much comes up. Just as she's considering typing something else, the phone trills: it's the station.

'DCI Day,' the force incident manager says into Julia's personal mobile – the one she always uses – and that's when Julia's heart begins its predictable descent down her chest. 'High-risk missing person just in,' he says, and it lands fully at her feet.

Julia sighs. No peri-peri chicken, no more banter with Genevieve. Just work. This is the job. This is the job, she repeats to herself. That has become her mantra after twenty years in the police.

After she's taken the details, she stares at the table. A twenty-two-year-old missing woman. No mental health history. Last seen on CCTV yesterday. Housemates phoned it in when she didn't come home. Those are the facts.

But sitting behind the facts is something else, she's sure of it. Something else. Something she can't yet name. A deep detective instinct tells her so. She shivers there in the dim restaurant.

'I've got to go in,' she says, just as her food arrives. Steami...ِ corn on the cob, mashed potato, chicken . . . she looks at it longingly.

As she stands, she glances at the maybe-murderer to their left. 'If you happen to see him leave,' she says in a low voice to Art and Genevieve, 'can you get his reg?'

* *.*

Julia has always been too soft to be a police officer. She is thinking this as she hurries into the station, ready to brief the team, but stopping to stare at an old informant of hers, Price, who Julia has always been too fond of. He is sitting on one of the benches, his features arranged in a surprised expression, paused as if someone's stopped the universe for just a second.

She is about to ask him what he's doing here. She can't help it; it's shot through her, no matter how many other tasks she has on. Cut Julia, and she bleeds curiosity for those she cares about, which is everyone.

Price has his legs crossed at the ankles, an arm slung across the backs of the metal chairs, ostensibly at home here, but Julia knows he will be afraid. Of course he is: he trades on information – the most dangerous of commodities.

He has auburn hair that he gels so thickly it darkens the red to inconspicuous brown. Freckles. Skin that burns and blushes easily. He's Scottish, originally from Glasgow, never lost the accent, despite moving down here twenty years ago, when he was seventeen.

'What're you in for?' she asks him, standing opposite him in the empty foyer. It smells of industrial cleaning wax and the stale dinners they serve the accused; many contain meat that somehow doesn't need to be refrigerated and has a use-by date of several years' time.

Most of the lights have popped off. Julia finds the station during these down times impossibly romantic, like it's an out-of-hours museum only she has access to, a still from a movie that she may wander around, just her.

'This and that,' he says. He's smart, Price, strategic; he won't be telling her for a reason.

'Meaning?' she asks. Price is hardly ever interviewed: he informs only to her. Quick, slippery, and funny, too, but never under arrest. Almost all of Julia's dealings with him have been in the outside world.

The custody sergeant arrives with a single cup of station coffee. Julia flicks her gaze to it. 'Just made one for you, then?' she says. The sergeant ignores her.

She looks back at Price, then sighs again as she walks towards the back office, stopping at the kitchen. She makes a tea, three sugars, loads of milk, partially to cool it down to make it less of a risk – steaming-hot tea is not allowed in custody, because it is a weapon. The cup warms her fingers. She's tempted to down it, has had one drink all day, in Nando's, but she doesn't. She has too much to do. She has to find out what's going on with Price. She wants to follow up on the murderer in the restaurant. And then, the main thing: it looks like she has to find a missing woman.

Price's hand is already extended out to her as she arrives back with it. 'Ohhh, miss,' he says to her, delighted. He sips it. 'The sugars as well. I owe you a tip. What's ten per cent of nothing?' He barks a laugh out. He's acerbic, but one thing is for sure: if their roles were reversed, he, too, would get her tea.

She smiles and avoids the gaze of the custody sergeant.

Better to be judged by a colleague for over-familiarity than to lie awake tonight thinking about Price and whether he's had a hot drink yet that day, that week. There is nothing Julia does better than obsess in the middle of the night. And, in fact, in the middle of the day, too.

'Good luck, okay?' she says to him. He raises the cup to her in a silent toast.

As she gets back to her office, before briefing the team, she checks on the murderer's file. It was John, John Gibbons. She gets a security guard to verify that he's still inside, HMP Bristol. It must have been somebody else. Julia cups her face in her hands, two jobs down, one to go, at pushing eight o'clock at night, and thinks about working in a supermarket. But, the thing is, she wouldn't love anything else. Not like she loves this. And nobody can have a balanced relationship with something they love.

* * *

Julia sticks the Polaroid photograph of Olivia on to the whiteboard in the briefing room. It's a tired, old room: suspended ceilings, awful carpets. For some reason, their cleaners don't tidy it as often as the rest of the offices, and it houses preserved, old coffee cups, the smell of Portishead's ever-present damp, and the paperwork scraps of old investigations.

The 1970s vertical blinds have shut out the night sky and, as Julia looks at them, she wonders if she has seen more evenings here than anywhere else. It isn't a warm Nando's with her kid, but, funnily enough, it is something almost more potent: to Julia, it is home. She removes her shoes as if acknowledging this, and leans into the investigation, into

11

who she has to become, at least for a while. A detective for whom everything else comes second.

The rest of the team files in, looking tired. Some won't have left yet. Some will have been recalled from dinners, date nights, parents' evenings. There isn't a designated Major Incident Team in Portishead. It was hastily assembled once the case was deemed high risk, detectives and analysts from other teams called in, and Julia hopes it contains some good people. She likes who she likes. She can't help it.

She stares up at Olivia's photograph. She is willowy and blonde, but with a strength around the nose that elevates her to striking. Julia reaches out to straighten the Polaroid. The Blu Tack it's been stuck up with is useless, old and dry; that's police budgets for you. It's her passport photo: her Instagram was too arty, heart-shaped sunglasses and peeking out from behind ice creams. She has a huge smile, crooked teeth. Perfect imperfection, that luminous quality that the young have.

Julia looks into her eyes and thinks that nobody is truly missing, not to themselves. Only to those left behind.

She may not know what Olivia's fate is, but she already knows her own: insomnia. Discussing the confidential details too much at home. Genevieve – already far too much like Julia – will start to fixate. Art will feel pushed out, though will never say so.

Two analysts are discussing a man who was arrested last night. 'It was ornamental Buddhas,' David is saying to Brian. 'Buddhas –'

'When Forensics examined them, it became *very* clear that he was putting them up his –'

'All right,' Julia says, biting back a grin. She knows *all* about that case. 'Enough Buddhas and –'

'Please say we've got a good, interesting one?' Jonathan, Julia's favourite detective, asks her. They have worked together for fifteen years. He started life as her analyst, then qualified into the force. Even when he was far more junior to her, in charge of telecoms reporting, Julia would eat her sandwiches at lunchtimes with him on the wall outside, glad to have found someone like her: a details person, somebody who always, always, always took the work home with them, emotionally or physically. After he qualified, she managed to keep him in the Major Crime Unit by calling in a favour.

Julia makes an equivocal sort of face, not answering yet. 'I'll take that as a yes,' Jonathan says. He is as dogged as Julia herself, seems able to magic up information in seconds, no doubt from his history as an analyst. His strategy is only that he asks and asks: phone companies, airlines, anyone. He simply repeats his request, then calls up again and again. His catchphrase is 'I don't mind holding.' He does much of his typing with a phone held in the crook of his shoulder, call-centre muzak softly detectable.

It's freezing in the briefing room, carpet tiles cold against her feet in their tights. It's late April, but still frigid, as bad as January. Nathan Best, her second-favourite Detective Sergeant, catches her looking out. 'Going to snow tomorrow,' he says. 'Fucking joke.'

'Snow is a great preservative,' Jonathan shoots at him.

'Let's not talk preservatives,' Julia exclaims. 'Let's talk finding living people.'

'Is this one similar to last year's? I can't do that again, honestly,' Jonathan says. She appreciates his honesty: she feels the same. A woman called Sadie went missing last spring, walking home, also seen on CCTV. The only hopeful element was that she'd taken her passport with her – though it had never been used at an airport. The investigation went on for months, with a sighting halfway through that amounted to nothing but upset everybody. They redoubled their efforts, searching wider and wider areas, ordering vast back catalogues of telecoms intelligence, arresting and questioning several known sexual deviants in the area, following less and less likely leads. Only recently, they talked about a re-enactment, but they knew so little, there seemed no point. Reconstructions only work when the general public can recall esoteric details about a disappearance.

Jonathan gestures with his hand so carelessly he slops tea on the carpet. That stain will probably be there for ever. This is life in the police. No high-speed car chases, no undercover assignments. Only a vague and constant feeling of spinning-plates pressure, stale office surroundings and, somewhere beyond that, a place hard to see, but nevertheless magical: life and death. And – beyond *that* – the trauma of it. Sadie was never seen again, despite Julia's very best efforts, which resulted not only in the missing woman's family accusing the police of laziness but in Julia's husband accusing her of marital neglect.

She remembers the day after they withdrew on the case so vividly. None of them could accept it. By the end, they were going over things they'd already looked at twice before. Just desperate. The day they withdrew, Julia went straight home and lay on their bed in the middle of the day, looking up through the skylight above it. She'd missed Art's birthday. The car needed its MOT. She hadn't attended four monthly book clubs in a row. The other members aren't police, and so don't understand. And all she could think of was that woman, and her invisible, grisly, assumed ending, and how Julia had failed her.

DS Poole enters the room. 'Sorry,' he says. 'I just bailed a dealer for this, so it had better be good.'

Something in Julia relaxes as she thinks of Price, going on his way, free tea and all. That guy somehow always lands on his feet. He'll be recalled, but he'll get out of it.

She grabs a red marker pen and draws an arrow across the whiteboard. It squeaks as she does so, and the room falls as quiet as if she has clinked a glass.

She begins to speak. 'Here's what we know. Olivia Johnson is twenty-two. Nickname Little O. She works in marketing. April twenty-seventh, she signs the lease for a house share. April twenty-eighth, the day before yesterday, she moves into that house in central Portishead.' She glances at Best, who looks concerned, and then at Jonathan, who looks up for a challenge.

'She spends that night in her room, unpacks a bit, then leaves the next morning for a job interview in Bristol City Centre at a marketing firm called Reflections. We don't know where she worked before yet, but according to her emails to her new landlord she moved from Walton Bay. She sends a text to her housemates, late that night, saying, please come. Signed with a kiss. No location sent along with it. Earlier that night, she was seen on CCTV on Portishead High Street. We've got the footage. This morning, the housemates reported her missing. It's taken a while to work its way to us, and meantime the father, who's been interviewed on the phone, has been helpful.'

The text to the housemates is what troubles Julia the most. *Please come x.* That text is a specifically female call to arms, sent with only one intention, Julia thinks: to be rescued. There are things you don't just know because you're police: you know them because you're a woman.

15

They go over what Julia knows. Olivia's friends, associates, regularly frequented locations according to her Instagram, and then Julia begins handing out tasks, thinking how interested Genevieve would be in this. 'What I wouldn't give to attend a briefing,' she'd said recently to her. Previously ambivalent, Genevieve is now positively obsessed with what she calls *true crime* and what Julia calls her job.

'Not on your life,' Julia had replied. Genevieve's intensifying interest in the police concerns Julia, given everything, but that's a conversation for another day.

Poole interrupts her before she can really start. 'Why is she high risk?' he asks. Julia isn't surprised: he's a contrary type, the sort of person who would argue against his own existence in the right circumstances. 'Just to play devil's advocate,' he adds, as if to demonstrate everything Julia is thinking. Christ. Is it not one of life's truisms that anybody who feels the need to play devil's advocate is seriously in need of a stiff gin and a shag? Get a life, she thinks caustically.

'No past mental health problems that we know of, an attractive woman presumably alone at night, a text sent to housemates asking them to come to her. Probably worth looking into, isn't it?' Julia says, instead of saying what she really thinks, her tone nevertheless sharp.

'All right,' he says, holding his hands up, brushing one over his bald head. 'No need to go all Julia on me.'

She talks over him, giving orders for CCTV and phone-records collection, interviewing the parents formally, questioning the housemates, fingertip searches. Her strategy, always, is to throw as much time – and budget – at a missing person's case as she can, early on. Julia abides by the golden-hour principles: get the immediate response right, and the rest follows. She doesn't understand why anyone would work differently. Information, to Julia, is crucial, and they need it in abundance. Eventually, it will tell them if Olivia is hiding, abducted or dead: there is no other outcome.

Julia walks eagerly back to her office to begin her own set of tasks, shoeless, semi-content, but thinking guiltily of Genevieve and Art at Nando's. Genevieve is only a few years younger than Olivia. It could easily have been her.

* * *

Julia likes her team to report to her one on one, and she likes to physically look at the things they show her, too. It creates much more work than a DCI should ever have, but she can't help it. You can't get a feel from an email, a dry CCTV report.

Jonathan is sitting in her office, looking implacably out of the blinds Julia paid to have fitted last year. She knows this is not normal behaviour, but the authorities didn't stop her, and now she has white wooden slatted blinds that she can close and shut out the world, or open up fully and let the sunlight in. The entire right-hand wall is windows and beautiful blinds just like at home. The rest of her office is a neat square, a corner desk, full of items she bought with her own money: a lamp from Next, an Apple Mac because she prefers them. In other words, it's a room in her house, transplanted to the office.

It's a couple of hours later, just after ten at night. Julia has been coordinating an ever-growing team of searchers, analysts and Forensics. She's pleased to see Jonathan, who has taken his large, black-framed glasses off and is rubbing at his eyes. His wedding ring hits the desk as he reaches to put them back on.

His wife had a baby only a few months ago. Julia had

to force him to take leave. He'd returned to work a week early regardless, his eyes bright, alive with the joys of his life having changed in an instant. He loves the baby, but he is addicted to the job. Julia was the same. The warm sugarloaf of a newborn not quite enough to kill her passion for this: solving things, piecing them together, helping people, and inching ever closer to that most elusive of things: the truth.

She sits cross-legged in her chair. 'All right, tell me what you know,' she says.

'Settle in,' he says. 'I'm afraid she is a quintessential member of the iGeneration.'

'I-what?'

'Vast internet presence. She's a Gen Z-er, but I'm sure she would say: don't put a label on a whole generation, guys, that's so not cohesive.'

'I suddenly feel very, very old,' Julia says drily.

'Allow me to start with Instagram,' Jonathan says. He's sitting on Julia's spare chair, which is designated for exactly this, nicknamed The Interrogation Chair. He brings up Olivia's Instagram grid on the computer and they look at it together. Jonathan also likes to show rather than tell, though that is because – as he once told her – he doesn't actually like talking to people very much.

The Instagram grid comprises selfies, flowers, stacks of books. Witty captions. 'Can you print them all for me?' Julia asks. 'Go through them anyway, but can I have them? And anything else, her emails, tweets, whatever.'

'Already done it in anticipation, my friend,' he says, lifting the file up to show a set of printouts underneath it. 'Though we have got to get you digital.'

Julia smiles a half-smile. 'No, no, no.' There is something authentic, to Julia, about leafing through the pages in bed.

Something tangible, as though any secrets hiding between each sheet will be released into the night air.

'Sure. So. Right. This last photo – clearly taken in the Portishead Starbucks, yesterday, yeah? See the distinctive branded window? She used a VSCO filter.' Jonathan is a middle-aged detective who specializes in the detailed machinations of the way the youth live their lives online. He knows about everything: TikTok trends, incels, Tumblr suicide pacts. And he has the best instincts of any detective Julia knows.

'Right.'

He zooms in on it. The photograph is of a distinctive lemon-yellow coat folded on to a stool, a laptop open in the window and a coffee. Caption: Pretending it's summer.

'We have CCTV of a woman in a coat like this,' he says, 'just a few hundred metres from that Starbucks.'

Julia swallows some emotion or other that she refuses to name. Since last spring, CCTV will forever remind her of Genevieve. More specifically, of what Genevieve did.

'They've got this, from outside the hairdresser's. Yellow coat, right? Woman walks up the street.'

It's grainy footage from up above, but it is in colour, and it is – to Julia, anyway – clearly Olivia. The same distinctively fair hair, a natural blonde, no roots. And the same coat from the photograph. She pauses it, zooms in. Did she know, then, that these would be her final moments in the before?

'Agreed. That's Olivia,' Julia says.

'Right. Eight thirty last night. Okay? Here's the weird bit.' Jonathan presses play again. Olivia turns right off the high street, and up an alleyway. He leaves the tape running for five minutes, people coming and going, late-night shoppers, the dribs and drabs of commuters, a handful of evening drinkers. As he often does, he allows his evidence to speak for itself.

'Okay?' Julia says.

He opens Google Maps on his phone. 'Here is that alley,' he says. 'Blindman's Lane, it's appropriately called.'

Jonathan angles Street View up to the alley. As Julia's looking, a text from his wife comes up, a photograph icon, and the message: *Bedtime, AGAIN*, she presumes regarding their baby.

'It's blocked up,' he says, flicking the notification away. 'Dead end. Look.' Sure enough, the alley ends in a brick block of flats, covering the entire thing. No doors, no accessible windows. Nothing.

'She doesn't come out. I have watched five hours of footage, sped up,' Jonathan continues.

'Is it still blocked up? Is Google Maps up to date?'

'Four uniformed officers have confirmed it. And I went myself – it's only' – he jerks his thumb – 'down there.'

'No ladder? No fire door? A shaft down to a basement?' Julia says, zooming in on Google.

'No, no, no,' Jonathan says. He closes Google Maps and opens the text from his wife. It is indeed a photograph of her and their baby, maybe four months old now.

'Seriously cute,' she remarks.

'He's got us wrapped around his little finger. Bedtime means nothing to him.'

'Well,' Julia smiles, thinking of Genevieve. 'He'll be sleeping until noon in fifteen, sixteen years.'

Jonathan's smiling eyes meet hers. 'We've bought something called a SNOO; it says it'll rock him instead of us.'

'Yeah, sure. Good luck with that,' Julia says. 'I need to look at this alleyway, too,' she says to him. 'Don't I?' He gestures economically to the door, like, be my guest, but then comes with her: he's nothing if not a gentleman.

It's a quarter of a mile down the road to the alleyway. As they leave, the station fire alarm triggers, as it does near constantly, and never gets fixed. They ignore it and walk there quickly, Julia's mind fizzing. 'Never once does the inner monologue stop,' Art, her husband – is he still, technically? – once said to her, a sentence that for some reason she has remembered for all of these years since.

It's freezing out, the air dry-ice cold, the streets quiet. Portishead's nightlife hasn't yet recovered from the pandemic, or perhaps nobody's has. The silent street ahead is frosted, the pavement tactile underfoot.

'I think it's going to be a big one,' Jonathan remarks. 'Lots of resources needed. Her social media is plentiful. Daily posts for over a year. And not a sniff of any reason to disappear.'

Julia asks him, 'What sort of person is she?'

'Hmm,' he says, and Julia waits. Jonathan is good at character. 'Opinionated. Lefty. Kind of – vivacious, her captions are all really sort of . . . voicy.'

Julia nods. She likes Olivia already.

The alley is obvious: sealed off with police tape, two PCSOs manning it. Everything's a crime scene until proved otherwise, but Julia's surprised they could get two: Portishead is small, underfunded like everything, ill equipped, each big case requiring a team cobbled together from Bristol, Avon and Somerset.

She stands and looks at the alleyway. The PCSOs acknowledge her with raised eyebrows, but nothing more. They will not be surprised by her sudden appearance here. None of the force would be, nor that Jonathan has come with her. Julia is picky about who she works with, apparently, though shouldn't everyone be?

To the left is a hairdresser's. Old stone stained with years of water damage. On the right is a pub, red brick, newish, but still probably four decades old. And in the middle, the alleyway.

It is a complete dead end. The back is bricked right up to the fourth or fifth storey. Julia comes back out and walks a slow circle around. 'The flats have no way of accessing that alley,' Jonathan says, as they fall into step beside each other. Julia isn't surprised that he, too, has done this exact walk. Some people want to know why things are the way they are, and some people don't. Luckily, Jonathan is the former.

He indicates the newbuild set of flats. They've been erected on to the back of both the hairdresser's and the pub, spanning the entire back of the alleyway. 'There is no way they're recent, is there?' she asks.

'What, like, finished yesterday?' Jonathan says with a laugh. 'Right.'

He doesn't need to answer her rhetorical question, and so he doesn't. They walk back around to the alleyway entrance. Julia's phone trills with a text from her brother. Open-hearted, always fun, a perennial child, Julia can't believe he's a lawyer. He moved from criminal defence into civil a few years ago, thankfully before they ever came up against each other. 'I can't tell you how happy I am – watching *Saved by the Bell* while drafting a particulars of claim,' he has sent. Julia smiles and pockets it.

She puts on protective clothing. By the book, by the book, by the book. It's another of her mantras. Somebody guilty will never walk free because of an error on Julia's part. And neither will somebody innocent be convicted, either.

She enters the alleyway, stooping under the police tape, and runs a gloved hand across the back wall, over the seam where the buildings meet. It's faultless. Not a single way in.

The first window of the flats is at least twenty feet in the air. Julia looks around it, her mind spinning.

There's nothing. No marks where a ladder would have been. No manhole covers. No drains. Nothing. Olivia wasn't carrying anything. According to Jonathan, no vehicle entered or left.

The only items in the alley are two industrial blue bins. Julia remembers a case on the news, years ago, where the Scottish police didn't check them in a case not unlike this one, with catastrophic results. They contained an unconscious drunken lad, who was taken to a landfill. Discovered two days too late.

'The bins been emptied?' she calls to the PCSOs.

'Nobody has been let in or out since we found the CCTV,' one of them, Ed, replies. He's young, barely twenty, is gym-obsessed, drinks tea with protein powder in it, which Julia finds incredibly endearing.

'Good. Don't,' she says. 'Nobody comes in or out.'

'Obviously,' he says, flexing a muscle at her.

'No messing with the bins, either,' she says. 'Not even to shoulder press.'

Ed guffaws.

She tugs at one of the bins with a gloved hand. It moves easily. She opens both lids, then stares in. Nothing. One pristine, looks never used, doesn't smell of cleaning fluid. The other has a single can of Carling in it, but the stain that's dribbled out of it is ancient, a dark brown fuzz.

She adds to her mental list fingertip searchers and forensics on the bins. This skill is now a living, breathing thing. The way tasks leap up the priority list. A mystical but methodical sort of sifting, the larger items naturally rising to the surface, the finer grains falling to the bottom. The list reorganizes itself overnight, in the shower, when she should be listening to her husband. She gets it right most times. But not enough.

She casts a gaze across the ground. Old chewing gum. A couple of bits of gravel. Nothing else. She's looking for blood. A weapon. Signs of a struggle. But there's nothing.

'Right,' she says to herself, taking another look before she leaves. She's freezing. There's so much to do, and none of it here.

Jonathan must have heard her, because he appears at the entrance, says, 'Incredibly odd, right?'

'Completely,' Julia says, bewildered. 'I can't think of a single credible explanation.'

'Rope out of the window?' he suggests, and this is why Julia likes working with Jonathan.

She pokes her head back into the alley, looking at the walls, looking for scuff marks, tiny holes, anything. But there's only clear bricks, mortar. Nothing else.

'I need every single bit of CCTV on this alleyway,' she says.

'Yeah,' he says slowly. 'Yeah. I'll send it. But I have watched it. I promise, she doesn't come back out.'

* * *

It's after eleven, and Julia leaves the station with gritty eyes that have watched four videos at a time on her monitor, followed by another four. She has covered every single camera, and every single minute. She has barely blinked, doubling up on Jonathan's work.

It can't be true, but it is: Olivia goes into the alleyway and doesn't come back out. Nobody else walks in there. The bins do not go in or out. At two o'clock in the morning, a fox enters then exits. And that's it. No cars, no people. Nothing. She's called the pub and clarified that the bins aren't used. She'll check with the hairdresser's in the morning. 'Why are they there, then?' Julia asked, and the pub manager couldn't give a satisfactory answer. Those bins are on Julia's list, somewhere in the middle, troubling her like a couple of nuisance summer flies. Think, she implores herself. Think outside of the box.

She is now walking to her ancient car, parked half a mile away, despite a reserved space in the station. Local criminals have been videoing which police cars go in and out, uploading them to YouTube, God knows why, but Julia has no interest in appearing in one.

She rubs at her forehead. Leaving Nando's feels a hundred years ago. Perhaps Art was right about her work–life balance. A pedant, a person who reads literary fiction on the toilet – Art is indeed often right, but that doesn't mean it doesn't hurt.

Out of guilt, Julia checks Genevieve's last seen. Two minutes ago. 'You up?' she texts.

Genevieve calls immediately, just as Julia wanted her to. 'Always,' she says.

'Same,' Julia says with a smile. How amazing that Genevieve, her posing toddler, once a fan of wearing sunglasses and a volatile expression, is now an adult she can call up for a late-night chat. A fellow insomniac. Julia closes her eyes. She doesn't regret doing what she did for her.

'How are the criminals?' Genevieve asks, as she often does. 'I got that reg. You want it?'

'You're a star,' Julia says, noting it down, knowing she probably won't use it. 'The missing person isn't much older than you, actually,' she adds.

'I'm guessing Nando's is off for the foreseeable?' Genevieve asks, and Julia considers her question. The thing with her daughter is that she doesn't say how she feels. You have to mine for it, excavate it, come up with theories by yourself based on remarks she makes. Even more so recently.

'Sorry – but yes,' Julia says. As her daughter's voice choruses down the phone to her, Julia thinks: it's okay. She's okay. 'Did you get me a doggy bag?'

'We ate it all,' Genevieve says, not even sheepishly. 'I'm doing mad cramming,' she adds. Underneath the snark, Genevieve is one of life's conformists, happy to work hard and buy into the system. And, underneath that, well, who knows?

Julia's breath makes cirrus clouds in the cold April air as she walks. She cuts through a park, the iron gate singing behind her, the sky a dark blackberry beyond. There's nobody around, except her; except them.

Art confessed to her the Christmas just gone. She should've seen it coming. She had hardly seen him all summer and autumn.

It was one of those milky-light mornings. The weather mild, rainy, intermittently sunny. Their street completely silent. The air full of the hum of nostalgia, of things only done once a year: cooking turkeys, East 17's 'Stay Another Day' playing, dusty decorations out that they'd had for twenty years. Genevieve unwrapping gifts, Julia peeling sprouts into a colander on the sofa even though it was ten in the morning. Julia remembers Genevieve saying, 'Not Mariah Carey, no,' to Alexa, right before Art got to his feet and walked into the kitchen. He did it so quickly, so without ceremony, in the middle of the present-opening, that Julia followed him in surprise.

He was looking at her as she walked in. 'I slept with someone,' he said. 'Else,' he added, because even in trauma he is a grammatical pedant. Four words. Five. The worst of Julia's life. The tips of his fingers blanched white where he leaned on them on the counter.

She'd done what she thought her past – and future – selves would have wanted, even though it had felt like she was in an alternate universe, without a brain, or any emotions at all. She'd asked him not to speak to her any more. And, really, since, they truly haven't. They're in a hinterland of a marriage. Julia hasn't asked him to leave. She is suspended in animation. They sleep either side of a thin wall, separate bedrooms, though each can hear the other.

Genevieve guessed it after a week. 'Well, *something's* happened,' she said, in that teenage way. They had no choice but to explain, and Genevieve turned to Julia and said, 'Can't people make mistakes?' and, Jesus, teenagers can be cutting, but Julia hadn't been braced for that. She felt like she wanted to put on a bulletproof vest. Of course, it was clearly about Genevieve's own mistake earlier that year, and Julia had wanted suddenly to just trade in that whole past year for something better.

'Where are you?' Genevieve asks now. 'Nearly home? I can make hot chocolates . . .'

'Almost at the car,' she says.

'Is it a bad one?' Genevieve asks. 'The misper?'

'Very.'

'Oh – how so?'

'Disappeared into an alleyway – only it's blocked up. No escape. Riddle me that,' Julia says, admonishing herself for sharing too much with a daughter who is already too interested, but unable to stop herself.

'Wow,' Genevieve says. 'That's so weird. You need the Tik-Tok detectives on the case.'

Julia has to laugh. 'Maybe I actually do.'

'What's that saying? You can't hide one body, but you can hide a body in a hundred pieces?'

'Jesus, Genevieve,' Julia says. Genevieve previously seemed to find Julia's career both mundane and frustrating, had the impression Julia spent her days missing family dinners in order to arrest petty criminals. But now look. She's coming up with disposal methods. The thought unsettles Julia.

'Right – home in ten. Love you.' She hangs up. It isn't even a ten-minute drive to home, new home, anyway. After everything with Art, they moved, even though it felt like the wrong thing to do, to uproot together, still as a family, while she and Art continued to sleep in separate bedrooms and ruminate (Julia can only speak for herself here). But she'd seen a house that they had been looking for for years. And Art came with them because neither of them could think of a better decision at the time.

But now they have the most coveted of things, even if it came at a price: a new semi-detached house overlooking Sugar Loaf Beach at Portishead. During winter storms, the sand glasses the windows and blows in the cracks. Julia finds it everywhere. It is unimaginably lovely.

She emerges from the park. It's surrounded by iron railings that blend into the dark air like the tops of mountains in mist, their sharp knife points almost completely invisible.

Footsteps.

Julia doesn't react, has trained herself not to. She reminds herself of the power the police hold. To arrest, to flash a badge. Julia should feel untouchable.

She keeps her pace measured, allows her phone to glow. If they want to mug her, let them, make the target bright and obvious.

She looks casually over her shoulder. It's a man in a hoody. A kid, really, maybe sixteen, seventeen. She hopes she has never arrested him.

Everything about his body language says that he has a problem with the world. Arms criss-crossing in front of and behind his body as he walks. Hood pulled down, pace slow, like he has all the time in the world. Julia has met many men like him. Has arrested them, pressed them for information. Has taken victim impact statements from them, too. Has met their parents, their children. He could easily be an enemy of hers.

She takes a quick left, just to see what he does. He smiles a half-smile, then walks on past her. Julia watches him go. He looks back just once. She hopes he has a home to go to with somebody who cares.

She reaches for her car keys, and only unlocks the door when she's as close to it as can be. She lets a sigh out as she gets in. It smells of Genevieve's McDonald's.

The fabric of the seat is cold against Julia's skin. She allows her heartbeat to slow, thinking of Olivia and where she could be. That distinctively female fear she must've felt, that text to her housemates. Is that what Julia would send, if she were in real trouble?

She starts the engine, turns her lights on, then the heat up. Her phone vibrates in the cup holder, but she ignores it. She knows it will be Genevieve, having thought of some suggestion or other.

As soon as her phone stops, she feels it. A presence. Or, rather, a lack of absence. A notion that she isn't alone.

She tells herself she always gets like this when working on missing persons cases, that it is because a young, attractive woman has disappeared, that it's because it's late, unseasonably cold, it's because Art both is and isn't at home waiting for her.

But then the back of her neck shivers with something more than just anxiety: instead, a deep, limbic part of her brain fires up a warning flare into the night. There is someone in the car. She counts to three, then raises her eyes to the rear-view mirror.

In the back is a man wearing a balaclava. He says only one word: 'Drive.'

2

Lewis

I don't know it yet, but I am about to get the call to say that you are missing.

I am in the back room alone, at work, quite bored, and so very seriously accepting an Oscar, this time for my role in a breakout film whose title I haven't yet decided. This will pass the forty-five minutes until my morning coffee. 'The person I'd like to thank the most,' I am saying as I seal up passport renewals into their designated envelopes, 'is my past self.' Hmm. Would even Hollywood think that was perhaps a step too far?

You used to find this hilarious, would join in sometimes if you overheard me. As I prattle on about the incredible special effects team who, really, made all this possible, I start thinking about how much you hated working here with me at the passport office. But I loved us being together: you were the jaded work playmate I had been searching for. You – twenty-one, just graduated, looking for better – couldn't believe this was how your father spent his days. I still remember you looked at me, blonde hair everywhere, a doughnut raised to your lips, and said, 'This is the highlight of my day, and it's not even a good fucking doughnut.'

We'd go home together and bore Mum with talk of our dysfunctional colleagues and their petty moves: name-tagging their staplers, and so on. We messed up a run of passports so badly we couldn't confess, took them home and hid them under the spare bed, both of us living in fear for several weeks that we'd get found out.

I stop my Oscar speech once the envelopes are done. Before the coffee, I have to check off some passport applications. New photo against existing passport. New photo. Existing passport. One more lot of twenty-five minutes until I can go and boil the kettle . . .

I've never had the kind of brain that can deal with any kind of drudgery. I never ever knew what I wanted to do. Not at ten, not at twenty, not at thirty. I've gone on countless after-work courses, locksmithing, social media, mostly to forget about work. I've learnt all sorts, over the years, but nothing I really wanted to do.

It's at this point that my phone rings. A string of digits, not a contact of mine. I have no idea what's about to happen.

'Hello?' I say. I walk from the back room with its poor signal and into the kitchenette. The door handle is wobbly, has been for years, and I steady it with my fingertips. The public sector: they never fix anything.

It smells of tannin in here. They're all tea drinkers. I recently suggested once again that we buy a coffee machine, and they acted as if I had said I wanted to take a shit in the kettle.

'Hi,' a female voice says. I can tell, immediately, that something is wrong. 'Sorry – sorry,' she says. 'It's – it's Molly. Er –'

Your housemate. We've never spoken. She only knows me because I guaranteed the rent. Why would she be calling me? My entire body goes hot. I try to count to ten, the way your mum says I should. 'God, Lewis,' she will say frustratedly. 'You always go from nought to one hundred – there is never any happy bloody medium.' Yolanda: the level-headed love of my life.

One, two, three. 'Is everything okay?'

'Sorry – sorry,' Molly says.

Murders, accidents, heart attacks, my mind suggests. Don't some young people suddenly drop down dead?

Four, five, six. 'We all have these thoughts, Lewis,' Yolanda sometimes says. 'But you have to ignore them.'

But then Molly says it. You are missing. Rather, she doesn't know where you are. The kitchenette blurs for just a second, the edges of it fading and then coming back technicolour. I try to concentrate on the things I can see to ground myself. A Costco industrial-sized sack of teabags in the corner. The fridge, covered in magnets that everyone here – for some reason – brings back from their holidays.

I take a breath. 'What? Since when?'

'She didn't come home last night – I . . . we don't know where she is. Sorry to call . . . I – I know we hardly know each other but . . .'

Images rush through my mind like cards being shuffled while I wait for the universe to reveal its grotesque hand. Twos, threes. The hanged man. The devil.

No, not you, my Little O – when you were a baby, your mouth made a lovely little happy O-shape. When you smile, it turns full Cheshire Cat. The Little O nickname stuck. You grew up, are now in your twenties, but you're still the same, really. Happy. Optimistic. Funny. Bit of a champagne social- ist, but, you know, lovably so.

'Where was she?'

'We don't know.'

'Tell me everything,' I say, closing the door to the kitchen tightly. Something thunks, somewhere, but I don't look to see what.

'She didn't come home last night,' Molly repeats. 'I . . . her phone's off.'

I check the clock that hangs – nonsensically – above the fridge, though I know exactly what time it is here, always, to the minute. 'Did you text her?' I bark it, defensive. You being missing is a problem to be riddled out, to be quickly fixed. A mistake.

'Nothing's delivering,' Molly says.

An image of you springs to mind. A selfie you sent me once, wearing one of those bloody awful sheet masks you love so much. A peace sign made with your fingers, your face covered in moist cloth like Hannibal Lecter. That's what I said back to you, and you sent a photo with your teeth bared.

'So she's out, phone dead,' I say now to Molly. A twenty-year-old woman I have actually not yet met, talking to me – I catch myself reflected in the microwave – forty-two, rail thin, and now about as panicked as I've ever been.

'We don't know whether to – whether to call the police?'

'Do. I will, too,' I say.

I turn to the window that looks out on to a tired square. Tatty, mossy pavements, dying plants even though it's spring-time, pale skies. As I look up at the world with a white blind drawn across it, I think of him, your boyfriend Andrew, and ask your housemate if they've heard from him.

'No . . . I'll try and call him.'

'Okay.'

'I rang her mum first, but got her voicemail. Didn't leave a message.'

'All right. I'll call – I'll call the . . . I'll call,' I say.

'Okay,' Molly echoes, her voice small.

I ring off, adrenalin flooding my system. Already, my mind is suggesting solutions, and aren't there plenty? You stayed out, met a nice new boy maybe. Lost your phone. Appendicitis. Car crash. Amnesia. But all of them involve a call from somebody. And you are the most communicative person I know. You'd ring, you'd arrange for someone else to ring, or someone would look in your phone and know to dial me.

I pick up my coat and walk in a stupid, useless circle around the kitchen.

I press the numbers like I'm in a film.

'999, which emergency service, please?'

'Police,' I say to the operator, leaving the kitchen, then leaving the office.

'What's your emergency?' she asks, and all I can think is how long it took to conceive you – nineteen months. The day Yolanda got her eighteenth period – and I'm sorry if this is too much information – I locked myself in the bathroom and cried, not knowing that, four weeks later, there'd be other bathroom tears. Two pink lines, happy tears, two souls, freed. That struggle – it never really left us. We weren't able to have another child, and we treated you like a glass bauble.

'What's your emergency?' the operator says again. But I'm not answering because I'm thinking that, really, for the whole pregnancy, I didn't believe there was a baby in there. Strange, but true. It felt so abstract to me. Right until you were born, placed on to Yolanda's chest, and reaching out a little starfish hand to grip my finger, holding on for life.

'My daughter is missing,' I say eventually. 'She – her house-mates say she never came home. I need to speak to somebody. Please – she's – this is out of character.'

'All right, okay, let me take some further details and then I

35

will get a patrol dispatched to you to take an initial statement – what's the address?' she says to me, I think kindly.

I'm outside. I don't remember coming out. It's fresh out, freezing. I'm breathing the same air as you – surely? – and it's only as I think this that I notice I have the handle to the kitchen door still firmly enclosed in my palm. I grip it tight, holding on for life.

3

Julia

Julia knows from victims that the following is true: in real crises, a chamber opens somewhere deep in the brain, and you cope. You cope with things you never thought you could. Julia notices this in herself dispassionately, through a haze of what feels like an eerie calm.

She meets the man's eyes again in the mirror, nods once and puts the car into first gear.

Right. It is her job to comply and, in the meantime, to glean as much information about him as possible so that, if she survives, she can phone this in, identify him and arrest him. All that without letting him know she's doing it: in crimes like this, many perpetrators kill their victim if they feel they are too good a witness. Too much knowledge is a bad thing.

'Where?' she says to him, indicating right to pull away with a hand that she can see is shaking but doesn't feel like it is.

His balaclava is close-cut, doesn't give anything away. He has nondescript brown eyes, so probably brown hair.

She flicks her gaze back to the road, trying to look casual. Then back to him. The outline of thin shoulders in his black coat. He's slim. His legs rise up off the back seats. So tall, too.

Her body begins to shake. Sweat tracks down from between her shoulder blades, sliding towards her lower back. She licks her lips, trying to think. He will want something. She just needs to work out what it is, and how to give it to him.

Julia looks at those brown eyes again. He must be an enemy. A suspect, a criminal, a gang member. Somebody she knows. God, she has too many enemies to count: all police do.

A couple of crow's feet around his eyes, nothing heavy. He's maybe her age.

After a beat, he speaks: 'I have an address.' Okay. He is disguising his voice. Deliberately gruff, farcically so. So either she knows him, or he's a smart enough criminal to know that he must be unidentifiable. 'Seventeen, East View Lane,' he continues. A chill moves through Julia's body: that is Olivia Johnson's address.

* * *

'Okay,' she says in a cool voice, progressing along the street at twenty miles per hour.

A civilian is driving behind them. She could stop abruptly, get out, flag them down. Her phone is just there in the cup holder. She could call 999 easily, has the entire police force at her disposal. And if they're going to Olivia's, it will be surrounded by officers.

Instead of finding all of this comforting, Julia finds it disturbing. This man will know all of this. He isn't mad. He is composed, informed. Knew how to break into her car. Is sitting collectedly now, in the back, in complete control.

Why does he think she won't get help? The road widens

into two lanes, and she moves over to the right to give her an excuse to check her rear-view mirror. She scans his body. He must be armed.

Panic finally begins to burn, quick and hot, in Julia's chest. She thinks of Art, and everything that's still unsaid between them. And she thinks, too, of Genevieve, and how Julia always wishes she had made the time to have another child, though she worried she would never love a second like she loves her. How could she? Julia doesn't feel as though she loves Genevieve because she's her daughter; she loves Genevieve because she is Genevieve.

She wonders, if he kills her now, if they will be surprised, or if they expected it, somehow; that one day the job would finally take her away completely, rather than partially.

'Why there?' she says to the man. Third gear. Fourth. They're doing thirty-five miles an hour, now, on roads that look totally, absurdly, normal. Ubers. A bus.

'You know.'

Fifth gear. On an A road, now. It is a blur of red lights. Busy, surprisingly so for the time of night. 'You'll park up outside it, where I tell you to,' he says. Julia recognizes his voice. She's sure of it. There's something familiar about it . . .

A roundabout. First exit. The man begins to rifle around in the back. The movement distracts her. He's hidden from the outside world by the suit jackets she's in the habit of hanging by the windows. They give him the perfect cover.

He is making a noise with something. Julia drives and listens intently. It's metal. Each hair stands up on the back of her neck, a fearful sweep of goosebumps, as she waits to see what he does. He's about to play his card, Julia's sure of it.

A car in the distance has rap music on. The beats reverberate along the road, obscuring whatever noises he's making.

Julia waits for it. She can imagine it precisely: cold metal on the vulnerable skin at the back of her neck. The cock of a gun. Her heart throbs along with the bass. Perhaps she's been waiting her entire career for this to happen.

They pass under a flickering streetlight which strobes the man's eyes in the mirror, dark oak to ash. Julia feels like she's dreaming, like she's taken LSD, like she's got a fever. The calm has disappeared, replaced with panic.

Olivia's house is off this next junction. Julia indicates left and moves over. The man in the back does nothing at all, but Julia knows he's going to do something, soon, before they reach the house surrounded by police. She tries to think, but it's impossible in this loaded, violent silence. All she can hear is her breath, and his.

She drives for two more minutes, taking glances at him in the mirror. Time ticks down slowly, sand through an hourglass, and Julia wonders in that strange, cold way that characterizes situations like these if these might be her final moments.

Olivia's house looms up ahead. Despite herself, Julia can't help but appraise it. Victorian terrace – good; hopefully the neighbours overheard something.

Two police cars sit outside it. A PCSO on the door; Julia can't quite make out who, but she thinks it might be a man called Harry who she knows well.

'Keep going, away from everyone,' the man says, flicking a hand in front of him, pointing down the road.

She drives, and a plan forms in her mind. Despite twenty years in the police, it doesn't come naturally to Julia to keep her cards close to her chest in this way. She is straight up. Everyone knows her for this. She doesn't withhold disclosure.

She doesn't tell lies in interviews. Julia believes everything is better when everyone knows the same stuff. But she can't do that today, not now.

The forensics van is parked up. Erin and her team will be inside, preparing to or having already started to search Olivia's room, to see what she took, what she left behind, and to check for signs of a struggle.

But what evidence does this man in Julia's car leave behind? Perhaps some unknown skin and hair fibres, her number plate seen on ANPR, him invisible behind the jackets, but nothing else. For all of her life, Julia has followed the evidence ruthlessly, but here is the real world, playing out in front of her, and what use would forensics be? If he took her now, nobody would really ever know what happened to her. Male DNA would be found, but, unless he has a record, it could be anyone. A friend. A colleague. A mechanic.

Her hand goes to her seatbelt, ready to leave, to run.

The man immediately grabs her wrist. He's wearing gloves.

This is exactly what Julia wanted to happen, but, nevertheless, her entire body blooms with sweat at the physical contact. Before he releases her, she does it. She scrapes her fingernail down his arm.

'You're not to leave,' he says softly, looking at his arm. But, if he's figured out what she's done, he doesn't seem bothered. 'Park there. On the right.'

'Okay,' she says, thinking that at least she now has something useful: concrete evidence, his DNA, underneath her fingernail. Whatever he's pulled out of his pocket, whatever happens now. If she dies, there are officially signs of a struggle that will lead the police to him. And if she lives, she can follow them herself.

41

She indicates, then slows to a stop on an empty part of the street, way past the house and the police presence. She kills the engine and the silence throbs, the air humming with fear. Julia's body is sour-smelling, the burnt-off adrenalin of terror.

A handful of people are coming home from bars, getting late-night food shopping out of their boots, making calls, locking cars. Everyone is still in hats, scarves, gloves. It looks like a winter postcard. The citrus colours of the streetlamps, the lit-up windows in the houses. Normal life orbits around them, and nobody has any idea.

'This is for you,' the man says.

The way he swings from *for* to *you*. That West Country *r*. So he's local.

He offers her a small metal box, but he only uses one hand to pass it to her. The other – in his pocket – could easily still be concealing a weapon.

'Your instructions are inside.'

He sits back as though his job is done. Julia's hands tremble as she fiddles with the catch. It's flipped shut like a lunchbox. She moves the metal clasp, cold against her fingertips, and opens it.

Inside is a piece of paper. A glass, double-bagged in a sandwich bag. A cigarette, also double-bagged.

She looks over her shoulder at him. His eyes are expressionless. She opens the letter.

Julia Day. It is now your job to convict Matthew James for the murder of Olivia Johnson. Enclosed are your forensics to plant. They contain his DNA. He resides at 1 Glasgow Place, Portishead.

Julia stares down at the paper, blinking fast. Her mind is in overdrive. Convict someone of murder. They've had training about this. Bribery. Corruption. Inside jobs. The first thing you do is tell someone. Phone it in at the earliest possible moment to the Professional Standards Unit. The helpful part of Julia's mind is thinking things of this nature: how to get out of it, the fact that the note is handwritten and can be analysed. The other, unhelpful, part, the part obsessed only with finding missing people, is thinking that Glasgow Place is very near to the alleyway where Olivia disappeared. Only one street back.

But, finally, she lands on the most important, most obvious fact of all: this man must know where Olivia is, dead or alive, and needs somebody framed. The clearest explanation is most often true.

It's all irrelevant, she thinks vehemently. She is not bribable. She isn't. She hasn't ever got into debt. She doesn't want money or power or drugs. She's off social media. All these things make you a target in the police, and she's never once been corrupted.

'You've got the wrong person for this,' she says to him. 'I won't do it,' she adds, her voice shaking.

'This isn't the way it's going to go, Julia,' he says. He sounds almost mournful. *Where* does she know that voice from? She closes her eyes, trying to play it again in her mind, but she can't. The calm has disappeared, the hurricane has arrived.

She opens her eyes. 'I cannot be blackmailed. I am not corrupt. Besides: I'm going to find Olivia, whatever's happened to her.' It's a bluff, but, bizarrely, one she almost believes. Her eyes keep straying to his left hand. Still concealed. At any moment, he could strike, and she'd be gone. But she can't bow down to him, wave a white flag, submit. 'You will see,' she adds.

43

The man pauses, looking at Julia square on in the mirror. She knows it's coming. His trump card. The reason he is here. Her instinct spots it before she really can.

And now he speaks a single sentence which changes everything. 'I know what Genevieve did.' After this, he adds another, so softly she has to strain to hear: 'And you.'

4

Julia

'What.' She says it with a full stop, intending to give absolutely nothing away in tone. He cannot know. This man cannot know. Two people in the whole world know what Julia did for Genevieve, and those people are Genevieve and Julia. Not even Art knows.

'I know you covered up what Genevieve did. The CCTV. Zac.'

Julia's mind stays as calm and frozen as the ground outside, but her body has a full reaction to this statement, specifically, to that name. Her stomach seems to set itself on fire. She actually glances down at it, expecting it to be hot, charred, smoking. It's the same shock she felt that night, the night Genevieve did it. Sometimes, when she's falling asleep, she still hears the particular slam of that particular door in the car park. It had a tone to it, as rich and nuanced as a human voice. A panicked, high jolt. When they moved house, she was relieved she'd never have to pass there again. The stories we tell ourselves: it turns out, she could never leave it behind her. Here it is, that door swinging from the past into the present, and bringing this man through it.

'How do you know?' she asks him directly.

He gestures wordlessly to the door, ignoring her question. Julia memorizes the movement his arm makes. There is something almost theatrical about it.

'You have evidence?' she says.

'Your daughter, on CCTV.'

'I'll need to see that,' Julia says. He can't have it. He can't. She destroyed it. She checked meticulously for other cameras at the scene. Didn't she?

'I'm very happy to schedule a viewing,' he says, and his tone chills Julia.

'Have you got Olivia?' she asks, hoping that, if he has, he hasn't killed her yet. If she were this man, and she had killed Olivia, she wouldn't provide only a glass and a cigarette: she'd provide a body.

Maybe it isn't too late for her.

He reaches over her seat, to her right, which makes her jump, and clicks her door open. 'Good luck, Julia,' he says quietly. He smells of the outside air, nothing more. His left hand has emerged: no weapon. She should feel relieved, but doesn't.

Because he is expecting her to plant the evidence. Right now.

And if she doesn't do it, he is going to tell the police – and the world – what Genevieve did.

* * *

Genevieve was mugged on a misty spring evening almost exactly a year ago. She went to pay for parking while Julia took a call she recognizes only now to be unimportant, about a charging threshold for a burglary. Genevieve was perhaps too full of sass, a tall and sporty fifteen-year-old to whom

46

everything had always come easily and, when a young lad approached her, she resisted. He firstly asked her for the time, then for directions. If Julia had been there, and not an entire floor away, one finger in one ear, the other listening to the Super, she would have told Genevieve to drop her belongings and run. Never a surer sign that you're going to be mugged than those clues.

But she wasn't there. And so the mugger, a petty criminal called Zac who Julia knew of, reached for Genevieve's phone. And Genevieve didn't want to give it. She took a swipe at Zac's neck with her keys held out between her knuckles, just the way Julia had told her to if she was ever attacked. Zac began to bleed, there in the stairwell. Genevieve had hit his jugular – a combination of bad luck and bad judgement – and fled to Julia, that door slamming behind her.

Julia raced up the stairs and called him an ambulance from a tired payphone in the lobby. And then she did three things, things that felt right, maternal, protective, but which in hindsight she knows look gruesomely selfish: she told Zac – bleeding out, barely conscious – that if he ever phoned it in, she would get him sent down for life for drugs offences. She thought they might be the last words he ever heard, and hated herself.

Then she broke into the CCTV cupboard and removed it, took it home and corrupted the footage. It formed part of the police file, and anyone who looked could see that it was useless. So how had this man seen it?

And then, she and Genevieve left before the ambulance arrived, presuming Zac would die. The whole journey home, she felt chased by him, the spectre of him: her guilt.

Only he didn't die.

Zac survived, had an operation and a blood transfusion,

and the only way Julia knew was because the police were told by the hospital that a stabbing had occurred but hadn't been fatal. Julia sat at her desk, blinking back shock, hoping he'd heard her threat.

He went to the station a few days afterwards, full of bluster, threatening to complain. But he eventually didn't. Because, four days later, he was admitted with an infection that became sepsis. And three days after that, he died. Julia will remember for ever the moment she saw it on the news: *Car Park Stabbing Victim Dead of Sepsis at 19.* Right there, in that single moment, a week after the stabbing her daughter became – somehow – a murderer. But – much to Julia's shame – the thought that followed this was one born out of relief: that it's much easier to get away with murder than with assault, because your one witness is dead. The only thing you have to do is work out whether he told anyone, and Julia had thought he hadn't, after a few weeks elapsed, then a few months. Now, she isn't so sure.

Genevieve's act caused his death, a jury would surely say, even though it hadn't felt like that in the immediate aftermath, when he survived, the cause and effect so disparate. Shit luck. Bad judgement, sure, but mostly shit luck. Genevieve might get some mitigation for having been mugged, but her actions went totally beyond a reasonable response, including leaving the scene: something Julia had thought was the right thing to do, but now isn't so sure.

The case had been referred to Julia, as all stabbings were, and she had closed it as quickly as she could: Zac was a regular user, a criminal, had plenty of enemies. Misadventure, she had concluded, after asking a few questions of his friends and acquaintances, her hands shaking as she took notes from them. She had gleaned enough to know they weren't aware of what had really happened. Enough to hope he hadn't told anybody at all.

Julia never told Art. Genevieve had asked her not to, in the car on the way back that night, her face white, eyes hollow and panicked. And Julia had agreed, for Genevieve's sake and her own. Her daughter's crime seemed somehow to cross directly with Julia's job, already something Art was scathing about. Julia wonders now if that was the wrong thing to do, too.

But, now, somebody knows. Somebody – when even her husband doesn't.

She looks at the man in the back of her car. He and Zac must be connected. Zac had several days to tell people. She'd assumed he hadn't, but perhaps he had. But why is it only coming out now? And what does that have to do with Olivia?

She tries to forget about how this man knows, about what he knows, and thinks, instead, about the choices facing her. She looks at herself in the rear-view mirror. Genevieve has her eyes. Pale blue. Her daughter who likes Walkers Sensations, delivering a great comeback and complaining about companies on social media in the hope of coupons. She wants nothing more than a job where she gets to wear a sharp suit and most of all – somewhat to Julia's shame – a husband. She doesn't give a shit about being popular, and therefore is. She is always the first on the dancefloor, or was, before last year. She once told Art she was 'certain' she could cope with a nuclear war. She leaves cat food out for hedgehogs in their garden. She regrets the assault so much – they never use the word 'murder' – she won't even be driven down the road past the car park, and won't talk about it, either. The topic, in the Day household, is as prohibited as a firearm.

* * *

49

Julia leaves the car and the man inside it and walks down the street like an autumn leaf blown on the breeze, carelessly buffeted this way and that. Her feet feel like she has on clown shoes. Nothing feels real. *Think. Think.* She's got to call this in. There is no way she can plant evidence to frame somebody.

But . . .

Think. Think.

But there's nothing.

If she doesn't do it, she is certain that man will tell the world about Genevieve, and about her. He has serious intent. He's broken into her car, he's sourced DNA for her, he's found out her most damning secret. Julia's back is against a wall, with nowhere to go, and no time to make a decision, either.

She glances back at the car. What could she do? Confess all, now, to her police officer colleagues? Genevieve would get a decade in prison, if not more, for both the brute force and fleeing the scene. Julia would get time, too, for using her job to cover up a murder. God knows how much. They might make an example out of her, give her a decade too.

The car looks totally normal, but he's still in there, somewhere in the darkness, silent like an animal lying in wait. She turns away from him and darts up an alleyway that runs between two Victorian terraces. The houses are joined on the first floor above her. The passage is unlit, black, the bricks are slick with the damp weather, the air eddying with cold air. Julia turns in a circle, her hands on her head, her body covered in sweat.

She can't. She can't become corrupt. It goes against everything she stands for. She can't convict somebody of murdering Olivia, who might still be alive out there somewhere. She needs to find her.

But her mind — she sometimes wishes it didn't work so quickly — has already landed on the answer: there isn't one. She has no choice. It's Genevieve or this. And nothing tops Genevieve. That is what motherhood is.

And so the decision is made. Until she can find Olivia: dead or alive. Corruption. Just like that. Like jumping off a cliff, only what Julia didn't realize is that she had been walking steadily towards it since that night in the car park last year. It took one more step.

The night is sharp with cold, almost painful against her skin. There are a few sleety flakes in the air, little currents of snow being tossed around the haze of the streetlamps. The weather feels suddenly inevitable, some kind of warning sign: no spring should be this chilly.

'All right,' she says to the PCSO on watch, Harry. She doesn't know what else to say. He's young, twentyish. Tall, angular, handsome. Julia is reminded of Art-at-eighteen. She's been married to him for so long, she hardly remembers life before. But she remembers him at their wedding, shirt unironed even though he swore he had pressed it, his eyes on hers.

She stops, ignoring the burn of this man's gaze behind her, and looks up at the house. Olivia's house. Blue front door, brass knocker. No Ring doorbell so unfortunately no amateur residential CCTV here, or on the two terraces that flank it.

'Going to get a look inside,' she says woodenly to Harry.

''Course,' he says. One syllable. A complete beat of faith, of trust in Julia, which makes her blush with ignominy. She signs the crime scene log.

Every police officer, in a big city or a sleepy town, has had the opportunity to become corrupt. Julia could have made

51

thousands of pounds. A nod here, a wink there, failing to stop and search. Passing criminals information. Weapons trading. The lot. It would've been easy for her; it is for any copper. And she never has. Has never even thought for even a second about it. Has only ever known one corrupt colleague, who siphoned off seized drugs and was sacked ten years ago.

She reaches for a stack of the protective outerwear and covers for shoes and pulls them on.

Already, she's thinking about how she can do it. Is this how it goes? Is this how every corrupt officer begins? First, they refuse. Then they need something. Then they start to plot how they can get away with it. Her upper lip begins to sweat. This isn't her, it isn't her, it isn't her.

Beyond the PCSO sits a typical student house. No familial touches, the stairs and hallway blank and communal in feel: no photographs, a tired grey carpet, a pizza leaflet the only thing on the entry table. Julia gets the same feeling she always gets when entering where somebody was last known to reside: she wants everybody out. Wants to walk around it herself, have it be preserved for her eyes only.

She catches sight of her reflection as she walks inside, past the hallway mirror that Olivia must have looked at herself in right before she left. Or before she was taken, by the man in her car. Julia doesn't look in the mirror; she looks at the frame. Clean of dust. Interesting: houses with multiple occupants are not often spotless in the communal areas. She looks behind it – searching for hidden drugs – a credible reason to go missing or to be abducted. She once checked for this in a show home, and Art had rolled his eyes and laughed.

She replaces it on the nail. As she does so, she can't help but meet her own eyes, but tonight she sees only Genevieve.

Olivia deserves better. Her parents, her family, a boyfriend, whoever her loved ones are. Julia will have to tell them. She'll have to tell them they have a suspect. For murder, for a murder that might not have even happened: there is no body yet.

Just as she starts ascending the stairs – bare wood, no carpet, two nails protruding – her phone rings.

'Hi,' she says. It's Jonathan, who Julia knows will have been diligently working away.

'O2 have released the phone records,' he says, sure enough. 'Brian is about to dig in.' Julia checks her watch. It's after eleven forty, but this is how it is. Any detective who gets the phone records of a missing person and leaves them until the morning shouldn't be looking for a missing person.

'But so far,' he continues, 'the phone was turned off at half past one in the morning – could be the battery, could be intentional. The last ping was by three roads – Glasgow Place, Patterdale Avenue and Selby Close, all by the alley. So we need to do door-knocking there.'

Glasgow Place. Matthew James's address. Julia's mind spins, trying to work it out. Is he merely an easy target, then? Someone who lives in the vicinity, or what?

'I'll send some people,' Julia says. 'Thanks.' She's reached the top of the stairs. The landing is cold, the front door left open. Wind blows through the crime scene, both Olivia's and now Julia's. The housemates are gone, interviewed by Julia's team. 'Anything else?' she says, scanning around. There's a felt-tip sign up on the wall saying GO AVA GO!!! With a car drawn underneath it in pink. A record player with a Pink Floyd record in it sits on the floor by a plug. Fairy lights made of white fake flowers are Blu-Tacked to the ceiling.

'Well. She upgraded her phone right before she moved, switched networks. There's a call to an 01275 number which matches Reflections, which is the marketing company – I've asked to see the correspondence inviting her for interview.'

'New house, new phone on a new network,' Julia says, almost relieved to find she still has her detective instincts, still there burning bright like a lighthouse that points towards home. 'Isn't that strange? Then missing.'

'It is strange,' Jonathan agrees. 'Suspicious. In a good way, though. A runaway, maybe? Though the dad doesn't think so.'

'Exactly,' Julia says, their theories bouncing off each other the way they always have. Julia thinks sometimes you become closer to colleagues than to anybody else. She could finish Jonathan's sentences more easily than she could most people's. Only this time, Jonathan has no idea what Julia is thinking, or about to do, either.

She hangs up and hesitates outside the bedrooms. It's clear which is Olivia's: all of the doors are open except one, the one at the end of the hall. She hears movement in there, and then Erin, the SOCO and one of her oldest friends, appears.

Her colleague of a decade is wearing a white suit and blue boots, and all Julia can think is that she is, unknown to Erin, clutching a metal box inside her coat that contains forged evidence. She meets Erin's eyes, and Julia can't believe she doesn't know, doesn't guess, that she's about to plant it here. 'We haven't started yet. Wanted to do the photo in the daylight. So feel free to go on in,' Erin says, gesturing to the door, to Julia's dual relief and shame.

Julia's hands are trembling, the metal box clutched tight. Erin is one of life's misanthropes, but she tells Julia almost everything. Julia knows how overdrawn Erin is – she has lots of children, which sucks her finances – and how often she has sex with her husband – not as much as he'd like. Julia looks at her and thinks she's never felt this ashamed and guilty in her entire life. 'Good, I will,' she says softly.

'Not much in there,' Erin says with a shrug, the white material crinkling up around her shoulders. 'She's unpacked, sort of. Half and half. No keys, no mobile phone, no purse. Left her ID. I guess the rest are with her.'

'As you'd expect for someone who left willingly.'

'Right. But most likely, anyway, that some man's murdered her,' Erin says with another shrug. She has good instincts, usually, if erring a little on the pessimistic side, and Julia can't help but look at her curiously. Erin folds her arms, tilts her head to the side. 'You know, her housemates didn't actually see her leave,' she says. 'You're going to want to interview them. I spoke to them briefly.' She indicates the other rooms, though her housemates won't be allowed back in them, will be housed elsewhere for now. 'They're not much help. She only moved in two nights ago. But, I mean . . . it's weird. That she texted them, out of everyone. Implies she was very nearby, perhaps?'

Julia nods quickly: the housemates can't know what happened when Olivia left, and texted them. Besides, they might be lying. Therefore, they are under suspicion. She winces as she thinks it. They won't get arrested, not by her. Even if they did it.

Erin gestures to the bedroom at the opposite end of the hall to Olivia's. It has a tiny balcony, unusual for a house of this size. It's wrought iron, empty save for a small table, a single chair and a dying M&S outdoor plant. A clean breeze rushes in.

They head out, and Erin lights up. This is a ritual of theirs. Erin smokes while Julia thinks. And, anyway, Julia has always enjoyed the juxtaposition of a clean forensics suit and a cigarette.

'Also, she hadn't locked the door to her room. She'd taken the keys, but not locked it.' Erin drags on the cigarette. 'Strange, given she's so new to the house.' She angles her head back and blows two plumes out of her nostrils, a dragon's breath.

Julia begins to shiver. From the cold or the deception, she doesn't know. 'Any theory in particular?' she asks. SOCOs are excellent vehicles for intel. People let their guard down around them in a way they won't around police. And Erin trusts Julia. Is happy to chat off-record, before her searches are complete. In fact, doesn't really believe in *the record* at all.

The lit cigarette draws a vertical line of smoke in the night. 'No blood spatter, no obvious signs of a struggle, nothing upended, nothing taken. Nothing significant left behind. No signs of a rush. I think she left here, intending to go somewhere, probably.' She blows another grey cone out. 'Who knows the fuck where.'

'Indeed,' Julia says grimly.

'Anyway, we'll get our lives back in two to four months.'

Julia says nothing, watching the fumes dance and disperse, and hating herself. She would usually quip back, but she doesn't tonight.

'Everything all right?' Erin asks lightly.

'Huh?' Julia says in surprise.

'Seem tense,' Erin says.

Julia stands at the crossroads this question creates, then steps over it seamlessly.

'Yeah, yeah. I'm going to take a look, if you don't mind,' she says, 'before you get all set up in there.' She pulls the box further into her body. Erin could reach for it, discover it, if only she knew to.

Erin stubs the cigarette out on the brickwork, then tosses it off the balcony, away from the crime scene, so it isn't collected by the fingertip searchers. Julia watches it freefall, thinking of what she's about to do.

'Sure,' Erin says easily, lighting a second cigarette.

'You taken photos yet?' Julia asks, wondering how well to conceal her items.

'Nope.'

Julia nods. The world swims. It's the perfect opportunity. Did the man know?

'Won't be long,' she says over her shoulder to Erin. Her voice sounds completely normal.

Down the hall and into the room. She closes the pale, stripped-pine door. Olivia's room is chaotic. A double bed pushed up against the wall to the left. Julia clocks it immediately: not a bed that is intended to be shared. Yellow bedspread with the starched, ironed quality of a new, out-of-the-box duvet cover. Julia palms her hand over it. Cheap. Low cotton count. Folds from the box still down the centre.

A poster of Che Guevara on the wall. A leftie, then, just like Jonathan said. She inspects the Blu Tack – recent, put up by Olivia herself, no doubt. She looks at the sash window – wiped clean, nothing on the windowsill – and in the old wooden wardrobe. One of the doors is hanging open. A mirror catches the light, winking like the surface of water.

She clutches the box the man gave her. The second she does this, she will have committed another imprisonable offence. And, worse, violated some law against – what? Nature? Morals? She doesn't know. If she doesn't do it, though . . . Genevieve would get custody, time. Ten years, fifteen. It would depend on whether the jury believed it was manslaughter or murder. Too big a risk to take, in other words, which Julia had known immediately that night. And Julia herself – she would get a few years inside, but, really, she would get life, because she would get beaten to death in prison for being a copper. She can't deny that self-preservation plays a role here, too.

Once straight as a rail, Julia, with no choices before her, now metamorphoses, right there in front of the looking glass. Already, she thinks she looks different. Blonde hair wild in the protective forensic clothing, jaw quivering with tension.

She begins to fumble with the metal box. She looks at the glass and the cigarette inside, and wonders if her search for Olivia is naive, whether it's simply the case that the man who gave them to her has murdered her.

Unless he's kidnapped her. Julia swallows. Olivia could be alive somewhere, and here Julia is, planting red herrings.

She feels her mind close off to what she is about to do. She is revulsed. Like somebody forced to make a cruel decision in the name of kindness, snapping the neck of something suffering.

Her eyes fill with tears. She brings her phone out and texts Genevieve, the forensic gloves not making contact properly with the screen. Her message comes out jumbled, but she sends it anyway. 'Just hel up with 1 thiNg,' she says. And even though she's not with Genevieve, even though she's left yet another meal with her, abandoned her, Genevieve texts back glibly: *I'll wait up to see you!* x

She's got to do it. She'll do it for Genevieve.

And, afterwards, and tomorrow, she will do everything in her power to find Olivia, and end this for everybody.

* * *

Julia wrenches up the sash window. Ivy climbs up the front of the house. The PCSO downstairs isn't looking at her. She glances across the street and around. She takes the cigarette out, careful not to disturb the end that will have been smoked. The end containing this man's DNA. Matthew, poor Matthew, whoever he is.

She places it on the outside sill, tucked into the corner so it won't get blown away. It looks like an offhand discarding by a cocky criminal. The search team will find it, for sure, and then the SOCO will test it.

It's so easy, this is so damn easy, it's amazing it doesn't happen more. Maybe it does, she thinks, as she gets the glass out. Rolls it under the bed, far enough that nobody will have seen it yet. Enough that they will conclude this man, this Matthew, was here drinking from it, right before Olivia left. Was taken.

That's all it takes. Two items. DNA. Planted. Faked.

They've had endless training about corruption. Julia remembers a particular session that they had been told was a stop and search exercise. Just before lunchtime, the trainer pulled a knife out on Julia's colleague, said he would go and kill her grandma if she didn't comply with his requests. It was a simulation, but terrifying nevertheless – he'd taken the information from their public Facebook pages. The names of their children, their partners, their parents and grandparents, in order to corrupt the officers. They'd all learnt the lesson, quick-sharp: don't show your hand online, don't reveal a vulnerability publicly that could compromise you.

But *had* she? It turns out you can stay off social media, you can never get into debt, into criminality, into any kind of strife. But sometimes circumstances come after you.

Julia stands back and looks. You can't see either item by looking in the room normally. Erin won't suspect a thing. It's done. She leaves, feeling transformed, the king killed, and awaits her fate.

'Pretty normal, right?' Erin says, as Julia lets herself out of the bedroom.

'Yeah. Strange case, though,' Julia says. Her lower back is wet with sweat.

She hesitates. She could tell Erin. She really could. That there's a man out there. His weapon isn't a gun, or a knife. It's a secret.

But she knows what would happen next. Julia wouldn't have to convict Matthew James, but she would have to convict her daughter, and herself.

'We'll get him,' Erin says. 'Sleep well,' she says to Julia as she sees her out. Orange streetlamps are hazy in the spring mist. Julia scans the street around her car, looking for him.

'We don't know who did it. Male or female,' she says to Erin, an afterthought, on the threshold to the house.

'Always a man, though, isn't it?'

'Yeah,' Julia says, thinking that Erin is right and wrong, both at the same time.

5

Julia

Julia trembles in the cold as she hurries towards her car. She tries the handle. It opens, but he is gone. The air in here is light again: she is alone. Relief sweeps over her like tiredness.

He has left a note on the passenger seat. It's handwritten, a looping, feminine style. She turns it over. Just a plain piece of paper – notoriously bad at retaining fingerprints, though Julia will run it through the system anyway – and five words:

Thank you for your cooperation.

She leans her head back against the freezing driver's seat, alone, thinking. No handwriting analysis system exists in the police, but maybe she could get it dusted.

She's got to make a plan. Julia needs a next step.

She drives home too quickly, full of adrenalin, trying to outrun herself. And all she can think as she speeds along is that that's two lives ruined. Hers and Matthew's. Three, if you count Olivia's.

* * *

Julia lets herself into her house. All of the lamps are on – teenagers – and Genevieve is still downstairs, in the small galley kitchen to the right, off the hallway. The kitchen spotlights cast a perfect rectangle on her hallway floor, populated by a single shadow.

'What time do you call this?'

Julia watches as the shadow puts its hands on its hips. 'Got waylaid,' Julia says weakly.

'Check this out. Ridiculous – and *rude*,' Genevieve rants, that spiked tone of voice so distinctly her that Julia wants to gather her close. She's been even more haughty since Zac. Some defence mechanism, Julia assumes. Already confrontational in nature, Genevieve is now positively combative at times.

'What's that?' she says, turning into the kitchen.

'An empty tub of Greek yoghurt in the fridge. Dad – if he wasn't hiding upstairs – would like to issue a confession, in accordance with the Police and Criminal Evidence Act,' she proclaims. Her blonde hair, just like Julia's – the exact same shade – falls around her face. Julia never stops being amazed at the things her child has inherited from her, things that were transplanted across, whole. Same hair shade, same texture, same section at the side that won't lie flat.

'I didn't expect to get PACE quoted to me at home as well as at work,' Julia says, surprised by how seamlessly she slips away from her own problems and into just *Mum*. It's always been the way. Like pregnancy birthed an entirely different part of her brain.

A voice comes from upstairs: 'There were morsels left.'

'It was the disappointment,' Genevieve calls back. 'I thought there was some left. And there was not. It is the emotional pain you owe me the apology for.'

'I think you'll recover,' Art shouts.

Genevieve pours boiling water into two mugs and adds hot chocolate. She leans back against the counter. The kitchen window is open. Julia can hear the sea.

'It's late for a school night,' Julia says. It's well after midnight.

Genevieve flicks her eyes to her mother, something she rarely does these days. Bravado, moaning, sure, but hardly ever anything that sits underneath that: vulnerability.

'I'm supposed to be revising cell mitosis but I'm googling old *Hollyoaks* characters,' she says, like it's Julia's fault.

'Oh, I understand that,' Julia says, still staring at her. And she does. Julia is either hyper-focused, or not interested at all. She doesn't know how people bring themselves to do jobs they're not personally invested in. Filing, answering phones . . . she would last half an hour. But, then, are vocations to be so lauded?

'It's so boring. Why would I need to know about mitosis? Do *you* ever use that?' She handles the mugs with a little too much force.

'Not often,' Julia says with a smile. She wants to ask her daughter if she ever told anybody about Zac, and then tomorrow she will try and trace who Zac's other associates were, to see if he had told anybody else. But she is actually thinking about Matthew James. When the DNA on the cigarette and the glass come back as male DNA, she still has to match it to him. She can't check because it would leave a trail, but if his DNA isn't on the system, it won't flag him. So how is she going to get a match?

'It's so mad. If I was designing the curriculum, I'd teach . . . something useful? Like – how to get a mortgage. Or how to drive, even,' Genevieve prattles.

Julia bites her tongue. The truth is, she entirely agrees, but doesn't want to rile her up. A couple of words of encouragement from her, and she'd go on strike. She probably *would* design a curriculum.

She lowers her voice so Art can't hear. 'I wanted to ask you something.' Step one.

Immediately, Genevieve seems to know it's about Zac. Her expression drops. 'What?' she says warily.

'Last year. And the – the incident.' This is how they refer to it. Carefully tiptoeing around it, like a frozen lake that might crack further at any moment. Words judiciously chosen. Never wounding. Never a killing. Never a cover-up.

Genevieve's hand reaches for the kitchen counter, perhaps steadying herself. She keeps her pale eyes on her. The bravado, the wisecracking, all gone. 'Yeah . . .'

'Is it possible – well . . .'

'What?' she says. Her lips look blanched. Her forehead takes on a sheen underneath the make-up. If she were a suspect, Julia would bet money on her guilt.

'Does anyone know about it?'

'Huh?'

'Like – did you ever tell anyone?' She holds her palms up. 'I'm not accusing you. But, if you did, I need to know.' She's got to trace the web of it. Three spindles stretch out from Julia, Genevieve and Zac, and one of them will lead to the man in the back of her car.

'God, *no*.' There it is. The defence mechanism. The pallor b⬛⬛ a flush. Julia watches it closely. 'Why would I?' she adds. ⬛gical to a fault, like her mother.

'I don't mind, you know. I just want to know. You're not in trouble.'

She skews her mouth to the side. Julia doesn't think she's lying. She's bewildered. Isn't providing the superfluous detail liars do.

'I didn't tell a soul.' Eyes to her. 'As requested.'

'Okay. Okay.'

Genevieve turns away from Julia. She doesn't ask why.

'Just thinking about it recently,' Julia explains needlessly.

'Me too, now,' Genevieve says.

'I'm sorry,' Julia says.

'Rather mugging than mitosis,' Genevieve says, and the joke is so unexpectedly dark that Julia smiles her first genuine smile of the evening.

'Sorry I made you think about him,' Julia says. Meaning: the man who mugged you, but also: the man you murdered.

Genevieve's eyes flash. 'Do you know,' she says. 'I think about him all the time.'

'Do you?' Julia says, but it must be too much, too soon, because Genevieve turns away from her sharply.

Later, Julia knows, these emotions will come out in an explosion, some small perceived injustice or other.

'Sorry to be a party pooper, but I'm knackered,' Genevieve says, her back still to Julia. 'Fill me in tomorrow? On the misper?'

'For sure,' Julia says, though she doesn't mean it. She doesn't understand the psychology, exactly, of Genevieve's increasing interest in the crimes Julia investigates. Only that she *is* more interested, since the mugging, almost obsessively so.

'Shimmyshaker,' Genevieve says, leaving the kitchen before Julia can raise it, and waving a hand above her head without turning around. An ancient greeting and goodbye, from a TV show she watched for hours and hours when she was little and Julia was trying to buy peace. *The Fimbles* – they'd watched repeats on YouTube when it was taken off air, that's how much they'd loved it. Their word stuck, in that way things in families sometimes do.

'Shimmyshaker,' Julia immediately says too, but her voice sounds weak and sad.

Art appears at the top of the stairs just as Genevieve begins to ascend them. The atmosphere immediately changes. Julia looks up at him and, as she has always felt when she sees her husband, time seems to stop for just a second or two.

Genevieve brushes past him. Their relationship appears unscathed after Art's infidelity. Julia sometimes wonders if it is because he doesn't know what Genevieve did. She is allowed to forget it, around him. And that is too precious to spoil with judgement over an affair.

'All right,' Art says calmly, walking towards Julia. As usual, his hair and clothes are all over the place. He just can't look neat, even if he tries.

Julia moves into the kitchen, busying herself. She listens to her daughter upstairs, lights flicking on, doors opening and closing. She can *feel* Art in the living room, even though she can't hear or see him. She thinks, as she often does, about the colleague he slept with. Elle. Julia couldn't believe it when he told her – two days after the first confession – who it had been. They had known her well. Dinners, one New Year's Eve spent together. But Julia had never trusted her. And rightly so.

She couldn't believe, either, that it was coincidence, that Art hadn't always intended to sleep with her eventually. Julia would see their text exchanges. 'I know, right?' Elle would have messaged Art. 'Total week seven vibes.' 'What's week seven?' Julia would say – Art was never secretive with his phone. 'Long story – inside joke,' he'd say.

Afterwards, Elle had left the school where they both worked. Art said he'd deleted her number, like that was that.

She wipes a kitchen counter for something to do – Julia has done more performance cleaning in the past four months than ever before – then straightens up the oven gloves, folded over the handle of the oven door.

She stops and stands there, alone, and that is when the enormity of what has happened to her descends, like she's opened a shaft to hell. She leans her elbows on the counter, breathing deeply. Jesus Christ. She doesn't deserve this. At every turn of her life, she's tried to do what a good mother and a good police officer would do – hasn't she? But, today, the two compete. Art is the only person on the planet who would understand, but she can't tell him. It's too late. In giving him her secret, she would be making a trade, she knows it. Confiding in somebody who has already taken her trust, and broken it.

She shakes her head, trying to keep it together, the keening terror, the shame, trying to think. After a couple of minutes, she straightens up, as though nothing has happened at all, and gathers the things she needs. The things she needs to find the man in the balaclava. To work out how he knows what he knows, to disarm him of that evidence.

She walks past Art, eventually, her body language stiff and awkward, and upstairs to the bedroom that she sleeps in alone. As soon as she enters, she thinks the same thing she thinks every fucking evening: about their old ritual, from the days before. There was a skylight over the bed in their old house, and they used to leave the blind open, look at the stars, debrief before sleep. Julia would tell Art her worries, and he would take them from her. Now, in the new house, there's no skylight, and there's no intimacy, either.

She hears him coming upstairs. 'Night,' he says to her, a word thrown out into the ether. She doesn't reply, even though he's one of the only people who would understand what she did for Genevieve, who would understand the dilemma she faces. But she can't. It's too late.

She can hear the sea beyond the windows. The tide's out. It ruffles like a taffeta dress. In and out, in and out, a ballroom dancer of an ocean.

She heads into the bathroom and finds the nail clippers. First, she rubs them over with alcohol hand gel she brought up from the kitchen. Next, she uses the tool to scrape, very carefully, under the nail she scratched her assailant with. She puts the scrapings into a tiny Tupperware pot she also brought up with her.

She's no good at forensics, but she must know more than most, and this might be enough, she thinks, descending the stairs to put the pot in the fridge. She holds it up to the light, then places it at the back, among the open pesto jars and bell peppers, like some science specimen. A small white curl of skin fibres, his and hers.

In bed, she puts on the reading glasses that she's only begun to need recently. The analysts will be going through Olivia's vast online presence, but Julia starts now, too. She'll read alongside them.

Because that is the only thing that will truly, truly help: finding Olivia. If she finds Olivia alive, the problem goes away. If she finds her dead, she can investigate her murder.

Art comes out of his room and goes into the bathroom. 'Don't *hog it*,' Genevieve shouts. And there it is: her explosion. Offence is her greatest defence, maybe. Art thinks it's teenage hormones.

'Shall I just use a bucket outside?' he suggests.

'I need to put my retinoids on,' Genevieve says.

'They sound like a disease.'

Julia's heart is full as she listens to Genevieve, and even to Art. She's glad Genevieve is okay, if sometimes angry. That she hasn't carried the burden of what she did too heavily.

68

That Julia has been able to protect her from that — whatever the cost.

She'd do it again, she thinks recklessly, as she turns the first page of Olivia's documents. She had no choice. Nobody takes risks with things that are too precious to them.

6

Olivia

Instagram photo: A clutch of peonies in a vase on a windowsill.

Instagram caption: Is it just me? No, it isn't. It's the entire world, I know. I am not the first person to be buying peonies in April and putting them in a watering can, no, however, I would say that, sometimes, being basic is the best way to be. Sorry not sorry.

Tweet: Watching my bf in a HIIT workout* at Portishead Beach while eating my eighth churro in a row, tutting at the disturbance x *High Intensity Interval Training, lol. For people training for . . . what? To sit at sedentary desk jobs looking hench, I guess.

Facebook: Recommendations for foodie nights?

Comment by Doug Adams: Pure Portishead.

Sent items:
28/04: LittleO@gmail.com to amymichelleP@hotmail.com
I mean, he's nice and all. I don't know. It's weird how he

sometimes is. Anyway, see you tomorrow? Gals before geezers x

28/04: LittleO@gmail.com to lucy@reflections.co.uk I'd love to. Thanks for this opportunity. Just checking, which documents will I need to bring with me to the interview? And can I check – though this sounds terribly worthy – what your company is doing to fight climate change? Sorry to ask but it's important to me.

28/04: LittleO@gmail.com to lucy@reflections.co.uk No, that's fine. I will just bring myself. Thanks for the info re renewables! Can't wait! O

Texts:

Olivia: Still on for next Thursday?
Dad: Hell to the yes.

Olivia: I'm excited to move in! I hear there's a CAT?
Annie: I know, so exciting. There is a cat but it's more like, I dunno, he just sort of hangs out here? But he doesn't live here.
Olivia: How totally cute.
Annie: He's a pain though – we've started buying cat food for him – lol.
Olivia: I'll get some for when I move in!!
Annie: OMG you move in super soonest.
Olivia: I knowwwwwwwww.

Second Day Missing

7

Emma

It's your second therapy session today. Your idea, not mine. *Matthew James, Room 104*, said the confirmation text.

We were in the kitchen when you first asked about it, and I swear, my heart plummeted down my chest. Because, the thing is, not everyone should tell someone all their secrets, should they?

'Oh, right,' I said tightly. 'Why?'

I didn't even mean it, not really. I was just taken aback. But it takes nothing to make you retreat into your shell – shy, elusive, something of a dreamer. You find life hard, and confiding even harder. So – it was my mistake.

Luckily, you took it in good spirits. You often do. It's the part of you that other people don't see, beneath the bashfulness, beneath the sometimes awkward demeanour.

'Oh, you know, to learn and grow,' you said lightly, only half joking. You laughed your quiet, understated laugh, leaned back against the kitchen counter, your arms folded across your chest, a mock interested expression on your face. Eyes blue, hair dark.

Therapy.

You blinked twice at me, two dark flutters of those

eyelashes I have loved for two decades, waiting for a response. 'No – no. Sorry, I think it's good,' I said lamely. And did I? I suppose I did. What's my coping mechanism, anyway? Working lots? Pissing around on Mumsnet? God, how parenting challenges you to look at yourself.

'Yeah?' you said, leaning your elbows on the kitchen counter. I bought that island myself – solid marble – the second year my business, Cooper's, turned a profit.

'Of course. Just – you know . . .' I said, leaving the rest implied: be careful who you open our private lives up to.

'It's therapy, not a cult,' you said. That smile again. I wished you would show it to other people. Never in the popular group at school, always coming home and telling me you'd eaten lunch alone. My heart used to ache with it, feeling fat and full, like a big, sad cloud in my chest.

And now here we are again, just like last week. Me waiting for you outside the therapist's office. It's nice, actually, to be here. Just lately, you've been out more. 'With friends,' you said shortly, when I asked.

The office is at the back of Portishead High Street. The instructions to find it are complicated: past the artisan bakery, left, past the Waitrose, find the green door. You want me to drop you here each week, so I do. It's been pure nostalgia, waiting for you. Toddler groups, football matches, school runs. They felt endless – not to mention annoying – until they faded away to nothing. And, in those days, I didn't know how lucky I was. Parenting felt so much like drudgery. I'd race through the days like I was on a timer, waiting for that elusive *free time*. For me, that was a single cigarette, smoked out in the garden after you were in bed, whatever the weather. I looked forward to it far more than I ever enjoyed it.

I'd go back inside afterwards, and work. Scheduling a

viewing here, calling for best and final offers there, but that's all gone, too: Cooper's sold last year. At least now at parties I don't have to hear the estate agent jokes.

You lope out of the green door, past the Waitrose, etc., and flop into the car.

'How was it?' I ask.

'Yeah, good?' you say. 'I think?' I don't expect you to tell me any more than this, to be honest. You have been the same your entire life. Even as a baby: soulful, somehow private, emotionally contained. You are the sort of person who remembers an insult levied two years ago, but pretends not to.

'Learning and growing?' I joke, but really I'm pressing you. I've always been able to make you open up more than most.

'Of a fashion.' You lean back in your seat, a hand on the beard you grew after everything last year. It makes you look totally different. 'It's like . . .' You fiddle with the radio, I think for something to do. 'Nice to have somebody who just listens – who doesn't know anybody you're talking about.'

'And who *are* you talking about?' I can't help but ask curiously.

'Oh, my vast mummy issues,' you say, a side-eye to me.

'Ha, ha,' I say sarcastically, though it's no laughing matter. Jesus. What if you're serious? I put the car into drive, thinking how I once had a manual car with three gears that cost seventy quid. It's funny to have once been a poor single mum, and then to have become a rich single mum, and now we're sort of poor again, because of everything that happened last year, and me leaving the business. I want to ask if you told her this, and the rest, but I don't. In a way, you know, it's you and me against the world – always has been – and I don't want you to let someone else in.

You hesitate, a hand to the radio dial again, then look

77

directly at me. 'I just feel – after everything. Well. I feel, like, good again,' you say. A swell of emotion crests over me, and I blink a couple of times. 'Like we can – move on.'

'I'm glad,' I say, and I am. God, I think, looking at your profile, so unlike mine, but mine nevertheless to look at. How much I love you. You'll never know it, either. You will only have some idea, if you have a child of your own one day, of the things you will do to protect them, of how deep and pure your love for them will feel, like, if somebody said, 'Jump in front of this train, right now, to save them,' you would: you just would. No hesitation.

'Oh, can we get Thai?' you say, clicking your fingers as you think of it. 'There's that – remember? There's that little place here we went once to – you had the sweetcorn chi–'

'Oh, but aren't you learning and growing?' I say with a smile. 'At the very least about takeaways?'

'This is absolutely therapist-recommended,' you say, and I laugh, and let a breath out, and keep on wondering if you spoke about last year in therapy: if you have told her yet.

8

Julia

Julia is plate-spinning. Doing things that are not the DCI's job – like watching CCTV – and doing things she should do, too, like reviewing the sequence of events pieced together by ANPR reports, telecoms reports and CCTV reports. She's been talking to the fingertip searchers, considering Olivia's boyfriend (*It's weird how he sometimes is*, Olivia had written in that email, perhaps about him?), and finding out exactly what the alleyway is ever used for.

And watching TikTok, too, while she makes coffee after coffee. Olivia's story broke on the national news last night, and, as these things go, on TikTok shortly afterwards. The theories are building: a helipad in the alleyway (unlikely), an SAS abseil rescue operation (nice) and, of course, a ghost. Julia had to give a statement to the press – fairly rare, and always makes her feel like she's in an ITV drama. All the soundbites are the same. Very concerned for her welfare, doing everything we can, if anybody knows anything . . . Julia wishes she could say how she truly feels, while standing there, outside the police station, mic'd up. *I don't know where the fuck she is, I don't know what the fuck I'm doing, I'm being forced to lie and cheat.*

She's also been looking up Matthew James. She can't use

the PNC – it leaves a trail – so she is left with Facebook. There are three in Portishead: two are older, forty plus. The other is maybe nineteen, twenty. Dark hair, smooth olive skin. Julia stares and stares at him, there on Facebook. Holding a beer up, sun in his eyes. God, she hopes it isn't him. He's just a baby. Let it be one of the other two.

Jonathan arrives at the entrance to her office. 'You look absolutely knackered,' he says. He is standing with his weight on one leg, absent-mindedly running a finger around the metal of the door knob.

'So do you.'

Jonathan grins. 'Straight up, as ever.'

'Likewise. Anyway – you do.' Julia smiles.

'Baby doesn't sleep,' he says. His glasses catch the lights as he looks at her, turning his lenses white for just a second.

'Oh, but they're so worth it . . .' Julia says, thinking of those honeyed newborn days, just her, Art and Genevieve. Terry-towelling babygros, milk-drunk sleeps. Fidelity.

'You know, everyone says that, but being up all night is still being up all night,' Jonathan says.

Their eyes meet. 'I know.'

'Sorry, just – tired,' he says, running a hand through his hair. He swings his messenger bag down on to the floor, then flops into The Interrogation Chair next to Julia. She remembers him before he fell in love with his wife, before he had a child. When he had no lines around his eyes and spent every weekend out. Now, suddenly, he looks forty, just like her. Funny how it happens.

He opens the bag and pulls out a mind map of people – called an i2 association chart – already populated with names and faces. 'My social network,' he explains.

'Good.' Julia is filled, suddenly, with the irrational kind of hope that sometimes punctuates periods of anxiety. Maybe Jonathan will help her to find Olivia. And, if she finds Olivia alive . . . the problem is solved. It must be. Then Matthew cannot be convicted. Nobody could demand a conviction for a victimless crime. Could they?

'I've messaged every single person here,' Jonathan says, spreading it out across Julia's desk. A DC's job, really, not a DS's, but Jonathan is just like Julia in this respect: a control freak. 'No answers yet. I've also populated it with people she's emailed and texted . . . I can't always find overlap. For example, she emails Amy De Shaun a lot, but I can't find her on Facebook . . . It might be this Amz woman here, but I'm not assuming.'

'ABC,' Julia says.

'Exactly.'

ABC: Assume nothing, Believe nothing, Challenge everything. One of the most important rules of being a detective.

'The boyfriend,' Jonathan says, 'the one she watched in the HIIT workout, and sent the email about.'

'Yep,' Julia says, thinking – full of shame – that the boyfriend might be her biggest issue. She will be expected to go after him. But Julia is also incapable of not looking into him: it's not always the boyfriend, but it's very often the boyfriend – however, this time, to save Genevieve, it's got to be somebody else, somebody called Matthew James. And it has to be murder. The hardest charge to get through. Julia knows she doesn't have quite enough. DNA at the scene is helpful, but there is no body. It's not unheard of to charge murder without a body, but it is difficult.

'Right, okay – I'll get the boyfriend in,' Jonathan says.

'Okay,' she says quietly.

'No? Thought you'd be after him.'

'I am, I am,' Julia says defensively. 'Get him in. See where he was that night, okay?' She then adds, to distract him, 'I'm reading the pack at night. All her social media. She's very . . . I don't know, she somehow manages to get her personality across in every single post.'

'Right?' Jonathan says. 'I really like her.'

Julia sighs, thinking about that boyfriend. What if it really was him? 'Do you have a contact? For the boyfriend?' she says, unable to resist a lead.

'Leave it with me,' Jonathan says, and she feels moment-arily, irrationally, better.

'Know if Forensics found anything?' she asks.

'They've got some items. No idea whose, or if any DNA has come up yet. Look – anyway.' He hands her the sheet. He has ticked in green and crossed in red everyone on there. 'I got failure deliveries for these,' he says, indicating the crosses. 'And these have delivered' – he indicates the green – 'and this one' – he ticks Doug Adams's box – 'just called me up.'

'Who is he?' Julia asks.

'He hasn't seen her for years, just casual Facebook friends, though only added her fairly recently, so he says. Her Face-book account is quite new – a year or so. Weird for Gen Z to set one up now – Facebook is so past it. Anyway, they worked a temp job together one summer while she was at university. He can't remember the company, said maybe it had Boston in the title, though it's London based.'

'What doing?'

'Data entry. It's helped to piece together a timeline, though. She went to Nottingham University before moving back here. Studied psychology. Then she did a few shitty temp jobs, one with Doug, before she moved into marketing.'

'Okay, well, all information is good information,' Julia says. 'Keep going. Weird, though.'

'What?'

'Well . . .' Julia takes the sheet from him. 'It's a small network, really, isn't it? And most people message their friends on Facebook occasionally, even if only when they've forgotten their phone, or whatever. Seems pretty scant to me – how few contacts she actually has on there.'

'She calls herself a neo-Luddite.'

'Right,' Julia says, blowing out a small laugh. 'Well, sure.'

After he leaves, she closes the door to her office and gets out the forensic scrapings she took.

She can't ask Erin. She'd have to fake a crime, say she was grabbed in the street. It would throw up more and more questions than she can handle. She needs to be able to control the process.

After staring at the white scrapings for a few seconds, thinking, she applies online, to a private lab. She uses a fake name, pays with a debit card still registered to her maiden name, gives them an old hotmail email address. She writes her fraudulent details in the letter, pays and packages them up to go.

She takes them down the street, to a post box on the corner, wind in her hair, gaze frantically checking behind her, hoping nobody sees her. Especially not him.

On her way back, she calls Price, her informant. It's the first time she's ever asked him directly for information, rather than him coming to her.

Their relationship never felt slippery, though it started out the usual way: he was caught dealing, but he had a knife on him. Julia asked for his suppliers in return for dropping the knife crime charge. He complied but, in time, seemed to undergo a kind of criminal metamorphosis where he actively enjoyed not belonging to either side. He liked the pursuit of danger, continued to snitch long after his charge was dropped, lived a kind of amoral code where he would talk about some criminals and not others: Julia was never clear on the criteria.

The only person who disapproved of Julia's relationship with Price was Art. He had a wide possessive streak and always thought Price had an ulterior motive.

'Zac Harper,' Julia says, when he answers. 'Thief, mugger. Got into difficulty last year and died.'

'Yep,' Price says, and Julia isn't surprised he knew of him: he's one of the most connected men in crime, and has an excellent memory. He's the best informer she's ever had.

'Were you in touch a lot?'

'*Más o menos*,' Price says.

'In English, please,' she says. Price has a habit of picking up and using foreign phrases, mostly designed to confuse whoever it is he's speaking to.

'Who else did he associate with?'

'He was a petty thief, at best,' Price says disparagingly, like it would be better to be a serial killer. Julia doesn't dignify this remark with a response. All she needs to know is who Zac is likely to have told in the days before his death. Surely that will lead her to the man in her car.

'Who were his mates – not just the close ones, but the other ones, too?'

'Think he had a brother. No real mates. Don't know the name, though. Brother's elusive.'

She sighs. 'Hmm.'

'S'on your mind, DCI Day?' he asks tenderly, Julia thinks. That's the thing about Price: Julia may not be able to work out why he is loyal to some people and not others, but she knows that he is devoted to her. He could easily stop supplying information, defect, but he hasn't. Nor has he ever – to her knowledge – used anything she's told him to pursue his own criminal interests, and he only ever informs to Julia. Price respects the delicate ecosystem of their relationship. He once sent her a bunch of daffodils early on in her career, when she alluded to having a hard time. He didn't leave a note. She watched him place them on her car windscreen, then leave, presumably not wanting to frighten her.

'Nothing – tough case,' she says.

True to all this, Price doesn't push her. 'Let me know,' he says: shorthand for whether he can help.

'Sure will.'

'And, Day?'

'Mm?'

'Take care of yourself, yeah?'

The exact same phrase her brother used, two days after Zac's death, when she met up with him.

It had been an unseasonable twenty-five degrees. The very tip of Bill's nose was sunburnt. Bill looks nothing like Julia. Where she is blonde, he is dark, thick-set, usually with a full beard, though not that day. He, the size of a bear, had given her a demure wave. He had bought two takeaway coffees, which were sitting on a wall.

'All right?' he said.

He passed her the coffee with one of his paw-sized hands. 'Need some off-record advice,' she said to him.

'Oh, make no small talk, why don't you,' he said with his characteristic booming laugh.

He was in a suit, no jacket, and trainers, which she assumed he didn't wear in the office, though she wasn't sure.

'All right, sorry,' Julia said, blushing. 'How's work?'

'Yeah, busy: too much off-record pro bono work,' he said,

side-eyeing her. She gave him a wry smile back. 'Otherwise, you know. Counting my piles of money. Shouting *objection . . .*'

'Of course.'

'And you?'

'You know, high-speed car chases, shoot-outs . . . eating doughnuts,' she said back. Bill laughed so loudly that the hot wind carried it right away.

They fell into step beside each other. The sun was high in a *Truman Show* perfect sky.

Their parents had died when Julia and Bill were twenty-three and twenty-one respectively, within two months of each other. Their mother to cancer and their father to suicide. Within a year of it, Bill had converted to law and Julia had joined the police. There must be a psychology in it, but she isn't sure what. Finding things out, perhaps. Seeking the ever-elusive clarity. Perhaps, if she had some expertise, she could have prevented at least her father's death. Been tipped off, somehow.

Bill is excellent at reading people, when he can be bothered, and, sure enough, he brought her back to what she wanted: 'What's the advice?' His eyes flicked to her.

They rounded a corner. The high street fell away into the marina. The wind picked up. Big sheets of it swelled across them, solid-feeling against their faces, as though they might be carried away on them.

'What is it?' Bill said. 'I have half an hour, I need to file some directions at the court.'

'Can't Sharlé do it?' Julia says. Bill's fancy new secretary. Bill had recently said Sharlé had whipped his entire life into shape.

'Up to her neck ironing my trousers,' he joked with a small smile.

'Let's say I got mugged, right? I lashed out – and assaulted the mugger.'

Bill deliberately sipped his drink, which is what he does when he's thinking. Sometimes, Julia couldn't believe it was him. Her baby brother in a suit. Despite the pretence, despite the jokes they have, despite him sending her memes of *The Simpsons* every day even though they're both in their forties, he has expertise. Related to the knowledge Julia has, but distinct, too. And he was trawling through it while he sipped that over-syruped latte of his.

'What kind of attack did the mugger instigate on you, what did you do in return, and did the mugger die?' he said. He kept his tone light, but his eyes were curious. They have that same trait. Used to love gossip as kids, and now have two of the world's most salacious jobs – theoretically, anyway.

The clear, green spring light near Portishead marina smelled like still water. Julia leaned into it, wanting to forget. 'Like . . . the mugger tried to take a phone, say, and then I used the hand with my keys in it – to . . . you know.' Julia made a gesture; a crude, criminal slash across the neck, and Bill's eyes widened.

'Why?' he asked. One simple word.

'Fear.'

'Did the hypothetical person believe the mugger was going to attack them?'

Julia grimaced. 'Maybe. In panic. But then – they left.'

'Hmm.'

'But let's say he lived. Wound not as bad as it looked. But he dies – later. Sepsis.'

'From the wound?'

'Yes. What're the chances of self-defence?'

'You can't kill someone because they take your phone.

Obviously. Julia?' Bill looked at her quizzically. 'It has to be a proportionate response . . .'

Julia dropped her head. 'I know.'

Bill sucked his lips in. 'You know this stuff, don't you?' he said softly.

'Yeah.'

Bill held her gaze.

'What would I get?'

'Life. Maybe ten years if mitigated.'

She'd already known it. She'd been spot on. But it was somehow both helpful and hurtful to hear it.

'Thanks,' she said.

'Any time,' he said, but he looked at her a little longer than usual, as they parted. A second or two later, he tapped her on the shoulder. She'd already started her journey back to the station. 'Juls,' he said. 'I don't know any of this – okay? My job, you know . . .'

'I know,' she said.

He met her eyes. 'Take care of yourself, yeah?'

* * *

Julia is supposed to be prepping to speak to Olivia's father, but really she is heading into the back, behind the offices, to the evidence room. Her favourite place. She has been following the evidence for twenty years and doesn't intend to stop now. Finding Olivia is the only thing that will truly help. She pushes open the heavy fire door, shoes off, and heads into the dim and the dust.

It's a large, warm room, and every single time Julia comes in here she remembers the one single time Art came over when she was working on the Sadie case, ostensibly to spend time with her during a long-hours stint, but in reality he ended up re-alphabetizing the shelves.

O. Johnson 1–10. She finds them quickly. Boxes one and two contain Olivia's clothes. The first thing Julia thinks is that this isn't many. Maybe the rest are in storage somewhere for the house move. Genevieve has ten times this amount of clothes. But then . . . maybe that's just Genevieve.

Julia fingers a dusty-pink blouse, old-fashioned, square cut, then pulls an Aran-knit jumper out of a clear plastic forensic bag. Sage green, huge. She spreads the clothes out on an empty metal shelf deeper into the room, where there is less daylight and the smell of old evidence boxes is even more delicious. A pink blouse, a green jumper. Two pairs of jeans, two black t-shirts, a slogan tee. Maybe she *was* running away, Julia thinks, frowning as she looks at them. That is hardly any clothes at all. She must ask the dad if Olivia had storage anywhere else.

She checks the labels. Huh. Some designer, some high street, but what really stands out is they're different sizes. Eights, tens, twelves, fourteens. One XL.

She was fashionable, according to her Instagram. Maybe wore things big. The forgiving figures of the young. She gets her phone out and calls Genevieve. She knows she shouldn't.

She answers on the third ring. Lunchtime. A buzz around her, clear air whipping through the microphone.

'Do you buy clothes in lots of different sizes?' Julia asks.

'Er, hi to you, too,' Genevieve says. She steps away, somewhere quieter, perhaps inside; the wind dies down. 'No,' she says, truly the daughter of a cop, good at answering questions without explanation.

'Not even, like, an oversized jumper?'

'No – usually you buy it in your size but the cut itself is oversized? Like a boyfriend cut?'

'Oh, okay. Boyfriend cut. Got it,' Julia says.

'That all, Detective?'

'That's all,' she says with a smile. 'Olivia has a range of sizes.'

'What range?'

'Eight to fourteen to XL.'

'That's so weird,' Genevieve says thoughtfully. 'Are any of them on her Insta?'

'No. Not really. She took photos of things, mostly.'

'What size do you think she was?'

'She's thin, surely an eight or ten.'

'Same as me. I wouldn't wear a fourteen,' Genevieve says. 'Not even if I wanted it a bit big.'

'That's what I thought,' Julia says, her gaze scanning over the clothes. Something about them isn't quite right, somehow . . .

They ring off.

There's nothing else of note in the evidence boxes. A few scant possessions, an old-fashioned alarm clock, a notebook with nothing in it but a few pages torn out. A pillow spray. A passport, clear photo.

Julia surveys the clothes, thinking. There are several odd things about this case. The new job, the new house. She noticed something on Facebook, too: that Doug Adams made that comment on Olivia's status about foodie nights almost a year after she posted. All things that could be something and nothing, but . . .

Maybe the man in the balaclava has been sent by Olivia herself, Julia thinks, folding the clothes and putting them back. She usually enjoys this sort of expansive thought that lands as if from nowhere. *What if . . .*

Would that make any sense? She works it through, standing there, alone, without a team to turn to.

Or, if somebody else has taken or killed her, why have they nominated Matthew, specifically, to be framed?

Maybe the housemates will hold some answers, about the clothes and other things. They're new to Olivia, but even so: they're witnesses. Interviewed once already by the team, but not by Julia. It feels good to be doing something that isn't failing to find the blackmailer.

Julia lets herself out of the evidence room, intent on visiting Olivia's house again. Jonathan is walking towards her along the corridor.

'Spoken to the boyfriend,' he says. He's carrying a hefty evidence box himself, Olivia's personal items, paperwork, jewellery.

'And?' Julia says, not expecting to see him, or for him to be discussing the problematic boyfriend. She can hear a tremor in her voice.

'He has got one of the best alibis I've ever seen,' Jonathan says dispassionately. 'He was out of the country. Passport moved through two airports either side of her disappearance. There's no way he was anywhere else that night, sorry to say.'

Julia's shoulders sag in relief. Jonathan might be sorry, but she isn't. 'Well, onwards,' she says.

'Indeed.' Jonathan pushes open the door of the evidence room with his hip, but turns to her, his gaze lingering. Ordinarily, Julia would want to know every detail of this alibi. What, why, where? But today, she doesn't.

'Have you looked into her former housemates yet?' he asks.

'It's on my list,' Julia says. Like many things, but she doesn't usually completely fail to get to them. She's got too much on, trying to find Olivia, trying to find her blackmailer, trying to protect Genevieve.

Jonathan turns away from her.

'What's he like?' Julia can't resist asking, just before he heads inside the room. 'The boyfriend?'

'Normal. Reserved.'

'Panicked?'

Jonathan turns his mouth down. 'Hard to say. Stiff-upper-lip type.'

'Right,' she says lightly.

'I mean – we could go further on him – surveillance, and all that, if you wanted –'

'No, no need,' Julia says sharply.

'All right?' Alfie, the Super, says to them, emerging around a corner, ostensibly drifting by, but perhaps keeping an eye on her too. Julia has no idea how long he's been there.

''Course,' she says.

'Not going to look into that boyfriend further?'

'No need,' she says. 'Cast-iron alibi. Right?' She looks at Jonathan.

'Right,' he says softly. They stand there in a small triangle, the three of them, in a barely used corridor.

Julia can't bear it. She makes her excuses, leaves, but she can still feel the Super's eyes on her back as she does so.

9

Lewis

Sunday morning, earlyish. You are now two nights missing.

We are in the station, waiting. I guess all we are doing is waiting, in all its various, torturous forms, now. We know we're here to give detailed statements, but our bodies think we are here to be told the worst. I swear, I would feel no different if I was about to be taken into that meeting room and shot. Yolanda is next to me, our hands clasped tightly together.

Yolanda wasn't answering her phone yesterday, after I heard the news from Molly. And so, when I got home, I had to tell her. She went through the exact same thought processes I had only half an hour previously: denial, there must be some mistake, surely she's . . .

That night, last night, we didn't go to bed at all. Like something from *The Twilight Zone*, we simply stayed up. Front door open. Waiting for you. Two, three, four o'clock in the morning. Nothing.

Yolanda and I first met when we got stuck in a lift together. A story you have always loved; *Like something from a romcom*, you once said. It was just the two of us for four hours, sitting top to tail, our backs against the walls, our feet stretched out in front of us, shoes off.

We ate the only thing Yolanda had – Werther's Originals – and we listed our favourite everything: films, food, books, weather. We had absolutely nothing in common. She likes rich, salty Italian dishes and hiding her emotions. I don't care about meals, will grab anything to fuel myself, and – as you know – I'm partial to *freaking out*, as you would say. She likes Booker winners. I like Lee Child. She likes twenty degrees and sunny. For me, the more dramatic the better: give me a storm, twelve inches of snow, a heatwave so mad it melts the pavements and gets on the news. She likes thoughtful, sub-titled films. I like stupid action thrillers.

But, nevertheless, we found, in that old-fashioned lift with its accordion doors, that we had that rarest of things: chemistry. I don't mean flirtation – don't panic – I just mean that spiced banter that propels a marriage forwards, that makes you laugh in the middle of arguments, that makes you tolerate long hours and sleepless nights and snoring, and, too, the things you thought would never happen.

But, today, we don't have it. We have nothing but the deep silence of the station.

Two burgundy rugs line the foyer, both scuffed at their ends. A mouldering coffee vending machine used by criminals and people whose lives are in suspended animation sits in the corner. Benches with holes in the back like colanders. The surroundings add to the chaos. If you don't already think you're fucked, having to sit on a bench nailed to the floor will only add to the *vibe*, as you would say.

'Come through,' a copper says, poking his head around the door. He's short, bald and relatively young. I can't help but hope he isn't DCI Day's right-hand man. I want someone strapping, or, no, perhaps a smoking alcoholic. Someone who makes corkboard collages of leads and has brainwaves in the middle of the night.

We are led into a meeting room with a grey carpet which smells new. There are three chairs, an empty table and a white CCTV camera in the corner of the room. There's absolutely nothing else except a female police officer wearing a suit, and using one sleeve to mop up a tea stain. She meets my eyes and nods.

This must be DCI Day, the lead on your case. Slight, blonde, intelligent eyes. I hope it is. She looks kind and very stressed, an excellent combination for a detective. 'DCI Julia Day,' she says, rising slightly out of her chair and reaching over to shake my hand. 'Call me Julia.'

'DS Robert Poole,' the bald man says. His knees click as he sits down on the chair. Damn, so he is her sous detective. He uncaps his pen, evidently not wanting to waste any time. Julia does nothing except look at us carefully, her expression unreadable. 'Interview commenced, nine thirty-nine. When did you last see your daughter?' Poole says, interrupting my thoughts about Julia.

'Three days ago. We don't live together.'

'Okay?' Poole turns his eyes to Yolanda.

'I didn't see her then,' she says softly, so softly I wonder if she regrets that. She was working late. You and I watched *Selling Sunset* – the episode where Christine wears a black wedding dress. You turned to me and said, 'Oh my fucking *God*, okay, we are watching an icon right now.'

'And when did you last hear from her?' Poole says to me. Still, Day hasn't spoken. Her eyes are on Yolanda, whose long, dark plait has fallen from her shoulder. She's fiddling with the end of it, not looking at anybody. Her hair's always been the same, that braid, but otherwise, the woman from the lift is long gone, right now.

'I texted her yesterday, about her coming over this Thursday, as she always does,' I say.

Poole's eyes are on me. He isn't writing anything down.

'Usually,' Yolanda corrects. 'It isn't every single Thursday, is it?' The muscle in her jaw twitches. She must be used to this, in a way, the precise nature of the questions. She attends many police interviews with her service users.

'How did she seem when you last saw her?'

'She was fine, normal,' I say. 'Chatty.'

Day speaks, now, for the first time. Her voice comes out hoarse and cracked, at first, and she clears her throat. 'What sort of person is she?'

'Er, she has a complete sense of self, doesn't she?' I say to Yolanda.

'Yes, totally. She's – ethical –'

'Left-wing –'

'Loves food. Funny.'

'Yes – and fashion. Shoes. The push–pull between being sustainable and buying what she likes,' I add. Day's eyes meet mine, and they look upturned, affectionate.

'I see,' she says simply, and I feel a rush of embarrassment, from nowhere, about how very much we love her. As though the world can see it, and so, too, see our pain.

'What did you do that night you last saw her?' Poole says, as smooth as that.

And that's when it suddenly occurs to me: we are suspects. That is completely clear now. Isn't the father often accused? 'Why is this relevant?' I ask, but Yolanda puts a hand on my leg underneath the table.

'We ate, watched television,' I say crisply in response to Yolanda's hand.

She removes it and places it back on the table. Her engagement ring has spun around, the stone hitting the table. She's lost weight, already. Her appetite is always the first thing to go in times of stress, even though her cooking isn't. She cooks and cooks and cooks, but doesn't eat any of it.

'What did you eat?' Poole asks.

Immediately, I begin to sweat. Jesus, the power of the police. They must never be able to ask anyone a single question ever, at parties, at parents' evenings, anywhere, without whoever it is thinking they are about to be arrested. 'Er,' I say. And then it comes to me – do you remember? The bloody saga that is Hello Fresh. Billed as timesaving; actually, a huge pain in the fucking arse. 'Butternut squash risotto,' I say. 'It's with this Hello Fresh, you know, they courier it all to you and you cook it –'

'I know it,' Day says. Two dimples appear on either side of her mouth.

'Nobody needs to know about how much you hate Hello Fresh,' Yolanda says, the first smile in what seems like for ever. A flick of her eyes to me, and there she is: the woman from the lift.

'Supposed to save time but actually you spend all that time opening tiny fucking packets of cheese,' I gabble.

'I would've cooked, if I had been there,' Yolanda says softly, which I'm glad of. It changes the mood, back to sombre, away from farce, away from my swearing (always out of control). And back to you.

Anyway. The risotto was rubbish. We have this thing where we text each other our meals – your recent Portishead beach churros, for example – then the other rates them out of ten. Once, you gave a croissant of mine an eleven. We both gave the risotto a two.

'What did you watch?'

'*Selling Sunset.*' This is the first thing Poole writes down, much to my humiliation. 'And then *Dogs Behaving (Very) Badly.*'

'Right – okay. And your daughter, she seemed . . . ?'

'Totally herself.' My eyes mist over. You were totally, utterly you. Ranting about ableism, about the unfairness of the housing market, reading out Taylor Swift lyrics to me. You ate two portions of risotto even though you said it had the texture of Blu Tack. Just you being you.

'No seeming off colour, no secretiveness, no shielding her phone from view?'

'No – but . . .'

Day's head snaps up, although she says nothing. Just looks at me. Her eyes do that thing where they look at your left eye, then your right, then your left, then your right, microdancing in front of me.

Yolanda sighs. She knows what I'm going to say. She is not prone to extremist thinking, but she can predict me.

'Hang on,' Poole says. 'What time did she leave, Lewis? Just for completeness.' He's making a note, now. The sort of person who is so fastidiously by the book that he is happy to miss the important details, I presume. Julia side-eyes him but lets him continue.

'I don't know.' The use of my name irritates me. This isn't *EastEnders.* 'She drove home, maybe eleven thirty?' I remember the way the outdoor light clicked on, illuminated your hair like a spider's web. The last time I saw you.

'Was it just you two?' he asks, even though he knows this already.

'Yes,' Yolanda says. 'We said. I had a client emergency at work.'

'What do you do?' Day asks, interested.

'Social work.'

Day nods in understanding, then looks at me. 'But?' she prompts, wanting me to finish a sentence from minutes ago.

'She has this boyfriend.'

It is as though I have passed a grenade across the table. Day's and Poole's body language changes completely. He sits up; she leans forward, eyes on mine. 'Tell me about him,' she says.

'Andrew Zamos. He's not a nice person.'

You met him a few months ago. At an after-work thing. You described it to me so well, do you remember? A meet-cute on a cold balcony, outside a wanky drinks reception, you said – par for the course in the corporate world, right? You escaped to look at the skyline, and there he was. Said you looked bored, which was correct. You stayed out there together for two hours, until your cheeks were pink and your feet numb. Your colleagues came and went, and still you chatted. Didn't catch a breath, you said. You didn't swap numbers but, a week later, he added you on socials.

I met him only two weeks after that. I thought he was leaning in to shake my hand, but he was reaching to push the front door open, behind me. Of my own house.

Two weeks after *that*, you said you were going to be together for ever.

Yolanda interjects. 'I'm not sure he's not nice. He's – you know, a bit insecure, socially awkward . . .' she says. She's seen a lot of *his type*, so she says, at work. Has more empathy than me, perhaps.

'He's an arsehole,' I say. But – in what way, precisely, he is

99

an arsehole is hard for me to say. Each anecdote sounds like nothing, as thin as gossamer, which I'm sure is his intention. Coercive control. That's what it is, isn't it?

Day takes Poole's pen straight from his hand and writes a perfectly formed bullet point. 'How long?'

'Three months, tops. It's volatile, I would say.'

'*Is* it volatile?' Yolanda says. 'Look.' She tucks a lock of dark hair behind her ear that's fallen from her plait. 'It's worth looking into. But, if you want to know, I have never worried about it.'

I cross my arms. 'Well, I have.'

'We'll talk to him,' Day says, looking at me. 'Okay?'

'Good.'

'But don't over-focus on him,' Yolanda says quickly. She looks at me, her expression saying, *Don't you dare fucking challenge me*, and I don't.

'What do you mean by "volatile"?' Day asks.

'It isn't volatile,' Yolanda says.

'They do fall out a lot,' I say. I'm trying to be measured. Even though I'm doing all this to help you, I still feel guilty. Like showing the inside pages of a diary to someone else.

'Why?'

'In my opinion, because . . . like, for example, he once said, *Are you going to come and watch me play football, or just not bother?* She said she already had plans – and he said . . . I will remember it: *No need to factor me in.* Then he got in her way on the landing, I saw it.'

'Okay, so physically blocked her way?'

'Yes. Exactly.'

'Would you say he's often intimidating?'

'He chipped away at her – mostly with those kinds of comments.' As I say this, Yolanda shifts in her chair. 'He accuses her of overreacting if she behaves in the same way as him. Obviously, you know – you can't control your own children . . .'

'Sadly not,' Day says drily. 'But this leads to arguments – between them?'

'Exactly. One time, he was mad she was late for something important – meeting his friends for the first time. He got angry, called her up, demanded to know where she was. She was with me. And it had been ten minutes? She had just been faffing before leaving.' I bite my lip. I can't conceptualize it for the police in a way that makes it sound as serious as it is. His dismissals of you. So careless, as though you were a fly, buzzing at his temple in the summer heat. His tone. His sanctimony. It's as intangible as smoke. Just thinking about it makes my temperature rise like I have the flu. 'Plus, whenever she has plans, he wrecks them. Gets food poisoning, or whatever, then miraculously recovers when she cancels.'

'Would you say he has ever taken his temper out on her?' Day asks. She has to raise her voice just slightly: the police station has a flat roof, above us, and rain has begun to hammer down on it outside.

'I don't know,' I say honestly. 'But it's a pattern of behaviour, isn't it? He thinks he can tell her what to do. One time when they were over, early on, her phone rang at dinner, and he reached out and declined the call for her.'

'Hmm,' Day says.

'Or what about' – I say, desperate now, desperate for her to see how it really was – 'another time, the two-month anniversary of when they met, or something, I heard him say, *Let me be clear – you're not seeing them tonight. It's me.*'

'So – controlling her friends?'

'Exactly. And right before she disappeared, he said to her – I thought jokingly, at the time – *Man, I swear to God, I'd like to just keep you somewhere all to myself.*'

Day's eyes flash at that. 'Said in what context?'

'I overheard it – a romantic missive. But . . . sinister.'

'To you,' Yolanda says.

Day turns her mouth down like, *Maybe, maybe not.*

That's the thing when you feel something emotionally. When you notice body language. When you *know it*, but you can't prove it. 'When he said that, he had hold of her wrist really tightly, I saw it. He saw me looking, and he dropped it.'

'When was this?'

'A week and a half ago?'

'So, pretty much a week before she went missing,' Day says, her eyes on me.

'Yeah.'

'Did he?' Yolanda says, looking at me. Her perfume wafts around the room as she moves, musky, old-fashioned, and I'm surprised she's put any on. 'You never said he dropped it when he saw you looking.'

'Er, yes. I did. Why are you doubting that?' I ask, trying to keep my tone mild, but failing. My own wife doesn't remember what I told her about our daughter.

'Look,' Yolanda says to Day. 'I'm not trying to be difficult. But she was out late, alone. She could be –' Her voice becomes coarse, like she's just knocked back a shot. 'She could be – *held* somewhere, and we'd be focusing on – be focussing on – because you are fixated on – the way you sometimes get –'

As always, when Yolanda is worried it has a full-bodied effect on me. I push my chair back. Bloody hell. *Held* somewhere. That word implies something so sinister. Kidnap. Worse. 'She'll be fine,' I say, semi-hysterically. 'She *is* fine.'

'We will look into all avenues,' Day says. 'Just – was the relationship fast, Lewis?' Thankfully, she ignores Yolanda's remark about my ability to obsess. *The way I sometimes get.*

'Yes. Definitely. From nought to sixty,' I say, not looking at Yolanda. 'They went from having just met to him being, like . . . just a completely central part of her life.'

'Okay. And was that why she left her job?'

'I don't think so,' I say. 'No. She was just – you know. Temping.'

'But she's seen much less of her friends, too.' Day writes something illegible on Poole's pad, at this. 'Do you know the housemates –'

'But – DCI Day –' I interrupt.

'Call me Julia.'

'Julia – I'm painting a picture that doesn't contain a lot of evidence, I know,' I say. I lean across the table earnestly, staring at the DCI, looking for answers. I notice suddenly that her fingertips are trembling. As subtle as a guitar string vibrating for just a few seconds after the song closes. 'But I didn't like what I saw.'

'Give us his details, we'll get him in. We need the house-mates in again, for formal interviews.' Day passes us a sheet of lined paper. 'Write everything on there – all her friends, her boyfriend, anyone you think might've seen her over the past few weeks. Okay?'

'Okay.' I write his name down at the top. *Andrew Zamos – boyfriend.*

'Noted,' Day says, as I underline it. I add a handful of your friends, then pass it to Yolanda, who adds two more.

'DCI Day.' Her eyes turn to me. 'What're the odds, here?' I ask. Poole shifts uncomfortably in his chair, but I'm not interested in him. Like the frontman of a band, like a CEO, like a sportsperson, Day is clearly in charge here, like any-body with charisma usually is.

Outside, the rain intensifies, like marbles on a tin roof. It lends a chaotic kind of atmosphere to the interview.

'Lewis,' Yolanda says. But I can't read her tone. Whether she wants the answer to this or not. I shouldn't have asked without checking she wanted to know, but I couldn't help myself.

'This is not the time for these questions,' Poole interjects. Immediately, I write him off as a gobshite.

'Ninety per cent come home unharmed, at this stage,' Day says softly, doing me a favour by answering. I'm surprised to see her eyes dampen. She blinks, sips her tea to cover it.

Ninety per cent. My shoulders fall as sharply as if some-body has pulled the skeleton clean out of me. Ninety per cent. I can work with ninety per cent. Ninety per cent is good odds. It's an A* in any exam.

'Thank you, thank you,' I say quickly, relief making me overly familiar. 'Ninety per cent.' I flick open my wallet, not really thinking about it. A small photograph of you sits in the window. You know the one, at the beach, heart-shaped sunglasses on, ice cream in hand. 'So retro,' you said, when I asked for the spare and put it there, but I don't care.

How can you be here, concrete, in my hands, in my wal-let, but nowhere else? I could rip this photograph up, I find myself thinking. Tear it and – like Dorian Gray – maybe you would emerge somewhere else, your portrait killed, your real self freed.

I look at Day. She is staring down at your photograph. 'She's lovely,' she says. Yolanda is steadfastly not looking at the photograph, her jaw quivering.

'I know. She knows it, too,' I say with a little laugh. I hope you don't mind that I say this. I mean, it is true.

As we're standing up, I think about it. Ninety per cent.

Ten per cent, therefore. This is how my brain works. First, the relief. Then, the *but*. The images begin to come: you're walking along a deserted street. It was rainy, the night you went missing. The slick street shimmers with it. A car offers you a lift. You're on the motorway before you realize the danger you're in. That the doors are locked. That your driver isn't who he said he was.

I touch my wallet as I put it away. Your eyes are boring into my hand. I can't close the flap and put you away. Tears clog my throat. I want to tell you. I want to tell you, the miniature you in the photograph: *Come home. Come the fuck home, Little O. We need you.*

'We have our very best investigators on this, Lewis,' Poole says. 'Keep your phone on overnight. I'm sure we'll have news.'

'We won't be sleeping.'

'. . . No,' Poole says, after a beat or two. 'No, of course. Well, if you do, put that phone on loud.' I glance at Day – far, far more endowed with interpersonal skills – but she's looking through the window in the door at an officer who's motioning to her with his phone.

'Sorry, sorry,' Day murmurs. Her brow is creased. She seems distracted, all of a sudden, by that colleague, by that waving phone. No, not distracted. What? I look closely at her. Fearful?

'Okay?' Poole says to us, an understudy finally taking centre stage, and I am struck by the thought that he might be about to say something horribly rousing, the stuff of Hollywood films, like, *Let's bring your daughter home, Lewis*, but he doesn't.

Instead, he gestures for us to go without anything further: they leave us to our own hell. The police station dribbles us out on to the wet street outside.

It's typical, blustery spring weather. The rain now spitting, sunshine appearing and disappearing on fast speed like a stop-motion film. Cold air, hot sun, freezing rain. Weather that doesn't know what to do with itself, like us.

As I look up, I remember something else. Feeling sure, the other Thursday, that you wanted to tell me something. You hesitated in the kitchen, a hand halfway to your hair, said *Dad* . . . but then said nothing else when I prompted you. As you looked down and chopped an onion, you were blushing, eyes smarting. You blamed the onion.

Nothing tangible, nothing that counts to the police. But still things nevertheless, like the clouds above. I keep looking up, searching.

You're out there, somewhere, alone.

Or, worse: not alone.

Later, after dropping Yolanda at home, I swing back by the police station, intending to tell them about you chopping the onion. But, as I arrive, DCI Day leaves, and that's the first time I follow her.

10

Julia

That night, Julia tries to find Zac's brother, but she can't use the Police National Computer without leaving a trace. There's nothing on Google. She cups her chin in her hands and thinks. She can't fathom why anyone who knew him would wait to act against Julia until now. Or what that has to do with Olivia.

Maybe Matthew had done *something* to Olivia, and she's now framing him . . .

Outside, the moon is up, a white haze around it, the streets quiet and black. Julia has decided to try and find the man in the balaclava. Where the sun set is striated and marbled pink and orange, a Jupiter sky. The air smells damp, as Portishead often does. It could be a January morning. It could be Christmas Day. She gets into her car but checks the back seats first. She wonders if perhaps now she always will.

The world carries on as normal around her. She's spent the day trying to trace Olivia's housemates. The dad has told her he will put her in touch. But, really, Julia needs to find her blackmailer. She stops at a zebra crossing. She fantasizes that it is he who is about to step on to the road. That she could get out, threaten him. Arrest him. Silence him, somehow.

She thinks about last year's investigation, and Sadie.

Genevieve's mugging happened right in the middle of the first week of that investigation, the day Julia was supposed to conduct all of the interviews with all of Sadie's contacts. She spent the days after in her back office, making sure Genevieve was okay, making sure Zac didn't come in (he did), making sure, making sure, making sure. But, evidently, she had been concentrating on the wrong things. Sadie had never been found, perhaps because of Julia's negligence – she had never missed interviews before. And then, a few days later, when Zac died, she had spent two days panicking and let Jonathan fill her in on the telecoms and forensics reports instead of looking at them herself. There is no substitute for first-hand. Still, sometimes, she looks guiltily at Sadie's Facebook, flicks through the photographs. A kind of apology, to her, from the woman who had been supposed to find her.

And it looks like Julia's efforts were thwarted, anyway, as somebody had found out about Genevieve. And now Olivia. Also missing, the investigation also bungled, for the same and different reasons.

An old couple crosses the street slowly, arms linked. Silhouettes against the blazing red, alive sky. Julia watches them go. Sometimes, on days like this, when surrounded by so much crime, she finds it amazing anyone gets to that age. Unscathed, happy. Neither a victim nor incarcerated. That's the skew you get from two decades in the police.

She drives her old car – she won't part with it – to the exact location she parked it that night, gets out and scans a slow circle around in the cold, just searching. The first thing any detective should do when arriving at any scene at all: spend five minutes observing. It's amazing what you see in that final minute.

There are several targets: Ring doorbells. A petrol station. A One Stop. They all have CCTV.

And so that's where she starts. Off record, painfully so, alone, but trying.

A bell tinkles in the Esso garage as she pushes her way in. It smells of newspapers and car air fresheners.

'I'm from Portishead Police,' she says to the owner. 'Could I please have access to your CCTV, in connection with a missing person?' An easy lie, or perhaps not even a lie at all. She doesn't show her badge, doesn't name herself. If it ever comes out, she will be on those very same cameras, unable to deny it, but anything she can do to stop herself being traced is for the best.

The owner of the garage blinks, looking at her in surprise. Perhaps shock at the police arriving, or perhaps he hadn't been expecting a copper to be slight and blonde.

He's maybe twenty-five, one hoop earring in, a black beanie on his head, the sides rolled up like a pie crust. 'Er, hang on, not my place,' he says, holding a palm up and disappearing out the back, past a row of cigarettes and scratch cards.

Julia takes a slow wander around the aisles of Pringles and chocolate bars and windscreen-wiper fluid, a Costa Express machine. But, really, she's just listening to the voices from the back room, and trying to look like she isn't. It's an old habit. You learn so much by looking uninterested while listening.

'Which days?' the owner says, emerging. Julia answers and he disappears out back just as her phone goes off, the jaunty tone she has for Genevieve. She opens it out of habit: 'It's going off on TikTok about Olivia,' Genevieve has written. 'So many amateur detectives with theories.'

Julia smiles grimly. She doesn't mind this strange facet of modern policing. Enjoys it, in fact. Most DCIs wouldn't admit it, but the Gen Z-ers contributing via social media very occasionally do assist. Not to mention entertain.

'Tell me a few,' she writes back to Genevieve, unable to resist, even though she should not be fostering Genevieve's interest in crime. The worst thing for everybody would be for Genevieve to join the police: Julia wouldn't wish that for anybody – like becoming an addict. She is a goner, but Genevieve needn't be. God, she wouldn't join, after committing a crime, would she?

She turns to the owner, a man with a round face and red cheeks. He passes her a USB, held between index and third finger like the offer of a bribe.

Julia, out in the cold again, works her way up the road that surrounds her car, shops, a clutch of USBs in her hand that she will copy the footage on to. She is thankful that the police system is full of chaos, of scattered, random USBs, that nobody will question what she's doing, that the search team has probably already done this once, only looking for a woman, instead of a man.

At eleven thirty she takes the USBs back to the station, where she begins to play them one by one. Another coffee. She takes her socks as well as her shoes off this time, puts her bare toes on the ancient carpet.

The motion-sensor lights go off around her. She doesn't move to reactivate them, is content to sit there alone in the spotlight of her computer.

She doesn't feel tired. Just lets the adrenalin burn and burn and burn, the only thing on her mind the survival of Genevieve, of her career, of their freedom.

On checking the fourth USB, she finds the man from her car. Or, rather, his gait. Julia's car is in the very bottom left of the frame, and the man, still in his balaclava, shuts her door behind him, and disappears, stage right, off screen. Eleven forty-seven.

There's nothing identifying about him. Julia watches the video over and over. He leaves her car confidently, easily, the same way, she assumes, that he let himself in.

He has a walk that is somehow quite gentle, slow, and he is slimmer than she remembered, but nothing else. All in black, only his eyes visible, two dark holes.

There's a logo in hi-vis on the bottom of his coat. It glows silver as he walks under a streetlight, but, no matter how many times she watches it, she can't catch it. Each freeze-frame is a blur. She watches twenty times, taking screenshots on the system every 0.1 seconds. None of them shows anything. She downs her coffee and sinks her head into her hands. He is missing, too.

As she goes to the bathroom, she sees Poole and Best together, their heads close, looking in her direction.

* * *

'DNA results in,' Erin is saying, walking into the kitchenette like it isn't almost midnight. Jonathan is making coffee and moaning about Meta – Instagram and Facebook – which has still not released Olivia's records to them. They can look at her social media, but they can't get inside it and see her messages without Meta.

Jonathan stirs his coffee and then Julia's. 'Sorry, yours will taste of sugar now.'

'What DNA?' Julia interrupts, the way she would if she hadn't put Matthew's DNA there herself.

Julia still doesn't know how she will get Matthew charged, and for murder. There's no body. Would his DNA being found in Olivia's room be enough for a charge of kidnap? And then to escalate it? Maybe. But how can she get to that point? There is unlikely to be a match on the system, unless he has committed an offence before.

'A cigarette and a glass,' Erin says, leaning her head on the doorframe. She doesn't seem surprised. To Erin, a scene always yields something, some clue. It's both the art and the science of forensics. 'Unknown person. Male. No matches on the system.'

Julia experiences an uncomfortable, unfamiliar emotion: how easy it has been to fool her old friends, experts in their fields for the longest time. How straightforward it is when you're on the inside. And how shameful that is.

Jonathan adds milk to his coffee and hesitates over Julia's. 'You are a details man, Jonathan,' she says. 'It's been no milk for two decades.'

'I remember only important details,' he says. And it's true. Jonathan has a wonderfully streamlined sort of brain, able to filter out useless trivia from important things to remember. Only last summer, during the Sadie case, Julia had asked him – after the sighting – what Sadie's exact height was, and Jonathan hadn't missed a beat before saying, '162 on Facebook, 160 on medical records'.

'The room, otherwise, is a DNA feast – the housemates',' Erin says, hands in the back pockets of her trousers. 'HMOs for you.'

She isn't wrong. Houses of multiple occupancy are always a DNA nightmare, but Julia needs to get the focus on to Matthew. 'Surely we can dismiss the housemates,' she says, though she knows it isn't what she would ordinarily say. She would usually go after them: every avenue, however unlikely.

'Why?'

Julia has no answer for this, and her brain stalls as she tries to think of one. 'Uh – just that it's natural their DNA would be there.'

'Not in her actual room, is it?'

'Oh – you said in her room?' Julia lies, trying to cover her own tracks.

Erin just looks at her, confused, saying nothing. Julia is never not on top of the facts.

The night behind Erin is black, the strip lights a stark, unflattering white. 'Anyway,' she continues, 'the cigarette isn't a match to the housemates. It had been smoked pretty recently, though I'm not sure if it's from that night; it had hardened just slightly. Maybe the night before. It had been stubbed out by the smoker, not stood on. The previous occupant of the room had moved out too long ago, so it isn't them, either. Anyway – I'll leave you with it. Miles has made a very late dinner.'

'How is he?' Julia asks.

Erin waves a hand. 'Yeah, fine, wants to move house again.'

Erin's husband is a restless type; he either likes to be planning a party or a renovation. They've moved four times in a decade. 'Where?' Julia asks with a smile.

'Bristol. He's found a Victorian doer-upper, has so much potential – blah blah . . .'

'Don't do it,' Jonathan says. 'We're having a bathroom put in. Baby up all night, builders in all day, listening to pissing Ed Sheeran.'

Julia smiles, at their chat, the normality. And then it comes to her. Right then, while trying to make small talk, late at night, exhausted, while amid the soup of keeping her head above water: how she's going to arrest Matthew James.

'I think we should do a voluntary DNA screening,' she says, almost jubilant with it, her own deception. 'Everyone on those three roads surrounding the alleyway, where her phone pinged, comes forward, offers their DNA. Males only. We'll see where we get to.'

'Oh, yeah . . .' Erin says slowly while she thinks, rocking back on her heels slightly, looking at Julia. Appraising her, Julia thinks. 'Yes. And if they don't come forward . . .'

'Well, that says something by itself,' she says, but really she is thinking: Matthew probably will, he has no reason not to. He has nothing to fear, or thinks he doesn't, has no idea he has a silent enemy.

A few minutes after Erin's gone, and Julia's finished her coffee, which *does* taste slightly of sugar, the Superintendent pokes his head around the door. Alfie Breeze, late fifties. Was once a great detective but has slid happily into management, budgeting, HR matters. He leaves at five o'clock, plays golf in the spring and summer. Somewhat disengaged, he regards his best years as firmly behind him. Tonight, he's passing through the office, not because he's working hard, but because he has been in a restaurant in Portishead, and still likes to abuse the free parking here.

'All right?' he says. He pulls his trousers up as he sits down opposite her in her office. Julia's slatted blinds tigerstripe him in the glow from a yellow streetlight. He smells of cigars. The charred, heavy smell used to make Julia nauseous when she was pregnant. A wave of nostalgia hits her, for back then. So in love with Art, who said it made him laugh how she was still solving crimes with a huge pregnancy bump.

Julia blinks, lost in the swirling smoke of the past, before it all went wrong. Before – Art would say; did say – she neglected him. Before he slept with someone else – *just once*, he yelled at her, his face bright red with anger, like a baby.

'How's it going?' Alfie prompts. Outside, it's strange weather. A kind of sleety, white rain, illuminated here and there by passing headlights.

'All right. We have some unknown male DNA at the scene,' she says woodenly.

'What do you think the chances are?' he asks.

Julia tries to forget everything she's done, looks out at the tumbling sleet and thinks only about Olivia. 'I don't think she's dead,' she says eventually, and is surprised to find she believes that. It doesn't make sense to Julia. She has no evidence, just a hunch. Maybe it's Olivia's vivacious online persona, maybe the strangeness of the alley, certainly the man in the back of her car, the lack of a body . . .

She considers, just for a second, what would happen if she told Alfie. He'd phone it in to the anti-corruption team. He'd charge Genevieve. She wouldn't be out until she was thirty. And Art would – what? Julia doesn't know, not at the moment. He's (usually) a fan of doing the right thing. He'd visit Genevieve, would be overly solicitous to Julia, maybe, before leaving her for an unproblematic colleague.

'Something on your mind?' Alfie says quietly. He stands and begins to tidy up, slowly and methodically. His signature soft-interview technique.

Julia had forgotten, in Alfie's benign semi-retirement, just how formidable he used to be, and she finds herself wishing, suddenly, that all of her friends weren't fucking police. She could tell a girlfriend this, a sister, but she doesn't have anybody. Work has taken that social life from her. All she has left is trained interviewers. Even her brother, previously her playmate, forever young with her, she hardly sees now.

'No, just want to find her,' Julia says lamely.

'Couple of the team have said you seem skittish. Not following things up.' Alfie walks over to the blinds, starts fiddling with the metal pole that closes them. He turns it, shutting out the sleet. 'Doesn't feel like spring, does it?' he says, not turning back to her. 'Snow in May.'

So that's why he's in here. Not checking in: checking up.

'Who's said what?'

'Just wondering if you need someone else to take it,' Alfie says. Julia closes her eyes. More than anything, she wants that. But that would be her death warrant. Or, rather, Genevieve's.

'Please don't do that,' she says. 'It's just complex. That's all.'

'So what's your plan?'

'Uniform are doing house-to-house inquiries. We're doing a voluntary screening for the DNA evidence. Anyone nearby and male to come forward. Question anyone who doesn't give it.'

'Big budget, that.'

Julia spreads her hands wide. She genuinely believes this is what she would do even if she hadn't been told to convict Matthew. 'You know me,' she says. 'I always spend too much. And I very often find the misper.'

'Except Sadie,' Alfie says. He walks away from the blinds, the room now darkened.

'Has something been said by Olivia's family?' Julia asks, ignoring the wound caused by Alfie saying that name.

'Let me know how you go. Hopefully the weather will warm up,' he says conversationally, walking across the room with one hand in his pocket, not answering her question.

* * *

Art and Genevieve have been to the theatre in Bristol. They're back late, almost one.

Julia is watching the car idle on the drive outside, sipping coffee in the kitchen and thinking about Olivia, awaiting the commingled joy and trepidation that now accompanies the homecoming of her child and husband. Respectively.

She has been a whirlwind of productivity tonight. Reviewing the fingertip-search results, chasing up Olivia's Twitter, Instagram and Facebook account releases, reviewing yet more footage that might include the alleyway. Her brother called her, too, for half an hour, said he was rewatching *South Park*, and Julia felt such a strong pang of longing it was almost like nausea. For that uncomplicated, free life. And for their childhoods, too.

And now she's standing here in the kitchen. The only light comes from under the cupboards. Her legs are illuminated in one clean, white slice, the rest of her is in darkness.

Lonely, alone, in solitude. Whatever you call it, Julia is an island. Somebody who has now done unspeakable, awful things that no one knows about. Suddenly, for the first time, she understands the desire some criminals have to confess. To end the uncertainty, and be punished. She closes her eyes as she sips the coffee, tips her head back as she swallows. Let it end. If it was only her, she'd do it. Take the jail term. But it's Genevieve, too. Genevieve's sentence, her own reputation, her own mistake compounded by her mother's.

Art turns the headlights off, then the security light illuminates them as they pile out of the car, turning Genevieve into a strobing picture, fragments of colour here and there, her outline a silhouette in the darkness.

'That sand is extra tonight,' Genevieve says as they come through the door. 'There's so much of it.' Sure enough, it crunches under their feet. Julia has never once swept it up, and she thinks guiltily that Art must do it. She suddenly misses texting and emailing him with a ferocious roar. Their relationship was so often conducted in writing – led by him. He is a texter, an emailer, a wordsmith. Out at dinner with other people, a text from him to her from the toilet: 'God, Janet is boring, isn't she?' and from her to him: 'I know! Share a pudding?' Words: the second love of Art's life, or so she hoped.

'How was it?' she asks, stepping out of the kitchen.

'Why are you lurking in there?' Genevieve says, and Julia blushes in shame. Teenagers. You can never conceal anything.

'Was just having a coffee,' she says lamely.

'You do you, Mum.'

Julia raises her eyebrows at her daughter. She sometimes feels her more argumentative persona is aimed precisely at Julia.

Art has on a wrinkled t-shirt and – somehow – wrinkled jeans. That shabby, comfortable, unpretentious way he always is. He once said he looked like a dog in a suit, and Julia knew exactly what he meant.

She thinks of her yearning to know anyone at all who isn't a fucking cop, and look: here he is.

'All right,' he says, avoiding her gaze. This week, she noticed he had moved his summer clothes into the spare room and out of what might once have been their bedroom, had things been different. An extra commitment to their estrangement.

'It was very long,' Genevieve answers Julia's question. 'Could've left in the interval.'

Julia catches Art's eye. She had said this exact sentence to him many times when they were dating. Funny how you pass things on you'd forgotten you even did yourself.

'I always think that,' she says. 'Three hours is two hours too long.'

'Two and a half,' Genevieve says.

'It's Tennessee Williams. You're meant to be bored,' Art says.

'And it'll improve your concentration,' Julia adds.

'What's wrong with my concentration?' Genevieve says sharply, so sharply that Julia wonders if there *is* a problem with it.

'No, nothing,' Julia says, holding her hands up. 'It was just a phrase.'

'Yeah.' Genevieve rubs at her forehead. 'Not been sleeping well,' she says. 'Sorry.'

Their eyes meet, and something is communicated between them, only Julia isn't sure exactly what. 'All right?' she adds softly to Genevieve, who nods quickly.

'I was just channelling Tennessee himself. I'm sure he took everything personally,' Genevieve says.

Art, oblivious, starts to smile, seemingly despite himself. The left side first, and then the right, temporarily lopsided.

Julia thinks of this as his middle-of-the-night face. Just a handful of months ago – eight, nine – they had been in bed together. It was the end of summer, the sky still pale in the window above them. He had leaned over and picked up his notebook, like he did every night. But something about that night had touched her. The sugared-almond sky above them. And the way he had reached for it, without even thinking about it, ready to take notes.

'All right, number one: this missing woman,' she had said. Sadie. She had shown him a photograph of Sadie she kept on her phone, despite police protocols not to. 'I just . . . I don't know, I feel bonkers about it. Keep self-flagellating, sure I've

119

missed something.' She had rolled to face him, looking at his features rather than the sky. He was tanned, the way somebody is who has spent all of the summer outside. His skin smelled of sap.

'And,' she had continued, 'I'm worried about Genevieve's grades. She is so confident, but what if she's wrong, and she gets disappointed? She thinks she'll get As. And I think the seabass we had was out of date. Pan-frying doesn't kill everything . . .'

'Okay,' Art had said, 'I have made the following notes . . . Bonkers: yes, you are, but you did your best. Genevieve: she is fine, and she probably will get As; besides, it's next year, not this.' He had glanced across at her. 'My final note is pan-fried. And it does. Kill germs. Okay? These worries are now mine. I will watch them.' And then: that smile. That half-smile. Sometimes, if you're lucky, it grows into a full-beam grin.

'Thank you,' Julia had said, into the blue-light air.

'You're not to revisit them,' Art had said, the notebook clutched to his chest. 'They now belong to me.'

Only, afterwards, Julia hadn't shared her biggest ever worry with him, and perhaps that is what does it now, as that small smile plays out across his lips. Because just like that, Julia's head is gone. She can't stop staring at his mouth. Just one, just one, just one, she thinks. Just one of those very specific, wide, sometimes goofy smiles. They're so rare for Art, and she never sees them these days. She doesn't make him happy enough.

'Bedtime for you,' Julia says to Genevieve, her eyes moving to the clock in the dimness of the kitchen behind them, her voice damp cotton wool. 'School tomorrow.'

'Have you found the missing girl yet?' Genevieve asks, her pale blue eyes on Julia's.

'No.'

'Missing in the dead-end alley,' Genevieve says. 'It's like a podcast.'

'A crap one,' Julia says, 'because I doubt there will be an answer to that, even if we find her.' She lets the subtext speak for itself.

Genevieve scoffs. 'Wow, how optimistic,' she says caustically. 'Shimmyshaker,' she adds, waving a hand as she leaves the hallway. Julia watches her go, thinking of her reference to insomnia, hoping it was just a one-off. Art remains, coat on, hands in his pockets. He looks down at Julia, and their eyes meet for the briefest of seconds. She wonders if he's about to leave. Or if he's just going to resume their depressing new routine, brushing their teeth alone and settling down to sleep on either side of a thin wall. Where, previously, they'd lie under the skylight talking, now, he goes to the spare room. A stopgap become permanent.

'Genevieve's incredibly interested in it,' he says now. 'Your misper.'

'I know,' Julia says. She can't explain to him the reasons why. Art hangs his coat up, glances up the stairs, his back to her. He's going to bed. She's relieved and disappointed. This man, here, who she has loved for three decades, who surely – somewhere? – loves her too. This non-cop, the keeper of her worries. She wonders why she didn't tell him about Genevieve, if, maybe, if she could go back, she might have. She had been fearful of his judgement of their daughter, but also of her. He would connect the two. It's irrational, she knows, but Julia wonders if Art would say that her job led Genevieve into trouble. Because Art hates Julia's job, she's sure of that. Julia fraternizes with criminals, to him, and now so too does Genevieve.

But was it something more than that?

'It's not . . .' Julia starts. 'It's not an easy case.' She doesn't know why she's said it. To get him to stay up? If so, how pathetic.

But.

He's the only person in the world who knows the real, full her; the mother she became, the girl she once was. He has known her since she was fifteen. Even if she falls in love again. Even if she marries again. Nobody loves their children like their mother and father, and Julia, right now, needs people to know how much she loves her child, in order to feel understood herself.

'Yeah?' he says softly, just hesitating, his back still to her.

'I should let you go to bed. I . . .' she says. 'I saw you moved your clothes.'

'Yeah,' he says, eyes downcast. 'You all right?' he prompts. Soon, he will go up to his bedroom and she to hers. She will hear him pull off his clothes, open the top drawer, find loungewear. The click of the toothpaste uncapped, electric toothbrush. A sigh as he gets into bed. The dry turn of the page of a novel. And then later, much later than when they used to share a bed, the click of his light going off. That's all they have now. Their routines, once together, now divided into solo sounds.

'It's . . . it's just a tough case,' she says, instead of all this.

'Okay.'

'She's – well. It's complicated. I'd tell you, but it would become your worry, too.'

He turns to her and smiles in surprise at the black humour, at the throwback to how they once were. And there it is. That smile. One side, then the other, a row of straight, white teeth, a little syllable of a wry laugh, beating down on her like a sunbeam. Julia stares directly at it, and after a second averts her eyes. It's painful to stare at the sun.

Olivia

Instagram photo: a golden retriever on a beach.
Instagram caption: Be still my heart. A sunny Sunday at Sugar Loaf beach, and, sunshine itself: a golden retriever, king of dogs. Bounding along like a fucking vitamin advert.

Instagram photo: An aisle of B&M bargains.
Instagram caption: Here is the new Zoflora – white linen. Yes, I have a Zoflora boner, but it's out of shot. I can't wait to polish the shit out of my table with this.

Tweet: At shops. Eye mask on, hair in messy bun, COLDSORE on my lip. If this were a film, I'd see an ex-bf right about now. If this were a romcom, I'd meet a hot but grumpy small-town guy in a lumberjack shirt who doesn't want me to be moving in next door to him from the city. As it goes, it's real life so absolutely f u c k all is happening.

Sent item:
26/04: LittleO@gmail.com to newt62930@hotmail.com
All right, I'm on my way to the bar and I can't get hold of you on phone or WhatsApp, are you going to be there?

Facebook post: Phone call with Dad – he just asked me forty cryptic crossword clues and I got ZERO.

Comment: Actually, you got minus one, because you got me to write an incorrect one in. x

Third Day Missing

I2

Emma

'Oh, sure,' you are saying to a man who is standing on our doorstep. You've just arrived back, and you wouldn't say where from, deflected when I asked. The hallway smells of a plug-in spring air freshener and the actual, real, outside, which is nothing like it.

'Sorry, what's this?' I say. It's the early evening. I'm eighteen weeks down some celebrity's timeline on Instagram, trying to see when they took their engagement ring off (for what reason? I have no idea), holding a laundry basket in my other hand. I am sure I used to be more interesting than this, though I can't quite remember in what way.

It's sunny out, but still freezing. You're in only a t-shirt, and the hairs on your arms have risen up. I see now that it is a police officer at the door. Plain clothes, but holding up a badge, just like he's in a TV show. Immediately, my heart speeds up. Back in my own hell, your hell, from last year, when another policeman knocked at our door. Different door, same police force.

'It's just this,' he is saying to you. He waves a transparent bag containing what looks like a swab. 'Wipe that around, er, the inside of your cheek if you could be so kind,' he says cordially, like he's just asked you to donate money to charity, not your DNA to a police database. 'Then pass it back to me.'

'Sorry – why are you . . .' I say, hurrying forwards, reaching an arm out to touch your shoulder.

You glance back at me. 'It's fine,' you say, blue eyes to mine. 'It's just a DNA thing. A voluntary screening – for that missing woman.'

The missing woman. I saw her on the news last night. Blonde, slim, early twenties. It was all too familiar. I heard the BBC News bulletin noise, and then the announcement, and I had to consciously remind myself: that was then, this is now. History is not repeating itself.

Still. She went missing in Portishead. I scrolled through the photos on my phone to the night the police say she disappeared, and felt my shoulders drop when I saw you were with me. This is the way it is. When you don't quite trust somebody any more life is actually much the same on the outside, except, internally, you spend more time thinking, assessing, checking. Going over stuff.

Something unspoken passes between us now. 'You sure you don't mind doing that?' I say levelly, unable to stop myself, wanting to ask a million more questions, starting with, *Why the fuck would you help the police out, after everything?* And ending with: *Do they know?*

'Happy to assist.' You say it so easily, taking the swab and running it around your cheek. I watch as you do it. Underconfident, not practised, at least. You cough slightly, then put it in the specimen bag. Panic begins to burn ferociously inside me. I stare at the back of your head. I have no idea if you're being tactical, or naive. You hide your emotions so well.

'We appreciate it,' the officer says. 'And just to check – do you know this woman? Ever seen her while out and about?' He holds up a poster. There she is, the woman I googled last night after I said I was so tired my eyes were closing and I needed to go to bed (See? The ways what we say differs from what's going on internally). *MISSING* written in red along the bottom.

'Nope,' you say easily.

'Sure?'

'Certain.'

'Okay, then,' he says hurriedly, 'thank you for your time.' He waves the labelled sample bag, goes next door to ring their bell. I'm relieved to see that. That it isn't just you.

I start unloading the dishwasher even though the plates are still steaming and burn my hands. It's for something to do, that's all. So that I can ask you the things I need to ask you with a veneer of housework covering them.

'You all right there?' you say to me. 'Laundry. Dishwashers. So productive. You should've been in the special services or something.' It sounds friendly, but it isn't: it's your own veneer, your own deflection. I've known you for twenty years, and you are never breezy. Awkward, often. Funny, very. But never really relaxed. It's just the way you're made. You came home from school once, aged sixteen or so, and said you found school so fake, and the people in it worse. We talked about it a lot, standing in your bedroom, you with your rucksack still on. The next day, you pretended the conversation hadn't happened, were embarrassed, I guess, at the intimacy.

'Are we pretending that didn't just happen?' I say.

You shrug. You actually shrug, then look directly at me, wounded, the way you sometimes are, my fragile, glass-bauble boy. 'I'm helping out.'

'But –'

'Do you remember,' you say, your tone frosted ice, 'that a year ago, I was actually exonerated?'

'I do.' I give you a tight smile, but my scalp is prickling in that way it does when you know you're in the presence of something important, something big, something dangerous.

* * *

It's late. We've been out to dinner, just the two of us, the way we often do. This is what people don't tell you about having a child: so quickly, so fast you almost miss it, they become a full, sentient, adult being. And this is when they need the most help, need the sacrifices. Breastfeeding versus formula feeding, crying it out versus co-sleeping, it doesn't matter then, though the hormones would have you believe otherwise. The time when your baby really, truly needs your emotional heft is now: the teenage years and beyond.

The Uber we're in smells of mouthwash commingled with the artificial scent of the air freshener, which dances every time we take a bend. You have just said to me that you want to get home and watch *DIY SOS*, even though that makes you a sad case, and I've said that it makes me love you more.

The conversation between us flows easily, but I'm thinking about last year, and what you said earlier: *exonerated*. That's the word you used. But, the thing is, you weren't, were you? Not really. Because your girlfriend disappeared, and you were questioned, and – yes – released. But she was never found. Can we call that exoneration?

I shift slightly away from you in the car. It's been – in a way – an easy problem for my mind to solve, at least intellectually.

The answer presents itself to me often: the police didn't go any further with it, so why should I? And that has been the answer I have given myself repeatedly, since last spring. Acting like the protective parent that I am – and I *am* – but, internally . . . well, something else.

Sometimes, when you're coming in late, or meeting friends I don't know of, or up pacing in the night, I think the flipside of my own reassurance: but they did question you.

You didn't ever fully discuss it with me. And it's been the same since this new woman, Olivia Johnson, went missing: nothing said by you. All over the news, all over social media, and . . . nothing. You haven't raised it, not directly, not with me. You gave your swab. That's all.

Nor have you mentioned how alike they look.

'Those bread rolls,' you say. You puff your cheeks out. 'I perhaps didn't need to eat forty.'

I can't help but smile. *They did release you.* You always did like simple food, even as a small child. Potatoes, chips, bread, anything beige. You're the same even now.

'It's the butter,' you say. 'How do they make it so nice? It's like – whipped.'

I close my eyes. The women have the same blonde hair. Similar circumstances. Similar location . . . stop thinking about it. Just stop.

'Plus, I think it's salted,' you say. You glance sideways at me, no idea of the transactions going on in my mind.

'We'll have to make some,' I say weakly.

We're pulling up, near to ours, and, just like that, the ambience dies.

That specific post-dinner feeling, blurred city lights, rain, alcohol, joviality: gone. You know why? Because the street is blue. A lit-up, phosphorescent blue.

And I can't believe it, but the first thought I have is that I haven't been wrong with my gut feeling.

No! I try to erase the thought the second after I've had it. It's just a misunderstanding. Bum luck.

All of my senses are trained on that blue. We don't look at each other. Perhaps this is what is most telling of all. We're not surprised. We're not even shocked. You are still and soundless next to me. We get out of the car like tin men.

'Ah,' a bald male officer says, striding over to us. 'Matthew James,' he addresses you.

'Sorry – what's the problem?' I ask, sounding authoritative, the me who can balance a profit and loss account on sight, who grew up with nothing, but I don't feel like that me. I feel like the real me, the me that lurks in every single one of us: someone for whom things fall apart.

'DS Poole,' he says, reaching out. As we shake hands, both of our wrists flash blue, strobed by the light from the car outside our house. 'Just a few questions for Matthew, if you don't mind?' He's standing there, next to the police car, with a blonde woman who introduces herself as DCI Day.

My job is to protect you from this. To believe in you, no matter what you might have done.

Neither copper wears a uniform. Both look tired and serious in the shadows of the pooled orange streetlamps. Unconsciously, I assume, the bald one looks around, expecting a father figure. I feel like telling him the whole sordid story, a high-school boyfriend who cut and run, sends a hundred quid every Christmas – laughable – but don't. I chose to bring you into the world knowing all of that, and so how could I let it define you? I never, ever have.

'Sorry – why do you need to speak to Matthew?' I say, guarding you despite my doubts. You're standing slightly behind me. I reach backwards for you in the dark but can't catch your hands.

'We just need a short statement from him,' DCI Day says, perhaps kindly, or something nudging close to kindness, anyway.

'What's going on?' you say, finally stepping into the sapphire light.

The first thought I have is absurd – that we're not presenting a very good impression. We've both been drinking beer. Not loads – two – but enough to smell them on us. Shame washes over me, that somehow I shouldn't be drinking with my adult child. This is what happens when you grow up poor: whenever you let your guard down, you think everything is going to be taken from you.

'Okay if we come in with you?' Poole says.

'Do you need statements from all of the houses? Who gave the DNA?' I say.

'Best if we do this inside. Always better on the sofa with a cuppa,' DCI Day says, as though it isn't eleven at night and they're not police. The hairs on the back of my neck rise up. I see now: the fake politeness, their unhurried manner. All is not as it seems.

'Okay?' you say, oblivious. Like: *go ahead*. You gesture to the front door and then unlock it. *No, no, no*, I want to say. *Do not trust these wolves in sheep's clothing.* But *do* you trust them? I can't read your facial expression. Always shy, perhaps secretive, it's gone up a level since last year. Now, you're practically a politician. Things glossed over, seemingly forgotten, treated as unimportant, as though that might change the facts of them.

You step inside, followed by the police and then me. As I turn and close the door, I gaze at our street for just a few more seconds, the rain flickering around the streetlights, my palm upturned to catch a drop, before everything shifts. Again.

You're all in the living room when I arrive, the officers standing right in the middle of it like grim reapers, their suits and wet shoes strange in the ambient surroundings. They smell of that intangible scent of outside, and it's all wrong: our living room is dark and cosy, jewel-coloured cushions, a big fluffy rug. It needs bare feet and Christmas slippers and faded old books, not this.

'No, no, we'll just have a quick chat,' Poole is saying while you brandish the kettle in the adjoining kitchen. 'No need for tea.'

'Sorry – why?' I say. 'Is this a formal interview? Or what?' My tone becomes hysterical.

Poole switches on our lights, which gleam on the wooden floors. 'Look,' I want to say. 'The lovely house we've worked so hard for – we're not criminals. We don't need to be interviewed.' Instead, I sit in the armchair and say nothing. As I look down, I see that my legs are trembling.

'We just have a few things we want to go over,' Poole says. A non-answer. He steadfastly directs his sentences to you, and not me. It makes sense. You're an adult; they don't know you're still my baby.

'Go for it,' you say, shooting a look at me that silences me, just briefly. I think about when we moved here, how the people you worked with in the bar back home said they didn't want to do solo shifts with you any more, not after what had happened with your girlfriend. I think how we cut and run. You got a new job, a new bar. It never happened again.

'Matthew James, your DNA has been found in the bedroom of the missing woman Olivia Johnson,' DCI Day says.

I am sitting in the armchair where I was five seconds ago,

coat and shoes still on. But, just like that, absolutely everything, everything, *everything* changes. I swear, I feel the earth tilt underfoot. DNA. You cannot argue with DNA.

Day's reading it off an email. Her tone is perfunctory, as if she'd rather be doing something else, like she isn't really in the room at all. She takes her reading glasses off and looks at you. 'All we need to know before we go is how you account for this?'

I feel it, somehow, in the physical way you sometimes do when you're a mum, when her eyes meet yours. She throws you a wobbly, encouraging smile. It's tone deaf. The gall of it.

I glance at you sharply. Your expression hasn't changed whatsoever.

'Account for it?' you say. You're playing for time. I know you so well, and this is the sort of thing you do while you think. It's what you did last year. I feel myself – I swear it – detach, floating upwards, just looking at you. The dark hair I've loved for two decades, the hand that goes to your chin in thought.

'Yes . . . explain it. Justify it. You know – if you did meet her, and what you said the other day was wrong, somehow, then . . .' DCI Day's tone is casual, but her words aren't. They're full of traps. Either you lied then, or you're lying now. You have two choices, both of them bad. Jesus, your fucking DNA – half *my* DNA – in a missing woman's room, one you say you've never met. Maybe it's your lack of father figure. Maybe I didn't instil a respect in you for women, maybe –

I look out at the rain, the drops on the windows lit orange by the streetlight, and realize only a few seconds before it becomes plainly obvious that this conversation precedes an arrest.

'I've never met Olivia Johnson,' you say. Panic breaks across your face like headlights sweeping the dark road outside. I think suddenly of the footage, all over the news. Olivia disappearing into that alley, never coming out again. How could that be? Is it possible you have the answer?

'Where were you on the night of the twenty-ninth of April?' Poole says. He sits on our sofa without asking, gets a clean pad out. He communicates something to DCI Day with his eyes, something we can't interpret.

I know this one. You went to see Linda, the therapist, and then we went out to Portishead One. I stare at this tangible fact like it's a mirage on the horizon that might disappear if I take my eyes off it.

'Er,' you say, thinking. 'Therapy? Then out with Mum?'

'Therapy,' Poole says, his fingers gripping a biro with a chewed lid. It's the first and only word he has written on his notepad.

I wish you hadn't said it, not the first part. I worry that therapy, to the general public, and most certainly to the police, means madness. Clinical rooms. Mental health problems. Some sort of darkness. To you, to us, it means Linda's lovely conservatory, softly lit. A kind woman who allows you to be completely yourself.

'Out where?'

'Portishead One.'

'And then?'

'Home.'

'At home alone?' Poole asks.

'Hang on,' I say, springing to life. 'What sort of interview is this? Have you cautioned him?'

'We're just trying to figure out the facts,' DCI Day says. 'How your son's DNA came to be in Olivia's bedroom.'

The mirage flickers and disappears. Your DNA in her bedroom. Alibi notwithstanding . . . how can this be? One false accusation is bad luck. So what is two? Who gets accused twice?

'What's her address?' you ask.

'Seventeen East View Lane.'

'I don't – I don't think I've ever been there?' you say, getting your phone out to google it. I'm relieved, because it's exactly what I would do.

'Erm,' you say, turning the map this way and that. 'Right, okay, one street off the main road – I mean, I don't think so? But I do . . . I don't know. I have been to some friends' houses and parties and stuff. I'm rubbish at geography.' A truth: you really are. Could not direct yourself to the Spar down the road.

Poole exchanges a glance with Day. It is as though you have agreed you are a criminal.

'When did you go to this house?' Poole says.

'I've never been to that house,' you say. 'I have probably walked past it, because I live around here.'

'When was the party?' Poole says.

'What party?'

'You just said you have been to some friends' house parties and stuff: when and where, and was one of them here?'

'No, I've never been there – that was hypothetical – just, parties in the past.'

'When was the hypothetical party?'

'There was no party,' you say.

'So why did you say there was?' Poole tilts his head to the side. It is interrogation masking itself as concern, interest, confusion even. He's tied you up in knots.

'So you're saying you've never been inside it?' Poole says. 'At these parties, and so on?'

'I don't think so,' you say.

'Certain about that?'

'Well, clearly not,' you say. 'But I'm as certain as I can be. Can you say for sure you've never been to a random house? I don't think I have ever been there,' you say. 'That's all I can say. Surely?' You look at them, and then at me, just the way you did when you were a baby making sense of the world, like, *This okay?* I nod at you. Your phone, face down in front of you on our driftwood coffee table, begins to vibrate, slowly skittering across the surface like a beetle. Everybody ignores it. I am struck with a sudden urge to pick it up, to see who it is, to get inside your interior, and know for sure. Before the thought is even finished, you pick it up, make a few swipes and replace it.

'Okay,' Poole says, his eyes on your phone and your fingers. 'A glass and a cigarette containing your DNA were found.'

My heart seems to explode with fear. A cigarette. You smoke. One of your only remaining vices.

'I hardly ever smoke!' you say.

But you do smoke. And socially, too. I'm saying nothing. It occurs to me, for just a second, that maybe I shouldn't be defending you. That maybe I, too, will end up on the news one day, complicit. Delusional. *His mother, thirty-nine, refuses to believe his guilt, even to this day.* Should I tell them? Should I tell them about last year? Do they already know?

Poole blinks, saying nothing, then shows you something on his phone. As you look at it, I stare at Day. Her eyes are on you, and they're . . . what, exactly? Mournful? Concerned? Not the expression you would expect to see from a police officer. Some sort of . . . I don't know. Longing, maybe? She catches me looking, and blinks down at her lap.

'That's the report. The chance this isn't your DNA is one

in one billion. So, maybe you saw her right before she disappeared, and panicked . . .' Poole says, letting his sentence drift. Eventually, he adds: 'If so, now would be a good time to tell us that. Given, too, that you were near the alley on that night, at Portishead One.'

'But he didn't go in that alley,' I say: I was with you.

'I haven't ever met her. Never even spoken to her,' you say.

'All right, then, Matthew. Nobody wants to do it this way . . .'

'What?' you say, gaping.

Poole springs to his feet. 'Matthew James, I am arresting you on suspicion of the kidnap of Olivia Johnson. You do not have to say anything, but it may harm your defence if you do not mention, when questioned, something you later rely on in court. Anything you do say may be given in evidence. Do you understand what I have just said?'

'I . . . I didn't . . . kidnap?' you say, aghast. 'I was with –' You gesture to me, your arm flailing.

'The reason your arrest is necessary is to allow us to conduct a prompt and effective investigation into this matter.'

'How can I have killed someone when I've got an alibi?' you say. The sound of your voice. Anguish. But the word, *alibi*, is all tactics: it's a defence.

I stare at you as you say it. Suspicion starts to creep up my body like a stealthy tide coming in.

DS Poole begins straightening papers, like they have just concluded a banal business meeting. Like it isn't night-time. Like this isn't life and death. 'Search?' he says to DCI Day, and she nods. He holds a palm out, and you hand your phone over.

'Kidnap. She's hardly in my basement, is she?' you say, bewildered, gesturing all around us. I send my hand out to the side to stop you speaking with a force that feels like telekinesis. It doesn't matter what I think.

The neck of your t-shirt looks tight around your throat. You pull at it uselessly. You begin to make gagging noises, losing all dignity there in our house. And then you turn to me, your mum, for help. Only I am helpless. As disorientated as you.

'I can't do this,' you say, gasping for air.

'You need,' I say, 'you need a warrant, don't you? He needs a lawyer?'

'Not when there's an arrest for an indictable offence,' Poole says crisply. 'Right, DCI Day.'

'I'll get upstairs done by the searchers,' she says. 'You do downstairs. Get one of the PCSOs to stay with him.'

Poole shepherds us into the kitchen, just you and me. He blusters off; understaffed, I guess. 'Touch nothing,' he says, and we stand there, like prisoners, but by our lovely marble kitchen island, displaced.

'Look,' I say to you.

'I have not kidnapped her,' you say. 'I don't know her. I haven't . . .' Your voice trails off, confused.

I hold your gaze for five seconds, ten. More and more police are coming through the front door. They must have been waiting for the nod, just outside, unseen.

You are looking back at me. Those soulful eyes. You blink, once, but say nothing. As ever. Until you do. A whispered confession to me. 'I have spoken to her. Online,' you say, sotto voce, so softly I have to strain to hear you. 'I deleted the messages just now.'

13

Julia

Julia has tears running down her cheeks. She has her hands cupped around the sides of her face, her elbows on a bar, heartbreak in her throat. She's just left Matthew's house. He's just a kid. Barely older than Genevieve. Julia shouldn't even have attended, but she wanted to see. Some voyeuristic, base urge had compelled her to observe the effect of her own corrupt actions.

The DNA matched Matthew earlier. Julia had tried to discuss upgrading the charge to murder, but the team had looked at her like she was an alien. She'd never ordinarily suggest that, especially in the absence of a body. She'd tried to justify it and couldn't. Then she'd arrested him. Then she'd left.

And now she's in a bar opposite the police station, alone, where she's wanted to be ever since his arrest. As she sat in that beautiful living room of theirs – hardwood floors, framed photos of Matthew everywhere, the scent of a bunch of lilies somewhere on the air – she had suddenly thought so viscerally about being here, this run-down bar she hardly ever frequents, that as soon as Matthew was checked in, she left, and came here.

And so now the natural order is this: Matthew is in the station, locked up, and she is here: free. That's the trade she's made. Julia's only child has been saved, and Matthew sacrificed. She shivers with it. She's done a deal with the devil. And, someday soon, she will pay.

It's an age-old tactic to arrest at night. Take them in late, interview early. Still compliant with PACE, but only just. Suspects will say anything to get released after that first night. Not something Julia usually has a problem with, until today.

His mum. She can't stop thinking about her. Matthew is her only child, too. She was beyond shocked. Stunned, her eyes bright, face red, like somebody had just slapped her.

Julia and Art had wanted a second child. They had waited, for her caseload to die down, for a good time, and it had never come. Not once. Then she had gone for the DCI job, and Art hadn't spoken to her for a week.

Julia doesn't come here very much. Coppers favour old men's pubs rather than this, an orange-hued bar, peeling leather stools, smeared glasses hanging and swaying on a rack above. Julia should be at home. And, yet, she is here, drinking fucking whisky, even though she's supposed to be driving. A cliché of a police officer.

She scrapes her hair back from her face. *Matthew, Matthew, Matthew*, her mind chunters. She thought the whisky would help her to forget, to at least numb it, but, if anything, it's revved her up even more.

She keeps thinking of Olivia. Through the trauma, and the guilt and the shame, there is a kernel of something that her detective mind is trying to get at. Something about her Instagram posts. You don't polish with Zoflora. Julia hates that she knows this, but she does. You don't go out in an eye mask. It's almost . . . what?

Her detective mind attempts this way and that, a burrowing animal trying to find its way in.

The bartender – forty, maybe, ginger man-bun – replaces an old pillar candle in front of her with a new one, which he lights. Wax soon begins to dribble down the sides like teardrops. The ambience is tape over a wound: the bar is tired and near empty. A candle won't do much. Julia passes a hand over the top of it, the flame just licking her palm; unfelt, but real.

It is this thought that compels her next action: she orders a second whisky, she flicks through Olivia's Instagram again, and then she calls Olivia's father.

14

Olivia

Instagram photo: Coconut conditioner.
Instagram caption: Trying a new conditioner out at the moment. Makes my hair greasy. Tried another. Makes my hair greasy. Washed it with just shower gel. Now look like Brian May. Thanks, hormones.

Tweet: Current fear: spontaneous combustion? A new one in anxiety's arsenal, but a goodie. Keep checking my arms to see they're not on fire. Did anyone else worry about this back in the 90s? I feel like it was such a thing then? Did anyone continue into 2023?

Tweet: Relationship status: boyfriend getting hench, I'm bench-pressing Daim Bars.

Instagram photo: A steaming bath.
Instagram caption: My horoscope said I'd get into hot water this month.

Sent items:

27/04: LittleO@gmail.com to amydeshaun@gmail.com

Hey you, how's things? Been a little while since university days. Just thought I'd email . . . don't have your WhatsApp? Though sorry if this reads like one of those round robin Christmas letters your mum used to get. Lololol. Old school. How're you, anyway?

All fine here. I've left ET. Getting a new job. Dunno if it'll be the right thing for me to leave with nothing new to go to, but – I don't know, you have to, don't you? Besides, my horoscope said to! Mercury is in retrograde!! I'm sidestepping into marketing. TBH, sales was not for me. Staffed by psychos.

Talk soon!

O x

Inbox:

28/04: amydeshaun@gmail.com to LittleO@gmail.com

OMG – let me call you!

Fourth Day Missing

15

Julia

'He's gone no comment,' Poole says, striding into Julia's office the next morning. Julia startles. She was thinking about Art, and how she overheard him this morning, after last night, telling Genevieve that theatre isn't boring, just misunderstood. Art and Julia had been to see a play together, a year or two before, and Julia had encouraged him to leave halfway through. They'd burst out on to the street in the interval and run home through the rain. One of the worries she had told him that night had been that she might have died of boredom in the theatre, and he'd laughed so hard the bed had shaken.

Poole is wearing a Reebok jumper and jeans, his eyes bright. She jumps. 'Could you knock?' she says sharply. 'Why are you dressed for PE?' She closes her screen down. She was reading about a David Harper, perhaps the brother of Zac, perhaps not.

'I'm apparently on annual leave,' Poole says.

'No such thing. How's it going, upgrading it to murder?' Olivia's dad is due to get back to Julia shortly, and she's tetchy, on edge, waiting.

Poole seems to just about manage not to roll his eyes. 'That's too high a bar, isn't it? Besides, the lawyer is Mr Jackson.'

'Oh,' Julia says, staring down at the desk. That explains the no comment. Mr Jackson is formidable. Leaves no stone unturned, and sees almost no cases through to conviction in the process. He roadblocks them. Each one failing either at first hearing or at trial. There is no way she will get this through on a murder charge. Not until there's a body.

'But . . . we have DNA,' Poole says, seemingly unconcerned. 'So the kidnap charge is okay. Maybe.'

Julia nods quickly, feeling sick. Poor kid, thrown into the legal system with no idea he's up against a corrupt police officer.

But the arrest is just the beginning. Charging him is just the beginning. He will plead not guilty – why wouldn't he? And then there will be a trial in a couple of years' time. It will hang over Matthew and Julia until then, the backlog of the courts ensuring it does. Lawyers and experts and jurors will pick over her faked, amateur evidence. She wonders where this will end, truly. In his trial – or hers?

Something tragic and instinctive compels her to go to the police custody cells and look in on Matthew. She moves past Poole, not providing an explanation. She can feel him staring at her as she goes.

The reception area contains a bank of CCTV, and each monitor houses a moving figure.

Most people in police custody simply do nothing. They sit and they stare into space. Some are drunk. Many feel frightened and stupid, because the police they have been running from for a long time – drugs, thefts, mostly – have caught up with them in ways they never thought they would.

Matthew is not a typical detainee. He is pacing, right now, a hologram version of himself above Julia's head. She watches him go this way and that, biting a fingernail, rubbing his hands through his hair.

He is clearly trying to work something out. Innocent people are completely bewildered. So sure that things are going to be resolved that they wait by the door. Guilty people mostly perform. Any distress is demonstrative; not like this, while alone. If Julia had to guess, she'd say he was not quite guilty, but not quite innocent either. Curious.

She wishes she could let herself into his cell, ask him: do you have any enemies? Is it possible we have one in common? But she can't. Was he chosen at random? A nearby house, close to the scene of the kidnapping. He was with his mum at a bar right off the alleyway, too. The perfect candidate: a guileless kid.

If not – then somebody's framing him for a reason. Once again, Julia's mind goes to Olivia. A traumatic encounter with Matthew maybe, once; maybe she wants revenge?

As she continues out through the reception foyer, she crosses paths with Mr Jackson.

She nods to him, and he acknowledges her with a raise of his eyebrows. 'DCI Day,' he says. She isn't sure whether it's a greeting or the beginning of a sentence.

Mr Jackson is old, weather-beaten, and one of the best lawyers she knows. He's a careful sort of solicitor, the type who doesn't think success lies in flashy clients or big-name cases. Mr Jackson's ethos is in the detail. He will go through every single piece of paper twice, never mind if it takes all night. He calls lawyers who don't do this 'first-page lawyers': those who read only the first page of the file.

The greatest lawyers aren't like they are in the movies.

They're not slick, expensive, big-picture types. They're like this: careful, considered, willing to read four thousand boring pages to find a small hidden error on just one, and they never lose concentration while searching for it.

'I was hoping to catch you,' he says cordially. 'We've had some disclosure but not all.'

'Well, those are the breaks,' Julia says.

'You have a duty to provide it eventually,' he says. 'Why not just do it now?'

Julia sighs. 'What're you missing?'

He consults a notebook in his hands. The hairs on her upper arms rise. The same animalistic fear that let her know the man was in her car is back. Another antagonist. This time, a lawyer who never misses a trick.

'The PCSOs manning the scene had bodycams on, but I haven't seen the footage. Can you arrange?'

'Bodycams?' she says. Her shoulders and chest go hot. 'Did they?'

'Yes, so the notes say.'

'Right, sure,' she says. She swallows. Her throat has dried up completely. Bodycams. She hadn't realized. PCSOs don't always wear them, she didn't check the notes . . . if the PCSOs had looked in the room carefully, it will be clear from the footage that the glass and cigarette weren't there, and time-stamped, too. She was the only visitor to the room after that, surely; she signed the crime scene log. 'I'll get that done,' she says, her voice dry.

'I will be going through that disclosure with a fine-toothed comb,' he says, enunciating this phrase precisely, not saying 'fine toothcomb' as many do. He has an issue with people who use the wrong words, not unlike Art. 'You have two pieces of DNA, nothing else.'

He leaves the rest unsaid. Julia nods quickly. 'I'd expect nothing less.'

'If you're considering a murder charge without a body, I would reconsider,' he adds over his shoulder as he leaves.

A throat clears behind Julia. It's Erin, who doesn't meet her eyes as she passes.

* * *

The fire alarm is triggered before Julia can get back to her office. It's still pouring with that fresh, sleety, wet rain, and standing in it with all of her colleagues in earshot isn't what Julia wants. Especially because there is somebody wanting to speak to her: Patricia, the CPS lawyer. Julia had called her earlier, advised her they had a suspect, but she hadn't been expecting Patricia to just turn up.

'Here's as good a place as any, I suppose?' she says to Julia, wandering over, one hand in a pocket, the other holding a pink folder. A studiedly casual pose.

Every inch of Julia's body is sweating. The backs of her knees are slick with it. Her spine. Her hands. All she is thinking about is bodycams. When she sees Patricia there, she wants to cut and run. Patricia is a by-the-book sort of woman, the kind who would say they are 'undergoing continued professional development' that evening. The sort to use management speak on nights out, to never break character, an old-school, boundaried type who would deliberately not laugh at a joke she found funny if it wasn't in an appropriate setting. Julia has therefore, quite predictably, never got along with her, favouring people who are their full selves in the office, emotional outbursts and all.

Patricia is short, and sort of ageless, somewhere between

thirty-nine and sixty, with bobbed, curly blonde hair, a wide smile, though not one offered up terribly often.

'About Matthew James,' Patricia says. She gestures with the file, its pink cardboard case gathering raindrops that darken to blood red.

'Yes,' Julia says.

Patricia, like Julia, is regularly lied to, and therefore has a serious radar for it. Julia tries to straighten her shoulders, wipes the sweat off her palms. She thinks suddenly of Art, and how much she'd like to speak to him right now. To text or to email him. Not about this. Just . . . the way they were. If not an email then a beer garden, the two of them. Sun. She wonders what he would say about all this: everything that happened with Genevieve, everything that she has made happen with Matthew . . .

'All I have is the glass and the cigarette,' Patricia says, without introduction. 'You say you want him for murder, not just kidnap?'

'Right,' Julia says: that is her task. Murder. She's got to do it.

'A guy with previously good character. Not at all known to the victim, so far as we know?'

'We're waiting on a few things,' Julia says hurriedly, sleet sticking to the end of her nose. 'Meta for Matthew or Olivia, not released yet. So we can't see their private messages. And Olivia's dad doesn't have her Facebook and Instagram passwords.' Julia's talking, but she's hardly listening, even to herself. How can she get that bodycam footage? How can she check it? How can she charge this kid with murder, when there's no body? She is sticking plaster after plaster over gaping wounds.

'I have to say' – Patricia folds her arms – 'I'm surprised.' Her hair is getting steadily wetter, drops covering the strands like miniature pearls. She doesn't seem to notice. 'You are usually cautious on charging.' She meets Julia's eyes right as she says this, a kind of searching quality passing across her face. Around them, their colleagues begin to murmur impatiently. The alarm is still going.

'He has absolutely zero explanation for how those items ended up in her room, though.'

'A room that had only belonged to her for twenty-four hours. Who was the previous occupant?'

'Jonathan went through it. He moved out ages ago – the room sat empty. Plus, Matthew says he's never been there – ever. It must be' – Julia swallows – 'a bare-faced lie. The DNA match is Matthew, not a previous occupant.'

'I don't think it's enough for kidnap, let alone murder, that's my honest feeling,' Patricia says, spreading her arms wide, gesturing with the folder. 'I'm not saying I won't charge him ever. I'm just saying we need a little bit more. Something to raise it. Any kind of further suspicious DNA, blood, a sighting, these things together . . . I'm not trying to be obstructive,' she adds at the end, which is exactly what somebody who thinks they are being obstructive would say.

A cobra has wrapped itself around Julia's body, squeezing her organs, her windpipe, her neck. This can't be happening. She has to convict him. She doesn't know by when. Only that she has to, and she's probably being watched until she does.

What's he going to do, if Matthew is released pending further investigations, rather than charged? Will he get back in touch? Or will he pull the trigger? He's already cocked the gun. Would she take the sentence herself, if it meant Genevieve would be okay? She probably would.

Julia blinks. 'All right, I'll do some digging,' she says. 'I'll find some more evidence.' She adds it without thinking. 'I mean – I'll . . .'

'I know what you meant,' Patricia says plainly. And, of course, it wasn't the initial statement that was the problem. It was Julia's panic. The alarm switches off abruptly, and the unexpected silence shivers Julia's ears. The receptionist stops checking everyone off, and they file back inside. Patricia waves to Julia and heads to her car. 'Short and sweet,' she says over her shoulder, and Julia nods.

Julia heads in with everybody else, but doesn't go to the back rooms. Instead, she goes to the docking station in the open-plan office where the bodycams are uploaded every day. She sees that the stations are empty, but nevertheless she searches around them, looking on the shelves underneath them, but there aren't any there.

Footage from three days ago will already have been up-loaded somewhere. She heads back to her office and finds it on the server.

She plays two at once, the PCSOs checking out the crime scene, talking shit together about some television drama with incorrect police procedure. She watches and watches. And then it happens. The PCSO bends down. The bodycam captures underneath the bed. No glass.

Julia's heart seems to zoom around her chest. She brings a shaking hand to her mouth. It's over. It's surely over. She's a goner.

16

Lewis

There are four steps down to our kitchen, an open-plan monstrosity that you and Yolanda love and I hate. I can't relax here, feel like a show-off simply for living in it. Slippery, dark, hardwood floors, bifold doors at the end there, a KitchenAid on the surface. *We are middle class, and we are utterly, depressingly conventional,* it says to me. I once expressed all of this to Yolanda and she said, eyes smiling, 'I thought it was just a nice food mixer.'

It's a Tuesday morning like no other. Yolanda is carefully rolling out pasta, a silver machine out and clamped to the counter, her eyes level with it as she feeds it through.

I walk into my study. It's quiet, the odd car passing outside, and the endless rain.

I open up my ancient laptop. You sometimes used it when you came here. Not often – always on your phone – but frequently enough for me to want to go and look at it, to fire it up, just to see.

It springs to life as soon as I move my finger over the trackpad, one tab open. I haven't been on it for days. It might be yours. Fucking hell, I should tell the police, but I can't help myself looking just now, for me. The private and the public. You are my daughter, and I want to know things first, before them. Before this nightmare turns from its ingredients – grief and love and confusion and searching – and into something bureaucratic and insane. Press, trials . . .

I delay it, just for a few seconds. Touching the mousepad and the keys. Your slender fingers must have rested here, too. Before. Before you left, or were taken.

Andrew Zamos

I blink, staring at it. His name, googled. And, worse, you had clicked on the news tab. But why?

I can't reach Julia, but I do get Poole. I tell him this – well, some of it – and he listens. 'All right, and you're sure it was her who typed it?'

'It certainly wasn't me or Yolanda.'

'Okay. I'll look into it. All right?'

But it sounds dismissive. 'Don't you agree that maybe she was googling him to try and get at his history? Was maybe worried about him? Like a Clare's Law sort of thing? I know it sounds like I'm some mad alpha dad, but I swear, I'm not.'

'Nobody thinks you're a mad alpha dad,' he says, his professional veneer remaining, even though he is forced to use my crazed language. 'It's just that he does have a strong alibi.'

'So – what? That's that? Do you have any other suspects?'

'I can't answer that.'

I let out a groan of frustration. 'Why aren't you coming to get my laptop?'

'We will send out an officer. This is perfectly under control.'

'Is it?' I say. 'So how come nobody's found my daughter?'

'DCI Day is –'

'Where is she?'

'She is completely focused on this case,' he says.

'I never said she wasn't.' His statement isn't lost on me. He pauses, too. He knows he's misstepped, said too much. And the smallest slips are sometimes the most significant. 'But I don't see the results,' I add, which I know is unfair, but I'm beyond caring.

'You have to trust us that we are on it, Lewis,' Poole says to me, but I'm not really listening to him. I'm thinking about how sometimes, people protest too much. *She is completely focused on this case.*

'Well, if you aren't – your supervisors will be hearing from me,' I say.

I hang up and stare and stare and stare at that preserved Google search. Then close the laptop, leaving it there, a museum of things you typed and felt and thought, even if the latter two are invisible. In the background, something I can't see. But there nevertheless. Like you.

* * *

'So he did pass it on?'

'Yes, we're on it,' DCI Day says, but her eyes aren't on me. She keeps checking her phone.

'Are you re-interviewing him? Andrew?'

'Look, Lewis,' she says to me, I think kindly, though still distractedly. 'It's a Google search.' Another glance over her shoulder.

'On the news tab.'

'Yes, on the news tab.' She looks back at the station, from where an older man is emerging. 'Look, I'll be in touch, okay?' she says. 'But remember, Lewis: Andrew has this alibi.'

'I know that.'

'There is no way he could have taken your daughter.'

'So that's that,' I say flatly.

'I have to go. Lot of balls in the air here.'

And, just like that, she turns and walks out of the station car park, and down into the evening air. A complete dismissal of me by the woman paid to find you.

I have no choice but to see where she goes. The first time I did it, I followed her for less than five minutes. Felt weird about it, my urge to know what the people in charge were doing with their time, and stopped. This time, it's longer. She heads to Portishead High Street, and I follow, just a few paces behind her.

I'm cringing as I walk along the street. This isn't me, is it? What am I doing? Trying to find you, that's what. No matter the stakes.

Day is weaving through the soup of shoppers milling around her, me several people behind her. I think it is that I want to know she is following a lead, not going out for dinner. You know? I want to know it really *is* in hand, that she is doing everything she can.

And there she is: the place where you were last seen, turning a full circle in the street, just looking. My shoulders drop in relief. After hours, staring at the ground, at the walls, at the cars passing, evidently lost in thought. I stand and watch her from my vantage point a few feet away, obscured by shoppers, by the busy high street, by life. Julia turns another circle, searching upwards now, for CCTV cameras, her eyes scanning carefully, checking them off against a list she pulls out of her pocket.

There's a lump in my throat as I watch her. Working as hard to find you as we are. I turn to leave her there, satisfied, carrying that heavy guilt of somebody who's taken a risk in order to prove something, and failed to. I'm a man going through my wife's texts, and finding nothing.

A young woman ambles up after a couple of minutes and greets her. Unmistakably her daughter: same hair, same bone structure. I hesitate, just watching them hug, but then leave them there. It's too much of an intrusion. God. I'm a normal person, and this is definitely, absolutely abnormal. They head together into a McDonald's, laughing, arm in arm, and I feel a dart of jealousy so strong it's like an arrow hitting me out of nowhere, fired straight at my back.

* * *

Tonight, we marked your disappearance for the first time. The time you were last seen by anyone, by the people who loved you, by the universe. By the person who took you. Unspoken, we sat there with a tea light burning as we marked the hour you went missing, an unofficial, unplanned vigil, but one that felt right. Gone, at this hour.

Now that Yolanda's gone to bed – she has started sleeping, here and there – I look at the investigation progress on Twitter. Share after share after share. No information, nothing useful: that's Twitter. Just virtue signalling, arguing, and retweeting the same old stuff to a pool of people who have already seen it.

These people, they don't know you. They don't know your politics, your feminism, your liberalism. They don't know how much you love candles, that you can't possibly sit and watch the television without ten burning, like you were some sort of effigy.

I flick off and back to Facebook. My message inbox is rammed. Old acquaintances. People I went to university with.

All expressing condolences, but there's something more, too. I click on to one of them, from an old colleague, Ray.

> Lewis, long time. Just wanted to express my sadness at what's happening. I hope she is home soonest. Anything I can do, mate, any time, do call. R.

I look at his timeline. He's shared the police's post about you, and added the narrative: *One of my oldest friends' daughters. Please help find her.*

I sit back on the sofa, one eye on the mullioned windows, still looking for you, still hoping you'll appear there, rueful, not really getting the big deal of your disappearance . . . and wonder why Ray's post has irritated me. Yolanda would tell me he is being kind, helpful: she sees the best in people. But is he? To me, that message is a horrified reflected glory. *I know them!!!* is the subtext of that share. I am not one of Ray's oldest friends: he's never even met you.

I log out of Facebook in anger but, just before I confirm it, I see it: suggested friend. Andrew.

I know I'm going to do it before I actually do. I resist it for a few seconds, eyes on the window, hand hovering over the button, and then I give in and look at his profile, as I have many times before.

And that's when the thought occurs to me. Arrives fully formed, as though not truly from me, but from someone else instead: Andrew would be good to talk to, but he will be more useful if he doesn't think he's talking to me.

17

Olivia

Instagram photo: A Diptyque candle in the scent Baies.
Instagram caption: Okay, but why do these smell so good? Isn't it so weird when high-end stuff genuinely IS better than drug store?

Tweet: Am I going to think this knot in the wood of my new stairs in my new shitty house share is a spider every single day for the rest of my life?

Fifth Day Missing

18

Julia

Julia is in her living room, staring at the emailed private DNA report, thinking about Olivia's use of the American phrase *drug store*. Strange.

The report came – fast-tracked, at a cost of £900 – but here it is. She reads it, and then dials Erin, holding her mobile between shoulder and chin. All it says is that her blackmailer is a man, then supplies his DNA profile. Outside, beyond her living-room windows, the relentlessly blustery spring winds carry litter on the air, right above the houses. Bags, fish and chip wrappers, the lot. 'Can you run a DNA sample for me?' she asks, desperation lacing her voice. She has problem upon problem. Last night, she recklessly tried ten times to delete the bodycam footage, but it's on a backend server. Each time she deleted it, it reappeared again when she logged back in, like a magic birthday candle that simply wouldn't blow out.

Nobody can help her. The Super? No. Jonathan? No. She could never put a friend in that position. Art? What would he do, anyway? Her brother? Well, he could defend her, maybe, but he can't help now.

She needs it gone. It's an obstacle that has arisen among a whole course of them, but it's still a hurdle she needs to clear.

She stands helplessly in the living room. A framed photo of her and Art's wedding is still on the mantelpiece. Neither of them has been so loaded as to take it down yet. She wonders if, when he broke those vows that he insisted on writing himself, he'd thought about her. But then – had she thought about him? When she chose work, time and again?

She turns her mind back to her other problems as Erin speaks. 'No preamble necessary. How am I, etc.?' Erin says. Julia can hear her kids in the background, Erin shushing them. 'God, sorry,' she says. 'Evening fucking chaos,' she adds. 'I'm looking forward to the quiet cup of tea that I'm going to have in a decade.'

'Sorry. How are you?'

'Great,' Erin says darkly. 'House move is go, you know, I just don't have the –'

'It's a cold case. Er – from last year,' Julia lies, ignoring Erin's chatter. 'I have a male DNA report.'

'Yeah? Okay,' Erin says, but her voice is confused. Rightly so: no normal DCI would be working on cold cases during the golden hours of a missing person's investigation. Julia hopes her dogged, multitasking reputation might precede her on this one. 'Any word on Olivia?' Erin says, perhaps passive-aggressively.

'Nothing . . .' Julia says.

'Jesus. I was looking at her Little O Insta last night. I think, if someone else hasn't killed her, I might. So annoying. She's like – I don't know. A parody.'

Julia's mouth twists into a grim smile. Gallows humour: necessary for survival in the job. When you've attended as many post-mortems as they have, you'll say anything dark for a laugh. 'I quite like her,' she says. 'Can you run it?' she asks Erin. 'The DNA. If I send the details.' One thing ticked off her list. She'll just have to screenshot it so it obscures the fake name she gave.

'No problem,' Erin says crisply. As Julia hangs up, she hears her bark an order at one of her children. Julia closes her eyes in relief that Erin was distracted, her attention immediately turned elsewhere. That Julia, surrounded by police, didn't hear that beat of Erin doing the worst thing possible: thinking. A damning, judgemental beat of silence: suspicious quiet.

* * *

'Not on the system,' Erin says, walking into Julia's office and sitting down in The Interrogation Chair. She sets a new DNA report down: a single piece of paper, curled at one edge. 'Sorry. You got any idea who it is, at all?'

'Nowhere?' Julia says, she thinks desperately. She can't do this. She is used to being outspoken, straight up. This subterfuge is the worst thing in the world to her.

Erin turns her mouth down. Her gaze is on the paper she's just set down on Julia's desk.

'No, sorry – never arrested, never cautioned.' A beat. 'Which cold case?' Julia's head snaps up. Erin's tone is interested, but in a studied way. Julia's detective brain is just as chilled by Erin's suspicion as she is by the notion that this unnamed, anonymous man has never once been arrested. He's either an amateur, or a consummate fucking professional.

'Oh, an ancient one,' she says quickly, not wanting to associate her assailant's DNA with anybody. She waves a hand casually. 'DNA came in on it, something got re-tested.'

'What got re-tested?'

'Just the – a coat, at the scene.'

'One of our lot tested it originally, then?' Erin says, and Julia knows she shouldn't have asked her. Forensic in occupation and in nature, Erin won't think anything of interrogating Julia.

'Yeah,' Julia says. Never complain, never explain. Whose mantra is that? Somebody famous. Erin hesitates, for just a second. Her gaze meets Julia's and something is communicated between them. A question from Erin's eyes, avoided, unanswered by Julia's. It's silent. It's invisible. But it's real. Both could attest to it. And, for a second, Julia is sure she knows, too. 'Look – I'm going to go to Olivia's. Interested in these housemates,' Julia says. She's read the reports but, as she learnt last year from the Sadie case, there is no substitute for the real thing.

'Sure,' Erin says easily, but as they walk out together Julia can feel her eyes remaining on her; she's biding her time, the way those in the police sometimes do. They walk past the bodycam docking station, and Julia feels as though each camera slowly turns, too, to stare at her back as she leaves. Mr Jackson will ask for the footage again soon. She's running out of time.

* * *

Only one of the housemates is in: Annie. Nineteen, a trainee in media communications, whatever that means. She is surprised to see Julia, and knowledgeable enough to comprehend her rank.

'The DCI, okay, Jesus,' she says, stepping aside and letting Julia pass. She's tall, with dark blonde hair, a narrow face and a friendly smile.

It's strange to be back here. The house isn't exactly as Julia remembers, which is often the way when you've visited only once. It's nice to see it in the daytime, when clear-sighted and not frightened. They walk through the hallway together, Julia ambitious and focused. She can't find the man in the balaclava. She's got to find Olivia. She has to. She glances at the stairs, and something about them bothers her. Her gaze lingers, but she can't work it out.

They go through to the long Victorian kitchen, bathroom at the end. One bedroom at the front, downstairs. Back door ajar, letting the spring air in. Hallmarks of the house-share life are dotted around – a chore timetable, flyers for a local club, coupons. Julia casts her eyes over them. So far so normal.

'I just – if you don't mind . . . I've seen the interviews, but I wanted to get a feel for . . . what you thought of her,' Julia says. 'There's some stuff to me that doesn't quite add up.'

'Oh yeah?' Annie says. It's nice to be treated normally. No *guv* or *ma'am*, no deferential behaviour, sniffing around for promotions. And no suspicion either.

She makes Julia a latte from a surprisingly upmarket coffee machine. 'This thing . . . so temperamental,' she says. Annie jabs a few buttons and milk begins spurting out. Annie and Olivia texted a fair amount after she had signed the lease and before she moved in. The latest: *OMG you move in super soonest!* Julia remembers it well.

'Like what – what doesn't add up?' Annie says.

Julia considers telling her about the different-sized clothes but they'd only just met. Annie won't know.

'She got a new number before she disappeared,' Julia says. 'A new house, obviously. And a new job.'

'Yeah.'

'Some kind of fresh start, or something beyond that?'

'Maybe.'

'Did you ask her?' Julia looks quickly at Annie, who begins

making herself a coffee, her back to Julia. That's when she thinks about them, the stairs. From Olivia's tweets – she thought the whorls in the wood were spiders. 'One second,' Julia says, breezing back into the hallway to look at them. And that's what had bothered her: the stairs are wood, but there are no knots in them. She walks up and down them, eyes to the ground, her body bent over, slowly, just looking. Nothing. They're cheap, MDF-type wood. And the tweet was recent, one of her last before she disappeared, right after she moved in. It was definitely about this house. The evidence in Olivia's case is strange in this way. Nothing tangible. Nothing she could interview on, arrest on. But things that don't add up, regardless. 'Sorry,' Julia says, going back into the kitchen. 'So, did you ask her? Why she moved?'

'No,' Annie says, seemingly not fazed by Julia popping off to investigate their house. A black cat arrives at the door and saunters in. 'He's not even ours,' Annie says. 'He comes to sleep in the downstairs bedroom.'

'Did she seem – you know . . . agitated, when she moved in?' Julia presses.

Annie actually steps away from Julia now, so much so the cat skitters back out and up the garden. It's a classic move of somebody who feels cornered; Julia's seen it thousands of times before.

'You know – if you know something . . .' Julia says, thinking how Annie is a direct communicator, the way she said *The DCI, okay, Jesus*, at the door. 'If you know . . . anything at all that would help us. It's a strange case for reasons I also can't disclose.'

Annie keeps her head down, looking at her socked feet, but flicks her eyes to Julia. The coffee machine hisses milk out and they both ignore it. 'The thing is,' she says, hesitating.

Julia waits. She could wait all day.

Eventually, Annie finishes, just as Julia knew she would. 'We were so worried about her, we didn't want the police to waste any time – we'd wasted enough. That text was – we were so spooked by it.'

'Of course,' Julia says, still waiting.

'So – what I mean is, when we called 101 to report it, the operator really pressed us on when we last saw her, and my housemate, she just – she just said it. She said we'd all moved her things into her room with her, just for five minutes. I mean – she heard her shower here – she just didn't . . .'

'What?'

'Well, we haven't actually . . . she moved in and we spoke a lot on text, but . . .'

'You haven't actually what?'

'. . . met her.'

Julia blinks. '*You* haven't, or none of you have?'

'None of us.'

'But you – you've given statements to . . .'

Annie turns and starts messing with the coffee machine, trying to turn it off. It begins cleaning itself, hot air rushing up the milk steamer. 'The thing is – once the housemate told the lie, it was . . . we had to pretend. She'd told the operator we'd all met her. So we didn't think we could go back on it . . . She only said it was five minutes. And we were so worried. The text – we'd chatted so much anyway, we may as well have met her . . .'

Julia stares at Annie. 'So you all lied?'

'We just said we'd met her when we hadn't. We WhatsApped loads, we *know* each other. We spent a night as housemates! We just didn't physically see her.'

'Physically seeing someone matters,' Julia says.

'Does it? I have loads of online friends I haven't met.'

'What did you think we'd do – not investigate?'

'Maybe. How could anyone say she's missing if she wasn't ever seen?'

Julia stares at Annie. She stares for so long that it becomes awkward. 'What?' Annie says, and Julia waves a hand in response. Is Annie right? Yes and no, Julia concedes. They would still have investigated. But they might not have started from this point: with the knowledge that these housemates had never, ever seen Olivia.

'So let me get this straight – she did move in, right?'

'Oh, yes – we *heard* her. She moved in super late, midnight. She texted that she was on her way, and then we all heard her unpacking, but we thought we'd say hi in the morning. Then one of us heard her shower. Then in the morning, she messaged to say she was going to an interview, and she'd see us later.'

Julia sighs. Meeting somebody *does* matter, for all sorts of reasons. The housemates now have no idea of Olivia's emotional state, actually. And the police have no true idea about her whereabouts. Who moves in at fucking midnight?

'Don't worry,' she says softly, thinking that some knowledge is coming about Olivia that Julia soon won't be able to unsee.

* * *

Jonathan is getting his coat on when Julia arrives back. He is folding up a Pret bag and putting it in his desk drawer.

'You all right?' he asks, looking closely at her.

'I need to brief the team about this,' Julia says. 'The housemates haven't sodding met her. Olivia.'

'What?'

'Yep. Clean lied about it.'

Jonathan pauses, Pret bag still in hand, looking at her. He passes Julia his phone, Olivia's Instagram displayed on it. 'I have been wondering, you know, if she has a second phone somewhere. Might be something and nothing, but . . .'

'Why?' Julia says in surprise. She grabs the phone and begins scrolling through the Instagram posts, thinking about the drug store language and wearing an eye mask outside and the bloody whorls of wood. It's like . . . some sort of persona.

'Almost everyone she has contacted on this phone, this WhatsApp, this email, this Facebook, have two things in common.' He puts the bag away. It's stained with grease. He eats the same thing every day: a pastrami deli sandwich. Not a bad choice at all, but every day? 'One,' he ticks them off on his fingers. 'A recent friend. Or, two, an acquaintance. Never an old friend, never a family member.'

'Right,' Julia says, nodding quickly. 'The housemates fit that too. When was her Facebook set up?'

'A year ago, same with Instagram. It's only her email – the Little O email – that goes back – way, way back. Almost a decade, though scant at times. I just wondered, though. It's all surface deep. I don't know. Women her age, you'd expect . . . in my experience,' he says, and Julia cocks her head, listening intently to him. Jonathan has serious expertise, the kind only gathered from doing this same thing, day after day after day. 'Deep chats, sometimes on voice note. A lot of texts. Close, close, close girlfriends. This is totally different. Like – her dad never did send us her old housemates' details, did he? And she hasn't contacted them?'

Julia blushes with shame. She hadn't followed it up. Another missing person. Another ball dropped. Both times, she had good reasons, but does that make it okay? She's been too busy trying to save her own skin, and her daughter's. Too busy, too, focusing on what really matters on this case. Trying to find Olivia with the hottest leads she's got, and trying to convict Matthew. Those are the things she has to do.

'And now this,' Jonathan continues, 'the housemates haven't met her. The only useful people have been the dad – who is kind of difficult, let's be realistic – and a guy she temped with, years ago? I rang a bloke she went to uni with, too. But – Julia, it's so flimsy.'

'Is she kind of a loner? Maybe? She speaks to her family, but . . .'

'Maybe. Often those with the largest online social networks are the most introverted and lonely in real life, yes,' Jonathan says. 'But – there is . . . I don't know. Something weird about it. The housemates add to that.'

'I know,' Julia says softly. 'I think meeting in person matters less to their generation, though. They texted a lot. They heard her move in. To them – that is the same.'

Julia puts his phone down, Olivia's Instagram still displayed. 'Don't you think her Instagram is – I don't know. Almost staged? The Zoflora, the overkill millennial slang, something in every single post . . . sometimes weird phrasing, like *drug store*.'

'That's because of YouTube. Beauty tubers,' Jonathan says immediately. 'All American.'

'Yeah. All right. But – I don't know? It's almost like – I don't know?' Julia pauses. She knows from the way the words taste and feel in her detective mouth that she's on to something. 'I don't know what I mean,' she adds, while she thinks that it isn't the lie the housemates told that bothers her: it's that they plain haven't met Olivia.

Jonathan picks the phone up. 'She says she saw a golden retriever on the beach near you – Sugar Loaf,' he says, 'but dogs are not allowed at that beach. I looked. I meant to say. Something and nothing. Do dogs go there?'

'People break the rules all the time. But it's things like that,' Julia says. 'She said she wore an eye mask out of the house. And – I mean . . . that is seriously bizarre. Almost like she doesn't know that?'

'How interesting.' Jonathan pauses, fiddling with the lock on his drawer while he thinks. Julia knows his thinking face well and, God, it's nice to be here, chatting it through with somebody rather than hiding things. He'd pull this exact face when he was an analyst who wanted to be an officer. Julia's so glad he made it happen. And she's glad she helped him, too.

'What's your gut instinct?'

Jonathan sucks in his cheeks. 'I'd say most incidental things like this do end up being connected,' he says eventually. 'Though not always in the way you expect. Also, you know. Look and you shall find.'

Julia nods. *Look and you shall find* is a common fact in any investigation. All you have is a snapshot. It'll naturally be full of red herrings. If anyone disappeared on any single day of their life, there would always be something strange about it. Human beings aren't robots. Taking a different route to avoid an old acquaintance. Getting a coffee and throwing it away because the milk tasted off. Julia has done both of these things recently, things that would look strange and loom large if a major crime unit were to investigate them.

Of course, Julia has since done much, much worse. If she is ever investigated, she's finished.

Jonathan is getting ready to go. Home to a wife and a baby.

Julia goes home to a daughter and a husband who won't brush his teeth in the bathroom with her.

'*Mañana*,' Jonathan says. 'Been learning Spanish on Duolingo.'

The foreign phrasing . . . that's what gives her the idea: a way to get rid of the bodycam footage. Maybe the decision to descend downwards into the criminal world was actually made the night all of this started, the night the man got into her car and forced her into corruption. The night that, only a few hours before, she'd seen Price. Her old informant. A man of the (criminal) people who can get you any service you require. All you have to do is trade your ethics. Again.

19

Emma

There is a lot going unsaid currently in this police meeting room, mostly by me. I keep going over and over it. Your hushed confession. You had been speaking to Olivia Johnson. A single line, uttered as if to a priest, and then you were whisked off, and here we are.

But the night she disappeared . . . I cling on to it. You were with me. You *were*. I collected you from Linda's. We went home, then we went out together, for tacos, at Portishead One. You said you were enjoying the new bar job. You like work like that – you seem to have zero ambition for much else, though, as with most things to do with you, I don't truly have any idea. You like the late nights, the quiet of the world after your shift.

And then, after the tacos, we came home, pretty late . . . but not so late that . . . do I know you were in your bed the whole night . . . ? It was the first thing they asked me. I tried to answer as forthrightly as possible. And then, after that, we got a lawyer.

And now you are sitting with me, and opposite is the lawyer who calls himself Mr Jackson. I quite like that formality. A proper person doing a proper job. Somebody who will untangle this nonsensical situation we find ourselves in. He got me in, too, argued you are so anxious you needed an appropriate adult as support.

You have spent the night in a cell. Your hair mussed, in police-issue clothing – a cheap burgundy tracksuit. You don't smell like you, like us. No laundry detergent. You smell like them. The State, the public sector. The sweat and stale odour of prison.

You look small, diminutive. You always did. At nursery you'd hang on to one of the key workers' legs, waiting for me, then transfer straight to mine, my baby limpet. Even last year, when you first met your then-girlfriend, you came home and you said you felt like a twat every time she texted you, you couldn't think what to say back. 'But you're so good with banter when you relax,' I'd said, and you'd shrugged. Forever insecure. I wish I could take that away from you completely.

'All right,' Mr Jackson says, uncapping a fountain pen. He smells of Old Spice, and I wonder if he strays into cliché. Pinstripe suit, ink cartridges, an understated watch bought indirectly by repeat offenders. It's only the same as me, I suppose, letting oligarchs outbid normal buyers and leaving the penthouse suites in Bristol and Portishead empty.

'Tell me everything, from start to finish,' Mr Jackson says to you. He's old, maybe close to sixty, white hair, black eyebrows. A throat-clearing habit that I try not to let irk me.

'The main thing,' you say, 'is that I have never been in that house.' Your gaze lingers on mine just briefly; it's drawn to me like a magnet.

Mr Jackson looks straight at you over the table. It's a standard-issue police interviewing room. Plastic chairs. Blue carpet. A panic strip halfway up the wall like a dado rail.

'DNA evidence is very rarely wrong.' He says this without

breaking eye contact with you for even a second.

'Okay. But I am not wrong, either.'

'I have had clients tell me they weren't there. It was their identical twin. They're being framed.'

Something leaden is making its way around my bloodstream. Some awful, creeping knowledge. Even this lawyer, this £300-per-hour defence lawyer, doesn't believe you, and he doesn't even know what I know, either.

I close my eyes. Images flash through my mind. Made-up things, hypotheticals, but so real to me. One o'clock. You get out of bed, in search of – what? Sex? A kill? You creep out, find her, follow her up the alley . . .

You don't dignify Mr Jackson's statement with an answer, only a sad raise of your eyebrows, and he continues. 'One thing' – he puts the cap back on his pen, like he won't even proceed a single step further until you tell the truth – 'that the justice system is good at is bringing everything out in the wash.'

'Well – I mean. I haven't got a twin,' you say. 'But – all of the above?'

I glance at you, dithering . . . deciding . . . I don't know the first thing about lawyers, about client confidentiality, about the situation we find ourselves in.

'You think it's a fix,' Mr Jackson says.

'I know that I wasn't there,' you say carefully.

'Isn't the main thing' – I talk over you – 'that he was with me on the night she disappeared into that alley?'

'The prosecution will infer that you're protecting him.'

'Right, so their evidence is cast iron, and ours is made up.'

'You have a cast-iron reason to give an alibi for your son.'

'Yes: because he was with me,' I say. And you were. You *were*. You went upstairs, after therapy, as you often do. I was in the garden, weeding. You rang me from your bedroom, as you also regularly do, wanting to go out to Portishead One, and we did. You met me out front.

'The issue,' Mr Jackson says tightly, 'is that Matthew can't account for why his DNA was found in Olivia's bedroom. If he had put forward some sort of story regarding the DNA, then we would have something to work with.'

'There is no story because I've never been there,' you say. 'If I had, given everything you've just said, I would actually tell you.'

'And you've never met her?' Mr Jackson says. The pen lid is off again.

'No,' you say carefully. Not a lie, not technically. God, I wish you had been more specific. That I had pressed you further while the chaos broke out around us. I currently don't even know the lies I am hearing, what their significance is.

'And you don't know who she is?'

This is the moment. I hold my breath.

'No.' You don't move as you say this. And that isn't the worst part, your lie. You know what is? It's that – if I didn't know – I wouldn't be able to tell you were lying. There is no clue whatsoever. You hold his gaze, your body still, face relaxed. Goosebumps break out across my back, a chilled, feverish, panicky feeling setting in across my body.

And so, after the meeting, I go home, and I begin to search your room.

* * *

Old schoolwork that you never threw away from under your bed. A payslip. Half a packet of Polos from your desk drawer. An empty can of Coke Zero. A used match – you like to light cigarettes the old-fashioned way, said it made you feel like you were in a book – and a pound coin. What looks like perhaps a PIN written on a piece of paper. I stare at it. How curious. It isn't your bank card; I know that one. This is something else.

So far, these are the fruits of my search, of the things the police left behind. You are still in custody, and I am here, alone. The way I thought it might end up last spring, when your girlfriend disappeared. Only I didn't think it would take so long.

The police discounted your involvement so quickly last year, but nevertheless, several newspapers ran stories about you, in the aftermath. Not nationals, only locals, only speculation, skirting as close to the line of libel as they could – *alleged*, *on suspicion of* – but people are people, and they began to talk. At your job, at mine, on our street. Eventually, we moved away, but only across town. I wanted to cut and run entirely, but you wouldn't, you wanted to stay close to Portishead. I wonder what you'd do now. You look different, with that beard, hardly get recognized. Maybe you're glad we didn't go far.

After the fruitless search, sweaty and grimy, I go elsewhere, across the hall to my bedroom – minimalist, modern – and out again, back downstairs, to the kitchen. Where would I hide something? Somewhere strange. I check the shed outside, cold spring air biting at the back of my neck like a pair of eyes. I check the garage. I check in the log burner, my fingers coming away covered in ash. I scrutinize it, but it's just firewood, burnt out. Jesus, what did I expect? Finger bones? Teeth? I turn away from it, revulsed.

I check in drawers containing light bulbs and chargers and old remote controls we've for some reason kept. I check in mugs we never use at the back of cupboards. I check along the tops of the kitchen cabinets, my ashy hands now covered in fuzz and grease and fat. I check along the tops of doorframes.

I check the toilet cistern, underneath your mattress, down the back of the sofa, like a Mafia wife, like a drugs baron, like a gullible fucking mother.

As I check and check again, mad places, looking for crazy items – what? Bodies? – I think of her, your girlfriend. Of Sadie, walking home one night and never seen again.

And, finally, I check above the bathroom cabinet. And there it is, the thing I've been searching for: evidence. A piece of paper, on it a QR code. It definitely isn't mine. It is a torn A4 page from a notebook, the QR code printed sideways across the lines. Without thinking too much about it, I get my phone out and scan it. It says, 'Bitcoin transfer incoming – I have Prudence Jones for you.'

20

Lewis

I have my head under the spare bed, in search of an identity. Do you remember? The summer you worked with me, we messed up that run of blank passports, shipped to the office from Holland ready for us to stamp, personalize, hologram. The passport office is, quite understandably, fastidious about disposing of bad runs, but we had ruined *so many*. We sneaked them out, put them under the spare bed, laughed about it every now and again, worried about it even more so. Passport after passport sits in there, printed skewed to the side, printed too lightly.

They're here somewhere, I think, rifling past drifts of dust and shoeboxes and lever-arch files until I find them: in the pink folder, exactly as I remember. I open it on my lap, sitting on the woven carpet that you chose with Yolanda. There are five copies of the same passport, a woman. Tens of other, different ones. I select one, open Facebook and finish setting up my new account, ticking hobbies, interests, bands my new persona likes. After that, I sit back, and look around me.

You were the last person to sleep in here but, already, it

has that chilled, dusty feeling empty rooms have. I try not to read into it. Try to stop being superstitious. A room's smell doesn't mean you're gone. It *doesn't*.

I return to Facebook, and find Andrew, under my new, female name.

Hi, couldn't resist messaging, I write. *Love your profile xx.* I then press *Add friend.*

Let's wait and see.

Yolanda walks into the guest room, hands on her hips. Wearing a strange outfit – sweatpants and an old winter jumper. Bare toes in the deep carpet.

'What are you doing?' she says plainly to me, but indulgently so.

'Nothing,' I say petulantly, like a teenager.

Yolanda isn't a suspicious person. For somebody who knows me so well, she sometimes seems to have no idea that I am almost always doing something semi-dysfunctional. Usually of the benign variety – ordering megapacks of sweets, et cetera. Perhaps she just knows this and ignores it. 'DCI Day called,' she says.

My heart immediately seems to expand widthways in my chest. 'And?' I say urgently.

'They're looking again at the place she disappeared,' she says. 'That's all. Well – almost. Did you know DCI Day didn't interview Andrew? She wasn't in that day – something to do with her daughter.'

'What?' I say, my world rocked. 'So – she just didn't . . . didn't bother to look at the whites of his eyes herself? How can they test his amazing alibi?'

'I know,' Yolanda says thoughtfully, her gaze on me.

'Why didn't she get him back in, then?'

'I don't know.'

'I . . .' I say, looking at her bare toes and thinking how like yours they are: long and elegant.

But, just as I'm about to reply to her, engage with her, apologize, Andrew sends me a message back.

Sixth Day Missing

Olivia

Instagram photo: A Starbucks peach tea on a bench in the sun.

Instagram caption: It may be March, it may be fucking freezing, but I have had fourteen of these peach teas in eleven days. And has the barista realized how addicted I am yet? No. Do they know my order, like I'm in a NYC-based movie? Also no. Maybe fifteenth time lucky.

Facebook post: I have about eighteen friends lol and am scared to post every day because of Zuckerberg's attitude to capitalism mostly, but I've got a new phone, add contacts below, please.

Comment by Michelle Smith: Text me, hun, I don't put my number on Facebook (for the same reason).

Comment by Doug Adams: Yet you'll use WhatsApp, which is owned by Facebook? Okay, then . . .

Tweet: Maybe this is just day thirty-two of my cycle talking but I really want to toast a loaf of bread.

Sent item:
26/04: <u>LittleO@gmail.com</u> to <u>returns@boohoo.com</u>
I've been trying to reach you on the phone but unable to. I wish to return order number #78304. They're trousers and they don't fit (sad face). Please call me on . . .

22

Julia

Price picks up on the first ring. 'DCI Day!' he says. Julia is standing a safe distance from the police station, cold wind whipping her hair around her face. Even now, standing on a frozen street still reminds her of her years on Response, when she first joined the police. Drunks, domestics, she loved it all. That first day, she stood on a street not unlike this one, and read out her first caution, later told the victim, who cried with relief, and that was it: she was in occupational love. Not only – she is slightly ashamed to admit – because she had helped somebody, she had stopped something, the way she hadn't been able to stop her father's suicide, but also because she had found it thrilling.

'Can I see you?' Julia says, no preamble, 'I need . . . I need somebody to be – I need some . . .'

'Spit it out.'

'Are you still at the same address?'

'Of course,' he says, Julia thinks jokingly, but isn't sure.

Julia saw Art this morning after seeking yet another extension to detain Matthew, this time from a magistrate, which she knows will be granted imminently but that she still feels uneasy about. It's rare for their paths to cross in the morning these days – sadly. Art leaves early, often before her.

But this morning, he was getting dressed in the spare room, the door ajar. Julia stood, just looking for a second. Not at his naked form, a body she knows as well as her own, but at his mannerisms. Their exact texture has faded, somehow, with the lack of intimacy that comes with a frosty marriage, where you can no longer openly study the person you live with if you want to. After a few seconds, he turned, saw her looking and closed the door. Julia sobbed while brushing her teeth, wondering what might happen if she could tell him.

A few minutes later, he texted her: always his favourite medium. Just a short sentence, but Julia read it over and over: 'Hope you're okay.'

'Thanks,' she says softly to Price, a man she's spoken more words to today than her husband. 'You in now?' she adds. So far, she's managed to withhold the disclosure from Mr Jackson, but she doesn't have much longer.

'It's the daytime, isn't it?' he says, a long-time joke among criminals, who tend to work at night, or often not at all.

'Yeah, no worries,' he says, not yet understanding: not yet comprehending that their careful give-and-take relationship is about to become something else.

* * *

Price lives in a top-floor flat in a tall block. His living room, he once told her rather proudly, has a dual aspect: two windows.

Price and Julia go back almost nineteen years, to when she was a PC. She worked regularly, then, with Covert Human Intelligence Sources: police-speak for snitches. Julia liked to use informants more than other officers. Perhaps it was her preference for real-time, primary information, perhaps something else, the careful nurturing of the relationship, the soft push and pull; she was good at it, and Price was, too.

He buzzes her in through a housing-association-bland front door – dark green, small white window, sadly not unlike a prison – and she finds her way through the unchanged, derelict corridors. The lift isn't working, and she seems to remember it hadn't been the last time she visited him either, about twelve years ago. The stairs are unpainted concrete, the smell distinctly multistorey urine, the handrail white-peeling paint.

'All right,' Price says at his door, Scottish *r*'s rolling.

He's a big smoker, and his small – although neat – flat smells of dry tobacco, of old wormcasts of cigarettes in ashtrays. Nostalgia hits Julia. Those were the days. Working as a PC. Dealing with Price. Cigarettes and calling the station on payphones and Britpop.

'DCI Julia Day,' he says, stepping aside. 'What's the situation? Twice in one week, a treat for me.'

'Just something and nothing, really,' she says lightly, though she knows Price is not so stupid that he will be lured into casualness. It doesn't matter what she tells him: he, like most people who live in the way he does, has to listen to more than what he's told, in order to survive.

He sees her through to his living room. Two brown leather sofas, an ashtray, and a cuckoo clock. He's recently dusted: it smells of Pledge furniture polish.

He makes a tea; Julia refuses one. While his back is to her, at his kitchenette, she starts to speak. 'My turn to ask you for a favour,' she says. She sets it up this way deliberately: within that sentence lies the subtext of leverage. Price cannot say no to her. She has too much on him. She knows that this specific fact won't bother him, though, so she has her trump card ready.

He says nothing, but turns slowly to her, leaning back against the countertop, teabag dripping from a spoon, eyebrows raised.

'Do you know anybody good at tech?' she says. 'I need some footage gone.' The sentence is painful to say. Not only because it extorts him, somebody who has never, ever crossed her, but because it extorts her, too. Evidence planting. Illegal CCTV searches. And now this: enlisting help, off-record help.

But criminals have access to things that the police don't. And Julia's run out of options. Here is her only remaining one: joining the world she's battled for two decades, at least temporarily.

'What kind of tech?' he asks easily. He gulps his tea. He takes it black. Drinking it must be for show: it's still boiling.

Julia shifts her weight on her feet, waits a beat, then answers: 'Someone who can delete something.'

'A hacker. Delete what?' Price says curiously, the *h* in *what* a surprised Scottish owl hoot.

'Do you have anyone on your books?'

'Is this errand personal, or professional?'

'Both,' Julia says honestly.

The cuckoo clock on the wall chimes twelve. As if on cue, the sun comes out, no longer the milky quality of winter but sharp and green, like spring. Dust motes dance in the air above the counters. There's not a single thing out on the surfaces, only two mugs on the draining board and a pink cloth which Price picks up and uses to mop up the minuscule drop of tea on the lino. He's a tidy person. Tidy surroundings, tidy appearance and a tidy, fast mind, too.

'Nice clock,' Julia remarks, raising her eyes to it.

'From my mum.'

Of course: his mother is German. It continues cooing, and he waits for it to stop, perhaps reverentially. 'Bavaria,' he says. 'Where she is – they sell them there for nothing – pence.'

He pauses, looking at her, cloth in hand, and Julia is struck that this is how a lot of criminal deals are done: in houses, neighbours just next door, kids playing outside.

Eventually, he speaks. 'Right,' he says. 'Okay. First and obvious question.'

'Right?'

'What's in it for me?'

She had expected this, too. And, of course, she has an answer for it.

'Well,' she says lightly. 'History.' She turns away from him and leaves the words there, hanging daintily in the sun-lit air along with the motes. Price is excellent at subtext: he will be in no doubt as to what she means.

To her surprise he bursts out laughing. 'Oh, DCI, DCI, DCI,' he says. 'I see now. Why didn't you just say?' His auburn hair catches the light.

'Say what?'

He shifts the mugs around on the draining board like a magician, then looks directly at her. 'Why didn't you say I don't have a choice?'

She shrugs, choosing not to answer.

'The long arm of the law, right?' he says.

'Exactly.'

He got to her trump card before she needed to play it: if he won't help, she will get him convicted of all the many crimes he's committed along the way. Supply, dealing, and the rest.

'Snitches don't do well in prison, Price. Especially if it's disclosed in open court.'

Price holds his expression where it is, open, curious, but she sees him gulp, just once, his Adam's apple moving very slowly, a funicular up and down a track. 'Okay,' he says cordially. 'Snitches get stitches, right? Well bargained,' he adds, like a teacher issuing praise. 'Let me find you a techy.'

'Let me know,' she says, trying not to sound too urgent, wondering if this is it, if criminals accept disloyalty more readily than police. She has the uneasy feeling of getting away with something she hadn't expected to.

'Report it into the station if I can't get hold of you, right?' he says, a test.

'Best to just come direct to me,' she says without missing a beat. She doesn't attempt to disguise it. And now, just like the tide that pulls in at one bay and pushes out at another, he holds the cards: he knows this isn't at all legitimate. He gives her a slow, knowing half-smile.

Whether he chooses to do something with that information now, or later, Julia can't tell. She walks to the window. She's never felt unsafe in his company, but she begins to this morning. Nobody knows she's here. The bright kitchen, the quiet surrounds, the towering view, tiny people on patchwork pavements below – they all become sinister.

Julia turns to leave, walking down his wooden-floored hallway to his door that doesn't lead to the outside world but to a maze of Escher corridors instead.

'Disappearing CCTV . . . people going missing a lot lately,' Price says casually from behind her.

Julia turns around, balancing her fingers on his hall table. It contains only an empty ashtray, the surface gleaming. Suddenly, she no longer sees Price, the boy who she started working with all those years ago, but a grown man, pushing forty.

'Always are,' she says. This is Price's way of telling her he knows exactly what she is working on, that he is capable of putting the pieces together.

He flicks his eyes to her. He's grown a beard, also auburn, more orange than the hair on his head. It obscures his expression, which Julia used to be able to read so easily. She wonders, suddenly, if she could ask him to find the man in the balaclava. He surely could: he could hack into Ring door-bells, intimidate people, follow people. He has all the avenues available to people happy to act illegally.

'DCI?' he says, wanting to ask something, perhaps.

Julia doesn't say anything. That one is a step too far.

'This is to do with the missing women, then?' he presses.

Julia notices the plural immediately.

'Women? Do you mean Olivia?'

'Someone went missing. Someone I work with worked with her.' Work: this is how Price discusses criminal enterprises.

'Who?'

'I didn't know her. She was blonde. They called her Mari-lyn. It won't be her name – just . . . the hair,' he says.

'When?' Julia says quickly, thinking of both Sadie and Olivia.

'Six months – ish? She was working for someone. Some ring or other,' he says casually. 'Then stopped.'

'Right,' she says, thinking how this is too long ago to be Olivia, too short a time to be Sadie.

'She stopped the work for them.'

'So not missing. Just no longer a criminal,' Julia says.

'No one saw her again. To be honest, I thought they'd killed her.'

'Why?'

'I just think that's what happens usually when someone leaves a gang . . .'

'Right.'

'Yeah – you know,' he says, and Julia can feel it. It distracts her entirely from her own thoughts, wondering who this woman could be, the arrival of his own trump card. 'I'm not sure I'm up for this errand. Thanks for thinking of me, though.'

'Why not?' Julia says sharply, perhaps desperately, though she tries not to show her hand.

'I want to know what I'm getting involved in here,' he says. Julia feels her body sag. It's fair enough. It's totally fair enough he would want to know that. She doesn't want to say what she says next, but she has no choice.

'I can't tell you anything,' she says.

'Maybe I can't do it, then. Send me down – I don't care.'

She reminds him of her own trump card: 'Sure you wouldn't want any of your contacts to know you've been informing on them?' she asks lightly. There are plenty of criminals she could go to. Both those on the inside, whose releases are imminent, and out. The threat to criminals isn't the law: it's their contemporaries. She winces as she says it. The first time she has ever, ever abused his trust, threatened him. Their symbiosis, ended in a single sentence.

'Fuck you, Julia,' he says. The Glaswegian consonants turn unpredictably like hairpin bends. He pauses, then adds, mostly reluctantly, 'I'll send someone.' Julia isn't surprised: most criminals don't fear prison, but they do fear death.

'That's all,' she says. 'Nothing else.' Sadness sweeps over her like a hangover.

Julia walks out without saying another word, thinking of a time in the future, and what her trial might look like. What the bundle of papers from the prosecution will say, and how this will all be portrayed. A single action by Genevieve, a year ago. And every slow-falling domino afterwards. It will look sordid, corrupt, but it doesn't feel it. All Julia feels is desperation, and love. God, Julia wishes Genevieve hadn't done it. She can rarely even admit this to herself, but she does. She knows it was an error of judgement, a rash decision that Genevieve has paid the price for. And yet – Julia simply wishes she hadn't done it. As plain as that.

'A mate will log in tonight.'

'Good.'

'Unlike you,' Price says conversationally, 'straight as an arrow.'

'Usually,' she says, then corrects herself. 'Still am. It's complicated.'

'Sounds pretty simple to me.'

She blinks back tears. She's good, isn't she? Despite doing unforgivable things? She's suddenly gripped by both terror and hope that the person blackmailing her is good, like she is. Despairing, but good. The kind of quality that can be worked with.

'Don't suppose I have a choice,' Price says. Her longest-serving ally. The blackmailed becoming the blackmailer. The oldest story. She hears Price's door close behind her after she leaves.

* * *

Olivia's dad has already spoken in depth to Julia's colleagues, and perhaps that's why he takes Julia's call today with an awful connection and an even worse attitude.

It's late, and she's spent much of the evening sending IP addresses to a hacker who calls himself B2.

'Sorry,' Olivia's dad keeps saying. The wind cuts through the line like a hand being repeatedly closed over the microphone, scratchy and rough. 'Sorry – terrible signal, as I said. I'm out looking for her. But – look. Let's keep it brief.'

Julia sits back in her chair, cross-legged, barefoot, and frowns. He's angry with her, she thinks. Has disengaged for self-preservation. From concerned and engaged to this: hard to pin down, poor signal. Excuses, Julia feels, if she had to say either way. Perhaps somebody who is up to something. Something he thinks will bring his daughter back, but won't. Whenever witnesses go off the boil like this, they are inevitably doing something stupid.

'Mr Johnson, we just have a few more questions about your daughter.'

'I know – it's just . . . if you . . . I know,' he says, the line so distorted Julia can hardly make any of it out.

'Can we set up a call somehow that'll be better than this? Maybe not standing in a gale?'

'Sure.'

'Do you use Zoom?'

'Can do, it may be a few days, though.'

'Right,' she says, thinking. 'You don't think I'm doing a very good job,' she says. She's seen it before. Sometimes, victims and victim's families have no choice but to disengage.

She looks at the streetlights slanting in through the blinds. Last spring, Genevieve injured Zac and, simultaneously, Sadie went missing and was never found. She still thinks about that day she sat in the back office, not interviewing key witnesses. And everything after it, too. Reviewing documents without fully reading them, instead going over and over who might know about Genevieve, what other evidence might one day bubble up to the surface like a body in an estuary. Julia blinks. The sighting that amounted to nothing, but perhaps because of her negligence. She can't let this happen with Olivia.

She allows her eyes to glaze over. Maybe she will leave on time, soon, watch a movie with her daughter, their legs tucked up on the sofa together, back doors thrown open.

'Just a few questions, though – if you can hear.'

He says nothing in response. 'I wanted to talk more about the boyfriend,' she adds. 'Olivia's boyfriend? I'm just wanting to follow up some more on this . . .' she says, thinking, as she often does during a missing person investigation, that all she has to do is leave no stone unturned, and then she will find them.

'Go on,' he says, and she can hear something shift in his voice, some anticipation. 'Do you have anything on him?'

'Not yet,' she says. 'But I want to ask –'

'I'll call – when I have a better signal, okay?' he says, though it sounds clear to Julia.

The line goes dead. Julia looks at her phone in frustration. She's definitely pissed the dad off, then.

She upends her pen on her desk, staring at her phone, thinking, thinking, thinking. Art's right: she can never turn her brain off. And, this time, it's homing in on something. She can feel it. Marilyn. Working for a gang. What if she tried to find her? She puts it into the PNC, but it returns too many results; hundreds of Marilyns.

'All right?' Jonathan says to her, passing by her room. For a second Julia sees him as the young analyst he once was, her as the sergeant keen to rise up through the ranks. They'd leave on time together occasionally, get fish and chips and walk to their cars. Julia would take some home to Art. He'd leave her messages on the wrappers for weeks afterwards. He was always good with missives, small things like that. The care and attention needed to maintain a relationship.

'Oh, yeah,' she says weakly, now that honesty, that integrity and innocence are long gone.

Her phone rings, interrupting the moment, and Julia startles. It might be Price, saying the footage has been deleted. It might be somebody in IT.

But it isn't Price. It's the desk sergeant. 'Someone here for you,' he says delicately, and Julia can tell from his tone that it is somebody significant. Immediately, her mind goes to Genevieve.

'Who?'

'She says she is Olivia Johnson.'

23

Julia

Julia cannot believe it. There must be some mistake. But as she walks into the foyer, there she is, in the flesh. Tall, blonde, a wide nose, slightly crooked teeth. Olivia Johnson. Julia feels like blinking, like pinching herself.

'Olivia,' Julia says, partly in wonderment.

Olivia nods, saying nothing. She's exactly like her passport photograph. A strong nose. Blonde hair. Eyes that crinkle at their corners, even while her face is at rest. Julia looks at her in wonder. Here she is: Julia's saviour. The mystery solved. So why does she feel like it isn't?

'I'm not missing.' That's the first thing Olivia says. Her voice is more clipped than Julia expected, her body language more self-conscious. This is how it goes when you meet somebody who's only ever put their best side forward online, Julia supposes. She cannot stop looking at her. Back from the dead: that's where everyone thought she was.

'Well – now you're ba–'

'I was never missing,' she says, cutting across Julia. Olivia's slender hands rest on her lap, both of them spaced evenly. Certainly not the posture of somebody returned from somewhere. Goosebumps sweep over Julia. *All is not as it seems,* the detective instinct says, and Julia listens to it. 'I should've come earlier, I know,' she says, holding up a hand.

'Why didn't you?' Julia looks at her closely. A couple of the lights in the foyer click off around them.

'Hang on,' Olivia says, digging in a satchel she has slung crossways over her body. She's in faded jeans rolled up at the ankles, must be freezing. Julia finds this sartorial impracticality not very surprising.

Olivia begins to explain, while Julia thinks about how Matthew must be released now, about how Genevieve might be okay now, but Julia doesn't believe it, feels uneasy at being let off the hook. Who knows what else might be demanded? 'I honestly thought it couldn't be real. I mean – I wasn't in that alleyway. I didn't disappear,' Olivia says.

'Sorry?' Julia says. Her gaze roves over her face. It's like trying to solve a logic problem. She ought to take her into a meeting room, take a formal statement. But, somehow, Julia already knows the answer to the question she needs to ask. 'Did you live in that house share?'

Olivia meets her eyes. 'No.'

'Were you in the alleyway – off Portishead High Street?'

'No.'

'What do you mean, it isn't you?'

'This is why it took ages for me to come in. The first night it broke on the news I thought, how weird, my name – but not exactly an uncommon one. Then the second night – the photo . . . it's my passport's. But I don't live where she does. None of the details fitted me.'

Julia's jaw drops. It isn't Olivia. Not the Olivia she's looking for, anyway. 'You left it several days, though?' Julia says curiously, needling at this. Anyone would have come forward, wouldn't they? So why hadn't she?

'We were away . . . a family wedding, five-day affair. Super-remote area.'

'I see.' Julia shakes her head. 'So the Instagram isn't yours?'

'No. I don't have any social media. You see?'

'But it is your photograph. And your name.'

Olivia hands her a passport, held between thumb and index finger, like a ticket. Julia takes it, and sure enough, it's the same photo: identical. Issued a year ago, in May 2022. The spring of Genevieve's crime. It's 2023 now, though it feels more than a year ago.

There's only one problem: Julia already has Olivia Johnson's passport in the evidence room.

24

Emma

It's taken me a full day to decide what to do, and it's one o'clock in the morning when I do, as it often is. At night, you can acknowledge things to yourself that you can't in the daytime.

I'm sitting at the kitchen island, and I'm thinking about your ex-girlfriend. I'm smoking a single cigarette. It won't matter that the house smells – you're not here; you're still incarcerated, extension after extension granted to your detention, while the police *make inquiries*. Vague speak, I suppose, for trying to find the evidence to charge you. So I don't need to hide the cigarette, or take it into the garden. I have out a single glass ashtray that I used to have with me when you were a baby and – forgive me – that single cigarette in the garden, late, was the best part of my day. Now, I watch the perfectly straight line of smoke rise slowly upwards and disperse to nothing.

Two women, both missing. Your ex-girlfriend, and Olivia, a woman you were messaging. And now a third woman, too. *I have Prudence Jones for you.* I have no idea what it means, what a QR code is in this context, what bitcoins are for. All I know is . . . what? What do I know? I stare at the smoke, trying to read it like tea leaves, waiting for an answer to emerge from the toxic mist. *I have Prudence Jones for you.* What else could it mean other than what it sounds like?

It's like swallowing an ice cube. There should be a name for that specific feeling that comes when you realize something is right but wish it wasn't. When you know you need to leave a job, a partner, a town, just like we did. We cut and ran last year, after everything, and yet still we couldn't escape it, not fully. We didn't go far enough.

I pick up the cigarette and drag on it. My fingers will be stained yellow. The kitchen will smell. It'll never come out, not truly. That's what happens with cigarettes. I'll remember this night, at this kitchen island, for ever.

Never once have you given me an explanation for your girlfriend's disappearance. And maybe there isn't one. But worse than that, never once have you acknowledged that I might wonder what happened, might have doubts.

Cigarette still in my mouth, I start to pull on my jacket and trainers, the names of the three women swirling around me like the cigarette smoke. Olivia. Prudence. Once is bad luck. Twice is . . . three times is . . . the cigarette feels like it's choking me. I can't believe this is happening. That these are my choices.

I have spent so long arguing with myself over your innocence I have forgotten something: that, sometimes, parenthood isn't an internal argument, assessing and reassessing your child. Sometimes, it is action.

Keys in hand, I press the button and watch the car blaze the street amber outside. Is this tough love? No, I don't think it is. It's something else.

Remember her father? God, you know, his heart was fucking broken. Absolutely cracked in two. That man would never be the same again. It was obvious. His whole body seemed to change, like the pain of losing her had carved him open and left him hunched over what remained.

He deserves to know what happened. Everybody does.

Outside, the streets are covered in moisture. It's been raining hard, now dulled to gentle tapping as the drops fall from the spring trees and bushes.

I finish the cigarette – God, I hate them, really – and toss it to the ground. It lands in a puddle still dimpling with rain. I get in the car and start the engine running, and it feels kind of apt, you know? Black rain on the windscreen, tears inside, and just me, alone. A single parent in every sense.

I looked up Prudence Jones earlier today. Nobody is missing who goes by that name, not that I can find, anyway. I have no idea what the bitcoin could be for, though I could make a few dark guesses. Kidnap, murder, trafficking. Which is it?

I idle at a pedestrian crossing on a timer for nobody when I could run the red light, and I wonder if you would. If we are perhaps just made of different stuff, even though I grew you for so long by myself, and parented you solo for all of your life, that it feels like you must be solely me. But maybe I've only been seeing what I want to see. Maybe you don't give a shit about other people, about red lights, about laws that say you shouldn't murder women.

And, of course, I think about your father. A waster. A man who is content to take flight at two pink lines. But what if he's worse than that? I blink as I pull away. I can hardly remember him. Suddenly, sleeping with him, being careless with him, feels like the biggest gamble of my life. Putting everything on red in a game of Russian roulette, without knowing what the bet is, what the stakes are.

The police station comes into view. Always lit up, one of

those grim places that never truly shuts, like fire stations, like churches, like A&E departments, places too important to close their eyes for even a minute.

I park up and take a few breaths, just for me: for you, too, I suppose, and I try to tell myself that handing over this QR code is protecting you – in a way: just from yourself.

My footsteps echo across the car park. The information I hold is in my hand, so weightless it feels almost insignificant, a damp and feather-light piece of paper, nothing more than that. It moves slightly in the cold breeze.

The automatic doors let me in, and there is DCI Day, right there in the foyer, a tableau of an overworked police officer, as though she is just waiting for me. I lift the piece of paper, ready to say my bit.

Day turns slowly to look at me, eyes first, then her head, then her body, like an animal.

'My son has been questioned and is still being held here,' I say. Her facial expression doesn't change, but her eyes seem to sharpen as I speak. 'I have some evidence that might assist you. And I wanted you to know: he used to be known as Andrew. Last year, his girlfriend, Sadie, went missing.'

25

Lewis

There's a man outside the police station, talking to DCI Day. I've come to discuss Andrew with her, to show her the messages between my alter ego and him, but I now stand, one hand on the hot roof of my car, the other on the door-handle, just looking, and watching it unfold.

It's something: more than a normal altercation between police and public. They're both emotional. He – in a parka, even though it's warm – is right up in front of her, like a drunk, like somebody at the end of a night out, his body a coat hook hanging over her. She's gesticulating, not a pose I've ever seen her make before. One arm across her body, the other held up in a stop sign.

She seems to have the final word, because he leaves, and as he turns I see his neck – a thick, white, NHS-issue gauze over it, steri-tape holding it down. Even so, the wound underneath has leaked through, a burgundy stain blooming across it like a poppy with a black centre. It looks unclean, uncared for, the edges of the gauze dirtied.

I watch him go, walking slowly down the street, wondering if he's a victim of a recent crime, wondering if he is as dissatisfied with DCI Day as I am.

Just as I think this, he turns, 'Fuck you,' he shouts, his accent wide and northern, like a blank winter sky. 'Fuck you and your corruption!' he says.

The words have a physical effect on Day. Her palm, facing out towards him, collapses, and she pulls both arms around her waist. She looks tired. She looks like she hasn't slept in weeks and weeks, purple eyelids, cut-outs beneath her cheekbones. She bends over slightly, as though gut-punched.

Corruption.

Corruption.

The second she turns away, trudging back to the station, I find myself hurrying after him. *Corruption.* What does he mean? My breath puffs out of me as I cross the car park. Following Day recently has somehow opened something in me, like this is a normal way to behave, to overhear, to accost, to tail somebody. I guess all I can say is that, one day, if you have kids, you might understand some of what I've done this past week. I miss you so viscerally it has become a soured, rotten part of me, right in the very centre of my body, like I have grown a new, sad organ.

'Hey, hey!' I shout to the man.

He turns and looks at me. Tall, with vacant eyes, angry body language, like somebody who it would take absolutely nothing to tip over into violence. 'How do you know her?' I say lamely. 'DCI Day?'

He rubs at his neck, which makes me wince. An old gesture, one that doesn't accommodate the new wound, and he startles as his fingers cross it, then looks at them, checking for blood. 'Yeah?' he says.

And that's when he says the sentence that changes everything: 'She tried to fuck up your life, too?'

'What?' I say, my voice carried away on the spring breeze,

213

fresh and scented. The verges of the car park are lined with cow parsley. My eyes dart to the police station, but Day's safe inside: they all are, in there in their ivory towers. Unthinking, unfeeling, unbothered if they don't solve the crimes, they still get paid, still get their final salary pensions. Meantime, we – the unfortunate – we languish, our lives upended.

'She can't do shit – and if you fucking challenge her, she threatens you. This is 2022, but the police are still fucking us over.'

'Huh?'

He gestures crudely to his neck, his hand forming a gun shape. 'Her daughter did this to me, mate,' he says, his voice hoarse, his eyes bright and feverish. 'So yeah – don't mess with her. She'll threaten you. Fuck,' he adds, turning in a circle. 'I shouldn't have said it.' He looks at me sharply, then draws his hood up, and lights a cigarette which illuminates his face perfectly in the igloo of his clothing. 'Don't say anything. Don't say I told you.' He points to his neck again, and then leaves me there, standing, reeling, thinking: *Exactly who is this DCI Day? And who is this man?*

'Hang on,' I say. 'Hang on.' But he doesn't wait. He sets off, loping down the street, then turns to me. 'She *did* try to fuck up my life,' I shout.

He turns slowly, looking at me. And that's when my mind presents the suggestion that he is both victim *and* criminal, like a lot of people. He comes towards me, to shake my hand – the first of what will become many – in a greeting, in an acknowledgement, and in a pact.

'I'm Zac,' he says.

214

26

Lewis

The house is silent and quiet, sleeping. But, for the first time, now a year later, it doesn't feel empty. It feels peaceful, like a cat by a fire. The rhythms of life have started coming back to me and Yolanda, so gradually you'd miss it, like a tide coming in. Yesterday I bought a bottle of wine and a sharing box of Maltesers. Such a small thing, but it means a lot: they resemble hope, to me. Not that you will return, but that there is life after you, instead.

I don't turn the lights on as I get up, just look at the sunrise, the clouds scudding and beautiful, printed with the footprints of a thousand toddlers' steps, the backdrop pearlescent. Nothing will be the same again, but that doesn't mean there can't be this: pockets of time when things are calm. Something has shifted. The tiniest pebble on a beach that moves and causes two more to shift and fall down, and then allows a trickle of water to seep into the sand. Grief that is the price I pay for having loved you so much.

I go out. Walking, walking, walking until my legs feel happy and wobbly and my heart feels full and strong. Sometimes, on the more optimistic days, I like to think about how alive I am. That your life was probably taken from you, but mine has not been, not completely, though it may feel like it has. The sky moves through its dawn, twilight in reverse. The light low and watery, slowly, slowly, slowly brightening up. I find my favourite rock.

Last year, after Zac's death, his brother, David, and I met up twice, he angry, me jaded. Zac had told him about Julia, and then, when Zac died, David found my details in Zac's phone and called me. He said if I ever needed any help to bring down Julia, or even just cause her misery, he'd help me. He, too, was a petty criminal, well connected. Able to do 'all sorts', he said, if I ever needed him.

Eventually, I told Yolanda that Julia had an enemy other than me, and she told me to drop it. We sat right here together, on this rock, our bottoms freezing and damp, and we talked about you. And we talked about us, too, and who we had become in your aftermath.

'I love her so much,' Yolanda said, 'it's like it has nowhere to go.'

'I know,' I said. 'A volcano.'

Yolanda nodded, saying nothing more, knowing, I hope, that I understood.

'If she doesn't . . .' Yolanda started to say, later, when the air was cooler and darker.

'I can't,' I said.

'Would we still be –' Her jaw began to quiver. 'Would I still be her . . .'

'Yes,' I said. 'Yes, God, yes. For ever you're her mother.'

Yolanda swallowed, looking at me as her eyes misted and then dried, the closest she really comes to crying. 'Thank you,' she said. 'For telling me that.'

I gulped, too, tears tracking down my cheeks the way they just do these days. We sat together for hours, until our muscles went stiff and our limbs cold and the air was black around us.

But, when we got home, you were still missing. We were still heartbroken. But – I don't know. Something. Life could never go back. We may have felt like we had moved to Mars, but we could go forward. And Yolanda made me see that. I've kept in touch with David only sporadically over the past twelve months, hoping maybe a criminal man on the street might uncover something about DCI Day's negligence that I could use as leverage in a real complaint against her, get the case reopened. But nothing happened. As far as I knew, David didn't do anything, either.

The only thing I've continued to do is update the fake social media profile, daily snippets that remind me of you.

There are now just shy of four hundred tealights on our windowsill back home. We look like hoarders. They litter the windowsill, five deep, seven high, spilling over like a waterfall on to the floor beneath them.

It's become a superstition. I know, I know, this makes no sense: they haven't worked. It would make sense to *stop* the candles, but we can't. They're your memory. Almost four hundred vigils, now, from that first April you went missing, through the summer, autumn, winter, and now it's spring again, though it doesn't feel like it. The miniature anniversary we commemorate every night when we light one at the time you disappeared. It means something to us that we can't explain. We have never missed it.

My phone pings shortly after eight. It'll be Yolanda, wondering where I am – still on edge, either that I have had some news about you or, worse, disappeared, too. I reach for it, but it isn't her. And it isn't you, either.

Hi, it says. It's on Facebook. Wait – but it isn't on my

account. It's on the other one, the fake me. *It's Andrew*, the message says, though it comes from somebody called Matthew. *I'm using a new account. I wanted to apologize for going off radar with you, I shouldn't have. I was – I was experiencing regret about something I'd done in the past.*

It's like electricity runs down my spine. My body heats up in the chilled morning air. It's him. Your boyfriend. Your ex-boyfriend.

Under a new name, Matthew. You've been missing a year, Sadie, and here he is, experiencing regret about something he'd done in his past. Talking about it to the woman I have invented: Olivia Johnson.

27

Lewis

I blink, staring down at my phone, unable to believe it. He is *experiencing regret about something he's done in the past.*

There it is, on a moody blue morning: a prelude, maybe, to a confession. A confession that could change everything. That could undo everything. My bad intention with the fake account. My promise to Yolanda to try to move on.

In the absence of the police, in the absence of any help given by anybody other than me, and on the freezing beach there – it's the coldest spring on record – I write back.

Me: Hey :) Nice to hear from you – what do you mean?

Matthew: Oh honestly, you don't want to know my dramas.

Me: Oh sure – we've all done things we regret, though – it's okay to talk about it!

Matthew: Hmm. Anyway – I'd love to meet. Feel bad about ignoring you last year. Trying to sort of – you know. Move on.

Me: Sure. Love to. You're local right?

Matthew: Yeah. Portishead.

Me: Same. So – why get in touch now?

Matthew: Thinking of some things I did in the past.

Me: What?

Matthew: Long story. I just – time to make some amends.

Me: Yeah?

Matthew: Don't worry. I can't say. But I'd love to meet.

That's it. That's all it takes. For me to act. If he hasn't told me what happened to you, he might have told somebody else. And, if he is arrested again, the police can look.

* * *

Adrenalin rushes through my blood. I haven't felt it for a full year, dulled by grief and constant disappointment. Suddenly, the Maltesers and the wine feel like a joke, a half-life. This – this is true purpose. Finding the man who took you. Bringing him to justice.

There was a sighting of you six months ago. Amounted to nothing, so the police said, but – God – that day. I thought my heart was going to leave my chest and fire up into the sky like a rocket. You'd been seen near the beach, near where we let you go, tried to consign you to the past, and there you were, again. Nobody else saw you to verify it. And, when questioned, the witness – an elderly woman, maybe seventy-five – became less and less sure. Definitely blonde, yes, tall for a woman, a coat just like yours, but nothing else. Not enough, not enough, not enough.

And that was that. Nothing since. The case isn't closed, it isn't cold, but it is losing heat rapidly. Fewer and fewer resources dedicated to you, updates dwindling to, so far this year, almost nothing. Just pure, undistilled pessimism. You're dead. It's written on their faces when they talk to us. Funny, even the real professionals are repulsed. You can tell. They don't want to get too close, lest it's catching.

But now. Here he is. *Experiencing regret over something he did in the past.* He is on the verge of confessing it to me, and only me.

Funny, it's all there, laid out for me, by me, past me, my subconscious, like I almost knew I'd do it one day. It's all there. Olivia has a passport. Accounts that I created. All I need to do is step into it. To them. To invent my character, and then to make her go missing.

28

Lewis

It makes me wince how easy it is for Olivia to disappear, just for a bit. Just enough to rouse suspicion. Just enough to investigate Andrew again. Just enough for the police to want to know the following: why have two women he knew gone missing? What did he have to do with the second, and what did he do in the past?

I open my laptop back at home, sitting in the place on the sofa you used to sit when we watched TV. Just before you disappeared, we got really into *Selling Sunset*. Jesus, that show really is trash. But compelling, I'll give you that. For Christmas, the winter before you disappeared, you got me a mug with Jason and Brett Oppenheim on it. It's my most prized possession; I never run it through the dishwasher.

A site advertising spare rooms has loads in the area, starting pretty much immediately. I try to find one that doesn't require any vetting, just replacing a tenant, maybe, but I actually find one where the landlord is happy to do *virtual checks*.

Dear Steve, I write, from my email. It's an old account, but I swapped over the name. And, later, I realized you could actually swap the email address to a new one, same domain name, and keep the history. Little O's email account is therefore peppered with my history, things deleted that sound like me, but leaving enough to look like a credible history: subscriptions to mailing lists, online orders, drafts.

I'd love to take the spare room in Portishead. I don't need to see it – I've just been let down and I'm desperate to move. I'd like to move in just as soon as you can, please? I attach a scan of my passport, hoping this suffices.

I glance over it, then season it with a few more of your phrases, just to make it sound like a young woman. But there's something else, too: your voice comes so naturally to me. It lives within me, the way you always will. The thought of this makes my eyes mist over on the sofa. How can you be so vivid but so . . . nowhere?

Hope this is okay :), I add. *Sorry it's scanned sideways, lol.*

You never scanned things sideways, but you did regularly forget to attach anything at all: emails from you usually came in pairs. And you did use lol as punctuation. You said it used to be uncool, and then people started to use it ironically, and then it just became cool again. 'Does it still mean laugh out loud?' I once asked you, and you said, 'Not really,' while lolling away.

The landlord emails back later, while Yolanda is cooking and I'm sitting at the kitchen island, fidgeting, or so she says. I'm not looking at the screen, not really. I'm looking at your mother's profile, side on, thinking that I know she would stop me. That this would take back from what has been so hard won: our reality, on Mars. But I am thinking, too, that one day, maybe she will thank me.

The landlord says Olivia can move in the next day.

'Need anything from the shops?' I say, standing with a start.

'Huh?' Yolanda says. 'You're going now? Why?' Her eyes stray to the clock: after ten.

'Just fancy it. The walk, the peace,' I say, and she doesn't question me any more. The thing is, since you left, even though it's been a year, we both still behave weirdly at times, erratically. It's not unusual for one or the other to excuse ourselves in the middle of a main meal in a restaurant, return embarrassingly late, with red eyes.

Tesco is not where criminal masterminds go, I know. I drive there too fast, then walk across the car park, still so cold, even right at the end of April. It's a supermarket within a mall, has an airport feel to it, or maybe that's just the time of day. Opposite is a Costa Coffee, populated by shift workers and those who need strange things at strange times, like me.

The Tesco Mobile place is open. Like something preserved from 2004. Little toy model phones tied to the desk with string. I take a box, just a cheap one, with full encryption. Am I really doing this? I wonder. But, yes, I am. For you. For justice, for you. And for future yous, too. Who will be swept away by men like Andrew.

I queue at the self-service checkout behind a woman buying gripe water. *It's just nice to be out, and away from it, tbh* she texts. I can clearly read it, though I pretend not to. The lives we lead online. The footprints we leave behind. Imagine if you were only those electronic footprints, and nothing more: would the world believe you were real? Could they?

The woman in front of her is buying flipflops and a bikini. And I am buying a phone for a fake person. I won't be able to populate this phone with your history, sadly. But what can you do? It'll have to be another hole in the plan. *Just get him arrested, just get him arrested, just get him arrested.*

I get outside, into the massive car park, dome of black sky

above me. It feels like it's just me in the world. Nobody to watch me. The anonymity of towns and cities. A gritter moves slowly along the street beyond the car park and a cold mist swirls around me like pollution. Somewhere in the very back of my mind is Yolanda. She is saying: *Lewis, this is crazy.* You'd agree, too, I'm sure. But I don't care, can't seem to. Imagine if he was arrested, properly this time: searched, cautioned, lawyers, the lot. Imagine if . . . no, I can't allow my mind to go there, that bright star of a place where you are found, alive.

I open the box and tip the phone out into my palm. It's a smartphone. No young person would have a flip phone – Jesus, you wouldn't countenance that; can you imagine the uproar if you couldn't access Instagram twenty-four seven? It's cold as it sits there like a pebble. Olivia's new phone.

It's so strange to me that I had it all there. The Facebook account set up a year ago to talk to Andrew. I'd followed him on Instagram. Found blurred selfies of models online that resembled Olivia's passport.

And then the strangest thing happened: even though I'd given up on bringing him to justice, I continued to maintain the account. Shots of artisan coffee shops, of peonies, of window seats you'd like to sit in. Things that made it seem to me like you were still alive. I'd check it, sometimes, and laugh at things I'd written in your voice. If I scrolled enough, it was almost like you were still here. A way of keeping you with me, I suppose. As though, if an avatar of you is out there on Instagram, your light hasn't yet gone out, not yet, not yet, not yet.

Olivia uses your phrases, as best as I remember, and she looks like you. Everything you liked, everything you said. Even that you'd left a job. All invented. Your funny phrases, your wit, your energy. My eulogy to you. For ever, Sadie.

The way you'd sit at the beach and watch HIIT workouts while eating churros. The way you always said you got a boner when you went shopping. All the things you did, the little things, the big things. All the funny things you thought and said. It was all there. Andrew didn't notice – men, eh? He probably thought everyone was just like you, just as funny and scintillating and sparkly as you.

It was easy, really. After all, what is an identity? I had loads of them. That box of dud passports that failed to print. I chose the one with the most anodyne name, Olivia Johnson, and the one that reminded me of you, Sadie, and that lovely face you used to pull as a baby, Little O.

And then I set up your profile, initially to catfish Andrew, later to pay homage to you.

Text me, I send to Andrew, now Matthew, giving the number of the new phone.

8pm day after tomorrow – here? he sends, adding a pin to a café you'd like. *It's dead near mine :)* I agree to it. We won't meet, of course. But, you know.

In the car, I set up five Facebook accounts, all pending ID, which I'll get from the box at home. I then message them from her, telling them the new number. I comment on a few of her updates, accidentally write on an older one as someone called Doug Adams. I email somebody called Amy De Shaun from Olivia, and then email back from Amy's account to Olivia's. I find somebody on Facebook who I can say is Olivia's boyfriend, if they don't find the messages with Matthew and believe he is dating Olivia. If the heat starts to turn to me, or it starts to look like they doubt Olivia's existence, I can say I am the boyfriend, this stranger, and that my alibi is that I was out of the country.

It's so easy, Sadie. It's so easy to make someone exist, I

almost wonder if I can magic you back. It's official: Olivia Johnson is about to go missing, even though she doesn't exist.

* * *

Early morning, next day, and I have a list of what makes a person seem like they exist. A house, a job, an email account, Instagram . . . and a wardrobe.

In the charity shop. It's musty in that way places only are on a rainy spring day, when the damp rises off clothes and hangs about in the air. An elderly woman behind the till, counting coins out into piles.

I begin to sweat. I'm meeting Matthew tomorrow. A self-imposed deadline, but a deadline nevertheless. Olivia has to be set up by then, by me, with no help from anybody.

I grab at this and that. Designer, off cuts, whatever the Oxfam shop has. A green jumper. A white top. Random jewellery. I clutch at them, then take them to the till, not looking at the prices.

I take the clothes to her new house, but as I idle outside, I see there's no way I can sneak in now. It'll have to be later, in the quiet, under cover of darkness. I can't risk being seen.

I go home, and write reams and reams of things I should do, setting her up so she seems rounded, a real person. I buy three burner phones to associate with fake Facebook accounts from a stall at an indoor market. I add them as Olivia's contacts. I fabricate the boyfriend and buy a phone to pretend to be him, too. Olivia can message these people and they will message her back. And, when the police call any of them: they will be me, because they are men. Doug, who temped with her years ago. A uni friend called Darren.

And her father. An elusive type, hard to get hold of, often has bad signal, otherwise the police might recognize him as me.

I email boohoo and pretend I have a return. I comment on a few more of Olivia's status updates. I clean up the posts, check them over, make sure they're authentic. Yolanda comes home, goes to bed, and then it's time.

After midnight, and I drive back to her place and move her in, having asked for the keys to be left in a safe space for me.

I plant the breadcrumb trail: add a few things to the kitchen, make some noise. I take a shower, bathroom locked so nobody can see who I really am. I use the shampoo and conditioner and leave the lids open. I put a toothbrush I bought by the sink. I send a few texts about the room to the housemates I know to be asleep.

When one knocks for me as I'm unpacking, I pretend to be asleep, my door locked. Nobody can see me. I rumple the bedsheets. I instagram the bed.

It's all evidence, evidence, evidence. The more people who see her, or think they see her, the better. She is an optical illusion.

I am almost ready. Olivia is almost missing. I go home and don't sleep a wink. Instead, I think about you. And how this nefarious, illegal activity is for you, to find out what happened to you, to find out what Matthew meant by his regretful message. *It'll be worth it, it'll be worth it, it'll be worth it*, I think, as Yolanda unconsciously reaches for me in her sleep and I grasp her hand the way I grasped yours on the day you were born.

* * *

It's just past eight, and Andrew will be inside the café – a pretentious, pretend-backstreet type, you know the ones. Used to be a warehouse, a yoga studio. Exposed waste pipes, asbestos raining down from the ceiling, you name it. Soon, I expect one will have a toilet just in the wide open, all in the name of hipsterdom. The café is lit up, an out-of-focus amber, Andrew safely inside. The air is cut-glass, spring-cold, winter's last bite. I hope you're not out in it, alone. I still think this way, even a year on.

I have fifteen minutes, or thereabouts. I reckon that's how long somebody gives a stand-up – don't you? He'll wait for Olivia until quarter past, minimum.

He drives the same car he always did, and it's parked on the street outside what I assume is his house. The moon is out, huge and low tonight, a swirling crystal ball. It provides hardly any light, dulled by the city haze. I look at it and wonder if I am on the right side of history here. Whether people will understand, and forgive me. Yolanda. You. Wherever you are.

I take a tennis ball out from the inside of my jacket. I have three items with me – this, a coat hanger, and a brick. The latter is an emergency measure, but might work if it looks like there were signs of a struggle from within the car.

I'm good at learning things, going on locksmiths courses, all sorts, and remembering them, and executing them, too. I've already cut a hole in the ball, and I set it now against the lock, creating a vacuum. As hard as I can, I bring down the heel of my hand on to it. One, two, three. The third time sends a shockwave down the door that I can feel, a private sonic boom just for me. And just like that, the vertical piece of plastic in the door pops up, signalling that the car is unlocked, as simple as that. I feel my shoulders drop in relief as I check my watch. It took two minutes. Thirteen left.

And now all I need is to send the housemates my location, then drop the phone in the boot. Two steps. Easy. It'll lead the police straight to him. And, when they come knocking, there'll be a text on Andrew's phone, arranging to meet Olivia.

I think about you suddenly, as I often do. Bound, gagged, forced to run away, raped, killed. Which was it, in this car? Each possibility beams onto the back of my mind like a movie projector, blazing me in its headlights. I hope you didn't die frightened.

I lean against the car for a second, winded by grief. It happens at the strangest moments. I catch my breath, then run around to the boot, but it doesn't pop.

My hands begin to sweat. I get into the front, run my palms over the dashboard, looking for a boot-popping icon, but they're symbols I don't recognize. Aircon, maybe. Fan heater . . . Jesus, where is it? I close the driver's door and pop the lock up and back down, but nothing happens.

Another minute down. I start to press every button. The hazards illuminate the street a bright, ice-lolly orange, and I turn them off again. Fucking hell, how old is this car? I don't recognize any of it. Maybe it's on the keys . . . which are with him. I think it with a sinking heart.

Olivia's phone buzzes, no doubt Andrew wondering where she is, and I decline it, then silence it in case he leaves the café and hears it ringing nearby.

I google it frantically. A site called Quora tells me it's underneath the passenger seat. I run my hands along it but they come away dirty, something muddy, no button found.

Fuck it. I'll go around the back. Have to try and force the boot myself.

But, as I lock the door and move around his car, I see him. I'd recognize that swagger anywhere. He's leaving the café, holding the door open for somebody behind him, and then loping over. The streetlamps cast a yellow haze around him. Time's up. He didn't give it long.

I duck down behind the car and scramble to send the text. It's all I can manage. *Please come x*, I send. Right, now, the location. Fuck, I forgot to look up how to do it quickly on this thing. FAILED TO SEND, flashes up. I go hot, then cold. I cannot fuck this up. The SMS has sent, but the location hasn't. Andrew is about ten feet from me. Fuck. This phone has no data on it. Only credit for messaging and calling. I thought it was all included.

The boot won't open, it just won't open, and I can't get back around to any of the doors without him seeing me. I haven't got enough time, I haven't, I haven't, I haven't. I've got to abandon it. I fumble with the phone, and it skitters away from my shaking hands, down a drain. One second's silence, then a dull splash.

I start to shiver, crouching behind his car. I practically have a fever, broken from nowhere. I've fucked up, I've fucked up, I've fucked up. My chance to do my best for you, and it's wrecked.

Andrew's approaching. I can hear him talking on the phone. 'Can we go out?'

A pause. 'Which one?'

'Okay – Portishead One. Got it.'

Experiencing regret about something I did in my past.

Experiencing regret about something I did in my past.

As I hide, I think about this sentence Andrew wrote to Olivia. If only, if only, if only. The truth is just out of reach.

He drives away, fast, engine revving, and as soon as he's

gone, I go to the drain, but it's deep, black, full of water. The phone invisible, probably now broken, switched off, water-logged. My neat evidence trail, linking him to Olivia, destroyed.

I stand there on the cold street, alone, without a plan, a woman now missing who I have invented, based on some poor woman who needed a new passport. God, maybe she will come out of the woodwork. I put my hands on my head, totally and utterly lost.

Before I can really think about the implications of it, I get my phone out and text him: David, Zac's brother. *Long time no speak*, I write. *Do you think you can help me with something?*

* * *

David instructed, I drive to the bar Andrew said he was going to, the one next to the hairdresser's. Portishead One. He's drinking outside, standing next to his mother, smiling at her in that awkward way that he always did. I park up and watch them for several minutes. It's late. David will be doing it right this second. He says he can take a blonde woman off a CCTV network available on the dark web and superimpose her onto CCTV of the high street, walking down the alley towards Portishead One, and threaten the hairdresser's to let him have the footage to do it and not to tell anyone. We talked for twenty minutes, me and him. He was all strategy, ready to fire into action on a minute's notice. Didn't seem to judge what I had done at all. The only thing that would bolster this even more, he told me, was something physical that placed Andrew at Olivia's.

Andrew stubs a cigarette out on an overstuffed metal grate attached to the wall, the butt falling onto the floor, still lit, a little ember, leading the way just for me. He sets the empty pint down on the pavement, right next to the wall of the bar where he drinks and works, checks his watch and gestures to his mother.

Something physical. DNA. A pint glass and a cigarette. Right there. Tomorrow, I'll wait until the housemates are out, and plant them at Olivia's.

* * *

The next morning, early. I barely slept. Yolanda is at work, and I dreamt all night of what I had done. Hidden phones, forged identities, subterfuge. At four o'clock in the morning she asked me – fairly acidly – if I was planning on writhing about any more, or sleeping, instead?

I make a strong black coffee now in our monstrous kitchen and turn on BBC News, which flickers to life on the television up ahead. I put that television up, and every single time I look at it, I think that it's wonky. The left side dips just slightly. Ever since I did it, Yolanda has maintained it's completely straight, even though I got out a spirit level to prove her wrong. 'Well, it looks straight to me,' she always says.

Nothing on the news yet, so I turn my laptop on at the kitchen island and go local, and there it is: Olivia's missing, phoned in by the housemates, just like I envisaged. But I can tell from the statement given by the police that my plan hasn't worked yet. They haven't arrested anybody. Julia's face looms on the local news website, the video playing even as I scroll down: 'Last seen heading into an alleyway,' she is saying, true to David's word: he worked fast and got it done, an alleyway by Portishead One. God, maybe we'll do it. Maybe it'll all be worth it, this mixing of my life and Zac's: a victim's and a criminal's, all bound up like two paint colours that eventually merge and become the same.

I go to another news story, headline: DEAD-END GIRL? and scroll down in surprise, shock like white lightning across my chest. Dead-end Girl.

The alleyway where David deep-faked his video. I stand up, then sit back down again and type it into Google Maps, which tells me it is blocked up. I told David it was the short-cut to Portishead One. But it isn't – not any more. It was blocked up several years ago. David didn't know enough to argue.

So she doesn't go to the bar. She disappears, like a fucking apparition. What have I created?

I slide my laptop across the kitchen island, wanting to punch something. I pull on the sleeves of my jumper. Fuck, fuck, fuck. I was almost there.

Experiencing regret about something I did in my past.

The pursuit of justice burns bright across my chest.

He's guilty. I know it. I think about the cigarette and the glass, carefully double-bagged when I got home.

I just need to make it happen.

* * *

I'm so naive, and no amount of criminal activity can solve that. The place is crawling with police. It's night, when I thought it would be quieter, but they're here in droves. Searchers walking out with evidence bags of the clothes I bought only the other day, talking on phones about foren-sics, two coppers standing like sentries by the doors, the tops of their heads bright white from streetlights. And me. In my car, afraid to get out.

It's incredible. I thought they would believe she existed for long enough to arrest Andrew. In fact, the opposite has happened: they believe in her existence so much they have launched a full-scale investigation, and they do not suspect Andrew at all.

There's no way I can get in there. None at all. Andrew's DNA sits on the passenger seat next to me, the final clue to the puzzle of your disappearance, and I can't use it. Can't do a thing with it. I drive in a useless loop around the estate, park up, then get out, the items held close to my body, inside my coat.

'Can I help you?' one of the PCSOs says as I walk past.

'No, sorry?' I say, trying to look clueless.

'Right – well, this area is going to be cordoned, now, please,' he says to me, though he doesn't mean *please*. He means *fuck off*. As I turn around, heading back to my car, I catch him get a good look at my face, the way the police do sometimes. It sends my body hot, panic flashing up and down my torso. I need to act. I need to get this evidence into that house, and I need to not do it myself, and arouse even more suspicion.

I drive in a slow circle around the estate, back on to the A road, past the station. And that's when I see her. Walking somewhere. Maybe to Olivia's.

Julia. Her gait is heavy, tired, jaded perhaps.

Experiencing regret about something in my past.

I pull my beanie down over my face, impulsively rip out three holes for my eyes and mouth with a Swiss army knife from the glove box and drive ahead of her.

The car she drove last year while investigating your disappearance is next to a park. I use my car key to lever the window down. It's depressingly easy. No tennis ball needed. Her car's old, creaky. I'll tell her I've got evidence of what she did. CCTV, or something.

I get inside and try to keep the tears at bay. For where I have ended up, for you. The things desperate men do for their daughters.

When Julia gets in, I spot the exact moment she realizes I'm there. Her shoulders stiffen, just slightly, by only a millimetre or two.

She seems to count to ten or so in her head, looking into her lap, psyching herself up. I wonder if this is how you felt, and I hate – I *hate* – the symmetry of it, that I, the victim, have become the perpetrator.

She meets my eyes in the rear-view mirror and, even though I'm sure she knew I was there, I think she's surprised, too. Surprised that she was right, perhaps an old anxiety, perhaps something she always checks.

Julia looks at me and I gaze back at her. I know I've got to speak. I can only hope she won't recognize my voice. I've used so many fake ones in setting this up, I've run clean out of them.

I take a deep breath, trying not to let the tears out. I never thought it would end up here. Never, ever, ever. My eyes are about to start smarting, I can feel it. Jesus Christ, I can't cry here. I can't. I swallow hard, then try to be as succinct as possible. I say one word only: 'Drive.'

PART II

SADIE

Three Hundred and Seventy-First Day Missing

29

Julia

It's half past one in the morning, and, once again, Julia has too much to do. She has Emma in one meeting room and Olivia in another. Really, she wants to be at home with Genevieve, who texted her an hour ago saying, 'This is too late for EVEN ME! Goodnight!!!'

Olivia really is uncanny. She is a walking avatar of the passport photograph that they have been looking for. Her eyebrows rise as she speaks, her mouth upturned slightly. 'I mean – I am here,' she says, gesturing to her body, to herself. A white t-shirt, faded jeans, a satchel. Even at this hour, even underneath the unflattering strip lights, she looks beautiful. 'My husband said, enough's enough – earlier,' she says. 'And I told him it was fine. But then I was lying in bed and thought – no. I've got to go. In case they still think it's me.'

'Look,' Julia says. And then she asks the question she knows she needs to ask to get the answer she needs: 'Where did you renew your passport?'

Sadie's father worked at the passport office in Bristol.

'Bristol.'

The very specific feeling of unlocking the truth floods Julia's system. She and Jonathan used to talk about this feeling all the time. 'Like electricity going from your heart,' he once said, and she'd nodded emphatically.

She catches her own reflection in the one-way glass, wondering when workaholism and passion turned into something else, something perhaps toxic, something destructive. Something that allows her to avoid her husband, maybe. Julia is only able to face these thoughts now she is here: excited, hyped up, full of good old-fashioned delicious police adrenalin that forms a protective ring around her. Can we only be truly honest with ourselves when things are going well?

Often in policing – and this is what truly makes Julia addicted to it – there really is one single moment that cracks open an entire case. A chance piece of information, a coincidence that feels a little too unlikely, a 'hang on' moment when leafing through tedious paperwork. It sometimes stops Julia in her tracks when she considers how many of these eureka moments might have passed her by, but she can't think like this – not tonight, when it's happened, once again: thank God it's happened.

The key that unlocks this case is so real to Julia that she can almost feel it grasped tightly in her hand, metallic, ancient, wrought iron. A key to a case from just over a year ago. A case during which she was distracted by Genevieve. A case where the father felt she betrayed him. Where the father would do anything to bring his daughter back. Or to cover his own tracks?

It springs open, and Julia looks inside.

Sadie.

She picks her phone up and googles the Sadie case. And there he is. A handful of less than salubrious news articles written about him. The boyfriend: Andrew.

Now Matthew.

He was questioned, on Sadie's first day missing, by a specialist interviewer, who was good, but who wasn't Julia. And who left shortly after, relocated, was no longer here to recognize him, not that that would be very easy – Matthew has a full beard now that obscures much of his face. Julia never met Andrew. Was too distracted by Genevieve and Zac to look too closely at the news articles, too. Just papers speculating that it's often the boyfriend. Nothing more, but enough to drive somebody away.

Andrew had a cast-iron alibi – his mother, multiple waiters, a Ring doorbell – and was immediately dismissed as a suspect. No record was kept of his interview because it wasn't under caution. His was one of the many interviews you conduct when looking for a missing person: you interview everyone they know, nobody under suspicion at first, and so nothing added to the PNC. Interviews with their friends, their partner, their parents. People they work with. People they used to work with. People they went on two dates with. Andrew, with an easy alibi, was called in once, interviewed informally by a colleague of hers, his DNA never taken. No matter what Lewis said – and people close to the misper often make demands the police have to ignore – Julia and her team hadn't thought it was right to investigate him. There was no reason to.

And so the informal interview didn't go on Andrew's record. It doesn't go on anyone's until there is either a caution or an arrest.

Andrew Zamos. Now Matthew James. Moved across town, new name, new social media. It makes sense. Julia might have done the same for herself and Genevieve, if they had been in the news. You can't hide from everyone if you don't go far, but you can hide from people googling you when you go for a job interview, or when you first meet somebody. You could tell those close to you the truth, but otherwise hide under cover. A pretty simple disguise that is capable of fooling the PNC – it would never tell you about a name change by deed poll. It's ancient, the software too creaky, the UK's lack of an ID-card system against it, too. God, how many others might have done it?

If Julia had been less distracted, she would've read the news stories better. Remembered them, and him, and avoided this whole mess.

'So there are two Olivia Johnsons?' Olivia says. Her hands are back on the table, a piano playing pose.

'No,' Julia says. 'There's just one of you.'

And here it is. The key.

Olivia.

No friends.

Housemates never met her.

A wardrobe full of differently sized clothes.

Her strange vocabulary online. Her blurred selfies, the way the passport photo was the only good one that they could use. She had a *voice*. Like a fictional character. Like a creation. She made mistakes – too long a menstrual cycle, the wrong information about dogs on Sugar Loaf Beach, believing you'd wear a moisturizing eye mask out to the shops, using the phrase *drug store* like women do – but women who are online, in America. Shoddy research, Julia thinks, smiling grimly. She can't help but feel a fizz and crackle of satisfaction: she's solved it.

She closes her eyes as it comes to her, like a sheet being drawn back off a body.

Two missing women, three if you count Marilyn. Sadie,

presumed dead. Olivia, presumed invented. Turns out, Julia had been looking for the wrong woman all along.

* * *

A constable in uniform appears with a cup of tea for Olivia and nothing for Julia, who looks on in envy. When was the last time she had a drop of liquid? She pushes her hair back from her forehead. She wishes Jonathan were here.

'The passport renewal,' Olivia says, continuing their conversation. 'Last summer. I got married. I was Olivia Davis.'

Julia nods quickly, thinking she should feel relieved. The clues followed, the truth chased down. But there's still a missing woman: it just isn't Olivia.

'Look – leave this with me,' Julia says. She needs to get back to Emma, sitting alone in an interview suite, having just given Julia damning evidence regarding her son. Julia rubs at her forehead. She can't even call anyone in, not yet. She needs to handle this alone, work out what it all means, and then instruct. That it is the middle of the night helps with this thought process, to keep it unofficial, almost like if it's two o'clock in the morning, it isn't really happening. It allows her to obscure the real reason: that, if she wants to do anything other than call off the Olivia investigation, she will need to keep it off the books.

Nobody in the police knows that Olivia is an invention. The most anyone knows is that she arrived back. Nobody knows that Matthew James was once known as Andrew Zamos: Emma has told only Julia. Nobody knows Julia was blackmailed, and especially, nobody knows that it was Lewis, father of Sadie Owen, who was behind it. Julia closes her eyes, just for a second or two, her head spinning with it.

'Will you tell me who cloned my passport? Will there be an announcement – that I've been *found*?'

Julia can't answer these questions. She motions to Olivia. 'All right,' she says. 'Give me the night.'

Olivia looks up at her, unblinking, saying nothing. Julia takes this as a tacit agreement and hurries down the corridor, to Emma. Only the desk sergeant and one custody officer know even slightly what's going on in here. She doesn't have a lot of time before word spreads. Time to do what? She avoids answering this question, even in her own mind.

'Sorry about that.' Julia gestures to Emma, inviting her to continue the confession she tried to start earlier.

Emma hands her the QR code.

'Right,' Julia says, looking at it.

'When you scan it, it's a bitcoin transfer, and it says *I have Prudence Jones for you*,' Emma explains. 'And . . . he had been talking to Olivia Johnson. Online.'

Julia looks at her closely – slightly sleep-snared hair, an unironed t-shirt.

'I don't know what it means,' Emma says. 'I'm just telling you.'

'Has the bitcoin been called in – collected?' Julia asks, ignoring the Olivia comment.

'I don't know. How do I tell?'

'Mmm,' Julia says, thinking. *I have Prudence Jones for you.*

She is thinking, too, that this morning, she thought Matthew James was innocent. Now, she wonders if he's trafficking women.

'You wanted me to see it,' she says to Emma, watching her facial expression. Emma looks down at her hands – cuticles ragged – then up at Julia, making direct eye contact, and nods. And that's when Julia understands: she and Emma are entirely on the same page.

'What do you think it means?' Julia probes.

Emma reaches across the desk, messing with the peeling Formica. As she moves, Julia catches her scent: she smells of fabric softener. Unlike Julia, who probably always smells of stale police stations, adrenalin and stress.

'Sadie was the first,' Emma says. 'He was questioned, you know. But he was with me. Olivia was the second. And I've been – trying to convince myself . . . he was with me both times, so it *couldn't* be. Couldn't – you know? But now this Prudence . . .'

Julia nods, cringing inside, but still not revealing her cards to Emma. 'He was with you at the time Sadie disappeared? You're one hundred per cent sure?' she says, her mind whirring about false alibis, but other things, too. How interesting that he was supposed to be with his mother on both occasions.

'Yes, he was.'

'But, regardless, you moved away, changed names.'

'The father's vendetta – you know . . . the press. It's always the boyfriend. They all just went after him.'

Julia nods quickly, looking at the QR code which sits on the table in front of them. 'And now Prudence,' Emma adds, but it's needless: it speaks for itself, along with her dejected body language.

Julia watches Emma, thinking of the very specific heartbreak of not knowing if your child is entirely innocent, and reaches for the QR code. 'You've done the right thing,' she says.

Emma looks up. 'I hope so.' She has wet eyes. 'What now?'

'Please give me a night,' she says to Emma.

Julia hurries in the night-time cold. She's not told anybody Olivia is back, nor filed any paperwork. Just hoping she has a bit of time to get to Lewis before anyone talks.

The pavements are lightly frosted, even in May, the streets totally empty, and Julia feels, somehow, like she will be here for ever, investigating these terrible, confusing crimes about dead women, missing women, where people flip between victim and persecutor on a second's notice. When she reaches her car, she presses the keys to open it, and, as the lights flash, she finds herself relieved – still – to find that it is empty, even though she knows now who was inside it. And why.

Lewis lives in a middle-class suburb on the outskirts of Portishead. He is – Julia now remembers – forty-something, rangy, tall, possessing a kind of wired charisma usually seen only in celebrities or sportspeople. The kind of obsessive character Julia felt an instant kinship with, but whom she now hates. How dare he – in his quest to frame and capture Matthew – involve her? She thinks of Emma and Olivia leaving the station to go home, coming back at nine o'clock tomorrow morning, bewildered, confused.

It's the small hours of the night, and Julia is firmly off record. She doesn't even have her badge with her. She is in her old, beaten-up car, no team with her, no team even in the know. It will just be her, here, the night air, and Lewis. Same as that first night, when Lewis got into her car.

It takes ten minutes to get to him. Funny how easy it is, once you know, once you have the key to the case. Here her blackmailer was, a couple of miles from the station, all along. She wonders what Jonathan would say about this. Often a fan of doing what's necessary to get answers, she thinks even he would judge her tonight.

Lewis's house is set back from the road, two columns either side of the wooden front door, clean driveway paving, a rose planted in a blue pot by a doormat that says *Welcome* on it.

As she knocks on the door, it begins to rain, a fine, cold mizzle.

She is surprised when he answers almost immediately, fully clothed in jeans and a t-shirt. He has bags under his eyes, not only the colour of bruises, but textured, too, three-dimensional, a half-moon underneath each, as obvious as if they have been gouged. He's aged a decade in the past year, easily.

He looks behind him, then back at her. Evidently, he makes a decision. It's easy to watch his mind work: he is a person who shows every emotion on his face, everything he thinks. He bites his lip, winces, then, decision made, he advances out on to the driveway, barefoot, even though the night's cold and wet. He raises his palms to her, white, bloodless, and Julia realizes that, although recognition and understanding haven't once flashed across his features, he knows exactly, precisely, why she's here.

'Evening,' he says flatly.

'You're the blackmailer,' Julia says, but she's surprised to find her voice is soft, like ribbons unspooling into the night air around them. 'You're the person that has ruined my life.' As she says it, she realizes that it's true. She is no longer in checkmate, like she once was; she is now in stalemate, instead: how can she ever phone this in, without revealing her own role in it? How can she ever admit Olivia isn't real without saying how she worked it out? How can she continue

249

to investigate Matthew, once people know that the missing Olivia doesn't exist and – worse – the evidence was forged by Julia herself?

She shakes her head angrily, disturbing the cold air that whirlpools around her. 'You threatened me and my family,' she says.

'He messaged me, thinking I was Olivia,' Lewis says tiredly. 'Said he regretted something in his past. I could tell you all the ways he tried to control my daughter. I could say that I'm pretty fucking convinced he has got something to do with her disappearance and that you – and your team – could never quite get yourselves together to find out what. You didn't even interview him yourself.'

He shifts his weight, crossing one leg over the other, toe down. He folds his arms and doesn't look at her, instead looking into the distance. His outfit is dark, only his pale face, pale feet and pale arms visible.

'So what *are* you going to tell me?' Julia asks, her breath a puff of white vapour that hangs and then disperses in the air between them.

He toes the blue plant pot, still not looking at her. The top of his foot is covered in rainwater. And that's when Julia realizes, and, once again, her perception flips.

Sure enough, he looks at her and says, his voice slow and laced with tiredness, 'Go ahead and arrest me for fraud, or whatever it is, DCI Day. I don't give a shit.' And then he actually puts his wrists together, barefoot on his drive, wife presumably asleep upstairs, daughter still missing, and Julia stares at him. His body is still, those wrists held firm in front of him, waiting to be handcuffed, but his jaw is quivering, just slightly, the way it does when you are heartbroken, and trying not to show it.

That jaw is the sign of a man so sad and mired in grief that he no longer cares, at all, about what happens to him. Her heart rolls over in sadness, the same way it does when she sees homeless animals, crying children, lonely elderly people.

Lewis was a despairing dad, and then a threatening blackmailer, and now, he's returned to that first persona once more. This man, without his daughter, has nothing left to lose. He knew he was about to be found out. The issue is that he doesn't care at all, has gone past the point of it in the way humans experiencing tragedies sometimes do. A parent without a child: there isn't even a name for it.

'Where did you get the passport?' she asks softly, surprising him. 'Work?'

'Yeah.' He looks at her now. 'Dud run. Printed loads accidentally. Didn't want to confess, so took them home.'

'So you took one – when you wanted to invent somebody?'

'Go on,' he prompts, nodding at his wrists.

'Who was it in the alley?'

'Doctored footage.'

Julia nods in understanding. 'Doctored before we collected it?'

'Exactly. Changed at the source. At the hairdresser's.'

'Nobody noticed. In the station.'

Lewis shrugs languidly. 'I had help.'

'Who?'

He meets her eyes now, and Julia knows she's about to find out more about who and how and why. 'Zac's brother,' he says.

Ah. The slow fall of understanding, like a demolition building that begins its topple long before you see it hit the ground. Zac's brother. She was both right and wrong to suspect him.

'I saw Zac – just after he confronted you, last summer. I'd gone to the station to speak to you, and I found you with Zac. He told me. And then when he died, his brother . . . he wanted to avenge that. His death.'

'I'm sure he did,' she says. 'His brother – he wasn't there when I interviewed people after Zac's death?'

'No. He avoided you. Went underground.'

Lewis nods to her handcuffs again, but Julia ignores him.

His front-room window, just behind him and lit orange by a streetlamp, is littered with what look like tealight candles, and Julia remembers now a story run by a local paper – one where he obliquely accused Andrew Zamos as carefully as defamation laws would allow – saying he and his wife, Yolanda, a stoic social worker, used to light a votive candle every single night at the time Sadie went missing. Julia feels some unnameable emotion as she looks at those candles. Something intangible, some unsavoury mix. Sympathy, maybe, but also revulsion, the way some people feel upon seeing tragedies, and the things humans do to deal with a catastrophic hand played to them by the universe. Some people revel in other people's misfortunes – thank God it's not me – and some people avoid them. Julia's never done either, until now. Lewis's pain, up close, is like staring at something taboo, something inhumane: a slashed wrist, a pair of grey feet in a morgue, the remains of a suicide pact. Julia's seen them all, but never felt quite like this.

'Go on,' he says again, his voice low and jaded. Julia looks at him, a man who has lost so much he's got nothing left, and she steps towards him.

'I don't want to arrest you, Lewis,' Julia says thickly. And then she says it, the sentence she knows, somehow, he has been waiting to hear. 'I should have found your daughter.'

He brings a hand to his forehead again, shielding his eyes from an imaginary sun. Julia can tell he's crying. Perhaps he always is.

'I will find out what happened to your daughter,' she says softly.

'She's lost,' he says, his voice as damp as the night air.

And all the anger she had felt for Lewis evaporates, there in the night, like the vapour from her judgemental words. She meets his eyes and finds herself thinking, if Genevieve disappeared, she might have done the same for her. Almost did.

And so now Julia sees him for who he is, who he really, truly is: a heartbroken parent, just like her.

30

Julia

Three o'clock in the morning, and Julia is fired up, a woman with a plan, on a mission.

She is used to running off little sleep, but she is at least usually in bed. Right now, she's in the custody suite, surrounded by other people's mistakes and other people's problems as well as her own.

Julia has never liked the custody suite, always felt an uneasy truce with visiting it: a place where human rights must be carefully granted, enshrined by law, because otherwise they would be forgotten. Row after row, blue door after blue door, detainee after detainee, and behind one of them is Matthew, a kid.

The lie comes much more easily this time. She needs a place to talk to Matthew with no cameras or recording equipment, as so very many corrupt police officers before her have required. Julia is disgusted to think of the traditions she's joining: forced confessions, roughing a suspect up before they talk – and worse. But this isn't that, she thinks: this is a mess. Blackmail and distraught fathers and missing and found identities and – this man. This boy. Somehow at the centre of it. And Julia is hoping he will talk.

'The media interest is too much, around Olivia Johnson,' she lies to the custody sergeant. 'So Matthew is being moved.'

'Okey-dokey,' she says in a bored tone. Julia checks her expression, but there's nothing. So she doesn't know. The custody suite isn't near the main foyer. She's got away with it, for now. The sergeant – iPhone in one hand, set of keys in the other, trust in Julia invisible and implicit somewhere between the two – hands her a key, not even looking up at her. Julia stops for just a second and notes this is another line crossed. Wonders if, since the first one, they have become easier to leap over, like she's acquired a rare and horrible skill.

'*Love Island* in a month,' the custody sergeant says, through chewing gum. 'Reckon we can repurpose just one of the CCTV screens and have it on?'

'Not really,' Julia says, and evidently her deadpan response is not especially out of character, as the custody sergeant just shrugs, and keeps scrolling on her phone. Julia and Art used to watch *Love Island* together when they could. Out of character for both of them; she thinks that is why they enjoyed it so much. The summer before last, Art turned to her and said, 'I'm going to apply next year, dad bod and all.' That night, she'd put it on her worry list, and their laughs had woken Genevieve.

Julia takes the keys, her fingers clutching the cold metal. She moves to get Matthew before she can think any more about it.

He's in the cell at the very end. She watches him for a second on the CCTV. He's on the edge of the bed, staring at the floor, arms folded over his knees. Like a painting. Like a meditation.

Julia will need to release him soon, she knows she will. She'll have to tell his mother, too. She can no longer detain somebody for the kidnap of an invented person, and she knows the desk sergeant will be busy spreading the word about that soon. She doesn't have much time. But she needs to keep hold of Matthew, at least temporarily, in order to find answers. About Sadie, and about Prudence.

She only hopes that nobody will notice they're gone, just for now, an hour in the dead of night. That nobody will look at the footage. That nobody will check anything Julia has done over the past week – ever. She knows, somehow, that this is not realistic, but Julia is being driven forward by a force much greater than caution, or guilt, or ethics: her detective brain is on the case, trying to find out what happened to Sadie.

'Come with me for a transfer,' she says through the hatch to him. He startles. He looks so small in the flesh – on the bed, still so childlike in so many ways, that Julia finds her heart roll over in her chest like a barrel.

'Why?' he says, meeting her eyes in the hatch, recognition crossing them. It is not a question most criminals would ask. Most would refuse, assume the cops are out to frame them, but Matthew seems only to want the facts. Well, so does Julia. He stands reluctantly, his body side-on to the door as he looks at her.

'I'll explain. Ready?' she says, and he moves quickly, his movements lithe and fluid.

Unlike other cells, his doesn't smell at all. Not of stale coffee and tea, not of the awful egg special ready meals, not of sweat or fear or anything: Matthew seems completely composed.

She leads him outside. The custody sergeant notices he isn't handcuffed, but says nothing. Whether innocent or guilty, Julia can spot a flight risk, and this isn't one.

Through the scanner and then the automatic doors, and

the night is like jumping into a cold pond. Julia watches Matthew begin to shiver, then try to pretend he isn't. 'Where's the transfer to?' he says.

When it becomes evident Julia isn't going to answer, Matthew walks slowly, perhaps stalling, perhaps thinking. It strikes Julia that he seems to consider every word he speaks, every step he takes: somebody with something to hide, or just the way he is?

Julia's car is parked half a mile away, and she won't say anything until they're safely inside it: the undiluted privacy she can provide.

Matthew doesn't ask any more questions. She can't work out if his compliance hints at something or nothing. Nevertheless, she doesn't say anything, either.

The flats above the shops on the high street all have their lights off. The shops shut up, some with roller shutters, others just darkened and locked. It's like a living museum, a homage to 2023, whatever that will mean in the future. Parked silent cars, faded social-distancing signs rubbed off the pavements, sodium streetlamps.

Matthew isn't stupid, and he starts to look uncomfortable, turning his head left and right, looking around him at the night air, the completely empty street, the lack of recording equipment, other officers, solicitors – anything. Realization breaks across his features: his eyes widen, his hand twitches by his side. They reach her car.

'Your mum found the QR code,' Julia says.

He says nothing, but his posture changes. His movements slow: he's thinking. Julia wishes that she could promise confidentiality, a bargain, or something, but she can't. She's always, always tried to be honest. Even amid everything that's happened. Pockets of the truth, folded in with her lies. She looks across at him as she unlocks the doors. His face in profile against the silvery wet night. He really is just a kid.

'I don't know what that is,' he says eventually. The oldest and easiest lie in the book: *I don't know.*

'Try again,' Julia says.

'Why are we not with my lawyer?' The whites of his eyes yellow as they catch the interior light as he folds himself into the car. She's surprised he gets in, but then, she supposes she would, too, if she were a young lad out only with a DCI.

She climbs in, too, closing the doors and feeling like a monster as she looks across at him: pink, still-teenage skin, the memories across his knuckles of where there were only dimples. She can just imagine what he was like as a child: shy, self-possessed, interesting. Julia would've done everything Emma has done, if she were her. Even the alibis, if they're false. Even handing Matthew over.

But she isn't Emma. Julia is Julia, mother to Genevieve, trying to find out what happened to Sadie for Lewis, and these facts somehow make some of them enemies: only Julia can't quite work out who's who.

She needs time. She needs to keep up the pretence of the Olivia investigation, just while she lines a few things up.

She needs to find out what happened to Sadie to end the mess they're all in: her impasse, that she can't tell her colleagues how she knew Olivia was invented, nor about the blackmail. She needs to protect her daughter. And she needs to find out what happened to Sadie to save Lewis: to bring him peace.

But, more than that, she needs to find Sadie because that is what Julia does. A mother and a cop: always the two, never just one. Her two great loves have been competing with each other for almost twenty years. It's only this year when it's become something more than emblematic.

'I told you. Transfer,' she says, thinking how the corruption of old – framing him, covering it up, interviewing Olivia's housemates off the record – felt wrong, but how very right this feels. She's chasing it down; it's animalistic. Julia is a lion, stalking a deer, out in the wild. She knows the truth is here, somewhere, among the closed shops and street silence. She *knows* it.

'If you don't take me back – I'll alert the –'

'The who?'

'I'll say you took me on a walk and asked me questions you shouldn't have.'

'I'll deny it. I have your transfer form right here,' Julia says, patting a pocket that contains nothing. 'The media interest in this case is too much. You needed to be moved,' Julia lies.

Matthew turns to look at her just as the interior light goes off. The car is a dark snow globe, alone on the street, nobody aware they're here, nobody looking. Julia regrets that he will be frightened.

'What fucking media interest?'

'Why did you change your name?'

'No comment.'

'What's the QR code? Who's Prudence Jones?'

'No comment.'

'What involvement did you have in Sadie Owen's disappearance?' she says, her tone angry. She knows this is illegal. She knows she's so close to the wire here. Over it. But she needs – like an addict – to reach out to the universe and find Sadie, find her killer, find the answer for Lewis, and heal his heart, just as much as she can. This urge is shot through her. Whatever Lewis did to her, whatever Julia's predicament, this – *that* – is her job, something she does even when it compromises her ethics, her family, her self.

Julia guns the engine and they set off, the same as she had that night – somehow? – only a handful of days ago. She drives them aimlessly, happy for Matthew to realize this is a trip to nowhere in his own time.

It takes forty minutes before he speaks. He has more willpower than even the lowest gang members who would be murdered for talking. You don't need coerced confessions or violence to be an effective police officer. You never did. You only need this: an awkward silence.

The sun begins to rise. In six weeks they will be at the solstice, twilight and dawn as close together as a pinch between finger and thumb. The tallest buildings catch the first rays, like they know something the others don't, their tips just slightly golden, so subtle you could easily miss them.

Matthew's feet are stretched out in front of him in the footwell, but it's the only element of his body language that is relaxed. His shoulders are tensed, he's sitting forward, perhaps eager, perhaps nervous, maybe both. Dark hair the colour of a black cat in the sun.

'I don't know where Sadie went. I don't know what the QR code is. No comment, no comment, no comment,' he says, his eyes meeting hers. And then he says something else, something that piques Julia's interest in a way she can't explain, but doesn't miss, regardless: 'If I knew anything, anyway, the police would be the last people I'd tell.'

* * *

Five thirty, now. A text from Genevieve: *I got up to use the bathroom and you're doing an all-nighter?!*

Matthew's back in his cell – an admin error, she told the custody sergeant: no space at the new place – and Jonathan's in early, before six. His morning, Julia's night-time. He's holding his Pret cup of coffee and one for her, too.

Julia takes it gratefully, either her third or her first cup of the day, depending on how you look at it. She boots up her computer and rubs her arms. Her skin feels raw from the shame of her failed exchange with Matthew. She didn't unearth anything useful from him whatsoever. No midnight-hour confession, no truth extracted painfully, through tears. Nothing. She was so sure there would be. What was she thinking?

And so now she's wide open, vulnerable, corrupt in every direction, waiting for Matthew to tell somebody.

'What's new?' Jonathan says, leaning against the doorframe.

Julia lets out a grim smile. 'Quite a lot,' she says to him. Immediately, he comes inside. 'Are Pret even open?'

'Always.'

'Did you pay for mine?'

'Got two free,' he says, and Julia isn't surprised. He once set up a business on the side selling records on eBay that nearly got him sacked for wasting (his own) police time. Jonathan can't resist anything free, anything he got for nothing.

'Er, guess what?' Julia says.

'What?'

'Olivia Johnson presented herself last night. Happened at one o'clock,' she says.

Jonathan puts his coffee down on Julia's desk and takes his coat off, folding it over his arms, then looks at her. 'Jesus – all I did was dispense milk last night. You solved a case.'

Julia pats The Interrogation Chair, and she fills him in, the way she often has, the sun rising beyond her slatted blinds. The way they have sat for years, picking things apart, solving them, turning them over between each other.

She tells him. She trusts him enough to tell him about the duplicate Olivia having been invented and who by, who Matthew really is, and about Sadie. She leaves out the blackmail, though she knows that soon Jonathan will begin to ask questions.

Jonathan puffs his cheeks out. 'Right.' He's staring down at his phone, but the screen is black. Inside, his brain will be technicolour, Julia is sure of it. He taps a finger on the desk. 'Photoshopped in,' he says. 'Into the alleyway. He some expert? It was seamless.'

'I'm surprised you didn't spot it. Sadie's father got – he got someone to do it,' Julia says, hoping his forensic mind doesn't home in too quickly on it: on the only piece of the jigsaw that she hasn't told him. The why.

'Who?'

'Some known criminal or other.'

'What? Why? How did he know them? Isn't he just a dad?' Jonathan says, Julia thinks disparagingly: somebody right in the trenches of new parenthood, who can't think of anything more mundane. In five years, he will realize that time was beautiful.

'I don't know,' Julia lies.

'What're you going to do – charge him?'

'I really don't know.'

'You know, I meant to ask you something about this case – not that it matters now,' Jonathan says.

'Go on?'

'I watched the bodycam footage of the PCSOs the other day,' he says. 'I thought there was something odd about it, but I couldn't put my finger on it. Then last night, up feeding late, I realized what that thing was.'

'Right?' Julia says, trying not to sound rattled. Trying, in fact, to sound impressed, the way she would usually be at this fantastic detective display: a clue, ruminated on, the significance of which became clear in the night. That's almost – laughably – how it should be.

But now, for the first time in their long careers, Julia is annoyed by Jonathan's scientific nature, his memory, his logic. *Fuck, fuck, fuck.*

'There was no glass on the footage. And when I went to check more recently, that footage had gone, which is doubly suspicious. I've been weighing up what to do. What to say . . .'

Jonathan folds his arms and tilts his head to one side, evidently trying to weigh it up. You can never take back an accusation, and he's never once made one against her. For fifteen years, they have been firm allies. From those first shared sandwiches on the brick wall all the way to now. 'You went to the crime scene, right? Her bedroom?' he says.

'Yes, I did, that night,' she says. She meets his eyes as they sit there side by side, and is glad he's not a mind reader, on top of everything else, too, as she tries to work it through. He can't know. Nothing links her to that camera. Nothing. She attends almost every scene. Always has.

As they're staring at each other, two minds working in overdrive, Julia's phone beeps. She sees it's Genevieve, but ignores it. God, the plates she's spinning. One is sure to drop, soon, and shatter; she only hopes it isn't the one that's made of glass.

'Did you not wear a bodycam?' Jonathan asks.

'No, I went kind of off the hoof,' she says. 'Just wanted to get a feel for it. You know how it is. Like we did with the alley.'

'Was it there when you went? The glass?'

'I don't know. Didn't Erin find it under the bed?'

'The thing is, though . . . according to the server, you accessed that bodycam footage twice, two days ago, once late at night. And now it's disappeared.'

Julia freezes. So he can connect her to that cam. She didn't know, hasn't worked at the real coalface since bodycams were introduced. Things are done for DCIs; you lose touch. Besides, she has never needed to understand the tech to cover her tracks: she's never needed to do anything underhand enough to warrant that.

She breaks eye contact. It's all over. It must be.

'I'm not wrong, am I?' he asks, eyes gentle, hands steepled together. Julia feels suddenly sorry for him, her strait-laced colleague who she has roped into this mess. Who now has a moral dilemma, as well as her.

'I can't remember,' she says lightly. 'I access all sorts.'

Jonathan throws her a silent but astonished look that somehow – he is so good at expressions – contains a high amount of scorn, too.

Something seems to settle in the air between them. Jonathan will know this is beyond his remit. Julia could shut it down easily, pull rank, but she never would.

'You don't remember,' he seems to decide to say. He doesn't need to interrogate her any more than this. It's absurdly out of character that Julia wouldn't remember something like that.

'Why don't we talk about this after we've sorted Lewis?' Jonathan says. Julia startles, meets his eyes, then realizes just as the morning sun floods the room properly, bathing them in it. She could weep for it. For his humanity. He knows exactly what's going on – or has some idea, anyway – and is giving her an out. A day or two, at most. A reprieve in which to decide what to do. His eyes hold hers, brown, soulful. A message communicated: a ceasefire.

'Let's do that,' she says to him softly.

'Let Matthew go. Andrew, whatever his name is. Let everyone know Olivia's back, charge Lewis with fraud. Hush it up, don't let the press in on it,' he says, while Julia's mind reels, spinning over what he knows, over what it means to her, over what he might do next. 'We don't need the vultures all over it. It's a tragedy, a bad decision, nothing more than that, isn't it?'

'But Matthew – he . . .'

'What?' Jonathan says curiously, but the words die on Julia's lips. She can't let Matthew go; she can't. But neither can she detain him further, or tell anybody why, truly, she suspects him. And she can't charge Lewis. She can't send a heartbroken man down.

Julia nods, mutely, saying nothing, thinking that, whatever she does now, she will be found out; she has been found out. Her corruption is now past tense, but that she became so controls her entire future.

* * *

Julia stares up at her house at six thirty in the morning. One room is lamplit. The room Art sleeps in. Genevieve will be asleep. She can imagine Art inside, just reading a novel. Like somebody from another time. He would never sit and scroll, or play a phone game to pass the time. If Art had been born in the 1800s, the 1910s, the 1950s, he'd still be the same Art he is today. He has always had that timeless quality. Julia supposes that is why his infidelity was such an awful shock. But then, perhaps he just behaved in a completely timeless way, actually, the way so many men before him have.

The outside smells like frozen seaweed. She walks to the front door, her coat wrapped around her, as lost and alone as a shipwreck.

She sighs as she walks into the empty-feeling house, then heads upstairs. She looks in on Genevieve, still sleeping on her side, one leg cocked, the way she always did even as a baby, when it terrified Julia. But, when Julia looks more closely, her eyes are open. 'You awake?' she whispers.

A single nod from Genevieve.

'Why?'

'Bad dream.'

'Yeah?' Julia says tentatively. Don't scare her off. Don't act too interested.

Genevieve shifts so that she is propped up on her elbow. Her eyes meet Julia's. 'I dream about him almost every night,' she says, seemingly out of nowhere. 'You know?' Her arm is trembling just slightly with the weight of her head. She seems so little, all of a sudden, there in the bed. A child.

'Zac?' Julia says, her voice low.

'Mmm.'

'Go on?'

'For ever,' Genevieve says, and Julia frowns, not following, until Genevieve finishes her sentence: 'I will have taken somebody's life. For as long as I live.'

'Oh, but –' Julia starts to say, wanting to correct her, to talk about Zac's decision to mug her, about sepsis, about causation, but Genevieve stops her.

'It's true,' she says. 'That's the way it is. But I dream about him – the blood . . .'

Julia drops her head. 'I'm sorry,' she says to her. 'I'm so

sorry I wasn't there,' she goes on, wishing she could add everything she's doing now to save her daughter.

'I wish I could atone without paying the price,' Genevieve says sadly.

'I know. I do, too.'

Genevieve swallows, saying nothing, but nodding, her eyes wet. 'Thank you,' she says, and Julia reaches for her hand, almost identical to her own, and grasps it. They stay there for a while, not saying anything, but this time not needing to, either.

Later, or the first time since Art had moved into their spare bedroom, Julia knocks on its door. He says, 'Come in?' in a kind of baffled voice, like he doesn't know whether he even has the right to grant her access to her own guest bedroom.

Julia pushes the door open. Behind him is a lamp. And a novel – Sally Rooney – splayed open on the bed. Her stomach turns over sadly.

He's in loungewear, a grey t-shirt and jogging bottoms. White socks pulled up over the cuffs. He looks comfortable and safe in the impersonal surroundings of their tired spare bedroom. A seascape painting, a pink lamp and him.

'You all right?' he asks in surprise.

'I'm not sure.'

He gestures for her to come in.

She closes the door with a soft click behind her. He sits back on the bed. There's no chair – the room is tiny, barely big enough for a double – and so Julia takes the floor, her back to a radiator, which heats her shoulder blades fiercely. Even the radiators think it's still winter.

Art folds the corner down on his novel and places it on the bedside table next to his alarm clock. He begins to work his socks off with his big toes. He isn't looking at her. Julia thinks about Olivia, and Lewis and Sadie, and Matthew and Emma, and Genevieve and, finally, about herself.

'What do you think defines a good person?' she asks Art.

Art, being Art, considers the question seriously. 'Selflessness,' he says.

Julia leans her head back against the radiator. Is she being selfless? She thinks so. She's trying to find Sadie's body. That's all she's doing; all she wants. And that will benefit Lewis, not her.

But is she doing it to cover her own tracks? And is she doing it in the right way? She thinks about Matthew's frightened, yellowing eyes lit by the car's interior light and shudders.

Art doesn't speak for several seconds, and then he says: 'What do *you* think defines a good person?'

'I'm not sure I know any more,' she says. And, despite everything, she is at home here, in Art's room, with him. Able to say anything, without explanation, without preamble. Nothing.

They lapse into silence. Art has a cup of tea on his bedside table, which he wordlessly offers to her. She declines it with a wave of a hand. 'Had too much coffee already,' she says.

'Always have.'

'Yeah. Have you slept?'

'A bit,' he says.

Julia leans her head back. The radiator creaks and puffs behind her. After a few minutes, she speaks.

'Would a good person go to any lengths to get justice?' she says, not sure if she's talking about herself, or Lewis.

'Is something going on?'

'Maybe.'

Julia cocks her head and looks at him. 'I'm at a crossroads,' she says. 'I need to investigate something but – I don't have . . .'

Art looks down at Julia from the bed. There is something strange about the atmosphere between them, about his uncertain expression. Out of place in the cosy setting, the lamp, the sea, the salted windowsill, the constant, unerring waves outside.

'Legal means,' she finishes.

To her surprise, Art shrugs, like it doesn't matter at all. That's right, she thinks. He isn't always judgemental. The law has never meant very much to him, actually. And perhaps it doesn't to Julia, a sickening but comforting thought to have after all this time.

'You'll figure it out, Julia,' he says, looking suddenly tired. 'You always do. And if not – you can always send me a worry list.'

Julia's eyes fill with tears, as she thinks about Matthew, about legality, about corruption, and about Art, too, and his allusion to the way they used to be.

31

Emma

You remain in custody right now, and I haven't slept at all.

I'm in your bedroom, but also somewhere in the hinterland between your innocence and your guilt, where I always am. Sadie, Olivia, Prudence. It's a jigsaw with no image, not one I can see. Or perhaps I just don't want to look at it.

I am sitting on the edge of your bed, trying to pluck up the nerve to call your therapist.

The bed is still a single. We bought it in a hurry when we moved, after we changed our names, after I left Cooper's – stepped back, withdrew as a director, retired, whatever we want to say. We've come up with so many stories for it, depending on who we're talking to. That's the thing about changing your name for the reasons we did; you have to tell people different things.

This bed – cheap pine, a blue checked duvet cover on it – was one of those things that seemed to take up more time and headspace than we intended. Messages back and forth about it, an arranged time to collect it that fell through, another one booked.

It's because we moved quickly. We'd decided, after the latest slur – HR taking you aside and saying there were a few members of staff uncomfortable with working the bar alone with you – that we had to go, and we found a rental and went fast. I wanted to go further – anywhere, really, Somerset, Devon even, Bristol at the least – but you only wanted to hop across town. I still don't know why. You never see anyone from your old life. But in the mess of it all, and the haste and the trauma, I've never felt able to ask why you wanted to stay so close.

And so we bought this bed, for ten quid, from Facebook marketplace, because I didn't want to spend the capital I made when I sold Cooper's. The sellers didn't live quite where we thought, and we got lost. It took all evening, and we left with it one cool early-autumn night, only just inches into September, walking slowly down the street, you holding one end, me the other. Right then, on the street, you said over the headboard, 'I have nightmares about the moment she went missing.'

'Do you?' I'd said, my shoulders up, thinking a confession was coming. I always thought that, though I tried not to let you know.

Sadie's father had called you five times the morning after Sadie disappeared. You were sleeping in. You hadn't been at work the night before, but you were still on a shift-work sleeping pattern. Sometimes I'd hear you come in around two or three, watch some television, have a beer, like a lot of people with a job like yours. You'd sleep until eleven or twelve, once called it your natural pattern anyway, which is true: even as a baby, you were a night owl, never had the unhappy, tired witching hour other children did. You were always at your happiest and most relaxed in the evenings, grumpy if woken before nine in the morning. The dream baby. The dream kid.

Sadie had been walking home by herself – hadn't called you, or anyone – but never arrived. Disappeared somewhere between Portishead High Street and her house share. As simple and as complex as that. Seen on one CCTV, outside a corner shop, and not on the next, around the corner. Multiple vehicles were traced, multiple men questioned, but none ever arrested.

'I dream about my phone lighting up when Lewis called me,' you said. 'I don't know why.'

I nodded, understanding. The trauma wasn't those Lewis calls, not really, but I can see why you have latched on to them.

The thing about a missing person is that it's an ongoing trauma. That's something I've recognized and learnt, over the past year. There wasn't one singular moment when you understood she was missing, probably in danger. It was – has been – a series of moments, each worse than the first. The first night she didn't return was a fluke. The second a warning, fired deep into the night. The third – a tragedy. And it went from there, until it became your tragedy, or maybe it always was.

'I'm sorry,' I said. I didn't know what else to say, didn't want to scare away this creeping revelation, either.

We'd had to park almost half a mile away, and we marched with the bed right up the street, like something from a *Carry On* film. It would've been funny if anything about it actually was. We'd moved into an unfurnished rental. You'd got a new job. I'd sold my stake, was figuring out what I'd do next. And the bed, that cheap, second-hand bed, was a shitty emblem of it all.

The weather was the spindly kind where you know you're on borrowed time, summer's gone, autumn not yet fully arrived. You were in a coat and I was in a t-shirt: the way we were – you closed and me open. One lone, thick, curled autumn leaf drifted down, and we both watched it, thinking – I'm sure – about how long she'd been gone.

'Do you wonder why she didn't call you?' I asked. You looked at me briefly, then away, down the street. It still had the last of that summer feel to it. Pale, dry pavements. Cut grass. But the air had cooled already, like somebody had begun to turn off the lights one by one at a party.

'No,' you said, and I tried not to judge. At twenty, to have a girlfriend disappear . . . I couldn't begin to imagine the effect it would have on your psyche. 'But . . .'

'But what?'

You shrugged, then, not wanting to elaborate. This is how it always was, with you, since she disappeared – how it's remained, too.

'I miss her, is all,' you said. Another shrug. 'Stupid sentiment, but a true one. The papers wouldn't believe it.'

'Fuck the papers,' I said.

You stopped, then, rested your end of the bed on the pavement and looked at me. Some anguished expression crossed your features. You bit your lip with just one front tooth, still staring at me. And, God, I swear, something seemed to pass between us, something significant, but then it vanished, just like the coming autumn season would, and the next. You picked up your end of the bed again, and we walked on.

We carried it all the way to the van. I didn't say much after that, and neither did you. That conversation, your sadness, had somehow made me more secure that you weren't lying. Until Olivia disappeared.

Now, I wonder if that sadness was really guilt.

I take a breath, now, on that very same bed, and dial Linda, your therapist.

'Hi, Linda Shepherd here.'

'Yes, hi. I was calling about – about Matthew James,' I say. 'I'm his mother.'

Linda says nothing and I prattle to fill in the gap. 'I mean – it's just . . . Linda, he was arrested four days ago. And I wondered if you knew . . .'

Linda still says nothing, a therapist's iron will forcing me to finish the sentence. 'If you knew anything,' I finish lamely.

'What for?' she says eventually. 'The arrest.'

'Kidnap. Of that missing woman. Olivia Johnson. And I found – I've found other evidence, in his room.'

A loaded silence plays out between us. Perhaps Linda is shocked, perhaps she is working something out, piecing some things together that I'm not privy to. Perhaps you never told her about Sadie, kept up your alias, your pretences. I have no idea. I've tried so hard to give you space, to respect your privacy. Perhaps too hard.

'So I just . . .' I continue.

'The court will compel me to give evidence if they charge him,' she interrupts, but she says it kindly. 'So I'm afraid I can't speak to you, Ms James.'

'But – are you as shocked as me?' I say. 'Just – tell me that.'

Linda doesn't answer. I sigh, wanting to sit on the bed again, cry like a child. 'I mean –' I add, then stop, not knowing what to say, thinking maybe I have gone just totally wrong somewhere with how I've raised you. Maybe it's the lack of a father figure; I was so determined for it not to matter, but perhaps it just does.

Eventually, Linda speaks: 'So he has been accused twice.'

'Only accused,' I say quickly, automatically, but I know she's right. It's the internal/external thing again. Externally, I defend you. Internally, I crumple.

'Linda,' I say. 'Has he ever mentioned a Prudence?'

'I can't say,' she answers. And, for some reason, I feel like this is more likely to be a yes than a no. Something about her tone, shifting like sand underneath my feet.

We hang up, and I stay there next to that bed that sometimes still smells of that late-summer/early-autumn evening when we bought it, the one on which I wonder if you almost told me something, but didn't – couldn't.

I hold my phone in my hands, still warm from the call, and google missing Prudences again. There are hundreds of thousands of hits, but this time I have the time to go through them all, piece by piece. I sink down on to the hardwood floor, my head resting against the edge of your bed, and scroll. None of them are missing. None of them are dead. I suppose I should find relief in that, but I don't.

Three Hundred and Seventy-Second Day Missing

32

Julia

Price is smoking a cigarette outside a nightclub called the Flamingo. It's early morning and Julia's had an hour's sleep. It would have been two, but she sacrificed one of them to eat croissants with Genevieve, who seems better. She went through some sort of catharsis, maybe, when she told Julia about her dreams.

This is where Price has agreed to meet Julia.

She told the team earlier that Olivia had returned, and that Julia had bailed Matthew, but wouldn't answer Emma on whether he'd be brought back in. How could she guarantee that, without knowing what his connection is to Sadie and Prudence?

Only Julia knows the full story: that this particular Olivia never existed. Only Julia knows that the evidence against Matthew is fabricated. It's a matter of time before somebody realizes – before the media get hold of it, before the real Olivia sells her story to a tabloid, before she chases up her stolen-identity case with the authorities, before somebody starts to ask Julia exactly how it all came to pass. Julia's on borrowed time.

She suggested here to Price precisely because she knows

it to be a CCTV blackspot. The club behind them operates as a drugs exchange. Julia knows it, everyone knows it, but they're not interested in small fare: footmen, suppliers, punters buying ecstasy.

In the morning light it looks tawdry, the flamingos graffitied on the side cheap, the chalkboard-black paint behind them mattified and dulled.

'Another favour,' she says as she walks up to Price.

'No one found your bodycam footage?'

'No. You always do a thorough job.'

Price smirks around his cigarette. 'Don't try to flatter me, DCI Day, when you're here to coerce me.'

Julia winces: she deserved that. It came to her earlier, on her bed. Everyone knows – even the police, *especially* the police – that criminals are better at some things than the coppers. The state, the establishment, the authorities, they're always a step behind. They're reacting. They find out what the criminals are doing, and then they try to stop it. It is the criminals who blaze the trail. The wrongdoers, the hackers, the scammers.

'What is the value,' Julia asks him, 'of a life, on the street?'

Price lifts his chin, appraising Julia, hiding a surprised expression – though she can tell. 'Of taking a life? Why?'

'I've got a man in. A missing woman. Maybe others. Pretty sure he isn't a sociopath or a sexual deviant. So I'm wondering if he's paid.'

'Are you sure he's a man if he isn't a sexual deviant?'

Julia ignores the joke.

'Who's the woman?' Price asks.

'His girlfriend. Went missing last year.'

'Not Olivia?'

'No, separate,' Julia says. 'Kind of.' Price's cheeks hollow as he drags on the cigarette. Julia leads him down the street. There's a black spot for another two hundred feet. Two Tesco bags buffet by on the breeze.

'And another. Maybe. Called Prudence Jones.'

His cigarette smells sharp, ashy, somehow slightly tantalizing on a spring day. It takes Julia back to way back when. When smoking was cool, when work was simpler, when Art loved her unconditionally, and wanted only her. She thinks, too, of a time before Genevieve, when love was so simple. Parenthood is beautiful, but hard, too. It's tough to exist in the world when there is someone going about their business who you would die for.

'Right – what you got on him?' He discards the cigarette, which bobs a few times on the pavement before it comes to a stop. He stamps and twists on the glowing end with the toe of his trainer, a seamless motion as they walk.

'Girlfriend disappeared last year. Suspicious circumstances – walking home. They were rowing a lot beforehand; her father thought he was coercive. He's been found with a QR code transferring bitcoin relating to Prudence Jones – it hasn't been downloaded, so far as I can see. It was not yet activated. So someone's looked at it, but not taken the bitcoin. After her name it said *I have Prudence Jones for you.*'

Price grasps it immediately. 'You want me to trace it.'

'Yep.'

Price seems to consider this. 'Give it to me. I'll see what I can do.'

'But, Price,' Julia begins as she passes him the paper. He lights a second cigarette instead of taking it: a petty power play Julia can't blame him for. She waits for him to take his first drag, and then he reaches for the QR code. 'If you cash in this bitcoin –'

'Get fucked, Julia, I'm in a bind but I'm not a fucking idiot,' he says, cigarette in his mouth, hands grasping the paper as he stares down at it.

'Fine.'

'Leave it with me,' he says. 'A third favour. But who's counting?'

Julia meets his eyes. A brutal but fair assessment of their damned relationship, ruined unilaterally by her.

Before he even finishes the sentence, he leaves Julia, puffing his cigarette on his way, leaving clouds of blue-grey smoke that billow behind him like memories.

* * *

Julia drives a loop, away from the Flamingo, back on to the high street, and goes into a pay-as-you-go stall in an indoor market. As she pretends to look at the handsets strung up on the wall, she tells herself she is good, she is good, she is good. She is doing this to find out what happened to Sadie.

She picks up a handset. Slim, blank, an old-style flip phone, burner SIM included, and pays cash, hoping she isn't recognized. If anyone ever asks, sees the CCTV, whatever, she will say it was for Genevieve. Some end-of-term present; her phone broke. Something. She is already concocting her witness statement as she leaves, phone in a small white plastic bag she wasn't charged ten pence for. As it swings down by her side, she wonders if Art bought one of these, in order to cheat on her. If he sent such beautiful text messages to his mistress, also.

'Have a nice day,' the owner of the shop says to her, just as she's opening the phone and sending Price her number. She nods, glancing up just once. She quickly checks she doesn't recognize and so has never arrested this man, as she almost always does when interacting with a stranger. When you work in the police, you are never not at work.

She leaves and looks at the less than salubrious surroundings. Two closed-off stalls – God knows what goes on in there – a shop selling knock-off designer t-shirts, a butcher's. Julia unconsciously memorizes the faces she sees, names of shops, the way she always has, the way her job requires her to.

'And I'll have a nice day, too,' the owner calls after her. Julia looks back at him. He only wanted her to be polite. Maybe he does just sell phones. Maybe not everything is a front for money laundering.

* * *

Julia is in Lewis and Yolanda's living room. Two hours ago, she asked them to tell her everything they remember about the night Sadie disappeared.

She spent the morning in her office, SADIE written on the biggest piece of paper she could find. She locked the door, feigned admin, told only Jonathan what she was doing. She pulled out the old CCTV, the old evidence files, the old statements, and spread them around her in a semicircle. Jonathan joined her, solicitous on the floor next to her, and they began sifting. He didn't mention their talk yesterday. Not yet.

She then came directly here, so nobody at the station would know what she was doing, and she's so far taken nine pages of notes with Lewis and Yolanda, the old-fashioned way. Tactile, the paper creased, curling at the edges, indentations on the flipside from the scratch of her ballpoint pen. It could be twenty years ago, and Julia is happy.

Nevertheless, it's odd to be back. Here, where she was a year ago, just as Genevieve's life – and Julia's – blew up.

Just as Art spent a summer completely alone watching *Love Island*, apart from her. At the end of August, on the very last day, he'd shouted at her, 'I put a hammock up in the garden in May and you haven't even noticed it.' He'd angrily torn his t-shirt off, and sure enough, he had a patchwork tan from the leaves above him as he lay in it. She couldn't tell him what she had done: rescued their daughter, buried the evidence.

And now here she is. A whole year later. Everything still in chaos, including, now, her career, too.

Sadie had been in between jobs when she'd disappeared. Had temped with her father, was waiting for a new job – Olivia's story was inspired by her. She had seen Andrew, a few hours before she disappeared, then went out to a speed networking event that she walked home from. She was seen on one CCTV camera, and had disappeared by the next. Her phone turned off immediately, which had originally pointed Julia to foul play. Andrew had been with his mother, then in a restaurant, then seen on a Ring doorbell.

The facts are as she remembered them, but it has still been useful to hear them again, to take notes, to look at the whites of Lewis's and Yolanda's eyes, and talk to them.

'Can you remember anything about these rows – between Sadie and Andrew?'

'He didn't want her doing things – did he?' Lewis says. He's cradling a cup of tea, hands either side of it, restraining it like it's a wild animal, and looking at her. He's never once levelled the threat that hangs in the air between them: that he knows she is corruptible. That he knows what she did; what she would do. And he might tell somebody if she can't find out what happened to Sadie.

'I'd say that's fair,' Yolanda says, perhaps with the distance a year brings, and Julia feels a wave of sympathy for her, stoic, must-be-bewildered Yolanda, whose daughter's case is being reinvestigated for no reason that she knows of. She is not unlike Art, whose stoicism and resentment of her career bubbled over into infidelity. Julia wants to tell them to guard it, their marriage. Visit it often: protect it from harm.

'They had a big one, only a few days before, about her going out too much. He grabbed her wrist. That's all I heard, like I said last year,' Lewis says, spreading his hands wide.

Julia nods. 'Uh huh.'

'He didn't like her to go to certain places, either. Bristol – didn't like it. Maybe because men were looking at her.'

'Did he say that?' Yolanda says, her body language entirely an echo of last year: a woman tired of reining in her husband, a woman not entirely convinced they were on the right path. But neither Yolanda nor Lewis knows about Prudence. There isn't a single missing woman on the PNC called Prudence Jones. Julia's searched twice now, and asked Jonathan. It remains a mystery.

'Well, he implied it. But he definitely said she shouldn't go into Bristol,' Lewis says. 'It wouldn't surprise me at all if he had somehow followed her that night, on the pretence of a lift home, and then . . .'

Yolanda gets up off the sofa and goes down into the kitchen. Julia doesn't follow her; the bereaved need time and space to escape situations if they want to. It leaves Julia and Lewis alone. She straightens her reams of paper and looks at him. 'Do you have any leads?' he says eagerly. 'Where is Andrew?'

Julia winces, and wonders how to say that they're looking for a perpetrator here – and a body. Nothing less than that, and nothing more, either.

'Not much yet,' she says, 'but I'm on it. I am interested in Andrew.'

Lewis cocks his head. 'Why?'

'All I have is what you have told me. But I have interviewed him now.'

'And?'

'He's a closed-up clam,' she says.

'He knows something. He did it.'

Julia makes an equivocal face. 'Maybe. Maybe not. But . . .' She hesitates. It might help. She's already acting illegally, off the books: it might help.

'But what?'

'Do you have any idea' – she says, trying to think carefully before she vaults over yet another boundary that should be firm but isn't – 'why Matthew would have received bitcoin money which said on the narrative, *I have Prudence Jones for you*?'

Lewis blinks, and Julia only hopes this doesn't reactivate him into doing something reckless – into doing something *more* reckless. 'Who?'

'A woman called Prudence Jones. A QR code transferring funds. The narrative said *I have Prudence Jones for you* – that's all. As far as we are aware – she is not dead.'

Lewis nods quickly. He sets his mug on the floor, then glances at the door his wife disappeared through. 'Don't we need to find Prudence, then?' he asks, then adds, more quietly: 'Maybe it isn't too late for her.'

* * *

Julia's eyes feel gritty when she arrives back at the station, her legs as heavy as if somebody has their hands gripped

286

tightly around her ankles. She is thinking that she can't set Price looking for Sadie and not have anybody find out. Nor can she investigate Sadie's disappearance alone, off the record, with no resources. She can't keep avoiding Jonathan's ultimatum. As though her thoughts have magicked him up, when she rounds the corner, he is sitting in her office. Waiting for her.

There is something about the inevitability of it all that makes her do it. That he is expecting an explanation from her. That she's tired of working alone, never confiding in anybody, a lone wolf who allowed herself to be blackmailed because she had no other options.

'All right?' he says. He looks tired too, around the eyes, two- or three-day stubble on his jaw.

'Not really,' she says heavily.

His expression is open. Eyebrows raised, elbows on his knees, sitting in her chair, just waiting for her. Her longest-serving sergeant, her colleague, her friend, Jonathan in his black-framed glasses.

'I kind of got myself into a situation,' she says.

He nods quickly, like perhaps he already knows the full story. 'It's –' Julia continues, thinking he might well hand her over to the anti-corruption team, he might tell the CPS, he might never work with her again. But, somehow, she knows he won't do these things. And, more importantly, she knows she can't lie to him any longer. Julia, straight as an arrow, comes back to herself right there in her office with the most prized member of her team.

'What?' he says slowly.

'Jonathan – you know I am not a bad person,' she begins.

'Absolutely,' he says, and the way he says it, with total conviction, makes Julia's heart sing.

She pauses just slightly, looking at him in the moment right before she tells him.

'Whatever it is,' Jonathan prompts, his eyes on her, 'we will sort it. Together.'

Julia closes her eyes, relief ebbing across her chest like a tide. 'Promise?' she says.

'Promise.'

33

Emma

You have been bailed, for now – that's what you said on the phone to me half an hour ago. And Olivia: found. It is as if a big, hopeful bird has taken flight in my chest. Momentarily, Prudence and Sadie don't seem to matter. It's irrational, I know.

I'm trying not to think that it might be you who has organized her safe return somehow.

And now, I'm here, collecting you, the way I have done a thousand times before. Only this time, it isn't football, or cubs, or the cinema: it's a police station, and everything that holds with it. Official forms to fill out, your belongings in ziplocked bags, picked over and sampled to see if you kidnapped and murdered a woman. And I'm wondering, of course, if you know that I handed you over. Your Judas.

But you didn't kidnap or murder her. She's been found. Evidently alive and well, according to the short news report. There's something slightly strange about it, slightly off, that I can't put my finger on. Maybe it's because women who go missing in these circumstances are not often found – I don't know . . . but they haven't said where she was, or how they found her. The police case closed, the media seemingly satisfied with a non-explanation. And, of course, you say you have no idea.

I brought you a change of clothes and – right in the foyer – you take the hoodie from me now and swap it out, evidently desperate to be out of the police-issue tracksuit. You immediately smell of home, and not of police custody, and I unconsciously step closer to you.

You're signed out and are told the police will be in contact, and it amazes me, this process. They don't have to tell you anything, even though it's your life, and it's their job. DCI Day is nowhere in sight. Just custody officers, receptionists, people writing your name on forms and swigging coffee and testing pens on pieces of scrap paper when they stop working. Just mundane work life – to them. Regardless of my own thoughts about you, you deserve better.

'Just waiting on the final few bits now,' an officer says to you, nodding to one of the banks of chairs where we've spent so much time recently. You sit in the very corner, one skinny shoulder wedged next to a coffee vending machine that has a sign on it saying OUT OF ORDER. You fold your arms inside the front of your grey hoodie, but you don't look at me. And that's how I know that you know.

'The QR code,' I say.

'I don't know anything about a QR code.'

I exhale heavily. 'It's the same stories,' I say softly. 'You deny all knowledge of everything, every time.'

You cross your legs at the ankles in front of you. Almost every time you do it, I remember the twenty-week scan, when you were doing just that. The sonographer said you had lovely long legs, while I laughed in total joy and happiness and thought I might just be okay: we might just be okay, together, the two of us; we already were.

'I don't know anything about a QR code, but I'm really very interested as to why you felt you had to tell the head of the fucking police,' you say, and, honestly, your tone chills me so much that I shift away from you just slightly.

An officer brings a final form over and you scribble your looped signature along the bottom without even taking the clipboard from him, just let him hold it for you like he's your servant. You're pissed off, and this is not the place to lose your temper. You stand up, ignoring me, and stride out into the spring sunshine. I have no choice but to follow you.

I don't unlock the car, which forces you to stand by it, doing nothing, but you still don't look at me. Hands in your pockets, gaze down. How has this happened? Until last year, you were shy, awkward maybe, but nothing like this. And now, accused twice. Has the system broken you? Or is it something else?

'What would you have done?' I ask. 'Two different missing women. A third – who is alive and well, apparently. Against all odds?'

If Matthew is surprised at the mention of the three women, he doesn't show it. 'What do you mean – against all odds?'

'Well, it's a payment for something, isn't it? The QR code – the bitcoin?'

You laugh softly, darkly, then try the car door again, but I don't open it. Eventually, you look at me over the roof, but again say nothing. The car reflects shards of bright white light that dance in my vision as I meet your blue eyes.

'What would you have done? You won't talk. You won't explain it. Everyone is just left wondering,' I say.

'Yeah – to think the worst.'

'Okay – what would be an explanation that sits in the middle, then?'

You turn away from me and look into the distance.

'You had spoken to Olivia Johnson. You were *dating* Sadie. Who's Prudence Jones?'

'I've said – I have no idea.' You look at me sharply, now, your gaze as direct as a snake's. 'I'm going to walk,' you say. You don't say anything else; you just turn those eyes away from me, and trudge across the car park, looking as defeated as I am.

I see you on the way home. It's only a couple of miles. You're on a side street, busy, a school halfway along it, and you're caught up in the throng of school-gate parents, kids, dogs. I slow the car and watch you, wondering, wondering what's going on in your mind, wondering if you're going where you say you're going, wondering if you're who I think you are. I idle in the traffic, glad of the opportunity to watch you. You sidestep out of the way of a kid on a scooter, smiling at him. It's nothing, really, something small, but something I've always taught you to do, to be kind, to be polite. And look: you are.

And yet.

* * *

Later that day and I have in my hands a prized possession, only recently relinquished by the police, only very much temporarily surrendered by you: your mobile phone. You were taking in an Amazon parcel, and I took my opportunity.

I have less than thirty seconds, but I've googled this, over and over. *How to tell if teen is hiding something. What to look at on teen's phone.* These searches throw up all sorts of things. I felt like a fraud reading them, articles aimed at mothers worried their children are doing anodyne teenager things like smoking, drinking and sex, not kidnap and murder, but I kid myself that it's a spectrum of sorts. That – whatever it is – it is somehow fixable, though I know some things just simply aren't.

Telegram. Kik. WhatsApp. Location services. TikTok. Twitter. Instagram. Facebook. Those are my hits, in priority order. There are messages to a couple of friends on Telegram and Kik, nothing more, which makes me sad, in a way: that whatever it was that happened last summer severed you so completely from your friends. If you're innocent, it's a tragedy. Maybe it is if you're guilty, too. I don't know, can't even consider it.

'Let me just take a photo,' the Amazon driver says to you.

'Sure,' you say cordially.

You're a member of a few football groups on WhatsApp, still message the odd person who was loyal to you when we used to live on the other side of Portishead.

No messages to women on WhatsApp. Well, good.

I open the settings, then location services. This part will tell me where you've been going.

'Yeah, thanks, thanks,' you're saying. The Amazon driver is handing you the parcel. I must have less than ten seconds.

Common locations – work: Portishead One. Home: 1 Glasgow Place. Other most frequent locations: 3 Streetsbrook Avenue, 292 Shirley Road, Tandy's All-American Diner.

I throw the phone back on to the arm of the sofa just as you arrive back, addresses memorized. 'Vitamins,' you say. 'Matcha,' you add, like that's a thing, tearing open the parcel to show me.

'What exactly is matcha for?' I say. 'Especially' – I reach to look at the packet – 'matcha collagen latte? *Latte?*'

You shrug. 'Seems to be good for you,' you say with a

293

moody smile. You saunter off into the kitchen, matcha vitamins in hand. You don't want to speak to me.

As soon as you're in the kitchen, I have the addresses up on Google on my phone. Number 292 Shirley Road is owned by Kevin and Beverley Rogers, one of your remaining friend's parents, and I instantly dismiss it. And Tandy's All-American Diner is exactly what it sounds like. Streetsbrook Avenue is a storage centre. I stare into space, trying to think. Have I ever seen a letter about a storage unit? Any way to know which is yours? Any way to get in?

Eventually, it comes to me: the four-digit PIN I found in your room the other day. Could it be?

Looks like I have two places to visit. Two places I had no idea that you went to.

* * *

The storage centre – called Boxes and More – is unmanned. There is something futuristic about it. I find it especially intimidating, as a woman who likes houses with owners and flowers on mantelpieces and freshly hoovered rooms in stripes. This is the exact opposite. A reception desk for nobody except a cluster of cameras that display your face and body at all angles as you walk through the foyer, presumably cleaned by robots, too, after hours. Stark metal floors, like a ship. Bright yellow plastic skirting boards.

I have the PIN I found, but nothing else. I have no idea if I'll be able to get in.

A yellow phone sits on the reception desk next to a plastic sign saying *Ring this for help*, so I lift the receiver and listen. Eventually, an operator answers.

'Hi there,' I say. 'I've, er, forgotten my storage number. I have my PIN if you need to know it's me. Name is Zamos.' I look up at the suspended ceiling, hoping it's under your old name. Hoping too that the operator doesn't ask for my first name – I can hardly say Andrew – or for ID.

I hold my breath and she clicks something on a keyboard. 'PIN?'

I read it out dutifully. '2740.' I decided to bluff it. 'The locker number's just gone clean out of my head.' A fake laugh escapes, no doubt born out of hysteria.

'Forty-one,' the operator says after a pause, evidently unconcerned by somebody who has the PIN.

'Thanks,' I say, slightly breathlessly.

Number forty-one is on the ground floor. The corridors twist and turn, always at right angles, no daylight, just rows and rows and rows of the same thing, roller-shutter doors like small yellow garages as far as the eye can see: an industrial horizon.

I stand in the totally empty, silent corridor and think that it could be anywhere. It could be a basement. It could be in America. It could be on Mars. What are you storing here? Old possessions from your life as Andrew? If so, I don't know about it. Like most omissions, it is a lie designed not to look like one. People only ever hide things intentionally, though they may say otherwise.

I take three long breaths in and out. Knowing that, really, this is the moment. The moment I find something. Something damning, something hopeful, some clarity. And, suddenly, I'm desperate for that. Whatever it is. Even if it's bad. It's better to know.

Now that I've had these thoughts, I feel ready: ready to spring it open, and to see what lies inside. Your locker is in front of me, the same as all the others, but containing God knows what. 2740. The numbers ring out little beeps on the keypad.

And I'm in. The door is mechanized, rolling up like a grotesque *Generation Game* prize, and I close my eyes and wonder what it is I'm hoping for. Old clothes. School books. Something anodyne. Or, even better: an explanation. Something to keep secret that isn't a murder, that explains everything so easily. A confession in object form, though I can't say what that would even be.

The storage box reveals its contents, and I blink as I look at them. Two passports. And a bundle of clothes. One by one, the hairs on the backs of my arms rise up. It isn't the passports. It's the clothes: they're bloodstained.

And, as if I'm not even really here, not experiencing this, I find myself thinking how ingenious it is. A storage centre that only you have access to. No worry about disposing of the evidence yourself. Keep it in your possession, but nowhere near you, so the police don't find it on their searches. How very clever you are.

I reach towards them, knowing my life is changing. First passport: Gail Hannah. Second passport: Sadie Owen. The clothes: a white broderie anglaise top, a pair of jeans, a pink cardigan. All three have blood on, dashed here and there like careless paint flicks. Stab wounds – signs of a struggle – kidnap – murder – I can't – I can't, I can't, I can't.

As I pick through them, something falls away from them and on to the floor. I bend to pick it up and see it: it's a lock of hair. My back and shoulders begin to shiver.

It's undoubtedly Sadie's, that fine, almost white-blonde. It's dry against my fingertips, cold, eerie somehow, like a very still animal.

I take the passports and the clothes and the lock of hair, my life changed for ever. My body is moving, somehow, my lungs breathing, my limbs working, all the while my heart is breaking. They belong to me now. I draw them to my chest and shut the locker.

The door closes with an echo that travels all the way down the empty corridor, and then back up, like the shout of somebody dying. Heard once, then echoed, even though by then it's far too late.

34

Lewis

Your things were returned to us forever ago, and so it's easy for me to look through them. I'm searching for anything to do with Prudence Jones. I comb through your emails. I ransack your hard drive. I leaf through the pages of the things left behind that never meant much to us – to-do lists, items you wanted to buy, jobs you were going to apply for. But there's nothing. Prudence doesn't even come up, only in obscure ways, like you having googled *Dear Prudence movie is it shit?* a year ago (lol, as you would say).

I google, too, as I'm sure DCI Day has, to see if any women called Prudence Jones are missing, but there aren't, nothing high profile anyway, the women Andrew specializes in: young, attractive, middle-class women walking home by themselves at night.

'It's funny, isn't it?' Yolanda says, arms folded by the door to my study. 'The police interviewing us again.'

'It's what we wanted,' I say, but I avoid her gaze.

'It must be about the woman who was found – Olivia?' She gulps, now, and I can't handle it. But isn't it better not to tell her? I would only be easing my own conscience. Isn't that what the guilty do? They confess, to get it off their shoulders, and put it on to someone else's.

'I don't think there's some – serial kidnapper of women out there,' I lie, but of course it's exactly what I think. Matthew could be trafficking women, could be hired to kill them.

'No. I like DCI Day, anyway,' Yolanda says. I wince, and spare Yolanda with a lie.

'Hopefully they will find something.'

'Hope so.'

She holds on to the door handle. In the time I've been in here, she's changed into soft pyjamas, flannelling material, a dusty pink. She looks about twenty-five, diminutive, peaceful somehow. You look nothing alike, but you do, tonight, just now. Something around the eyes . . . more a facial expression than anything else.

'You look like her,' I say. 'Standing there.'

I close the laptop and stop the Prudence Jones searches, leaving it to Julia. Yolanda smiles, says thank you and takes my hand as we head into the kitchen. It's late, after nine, but she starts cooking. And, for the first time, I stay with her, sitting on the bar stool as she chops and fries.

Our neighbour's children are in their garden, even though it's past their bedtime. They have a slide and swing set that they're scrambling over. Their parents are talking, not keeping an eye on them. I want to shout out to them: tragedy can strike at any time. It could be you.

Yolanda begins to make a marinade, satay maybe. I wouldn't know: I'm a rubbish cook. But it's a dark split-pea yellow. She whisks it with cream.

'I think all the time about whether she tried to call us,' she says. 'You know? If she was taken . . . if she tried to make a call. And if it'd have been us.'

'Of course it would have been,' I say, my voice thick. 'We were always – you know.' The words come easily to me, and it's like it's last year again, when we talked about you, and where you were, all day, every day. DCI Day's investigation has reopened, and so has our wound.

'I think so too. She trusted us, didn't she? To make everything better. To keep her safe.'

'Don't use the past tense,' I say. The past tense is a betrayal of you.

Yolanda sighs. Her breath is almost invisible in the warm kitchen air, but not quite. It disperses, unseen, unless you're looking closely for it. It vaporizes on the bowl she's standing over.

'What're you making?' I add softly.

'Katsu.'

I leave it for a second, then ask, 'Do you think she's alive?'

For a while, I think she hasn't heard me. The whisk is the only sound in the room. She dumps a bag of pre-chopped chicken in it and covers it with cling film. For a long while, I think she isn't going to answer me.

Eventually, she speaks. 'No,' she says. Her voice is thick and lined as she says it. A pair of curtains on her grief. She darts a quick look at me, and I wish I hadn't asked it of her. 'I just . . . there is not an explanation, to me, that is good.'

'She might be okay.'

'She might,' Yolanda concedes. She looks at me now, and I think I see sympathy there on her face. 'But – Lewis. She isn't. You know what we said at the beach.'

'I know. I do know that,' I say, and I do. I really do. I would know if you were still alive. I think we both would. I heave a sigh, trying to shift the sadness off my chest, as I stare directly down the barrel at life after you.

Yolanda turns her mouth down, and I can see it then. She has always been able to distinguish between what is true, and what she wants to believe, and is an ardent atheist for this reason. 'Heaven would be great,' she once said, 'if it was real.'

It's dusk. The sky outside is stained-glass blue. I stare at our garden as the neighbours call their children in. Their security light blinks on as their little bodies run past it. God, they have so much time ahead of them.

'You felt that if you could prove Andrew had done it, we might be able to get her back,' Yolanda says simply, succinctly. I blink. The bowl of chicken is on the counter between us, and I reach and rotate it, the ceramic still warm from Yolanda's hands. How perceptive that she would say this now. Almost like she knows what I've been doing.

Thank fucking God we have each other.

I stare at the place where the sun went down. The sky is bleached white. The sun is gone, it's an optical illusion, but it's still there, out there somewhere, somehow, like rainbows, like sun flares, like souls.

'Come on,' Yolanda says. She stands up, extends her hand to me, and I take it. 'We can watch *Selling Sunset* if you want. While the chicken does its thing.' I grab on to her hand, and to normality, gladly, momentarily happy, momentarily okay, in that way we are sometimes these days, little chinks of light in a dark, dark room. I sling my arm around her shoulders and pull her to me.

'I'll love her for ever,' I say, a sentence so true, so pure, that it doesn't even need a response. Yolanda nods into my shoulder. 'And you,' I add, and Yolanda leans right into me then, the way she used to, the way she did that day in the lift, right before we were rescued. And now look at us: rescuing each other, in grief.

It's at that precise, relaxed, poignant moment that I realize how to find out who Prudence is: work. The passport office.

Three Hundred and Seventy-Third
Day Missing

35

Julia

Julia has never once slept at work, but she does, today, after resting her head on her forearms and thinking about Jonathan.

'It's your kid,' he had said, when she had finished, biting his lip. 'God, Julia, of course you did it.'

'Do you really think that?' she said, her voice as viscous as cough medicine, emotional with having finally told somebody, with having been understood at last as *good*.

And then he said it: the sentence she didn't even have to ask him to say: 'I'd have done the same.'

'Would you?'

He blinked, took his glasses off, as though he wanted the barrier gone, his gaze direct on hers. 'Without a second's hesitation.' He paused. 'I remember Zac, when he died and you got that case. I remember thinking – well. Nothing of it. Probably died committing crimes. And didn't he? On your daughter.'

'That is not the way a jury would see it.'

'No.' He looked out of the window for a while after she said that.

Eventually, he turned to her, and said: 'So now – how do we sort it?'

'I have no idea. What about – you know . . . do you feel you have to tell somebody?'

'I can keep your secrets, Julia. But now – we find out what happened to Sadie.'

And so, today, Julia is ostensibly tying up loose ends on the Olivia case, actually working on Sadie with Jonathan's assistance – he's in Scotland for his wedding anniversary, but working from there – and actually, actually, having a thirty-second nap at her desk. The world takes on that strange quality as she drifts, her body jolting as though falling, her thoughts crossing over into dreams, not knowing what's real. The heat of the room, the smell of stale coffee, the light from her lamp . . . . just one minute more, two minutes, five.

She begins to dream of Price, and everything she's asked of him. She in his flat, then he in her house; the images pass by, unexplained. And that's when he turns to her, his silhouette moving in some darkness she can't make out, and says it: 'Another missing woman, blonde, goes by Marilyn.'

She opens her eyes. Marilyn.

She'd been distracted by how the timings didn't marry up with Marilyn being Olivia. Then distracted by her return. Then couldn't trace Marilyn, anyway.

But what if Marilyn is Sadie?

Her chin sticks to her forearm as she lifts her head, checks the time: five past nine at night. She must've been out for over half an hour.

Marilyn. What if Sadie was involved with a gang, then left it? What would happen to a woman who made that choice?

She shakes her head, trying to break the sleep inertia. She's been all over the place. Distracted by blackmailers, by finding her assailant, by covering her tracks. Sidetracked, too, by being duped into looking for the wrong woman.

She leaves the office, accepting she will finish nothing useful tonight, not while sleeping at her desk, anyway. She texts Art spontaneously, not thinking, just acting. *Coming home :)* she sends. A nod to everything, she hopes: her workaholism, perhaps selfishness, expecting him to run a home without her. He replies immediately, sends her a single kiss, and Julia presses her phone to her chest, breathing deeply for a second, then uses her pay-as-you-go phone to call Price.

His phone rings and rings out. Outside, it's twilight, still and quiet. She walks quickly, past the shut-up shops, past the alley, thinking of the night that started it all.

Price doesn't pick up. He will be working. Doing whatever he does. Supplying drugs, dealing drugs, buying drugs, Julia doesn't know for sure, only that it goes way beyond informing.

She tries him again as her car looms into view, but doesn't risk a voicemail. The streets are black, slick with rain. The night-time scene is an oil painting, the dim lights of the flats above the shops, the marina in the distance, but Julia can't relax. She's on the trail. Find Sadie's body. Find out what Price meant. Find Sadie.

A bus-stop light is flickering, a strobe from Julia's long-ago youth. She watches her feet move jerkily as the light illuminates and darkens each step as she walks, thinking. She tries Price again, the third time. Still nothing.

She leaves the high street behind her, heading towards her car. The remaining light slowly falls away, streetlamps becoming further and further apart, living rooms turning to darkness as people go to bed, and, just as Julia thinks about going to Price's house, it happens.

A light step, maybe ten feet behind her. She doesn't turn around. The sound is very distinctive to police. The noise of somebody trying to cover up the echo their steps create. Somehow, Julia can feel the intent, fired through the night air and right towards her.

They get closer. Julia casts a panicked glance around her, trying to think. She doesn't feel as powerful as she does usually. It must be because of Lewis. The worst happened to Julia, that night in her car, and she can't forget it.

There's nowhere she could go. She gets her phone out. It lights up the night in a white haze, and the motion of doing so must force the person following her to act.

A hand around her wrist, as tight and as powerful as a handcuff. A voice in her ear. 'You say nothing.'

Julia freezes, purely calm now, for the second time in as many weeks. She does as she's told, but looks down at the hand: gloved.

'Stop looking for her,' the voice says. 'And, when I release you, don't look back.'

* * *

Julia is freed. The streets look the same. Bus stop still strobing. She doesn't hear the man's footsteps as he leaves. She lets out a breath, counts to twenty, and then turns around, but there's nobody: it's as if it didn't happen.

The cold night air makes her feel feverish as she walks to her car on shaky legs. Not knowing what else to do, she gets in, seat freezing against her back, and thinks.

Who, what, why, her detective mind asks, and she rests her head against the steering wheel, not wanting to think, not wanting to have to keep pondering endlessly over these poor missing women, and the people who miss them, too.

Somebody knows she is looking for Sadie, and wants her to stop. Probably Sadie's killer. That's the why. But what about the who?

She lifts her head up, eyes stinging in the glare of an orange streetlamp, and tries to think. But how can she possibly know?

The strong gloved hand, the voice. Julia didn't recognize anything about him. Not Lewis. Not Matthew.

She tries Price again and, this time, he answers. She talks quietly to him for over ten minutes and, afterwards, sits back against the cold leather of her car seat, thinking. Thinking about what she's just learnt. How it might change everything.

Just as she's deciding what to do, her other phone vibrates in her hand and she picks it up, assuming it's Price again, even though it's the other phone. 'Hello?' she says.

'DCI Day.' It's Lewis. He sounds just like she does: too much adrenalin, not enough sleep, his words laced with a kind of rushed quality, like somebody one glass of wine in, but no more.

'At your beck and call,' Julia says, not intending to sound sarcastic.

'I have some information. I think. I think I know something.'

'Shoot,' Julia says, and she notices she says it without thinking. *Find Sadie.* She stares out of the car window and into the night. This is who Julia is: no matter the danger to herself, the personal sacrifices, the marital breakdowns, the costs she pays. She isn't sick of it. She isn't tired of it. She might be in more danger than ever, but Julia pays these costs happily, like a tax, because, in return, she gets this: this feeling. This feeling she is addicted to, that all police are addicted to.

'Go on,' she prompts Lewis.

'I know who Prudence Jones is. I went into the office . . .
I looked.'

'I'm listening,' she says immediately, in a low voice.

Three Hundred and Seventy-Fourth Day Missing

36

Lewis

It's the cold light of morning and Yolanda still knows nothing. I'm sitting in my car, with DCI call-me-Julia in the passenger seat. We are both deep in thought – at least I am. Thinking about you, and what might have happened to you now we know what we know.

Prudence Jones is dead. Her passport came in last spring through the Tell Us Once initiative. A relative sends the passport in along with the death certificate, and we confirm it and cancel the passport. She'd been seventeen – unusual name for a young woman – and it had said *Cause of death: car accident*. I shuddered at it, imagined it was you – of course.

This is what I told Julia. To which she – sharp as a pin – said, 'Did Prudence Jones live anywhere near Andrew?'

'Local-ish,' I said. 'Couple of miles from him.' Julia had nodded, evidently thinking, trying to connect Andrew to these missing women.

Julia indicates my workplace now. She's brought me here, wants more information. The morning glow of sunlight gilds her hand. 'All right,' she says. She holds a palm up.

My body fizzes with the knowledge that we're about to discover something. What happened to you.

'I want to know what happened right after her passport was sent in?' Julia asks.

'I don't know,' I say. 'What usually happens is we then cancel it.'

'Can you trace it?'

'Not officially. But I can pull some strings.'

'Lewis. Information is king here.'

I reach for the handle to get out. The moon is still up outside, the sky around it eggshell blue. Our breath puffs visibly in the car. 'Julia?' I ask.

She looks at me wordlessly. 'Thank you for doing this,' she says. 'You don't need to do this.'

'I don't care,' I say honestly. Her eyes are on me. 'Do you think – if you had to say . . . in percentage terms . . .' I ask it in precisely the way I did the first time, all those months ago, when we were adversaries, or felt like it.

'I don't think she's alive, Lewis,' Julia says. She holds my gaze as she says it, and I appreciate the honesty. Nobody ever regrets knowing something, no matter how tough. The worst thing in life is to be bullshitted.

'But we might find out who killed her. And if it's Andrew,' she says simply. Her hand moves to her hair. 'But, first, we need to know what happened after Prudence's passport was sent in. Who it was that said she was dead.'

'Do you think she wasn't dead?'

'Leave that to me.'

37

Julia

Julia is hoping what Lewis finds will assist her. She wishes she could discuss it with somebody, with Jonathan, maybe, though he's still away, revisiting the Sadie file in the evenings, looking for clues.

She is just down the road in a pub, meeting a contact of Price's. Nobody has followed her here, so far as she knows. The last thing Julia needs is to make another dangerous acquaintance, but she has no choice now. Isn't even really acting consciously, is just the lion chasing down the deer, everything else be damned.

The pub is called the Sparrow, and is very much not her style. It has a sign outside that swings and creaks in the wind. Inside is old-fashioned: ugly carpets, swirls of brown and orange to hide the stains. Four exposed-brick columns. A dark-wood bar. High-up windows threaded with lead. Tatty green velour-covered stools. Almost empty, the chilly sun from outside heating the insides so the carpet begins to smell sour. So retro, as Genevieve might say, meaning: oh-so-ugly. The thought makes Julia miss Genevieve, and she sends her a text saying so, which Genevieve reads straight away. *Oh, well, I would miss me too!* she writes back, and Julia fizzes with affection, and even more so when a second arrives: *We'll have a lovely day together soon x.*

It's the middle of the day. The door is propped open, bringing a light breeze inside. She turns in a slow circle as she tries to work out if he's here yet. When she sees him, it's obvious: the man at the table in the shadows near the back is so clearly a criminal he may as well be carrying a swag bag. A heavy coat even though the weather doesn't demand it, all the better for hiding things in. A steady gaze, right on hers. Two phones.

He is tall, elegant. Long white fingers, a straight spine. Cropped grey hair. In front of him is a glass of what looks like Coke, no ice, a full pint, the surface of the liquid right to the top, untouched, a black, glassy, distended meniscus. Next to that is the *Times* cryptic crossword.

'Thanks for meeting me,' Julia says, reaching a hand out.

'Pleasure,' the man says simply. He has filled in half of the crossword. Next to it, he's written the date as though he intends to cut it out. A daily habit, then. Well, good.

She glances at her phone. A text from Lewis has come in: Prudence Jones's passport was never cancelled. It was sent in to be cancelled, but the application was never completed. Just as she suspected.

The man meets Julia's eyes. His are colourless. Maybe blue, maybe grey, maybe hazel but, really, none of them. 'You're interested in supplying one of my patches,' he says.

'Sorry – you go by . . .?'

'Nines,' he says. He is affiliated with a gang called 4Place, the most notorious in Bristol. Nines doesn't deal in drugs, or arms, or trafficking. He deals in the very essence of who people are.

Clouds pass over the sun outside, plunging the pub into shadows. Two men arrive, half-cut already, at noon on a weekday. It's a dirty old pub for dirty old men, and Julia feels completely alien here. When she gets home, eventually, whenever that is, she will run a shower, fast and hot, and stay in there for half an hour, until her feet turn pink. And then she will try to forget that she has accepted this instruction at all.

'Yes, I'm interested in supplying your patch.'

'You got the necessary documents?' he says. He means passports, but doesn't say so. If Julia's hunch is right, then Nines is going to lead her to answers.

'Yes, I do,' she bluffs.

'Never met a bent copper before,' Nines says. 'Pleased to make your acquaintance.' He reaches out wordlessly with his hand. Julia shakes it. It feels skeletal in her grasp, a dead man's hand.

38

Emma

I set the passports and the lock of hair and the clothes down on the coffee table in front of us wordlessly. You're on the sofa, feet tucked up under you, a hand underneath your top, resting on your stomach. Ostensibly relaxed, the portrait not of a twenty-year-old bailed pending further police investigations but somebody on holiday, instead. Somebody lazing around on a Sunday morning. Somebody the day after their exams have finished.

You don't see what I've done at first. Eyes down on that phone that holds your secrets, only some of which I have managed to unearth. It's dusky outside, just before ten at night. We're almost at the part of the year where it doesn't ever feel like it gets truly dark. The lamp is on next to you, illuminating one side of your face, the other in shadow. Navy wall behind you. Jewel-green sofa. And you: sitting there, the sometimes-guilty love of my life.

I notice the exact moment you spot what I've put between us. Your body – not exactly moving a lot before – stills in an animalistic way; a rabbit stopped in the wild, listening for a predator. You turn only your eyes up to me after a few seconds. The rest of your body stays exactly where it was.

'I found them,' I say simply. I look at you, waiting a beat. I can see the crown of your head from up here, standing over you. When you were a baby, for maybe eighteen months, your hair grew only outwards, totally straight, like you'd touched a static balloon. I called you my baby hedgehog. Funny to think nobody will ever know about that: you can't remember, and single parents have fewer witnesses. We have only the photographs we had the time to take – not many, all blurred, none posed, none just the two of us – and our memories.

'Right,' you say, and it's at precisely this moment that I realize you're not going to explain anything to me. No matter what.

Nevertheless, I look searchingly at you, and you stare back up at me. It occurs to me, now – a thought I used to have often – how unalike we look. You're all your dad – as far as I can remember, anyway. That blue gaze, that dark brow.

'Right? A lock of hair? Bloodstained clothes? The only remaining question is – where is the body?'

To my surprise, you shoot to your feet like the sofa's burned you. 'Don't you think I'd tell you?' you say.

'What? Where the body is?' I take a step back from you, startled. You've basically just admitted it. You notice this immediately, but rather than your anger burning brightly, your face only falls in disappointment as you realize: I am afraid of you.

'Fucking hell,' you say. Your hands are on your head now, and the atmosphere crackles like there's a storm surging. Thunder, lightning, anger, regret. Everything is here in our living room with us. And even though I'm afraid of what's about to happen, I'm ready for it, too. The gasoline has been laid since last year, but finally, now, you're about to light it. 'Fucking hell,' you shout now. You pace out from between the sofa and the coffee table. 'I'd tell you,' you say. 'If it –'

'If it *what*?'

You don't answer this. It occurs to me that the no-comment interview Mr Jackson recommended would have come so naturally to you anyway. You have no-commented since the moment Sadie went missing. Only none of us can work out why. Or, rather, we don't want to consider why that might be.

'If you got arrested? If three women disappeared? If damning evidence after damning evidence appeared?'

I glance desperately around the living room. Suddenly, I want an ally. Not your father, but someone else, somebody useful. Somebody I got intentionally pregnant by, aged thirty-five. Somebody with a good job with a briefcase and a commute. Somebody who would have a plan. And, most importantly, somebody who would be able to say, 'No, you did everything right. It's not you, and it's not your fault.' Or even, 'If we fucked it up, it was both of us, and not just you.'

'You shouldn't have said you were my alibi for that night,' you say. 'I was out when I called you. I said I was upstairs, but I was just arriving home.'

A terrible shudder moves through me, like knowledge imparting itself into every cell of my body. 'For Olivia?' I ask. 'But she's been found?'

'I'm just saying you don't always know what's been going on.'

'Where did you put Sadie?' I say. I can't stop staring at the lock of hair. Such a gruesome token; worse, somehow, than the blood on the clothes. I wonder if you snipped it off while she was still alive, or after she had gone. The thought makes my stomach heave over, an internal avalanche.

You still haven't looked at the pile of possessions since that first time you noticed it.

You rub your nose roughly, saying nothing. The rims of your eyes have gone red, like somebody has lined them delicately in rose pink. The way you get when ill, when tired, when you've been crying. And when you're angry, too. Funny. You used to have tantrums over not being allowed chocolate biscuits, and now look what they're over.

'I was supposed to meet Olivia, but she didn't show,' you say in a low voice.

I groan, a painful, guttural moan, the kind I made in labour when I birthed you. 'Please explain to me – everything,' I say.

You say nothing.

'These will be going to DCI Day,' I say eventually, loyalty severed. My actions are no longer in your best interests. They're for these women, these poor, dead, missing women. Prudence Jones. Olivia Johnson, returned. And whatever happened to Sadie Owen?

'Fine,' you say, your voice as tense as a tightrope. Even in your monosyllables, there is zero vibration, no shaking, no hesitation. You have total conviction in your staunch denials.

'Fine?' I say. I get my phone out. 'Sure?'

'Tell her what you want. Pretty sure she wants to re-arrest me anyway for whatever the fuck she can.' You look at me now, standing a few feet from me. Your hands are in your pockets, shoulders up. Feet bare. Waiting. For what, I don't know. 'Odd,' you say. 'Both nights, I was with you almost all of the time. And yet, in your eyes, I'm still guilty.'

That's enough for me. 'Two arrests. Bitcoin transfers. Two passports. A lock of hair. I mean . . .'

'You're my mother,' you say, and I realize now: your voice is so tight because you're trying not to cry.

'So tell me your side of the story.'

You turn away from me. 'I shouldn't have to,' you mutter.

And I have no choice. I must have been doing it wrong all of these years. Cutting you too much slack. Not demanding enough from you. Giving you always the benefit of the fucking doubt.

You walk away from me.

I find Julia's number. The tones ring out between us as I tap. You stop, but you don't turn around.

'Also odd,' you say. 'You're proving exactly why I can't tell you.'

'What?' I say, four digits dialled, the rest unsaid.

'Evidently, I can't trust you.'

'Is that why you go to that diner so often?' I say. 'To get away?' I went, but it was nothing. Just a diner.

Your body stills again. Very slowly, you turn. 'Do not tell Julia about that diner,' you say.

And that's all it takes. Gasoline a river between us, I strike the match, and connect the call.

39

Julia

It's Genevieve's birthday today, but Julia is driving home to an empty house. She had said goodbye to Art and Genevieve earlier – they had called into the station on their way to Bristol for the last part of the evening, to play Ghetto Golf. Art had waited in the car, while Julia took Genevieve to get fish and chips. It was the best she could do; a poor token offered up for her daughter's birthday.

Outside the station, the evening sky had begun to darken. 'Chips is a good birthday present,' Genevieve said, Julia thought sincerely.

'I didn't only get you chips,' Julia exclaimed, thinking of the piñata cake she'd had delivered that morning, of the Ray-Ban sunglasses and the Beauty Pie delivery. All things bought in haste, online, but still purchased with love in mind.

The moon was up and casting a gilded finish on a patch of road. The sky was a Sistine Chapel, an Italian Renaissance painting, peach, pink, neon. Genevieve had scuffed her shoes uncharacteristically as they walked. She didn't look much like herself at all, actually, Julia thought, studying her. Unwashed hair. Unusually plain clothes. Julia hadn't noticed until then.

It was stormy, all-over-the-place spring weather. Violent winds, fierce sun in the day, freezing temperatures at night. Genevieve looked cold, slim shoulders hunched. She stared at Julia from within a black hood she had pulled up. 'Is everything all right?' Genevieve had asked directly.

'Yes,' Julia lied.

'I have been thinking about – you know . . . Zac,' she said simply. 'Since we talked about my dreams.'

'I see,' Julia said, looking curiously at her daughter.

The street unfolded in front of them, undulating and clear. It went this way and that, a direct contrast to the mess they found themselves in. The sun had dipped beyond the horizon. The air was darkening quickly like music on slow fade. 'I just wonder if I should have just confessed,' Genevieve said, seemingly out of nowhere. They turned up an unlit side street. 'I wonder if that's why – why I dream about it. Because it's never about what he did to me. It's always about what I did to him.'

'Nobody asks to be mugged, Gen,' Julia said. They walked in silence for several minutes as the universe turned the lights out. Eventually, Genevieve looked at Julia. Her face was a blue, underwater blur in the complete black. 'You did what – what you had to do.'

'No, but –'

'But what?'

'But if we hadn't covered it up, we'd have something else now.'

Julia didn't answer for several minutes. 'What?' she said eventually, thinking that she didn't want to be having this discussion, not now, not now she was so far down a line.

'Freedom,' Genevieve said.

'No, Genevieve,' Julia had said. 'You wouldn't. We wouldn't.'

Genevieve shrugged. 'I'm just – I'm scared, that's all.'

'I know,' Julia said. 'But I promise – it'll be fine.'

'In all of your cases . . . you know, not once have someone's actions been understandable. So I kind of think, why do I think mine were?'

Julia nodded, thinking. The obsession with the cases, the police. A slow, anxious sifting: are any of these criminals like me? No. More searching. Here, now, this behaviour makes perfect sense to her.

'What are you scared of?' she asked her daughter.

'That we made it worse,' Genevieve said immediately.

'We didn't,' Julia said through a sigh, but her shoulders felt heavy. 'I promise, we didn't.'

'Well. Who knows? Look – sure you can't get away?' Genevieve said, her eyes darting to Julia: one final ask. Julia winced with it. The maternal guilt was a well-flexed muscle, but that didn't make it any less painful. In fact, perhaps more so.

'I'm sorry,' she said, the words sounding lame.

When they had arrived back, chips in hand, Art was standing in the dark foyer. The lights were on timers, and in the absence of anybody being checked in, they had switched off. Genevieve wandered down a back corridor, keen to explore, or to get away from the emotional vulnerability she'd just shown Julia, perhaps.

Art had on a pale denim shirt with the sleeves rolled up.

'Sorry I can't be there,' she said.

'Yeah,' he said. Funny how two people can view the same events so differently: she thinks he cheated on her, he thinks she neglected him, their marriage, everything. Both versions are true. 'Sure you mean that,' he said.

'I do.'

'If you were sorry, as in, *regretful*, you'd come,' he said. And it's as easy as that to Art. Perhaps to everybody except her.

Because it feels as complicated as algebra to Julia. The minute she found out who her blackmailer was, she should have phoned it in. Called it all off, and released herself, forgotten about Sadie Owen and Matthew James. But she just couldn't do that.

The lights around them began to click off.

'Right,' she said, thinking how much was unsaid between them. Everything about the affair, everything after it, their future in question, and now everything with this case, too. She stood there in the dimness, feeling her full shadow self. 'I'm dealing with a hard case,' she said thickly.

'I know,' he said. That simple *I know*. Nothing more, nothing less. Just that he'd observed her from his perennial position on the side lines, the way he always had, and worked her out: *I know*. He saw her, he understood her, he *knew* her. That, even if it was for work, it was also for them, for Art and Genevieve.

Julia nodded quickly, saying nothing, wanting to say so many things to him. That she *was* sorry. That she missed texting him. Emailing him. Writing to him, in all the forms they had. That she had never been as hurt in her life as that Christmas. That she had done her very best to save their daughter, and Genevieve had just said she didn't even want saving anyway.

But she didn't say any of it.

The final light went off, and they were in darkness. Shapes came into focus. The lamplight from the custody suite rose through the window like vapour, gleaming a single gold square on the floor. In the gloom, Art reached for her hand. He hadn't done anything like that since Christmas, that milky light, that awful secret that he had detonated in the middle of their marriage like a landmine. And, suddenly, Julia

326

found herself wondering . . . had she lit the first match that had caused it all, by keeping Genevieve's secret from him? Had she provided the conditions for an affair? Or is this just something women think about themselves when men cheat? She looked at Art, whose expression she couldn't read in the dimness.

'Are you losers coming?' Genevieve called through, back to herself, intimacy about Zac swiftly covered over, and they broke apart.

But, God, she had missed it. She leaned into him, but she forced herself to drop his hand after just a second, like it had never happened at all. To return to the job, where she belonged.

And now. It's late. She's almost home. Nines has been instructed. He is in the right kind of business. Identities. Trading them. She only hopes she's right to be following this line of inquiry.

Julia arrives home and unlocks her front door, exhausted, just as her phone begins ringing and her head starts swimming with the mess they find themselves in. 'Julia Day,' she says to Emma, one eye on her hallway. Something about it feels – what, exactly? Art and Genevieve are coming home from Ghetto Golf in Bristol now – and maybe it's just this: the strange feeling a usually full house takes on when it's empty. Julia feels a glob of sadness slide down her chest as she thinks of her daughter. Had she truly meant what she said: that Julia's cover-up had made it all worse?

'I'm listening, Emma,' she prompts, wishing for a second that this job was like other jobs. Even when she's on record, and not off like at the moment, she could never not take this call.

'He's got a storage locker. I found four things in it,' Emma says, and it's at this moment that Julia realizes it isn't an ordinary call. Not housekeeping, not checking up if they intend to charge Matthew with anything, not trying to find out how and where they had found Olivia.

Julia stands in her hallway, the sand from outside still on her shoes, crunching like glass. The lights are off. She's in total darkness, but she doesn't care. 'What?' she asks Emma.

'Two passports. Sadie's and another woman's.'

Julia feels a flash of something zing up and down her body. A doctor would say it was adrenalin, nothing more, but to Julia, this is pure instinct, and, more than that: it's knowledge. Sadie's passport. They searched so hard for that during the investigation. It had never been used, that they were sure of, but they had never found it. And now – over a year later – here it is.

'Whose was the second? Prudence?'

'A woman called Gail Hannah.'

Julia walks into the kitchen, phone held between shoulder and chin, the exact place where it gives her neck ache, and writes this down on a piece of paper. 'Okay. I'll look her up. What's the third item?'

'A lock of blonde hair,' Emma says, and, even on the phone, Julia can tell Emma feels this has a relevance. A final reveal. But it doesn't, to Julia. Because Julia has a theory, and this plays into it. 'Fourth?'

'Bloodstained clothes.'

This Julia was not expecting. 'How bad?' she asks.

'Bad.'

'Okay – bring them to me,' she says. 'Double-bag them.'

'Also – he's been visiting somewhere other than this storage centre. A diner. Tandy's All-American Diner. He didn't want me to tell you.'

Julia writes this down, too. 'Come over,' she tells Emma again. 'Come over and we'll discuss it. And you can show me them.' She hesitates, then adds, 'Here, and not the station.' Another line crossed.

Emma's silence may be judgemental, she may just be processing; Julia isn't sure. Her mind is suddenly elsewhere. Momentarily distracted by the call, it's now homed back in on what it was thinking about before: that her house doesn't feel normal. It isn't that it's empty. It's that it's supposed to have that empty reverence of nobody being in it, but it doesn't, tonight. Julia listens to these instincts. They're usually telling her something, whether she wants to hear it or not.

The hallway is cold, colder than she would expect, actually, but everyone's been out, no teenager flicking the heating on. Nothing is disturbed. Shoes in a pile on the shoe rack. Coats hanging on the balustrade. No lights on in the lounge. Art usually leaves one on.

'Okay,' Emma says. 'Okay. Where are you based?'

And that's when Julia sees it. A twitch, just in the living room. Somebody all in black. A hot flash runs up Julia's arms and down to her hands. She has no time. She has five seconds, ten. She could use it to tell Emma her address, to call a police officer. To save her own soul.

But she doesn't.

The figure has noticed that she's seen him, emerges and advances towards her. No balaclava, unlike the first time. Gloves. Black clothes. And a face she knows well. He snatches her phone, pockets it, and passes a hand across her mouth, silencing her entirely. He's dragged her out and into his car less than five minutes later.

PART III

JULIA

First Day Missing

40

Lewis

Julia's phone rings out and out. The text message she has sent is cryptic at best, deliberately misleading at worst. *Welcome to the Vodafone messaging service*, it says over and over when I call her. It reminds me of when you went missing, though, of course, nothing compares, really.

It's midnight. Why would Julia send that text, and then do nothing? I stand in my kitchen, not wanting to wake Yolanda, not wanting to make a decision, really, just staring at those words. *Tandy's All-American Diner*. According to Google, it's a beaten-up American-style outfit the other side of Bristol, at least an hour's drive away, open twenty-four hours, frequented by truckers, port workers, people going nowhere. One of the Google reviews says, *Shit coffee, shit atmosphere, shit food*, which seems pretty accurate, from the photos.

Am I supposed to go there? I walk around my kitchen island and, I swear to you, Sadie, it is one of those situations where I know what I'm going to do, I just have to justify it to myself first. So I call the station and try to get hold of Julia, but, of course, that's impossible: like trying to speak to MI5, or, even harder, an NHS GP. I don't wake Yolanda, because I know what she'd tell me: don't bother, don't go there, ignore the text message. Or, worse, the refrain of the calm person: *Why don't you wait and see?* But I can't. It isn't me.

So on my second lap of the kitchen island, I admit it to myself: I'm going to Tandy's All-American Diner, whether or not I should, whether or not it's midnight. Because the police officer in charge of finding your killer has told me to go there.

* * *

A diner in the very centre of Bristol, a backstreet two alleys away from the river. An inconspicuous kind of place. Not so tucked away as to draw attention, become some hidden gem. Not so obvious as to have large footfall.

Nobody knows I'm here. Only Julia, I suppose.

It's American-style, but actually Americana: an uncanny approximation of American culture that probably bears no resemblance to the reality. It sits in between a bathroom shop and a white-painted pub called the Swan. It has a red-and-white awning, a neon sign and a blue-and-white striped door. It looks more like a movie set than a café.

Just as I reach to push open the door, I think it: what if Julia didn't send that text? What if someone else did? And set me up? I shiver, and dismiss it. Well, you know? So be it. I'm here.

A bell trills above me as I enter. The place is deserted, as you might expect at one o'clock in the morning, and I quake with it. With – what? With something. Some knowledge that something is about to change, for good or for bad. I scan the bar, just looking, but there's nobody. Five stools covered in cracked red leather. A jukebox. A milkshake machine, endlessly stirring pale sludge for nobody. Striped straws in sundae glasses. Ten or so booths, a handful of red tables with menus on, plate glass windows that look out on to the black street, but not a single person.

The room to the back is empty, so I head there. It houses a storeroom that looks like a kind of messy, industrial pantry. It contains ready-made everything. American-style pancakes. American-style milkshake mixes. American hotdogs in cans, American-style foot-long buns packed away in cellophane, bursting out of the shelves like foam fingers.

There really is nobody here. My back begins to prickle, like somebody has run their finger down my spine, a single, sharp stroke. Why am I here? Have I mindlessly trusted Julia?

The door bangs behind me, the door to the toilet. Footsteps. I hold my breath. I close my eyes and wait, content to stand and do nothing. This is what happens when you lose everything.

And then I turn around.

And – I must be dreaming, I must have died and gone to heaven – because it's you.

It's you. It's you, it's you, it's you. I'm awake. I'm here. And you're real.

I feel my soul rise up out of my body as I stumble towards you, drifting unsteadily like a happy hot-air balloon buffeting this way and that. And, oh, my God, the flesh on your arms is real. The tears you start crying are real. You are warm-bodied, alive you. 'Dad,' you say, your voice thin and watery. You're skinnier, your hair dyed dark.

'It's you,' I say. Is all I can say.

'It's me.'

In response, I simply sink to my knees, holding you, your wonderful, real, yielding body, and I thank every single lucky star in the sky that you are here, that you're mine. That you're you.

41

Emma

'What did she say?' you say to me. 'Is my arrest imminent?'

I stare at the phone in my palm. 'She's – gone,' I say, not comprehending it. The *call failed* notification. I try to call her back, but it goes straight to voicemail.

'Gone?' you say.

'I – I don't know. She just – went. I was saying what I found, the diner . . . and she – she disappeared. Off the line. There was maybe a – I don't know? A scuffle? I heard something . . .'

To my surprise, your fury, your desperation, seem to evaporate. 'A scuffle?' you say. 'What kind of scuffle?' You step towards me. A passing car lights up our living room in a brief white flash.

'I don't know. We were talking and then she went.'

You walk this way and that across the room, your thumbnail in your mouth. In this whole debacle – after Sadie disappeared, your initial interview, Olivia, your second arrest – this is the first time I have seen you truly unsettled. You've been irritated, gutted sometimes, but nothing like this. It's like you're walking on knives, your gait is strange, your movements quick.

'Is she okay?' you ask.

'I have no idea,' I say plainly, factually, caring more about you than about DCI Day. The nonsensical way parents feel. It wouldn't matter who you were, and what you did, whether or not I handed you over to the police. I would always love you, the boy who grew in my body.

You glance at me across the living room and – I can't explain it – it feels like the first time we have made eye contact in months. Maybe in over a year. Your blue, intense stare burns on to mine like laser beams. 'I . . .' you start to say. You're still looking at me.

'What?' I say, but I only whisper it, not wanting to frighten you. Another car streaks by outside, too fast. We both watch the brake lights disappear into the distance, observe the darkness redescend, rain seen tumbling only in the glow of the streetlamps.

'She can't go to that diner,' you say.

'Why?'

'She's in danger,' you say. 'We all are. Anyone who knows.'

'What?' I stand, my body as quick as an animal's, ready to defend, to protect you. Ready – at last? – for answers.

You pause, swallow, looking at me. 'Sadie's at that diner. And Day – if Day finds her . . .'

I gape, absolutely speechless. It's something people say, isn't it, but it's never once happened to me. Zero ability to find any words. All I can do is stare at you. My whole body goes cold, my teeth begin to chatter. 'Sadie's alive?'

'Julia will be being watched, if she's trying to find Sadie,' you say.

'Why is Sadie there?' I say, still unable to comprehend it. Alive, after all this time. And it's a surprise only to me, evidently.

'Listen to me,' you say, frustrated, anxious. 'I promise, this is life or death. Someone will follow Julia there.'

'Who?'

You look straight at me, now. 'Was Julia at home?'

'Yes.'

'Do you know her address?'

'No, I . . . I barely know . . . she was about to tell me.'

'Was she going to go to the diner?' he asks, but we both know the answer: of course Julia would check out the diner.

'You're going to need to explain this to me,' I say.

'There's no time.' You rush into our hallway, begin putting your trainers on. You struggle with the laces, then the tongues, pulling them out, irritated. 'We need to find out where she lives.'

'She once said it's near the beach – I . . . maybe the police will tell us?' I say.

'Let's ask them for her address on the way,' you say urgently. That laser-beam gaze again.

'Andrew,' I say. I blink back tears. I still need to say it. I need to say it before I come with you – before I engage with you. 'You didn't kill her,' I say softly. You're pulling a coat on, but you stop and turn. Those eyes rove to me again.

'No.' You lower your eyes to the ground, start putting your coat on. 'I didn't kill anyone,' you say dejectedly. I reach for you, now, and I wonder if this is enough. This gesture, this olive branch, born primarily out of my own relief. If it will make up for suspecting you. If you can possibly understand how it all looked. And how, too, I suspected you primarily because I suspected myself: of inadequate parenting.

'I was protecting her,' you add. 'From all this.' You wave an arm, though I don't understand what the gesture means. 'Trying to,' you add softly, and I see now that your eyes are glassy. I close mine in response, lean into the glorious, glorious feeling flooding my blood: calm. You haven't killed anybody. And, more than that: you are good. So good that you will take these accusations and do nothing with them, in order to help her.

'Who is watching her? Who is watching Sadie?' I ask.

'Somebody bad,' you say. Trainers on, one arm in your coat, you blink.

'Who?'

'The police,' you say.

42

Lewis

We're in the backroom, the one full of mad pancake sauces and tinned hotdogs. There hasn't been a single patron since I arrived an hour ago, which is good, because I can't stop fucking crying.

I can see your collarbones, your shoulders a perfect coat-hanger shape. You've lost so much weight, lost the lustre in your now-dark hair, lost the fat in your cheeks. But you're here. It doesn't feel real, but you are.

You're wearing black ballet flats and a skirt that comes to your skinny knees. For the first time in your entire life, I don't see you when I look at you: I see me. You're sitting on a box of Annie's Mac & Cheese, one foot bobbing nervously up and down, the same way I do, and you're looking at me.

It's you. How is this possible? Surely, people don't get as lucky as this? I have never once thought I might be dreaming, but I do, today. My arm has pinch marks on it. I'm too scared to tell Yolanda. I'm too scared to do anything, lest you disappear again, a mirage on only my horizon.

'It's me, I know,' you say, and, as you say it, your mouth forms it: that perfect Little O I had missed so much.

'How did this happen?' I say simply, reaching out a hand to you. It's warm in mine, like a little pocket of happiness.

I scoot over on my box – of graham crackers – that is slowly bowing under my weight. I put mine next to yours, and now we're here, hands linked, and I'm listening, Sadie, I'm listening, but there's nothing you can say that will make me not pleased you're back, and okay. Nothing.

You have gone white. The texture of your skin seems to change with it, becoming dry, lined around the mouth, like a smoker's.

'Are you in any danger?' I ask.

'Yes.' You glance at the door we came in through, and then at another door, a fire door with a wide metal push bar across it.

'From who?'

'I knew it'd happen,' you say. You turn your gaze to me. 'I . . .'

You raise your shoulders to your chin, begin fiddling with one of the chocolate-pudding cans just above your head height, not looking at me. Everything you are doing is so quintessentially *you* that it hurts my eyes. It's so real it's almost technicolour. I have lived with your avatar, Olivia, for a year. My only connection to you invented social media posts born out of bastardizations of phrases you once used. And now you're here.

'I can't come back,' you say quickly to me. 'I can't.' You catch my gaze.

'Why?' I press, but I'm not worried: of course you're coming back.

You close your eyes. 'I can't.'

'Sadie,' I say, and suddenly, I'm a parent again, just like I told Yolanda we would always be. 'We do not care what

343

you have done. We – we have had our hearts broken. And mended,' I add, in case you think I'm blaming you. I don't have it in me to blame you. Don't care enough. I'm punch drunk, a guy so in love he doesn't mind anything at all.

'I know.'

'Have you been here the whole time?'

You nod. 'A grim flat share. Cash in hand.' You tuck your brown hair behind your ear. There is a pale row of roots above it. You've become slack with your disguise, perhaps. Relaxed into it, after over a year.

'Why?'

You rub your forehead. 'You can't protect me,' you say.

'I can,' I say firmly, thinking of everything I've done to find you. Tracking down Andrew, inventing a person, bribing a police officer, forcing her into an off-record investigation, coming here, tonight. How did Julia know? I can't work it out. Don't even want to. I'm happy for this to remain unsolved, for ever, if I get to keep you.

There is nothing I won't do to help you: there is nothing I can't do. All parents are superheroes, for this very reason.

'The summer before I – went missing.'

'Yes.'

'Well, one day – it was hot, you know, pavements-melting-on-the-news kind of hot. Do you remember that heatwave? I left work early, the air con was broken, they sent us all home?'

''Course.'

'There was this woman outside. Two kids, about to be deported. They were just babies.' Outside, someone's foot-steps sound near the door, and you jump. I automatically stand and block it, my back feeling shivery and wary. You glance backwards.

'Are you here alone?' I ask.

But you're too skittish to answer, glancing over your slim shoulder repeatedly. 'Is there someone here with you?' you whisper, and I suddenly realize how this past year must have been for you, in hiding.

'I don't think so,' I say. 'Do you run this place alone?'

'Not usually – but my boss had to go home.' You're completely still, just listening. One more glance is all it takes. I extend my hand to you.

'Come with me,' I say, and you take it. We leave through the fire door. The car park is empty, breezy, and we hurry to my car. You look behind you repeatedly, but I don't look once, my eyes only on getting you inside, to safety.

'Thank you,' you say, as we reach the car, your hand on the door. As your eyes catch the streetlights, you look just like Yolanda.

Inside, it's quiet and dark, and I want to reach right back over this past year, and tell all my past selves that, this spring, you come back. You sit right here in the passenger seat. Home.

You seem keen to explain. You switch off the interior light like it's second nature to hide in darkness – and take a breath and say, 'She needed a passport off-cut, you know?'

'The woman?'

'Yeah. So I . . . we already had some.' You cross your legs at their ankles, the way you always did.

'The dud run,' I say.

'Exactly,' you say, your eyes lighting on mine briefly in the gloom. 'We already had them. It was easy. Anyway, next day: she was there. And the day after. And – well. Eventually, I did it.' A small shrug, just like that. A confession.

'You gave identities to illegal immigrants.'

'Yeah. One first, just that one. Then her kids. I used

to wait for a good match to come in, you know – right ethnicity and stuff . . . and then started deliberately printing dud runs for people *she* knew. Such a slippery slope. Stupid, really,' you say, wiping your nose on your hand, 'but it made them – so happy.' You flick your eyes to me again, assessing me. 'I couldn't resist.' You toss a hand out to your side and it falls aimlessly onto the gear stick. 'Always been a lefty.'

I half smile. You have. And you have no idea, Sadie, that I just don't fucking care. Send me to prison for life, if you like, to have you back. I just don't care. Tell them I did what you have done.

'But how did that bring you here?'

'Someone found out,' you whisper. 'I think someone put it online . . . the dark web, maybe. Someone found out what I was doing, just for those people who really came and begged, and it grew. Someone showed up outside, started to blackmail me, taking a cut. They needed twenty passports, they said, or they'd report me. And on and on. It became – a supply chain.'

Your eyes are on the floor again. Your ankles are so slim, the bones either side like ping-pong balls. God, Yolanda can feed you right up. Doughnuts, churros, whatever you want.

'Not what I had in mind for my first graduate job,' you say, a small, dark slice of your humour. 'They threatened all sorts. To make it look like you were doing it – unless I complied. It got completely out of hand. Fifty passports on order, a hundred. I don't know – you know when you actually don't know how something has happened?' you say, a tiny, wry laugh escaping. That one exhalation contains just a speck of your personality, the one I used to create Olivia, like a diamond that catches and refracts rainbow light for the smallest of seconds.

'I know,' I say, understanding that all too well.

346

'Then we realized that when people sent in the passports of people who'd died . . . rather than cancelling them, we could sell them on. God.' She rubs her forehead. 'It was so stupid. Anyone could have seen I was doing it, if they'd looked on the system. There will be people all over the country living under identities of people who've died, Dad.'

Prudence, I think, but don't say it. So it was you who cancelled the application.

'Who's the guy? A gang?' I say urgently, instead.

You bite your lip, saying nothing. 'I can't,' you say. Your eyes stray again to the diner.

I reach for your shoulder, not letting you go, not ever. 'It's time.'

'But – Dad.' You catch your breath. 'He said he'd kill me.'

'Who? Sadie, we've got to tell someone. We've got to tell the police.'

'But he *is* the police. He's called Jonathan.'

43

Julia

Julia is in the boot of a car. Her assailant parked up somewhere – she has no idea where. She tried to keep track for a mile or two past her house, but she lost it after that. Jonathan hasn't done anything clichéd to her, her old colleague and friend. No gag, no binding. All he has done is betray her, a Brutus to her Julius, happy to dispose of her in pursuit of an enterprise, money, a dark-web syndicate of stolen passports. No wonder he was so content to help her. To help her to cover up and hush up what Lewis had done. To quietly drop the Olivia case. By this time, he knew: he knew she was on to Sadie.

Julia's not yet given up, even though she knows it's futile.

For the first time, in the eye of the hurricane, Julia is terrified. There is no calm any more. She knows she isn't going to be found. Wherever they have arrived is almost totally silent. She can hear only the noises of nature at night. Maybe the distant sea, but it could just be the river, or the wind. Either way, Julia is in no doubt how she is going to end up: dead, and disposed of, by a consummate professional. A man with two decades' experience of what he is about to do.

She hears gravel move underfoot. She listens so intently her ears strain. Is it gravel? It's something loose. Shingle?

With nothing to lose, Julia calls his name: 'Jonathan?'

The footsteps pause. He's listening.

'How could you?' she says. A simple and loaded question all at once.

'It's not personal,' he answers, his voice chilled.

'But it is. It's me – it's – we work together . . . I thought . . .' Julia doesn't know why she is bargaining with him, her old friend. It was obviously never real, never genuine. And arguing with criminals hardly ever works.

'It's a business opportunity,' he says simply. 'It's come a bit unstuck is all.'

'You don't have to do it,' she says simply.

'Julia, this is not your concern.'

'But how – how did you start running these people for identities? Have you done anything else?'

'My whole career,' Jonathan's voice says, disembodied, somewhere outside of the car. 'I have had many mini enterprises,' he says, perhaps a gloat, but that's how Julia knows he intends to kill her.

She blinks, turns her head away from the sound of his voice. She can't bear to hear it. Those supposed detective instincts: duped by her right-hand man.

As she hears him walk away somewhere, she lies back against the cold, hard boot, and she thinks about the moment she worked it all out.

'A question I've asked before,' she'd said to Price, when he finally returned her call. 'But with a different meaning this time. How much for a life?'

'The price to kill?' Price said, same as last time.

'The price to buy,' she had said. Matthew might have

appeared suspicious, but there was something crucial that Julia hadn't been able to overlook: Sadie had worked at the passport office. And Prudence Jones's passport had been sent there. It was that thing again, that piece of information her detective mind went back to over and over again. It was too much of a coincidence. And coincidences don't often happen in investigations unless they mean something.

'How cryptic,' Price had said, one of the few people Julia knew who was exhilarated, rather than frustrated, by obscure communications.

'A life including a passport. How much would this be – on the market?'

'Ah, dealing fullz, are you?' he said seamlessly, and Julia had tilted her head back and closed her eyes, her antagonist forgotten. This was why she dealt with Price: he's a specialist. Only, while her niche is stopping crime, his is committing it.

'Fullz?'

'A full identity. Off the rack, ready to go. A grand, maybe?'

'So – lucrative, then. Second question: what happens to a woman with access to these, dealing in these, who doesn't deliver?'

'Death. No question. Betrayal in gangs is the worst thing you can do,' he had said softly before he hung up.

She knew she was right: Sadie had been trading passports. Matthew was protecting her, happy to look guilty himself when, in fact, he had been trying to stop her. That is what their arguments had been about. That is what the bitcoin transfer was, and why Prudence wasn't ever missing, or reported on the PNC. Prudence was a sold identity, that's all, that's why it said *I have Prudence Jones for you*. She was never a missing woman, only a passport. Half of the missing women in this story are illusions. Half real.

And Matthew had been happy, too, to take away that evidence for Sadie: the dud runs, the bitcoin transfers, the passport she was living under: Gail Hannah's.

Because that is the only reason Matthew would've kept her goods: if she wasn't dead but somewhere waiting for them. A lover's talisman, not a murderer's. And he kept frequenting an anonymous diner. It had to be worth a shot. Where better to disappear, to be paid cash in hand, living under an assumed name that – of course – she had the passport for?

Julia had known some of this before Lewis told her that Prudence's passport had never been cancelled – a sure sign identity forgery was taking place – but she couldn't let him know of her hope. Let him believe he was trying to find Sadie's killer, when, really, Julia hoped they were still trying to find Sadie. She hopes he's reunited with her now.

And when she worked it all out, before and during her phone call with Emma, that is why she sent that final text message, before Jonathan took her phone. Not a text calling for help, not a text to Art, or even to Genevieve: she had protected Genevieve, done her best by her. With her final words, she instead sent a text to Lewis. Not only because this is Julia's job, but because, with her final moments, it was the very best thing that she could think to do: reunite father and daughter, herself be damned.

And here she is, in the boot of a bad man's car, surely damned.

She closes her eyes, ready. Jonathan. So careful with money. So keen to keep it. Of course he found another enterprise.

At first, she thinks it's only her imagination. Cool night air piping in. Noises. She thinks that perhaps she is delusional. Hallucinating.

351

But she isn't. The clunk of the boot. She winces, eyes still closed, hoping Jonathan will be quick.

Another noise.

But Lewis and Sadie are reunited.

And Emma will know that Matthew is good.

And isn't this a happy enough ending? Hasn't Julia done everything right, in the end? She started out on this journey by putting her family before the job, and ended it by putting her job before her own survival, a goodbye to her own family. Neither is right. That's the position she's forever been in.

The smell of the outside air. The slow lifting of the door, like a helium balloon rising up, up, up – and then.

Jonathan.

A single gunshot rings out in the night, a real, full-bodied two-syllable shoot and echo, like close-range thunder, and, after the shot, and after the echo, then there is only the aftermath.

Nineteen Months Later

44

Julia

'All rise,' the judge says, and Julia stands. She is in Courtroom One of Bristol Crown Court. A grand, pale stone building with a balcony out the front that looks more fitting for a royal wedding than a trial.

Still, Julia had often thought it might all end here. The courtroom is where most catastrophes have their grim conclusion, including – as it turns out – her own. Ending in her trial for Zac's murder. Genevieve's crime, dressed up as Julia's.

It's deepest winter. Early December. Outside, it's hard to tell if the sun's only just risen or is about to start going down again; near to Christmas, they merge together, the world in perpetual dawn/twilight. It's later than she wanted for day one to begin. Listing problems, absent jurors; this trial has so far had every setback it's possible to have.

She looks at the bench – a single judge, wearing lavender robes with an absurd red sash – and then at the lawyers, sitting in the bowels of the room, the people expected to defend and prosecute the worst. The defence lawyer is Bill, her brother, in a wig and a robe. He texted her this morning to say he had to get new criminal robes, that he had to get size XXXL. 'I'm honoured,' she had told him, and she had meant it.

'Approach the bench,' the judge says to the lawyers. Julia glances up, towards the public gallery, where Genevieve and Art are sitting, their faces impassive.

The judge is a circuit judge called Daniel Dever – pronounced Diva. Despite his fun name, Julia has never once observed him having a sense of humour, and she could really do with some today.

'If I may begin,' the prosecuting lawyer says, rising to her feet. It's Patricia. She has rights of audience – permission to speak in open court – so doesn't ever use a barrister, but, nevertheless, seems to transform into somebody else when in the courtroom. Her voice a deeper register, her body language more upright.

'Please do,' the judge says, his voice clipped.

Bill looks up, and Julia feels a crest of hope ride up and across her chest. She trusts him. She trusts hardly anybody, but she trusts him with this: her freedom.

The public gallery where Art and Genevieve are sitting is elevated. A wood-panelled box suspended above everybody else. Up there, next to the rafters with the public, the police and the journalists, Julia can see a window to outside. Christmas lights just appearing in the lanes off the high street, spitting winter rain blurring them into kaleidoscopes.

She wonders if her family are ashamed of her, or proud of her, like they say. She can't tell for sure.

The night she got back after being questioned, the night everything changed, she emailed Art, the way she always used to. Within one minute, he'd read it, and called to her to come into his room. She told him about the mugging – a version of it, anyway. Sitting with him in that shabby little guestroom, both on the bed. He listened in the way only Art can: fully.

'What?' he said when she had finished, at first genuinely not seeming to comprehend.

'It was in a multistorey,' she'd said. 'He came out of nowhere. I used too much force.' The lie had come easily to her. She hoped this was the solution Genevieve could live with: a way to pay the price, without paying it herself.

Art had lifted his chin as he looked at her, digesting this.

'I didn't tell you because I was ashamed,' she said, and this sentiment must – of course – have appealed to him, because he dropped his head, rubbed at his hair.

'But . . .'

'You blame my job,' she said.

'Only because it takes so much of you,' he said, and the pureness of his honesty had hit Julia like a clear spring sunbeam.

'There's a lot left for you,' she said simply.

'Why are you telling me now?' he'd asked.

'I need to – I need to . . . it's been hanging over me. Somebody knew,' she said.

'I see,' he said, quietly, in that way that he did.

She leaned her head on his chest, not looking at him, and then she said it: 'It wasn't just that you slept with her.'

Art heaved a sigh that moved Julia's head up and down slightly. 'I know.'

'It was who she was.'

'I know that. If I could go back . . . it is the one thing I'd change. Not even what I did. It would be that,' he said.

'Thank you. Thank you for saying that.'

'It could've been anyone,' he said. 'I was so drunk. I would've – I would've fucked a – a mop.'

A burst of surprised laughter had left Julia's throat and landed in the room like a spark. 'How?' she asked.

357

'It wouldn't even have mattered to me.'

Julia had left his room shortly after that, the unsaid things spoken. But she returned there the next night. And the night after that. She has returned every night since, and hopes she will until – until she's put inside, and can no longer.

Julia turns her gaze back to Patricia. 'The State has a submission they'd like to make,' Patricia utters as she rises to her feet. Julia blinks in surprise. A submission at the beginning of a trial isn't normal. She tightens her hands in her lap, and holds her breath, her eyes only on the lawyers, waiting.

'Go ahead,' the judge says benignly.

'The State would like to withdraw its case. And the charges against Julia Day.'

45

Emma

It's a crisp December day. The air sharp and painful, the rain black outside. But we're here, together. Just us two, tapas, two beers. You're good company. When you were little, I always imagined that we might do things like this, you sitting opposite me, opinions, witticisms, all that, all coming out of the body that I made with my own and that continued to grow outside of me. Sometimes I think people have children to have this sort of moment with their adult child. We made it. We're through. You still need me now, but not like before, when you were little. It's different. Good-different.

A waiter brings us another dish we've ordered. 'Literally, what planet are we on?' you say, making room. 'This is enough for ten people.'

I wave a hand. I've gone back to Cooper's. Money flows plentifully into our lives again. We got rid of the Facebook marketplace bed: gave it away, to somebody who looked like they needed it.

You decided to protect Sadie, despite the risk to you. Despite Jonathan having lashed out at her, bloodied her clothes. She'd left, then, living under a false passport. She'd left you a lock of her hair; a promise she would one day return.

And, you know, when I found this out I thought: God, you are good.

You spent the springtime a year after Sadie's disappearance making amends. You thought you must be a shitty person, for those newspapers, and Sadie's father, to be so sure of your guilt. When you told me that, my heart cracked clean in two. You reached out to anyone who might have got the wrong end of the stick about you, including Olivia: a woman you gave the brush-off to when you'd first been chatting. You got back in touch to apologize for being rude. You apologized to hundreds of people that spring.

But you aren't a shitty person. Every single thing Lewis accused you of was because you were trying to protect Sadie. Stop her selling passports. Stop her associating with the gang in Bristol. Everything.

'I've quit the therapy,' you say to me, out of nowhere. Like all confessions, pieces of information, small nuggets; from you, I welcome it.

'Why?' I ask.

You shrug. 'You don't need so much therapy when you have – I don't know,' you say.

I wait, leaving time for you to say it. 'Your life back,' you finish, eventually. You smile, then, a small, private smile, meant only for you, but, really dedicated to Sadie, who is back, and who is firmly, fully yours, once more. Not that she ever wasn't.

'You know?' you say to me, putting patatas bravas into your mouth.

'I know,' I say.

'You all right?' You cock your head. 'You look – I don't know. Weird?'

'You know, I think I am all right,' I say, thinking that Sadie is the reason you never wanted to move far away. Your own safety from persecution be damned. You stuck around for her. My boy.

You smile, a goofy child's smile, mouth full of potato, and the moment is so normal, but everything that came before it has taken so long that time seems to hover, suspended, for just a second. And then it breaks, and you reach across the table and cover my hand with yours, where it belongs.

46

Lewis

You are here on the sofa, where you belong. You've moved back in with us, and this is what we do every single night. You on the left, me on the right, Yolanda in the chair, the television on low. Sometimes Andrew is here, sometimes not. He's welcome whenever. People still talk about him – about you – but you've got each other. And so you don't care. You wear your love like armour against the world. The gang fell apart after Jonathan was murdered. Nobody wanted to pay a similar price for identity stealing and selling.

'*Come Dine With Me*, no fucking way. The narrator . . .' you say now, bowl of popcorn in your lap, remote control in your left hand.

'He's funny!' I protest, while Yolanda laughs. The back doors are open, even though it's December, freezing. It took us ages to do that. To let the world in again. To feel safe. But we do it, tonight. Winter sweeps its dank smells in, rustling the curtains, but we like it. It feels like freedom, to us.

You shift and stretch your bare feet out across the sofa. The oven timer goes off, and Yolanda gets to her feet, coming back after a few minutes with three full plates that we will all finish. She hovers in the doorway for just a second, a plate in each hand and one on her wrist, the way she's always been able to carry them. I know what she's thinking, because I think it every time I see you, too: we just stand and marvel at how fucking lucky we got.

'The narrator is full of snark,' you explain, even though I had forgotten what we were talking about. 'Snark is over. Earnestness is in, now.'

'Noted,' I say. 'Another opinion. One from the 'gram?'

You glance at me quickly, charmed. Yolanda still doesn't know about Olivia, and we intend to keep it that way.

'Put it on your own,' you say, quick as a flash, your face forming that amused Little O, then a smile, finally, finally, finally.

47

Julia

'It is the prosecution's view here today that there is no case to answer,' Patricia explains primly. A surprised murmur travels around the courtroom.

Julia's chest pops clean with shocked relief. No case to answer. How can that be? The CPS won't bring a case if they don't believe in it. Something must have changed. Julia stares and stares at Patricia, trying to work it out. How can it be that a bullet has sailed past her, just missing her? She's been lucky enough to see it, and feel the shiver as it passed.

She blinks, shakes her head.

Outside is pitch black now, night fully descended by half past four. The courtroom is overly heated, stuffy. Julia waits for the prosecution to confirm what they mean.

'It is the prosecution's view that the evidence against the defendant is insubstantial,' Patricia continues. Julia blinks. She isn't dreaming. It's really happening. 'Despite her full confession and the evidence of the victim's brother, the defence is likely to say, at the end of our case, that there is no case to answer, and so the State is minded to do so now, to save a jury's time, and everybody's costs.' Her jaw is set into a hard line, as though she is tense. Julia tilts her head, looking over at Patricia and thinking.

'That seems like fairly substantial evidence, to me,' the judge says.

'Not so. The confession won't be admissible. No other witnesses. Evidence Mr Zac Jones's sepsis was exacerbated partially by poor wound care and subsequent substance abuse.'

'But you brought the case to trial,' the judge says mildly.

'At this juncture, we don't believe there would be enough to convince a jury beyond all reasonable doubt,' Patricia says, but her expression is sour.

'So your submission is – the State drops all charges against the defendant now?' the judge asks. 'On a causation point?'

'That's right,' Patricia says crisply.

'Very well,' he says. He takes his glasses off. 'Though one wonders why we got this far at all.'

'Your Honour, sometimes things become crystal clear only when one is faced with the immediacy of them,' Patricia says evenly. 'Many a defendant has changed their plea at the door of the courtroom.'

'All right, then,' the judge says slowly, wiping his glasses with the end of his red sash. 'So be it,' he adds. Julia understands the logic – many defendants *do* plead guilty on the day of trial, and they get ten per cent off their sentence for doing so. But none of this has come from Julia. Is news to her, in fact.

'Julia Day,' the judge says. 'You are free to go.'

At this, at these unambiguous words, her head drops on to her chest, like somebody's cut a string that was holding it up. Who cares about the logic, the reason of it? There was never any logic to any of this mess that started with Genevieve's crime and ended with Price's. Julia, for all her cynicism, for all her doggedness, is trying to learn to trust the good news when it comes her way, to treat it like a friend, to regard it without suspicion.

That night, the night it all unravelled, Price had arrived. He'd been following Julia, worrying about her involvement with Nines, a gang member selling fullz on the black market who Julia was sure could lead them to the person behind it all.

Price had used the element of surprise to grab the gun from Jonathan, and had shot him in the head, close range, right there, near his house on the beach; nobody knew it was him except Julia. The police would assume suicide: Price had used Jonathan's gun, cleaned off his prints and left it lying beside him, in his right hand. They would conclude that Jonathan had realized Julia was on to him, and took his own life rather than go to prison.

It didn't seem to matter to Price that Julia had betrayed him. When he found out she was in danger, he acted to save her, and take her home to safety. Nobody would ever know she'd been there. It was the same way he had always been with her: acting from the heart. As loyal as they come.

It would have been easy to extricate herself from corruption, morally: she knew she had found Sadie. She could find plenty of evidence that connected Jonathan to Sadie, and she knew Matthew would testify, too, now that Jonathan was dead.

But doing the easy thing doesn't come naturally to Julia and, that night, she kept herself awake again, this time thinking not about Sadie or Lewis or Andrew or Emma but about Zac, instead.

And, after that, Julia had thought: this is enough. She was blackmailable, corruptible, bent. It could never happen again. She could never allow herself to have so much to lose again.

'I've got to come clean,' she'd said to Art that night on their bed, imploring him. And she had meant it, only her crime had been protecting her daughter, and not herself.

To her surprise, he hadn't judged her. Hadn't suggested that her occupation had finally pulled her into the under-world she'd spent two decades fighting. He'd simply said: 'I know. I love you. I wish you'd told me.'

And Julia does, too. The fractures in their marriage had begun long before his affair. Cracks born out of her work and his resentment, and then her secret-keeping. Julia didn't know the answers to these problems yet, but perhaps Art did.

So she had handed herself in, said she stabbed Zac, that she'd threatened him. She knew his brother wouldn't care whether it was her or Genevieve: she is his true enemy, after all, clearly.

And now here she is. In the dock, her family up there in the public gallery. Art's looking down at her. Last night, before the trial began, he showed her something he had ordered for their bedroom: a skylight, just like at their old house. 'To sleep under. And to worry under,' he had said. 'Builders coming next week to do it.'

Julia had leaned against him like a baby animal with no strength in its legs. Both because of the gesture to save their marriage, and because of the faith that she would be found innocent, would be sleeping in their bedroom again any time soon.

'I won't change,' she'd said to him, their hands linked. 'If I get off – if I stay policing. You know? It won't change. You marry me, you marry the police.'

'I don't care,' Art had said, Julia thinks genuinely. That was the moment she had realized that things may change between them. He'd read every newspaper article about the Sadie story, about Julia's role in uncovering it. And he'd witnessed Lewis's blissful happiness himself, when he had come over to thank Julia.

Art, that night, had said to her that he finally understood it. Both who she is, but also what she does. Which are, to Julia, the same thing. Why she can never do anything else. Why she has to carry on. Why she will be police for ever – hopefully. Art finally seemed to comprehend it.

Julia leaves the courtroom on wobbly legs. Out in the foyer, Art and Genevieve lope towards her. Julia regards them steadily. Her daughter had never wanted her to cover up her crime – initially, and afterwards, too, she said – but Julia thinks she will understand it, one day. Perhaps if she chooses to have children of her own.

She seems happy her parents are talking to each other again, sharing a bed, laughing over morning coffee. She's accepted it in the simplistic way of the young. Only a few weeks ago, she'd said to Julia: 'I wasn't on his side, you know. It was just a stupid comment. I'm not on his side.'

'I know,' Julia had said, even though she hadn't.

'The dreams have stopped,' she'd said. 'Thanks to you, I think.'

And Julia couldn't help but smile. Smile and hope – that she'd got it right. That she is some sort of role model for her daughter, however imperfect.

As Art and Genevieve pass the automatic doors, they judder open, slow and unsteady. A cold snap of December air breezes in as they reach each other, and they stand there, together: free. 'Shimmyshaker,' Genevieve murmurs. 'And thank you.'

* * *

Back in her office, back at a desk – though not her own, following a demotion – and after a long absence, too long, Julia feels truly herself. It's been like pining for an old friend or lover.

A stack of cold cases rests on her desk, and she can't remember the last time she saw anything more beautiful. The curled pages, the coffee rings on the files, the faded cardboard sleeves. She feels a firework of happiness shoot up through her: evidence boxes and forensics reports and crime scene details. Illogical jigsaw pieces eventually fitting together into a thing of beauty. She's home.

Julia starts leafing eagerly through them. She had recalled each one of these, and she hopes her reasoning is correct.

File one. Page one. A missing woman, two years ago, never found, like so many cold cases in the police. She gets the second file out. Page one. A missing man, three years ago, never found. Page two. Nazima Dawood, went missing two years ago. Each person surrounded by Venn diagrams of family, friends, partners, siblings, daughters, sons, parents. Julia, tired already, pushes the hair back from her face. Onwards. Each one at a time.

Because the thing is, Jonathan had worked on every single one of these cases, each one not a file, in fact, or an avatar, or a case reference number. Each person a full-bodied, fully missed individual, and it's Julia's job to find them.

She takes her shoes off, and she gets started.

Yesterday

48

Lewis

Lewis meets Price on a dark street corner. It's lateish, nine o'clock at night, the evening before the trial, and the Christmas-frosted air is dense with favours owed and questions of loyalty.

'This the house?' Price says, gesturing to it.

'Yep.'

'Okay, ready,' he says. Lewis sees just a glimpse of fear cross his features, and he regrets instructing Price, but not enough to call it off. Price would do anything for Julia, Price killed for Julia, she told Lewis in confidence, and Lewis is happy to abuse Price's Achilles heel, tonight, to get what he wants.

'You know – Price?' he asks. 'Why do you do it?'

'What?'

'The informing. You know – you must end up . . .'

'In all sorts of scrapes, you're right,' Price says, but he says it cheerfully enough. He looks at Lewis, just for a second. 'Julia's never once asked me that.'

'She thinks you enjoy the intellectual challenge of it.'

Price's mouth skews to the left in a half-smile. 'Maybe I do,' he says, 'but, really, I send the money to my mother. That

I make,' he adds. 'She's in Germany, but she's very poor.'

Lewis nods in immediate understanding. Family: people will do anything for it.

'All right. Going in.' Price pulls on a balaclava. 'Going in,' he says again, looking at Lewis for just a second. As their eyes meet, Lewis finds himself wondering if Price is ever angry, or if he's happy with the hand he's been dealt, the hand he's chosen. 'Patricia, right?' he asks.

'Right,' Lewis says softly. He reaches a fist out to Price's, who bumps it without hesitation.

'For Julia,' Price says. 'Who still keeps my biggest secrets.'

'For Julia,' Lewis echoes. 'Under no circumstances is Patricia to proceed with the trial against her tomorrow. I don't care what you have to do,' he says. 'All I care about is that she understands that, and she doesn't know it came from me or Julia.'

'A simple threat will do it,' Price says.

Lewis nods. Price knows she was assisting Jonathan's gang, taking a cut of the profits in return for failing to bring prosecutions. He was happy to keep quiet for her, but he's not now.

Lewis gives him a single salute, and then leaves, having done the wrong thing, but the right thing, once again, once more.

Acknowledgements

Over my now eight novels, these acknowledgements have served as a sort of (weird) personal diary, and here's this year's instalment. Last year, I wrote these the night before my wedding. This year, I write them at thirty-seven weeks pregnant, about to find out whether this parenthood business I've been writing about for so long is as I thought it would be.

I wrote this novel through two pregnancies (one lost), a book tour, a house move, a delayed wedding party and my previous novel becoming a global bestseller. I wrote more drafts of this book than for any other, perhaps because of all of the above, but most likely because of that midpoint twist that I was so wedded to, so wanted to make work. I hope I have succeeded. I always hope I have succeeded. I labour and labour over these plots, and I hope you can tell.

As always, I owe a great debt to my agents, and no more so than this year. Felicity Blunt and Lucy Morris mean more to me than almost anyone in my life. I cannot tell you how hard we have worked over the past four years together. This time last year, I delivered *Wrong Place Wrong Time* to them, and we knew something huge was about to happen. As I write this now, it is a *Sunday Times* bestseller, a *New York Times* bestseller, a Canadian bestseller, and has sold into thirty-one countries, and going up by the day. None of this would have happened without them, their careful, pure, wholehearted guidance: everything comes back to the novel. They edited this one with me, and because of them, and their honesty, and their (sometimes) brutality, but also their humanity, I can very honestly say I will never, ever write a substandard novel: they would never let me. That means more to me than anything. Huge thanks, too, go to Jake Smith-Bosanquet, Tanja Goossens and Luke Speed at Curtis Brown: my life has changed because of you.

I am equally indebted to Maxine Hitchcock and Rebecca Hilsdon at Michael Joseph, and the whole wider team of marketing (Jen Breslin), PR (Ellie Hughes), sales and Clare Bowron. We are now on seven for seven bestsellers, half a million sales, a Richard & Judy pick, a Radio 2 Book Club Pick, one tour (thank you to Ellie for looking after me so well in my first trimester! I have strangely fond memories of eating too many crêpes and napping in my hotel room a lot), and the rest. I have never been edited nor sold so well.

Thanks, too, to Zoe Sandler at ICM and to the team at William Morrow. My editor, Lyssa Keusch, Lisa McAuliffe and Jamie Lescht: you took this book on out of nowhere, by an author with poor track, and extremely casually launched it at number two on the *New York Times* bestsellers list. I will remember that late-night call for the rest of my life.

Though it feels incredibly A-List to do so, I must also thank Reese Witherspoon and the Reese's Book Club team. What happened with *Wrong Place Wrong Time* this summer was extraordinary. I think it was the happiest time of my life.

I am indebted to many people who helped during the research of this novel, but none more than Neil Greenough, who this book is dedicated to. He is on hand every day (and night) for police procedural questions, and I couldn't be happier that we met. There is no one better to send a WhatsApp to asking 'How do I buy a gun?' than an ex-cop who knows you're not a criminal.

Huge thanks, this year more than most, to the people who surround me, who love me for who I am. Lia Louis, Holly Seddon, Lucy Blackburn, Becky Hartley, Beth O'Leary, The Wades, Phil Rolls and Lindsey Davies. In pregnancy especially, women need a network of people who will hold how they feel, and I have this in spades.

The twist in this novel belongs, like many things, at least in part to my father, who said very casually over dinner, 'Be cool if she didn't really exist, though.' So thanks, Tone, for the eight drafts it took to nail that, the year of headaches, and the brutal edit from my agents, too. Keep them coming . . . Tandy's All-American Diner belongs to him, incidentally: named after his new dog.

Usually my final thanks, now my penultimate thanks, go to David, the most elusive man to most except me. My now husband and father of our child. I shiver with the thought that it would be so easy for me to have never met you, and my life would be much worse, unimaginably so.

And my very final thanks and hello go to our baby, not yet here, but eagerly awaited. Let's get started. (If you could sleep, that would be great, as I have a new book to write . . .)

'An incredible, gripping, thrilling read'
LISA JEWELL

The new novel from Gillian McAllister

FAMOUS LAST WORDS

'*FAMOUS LAST WORDS* blindsided me with twists and surprises
that had me gasping…and with a poignancy about relationships
and love that one rarely finds in the genre. A brilliant, brilliant
book'
JODI PICOULT

EXCLUSIVE FIRST CHAPTER OVERLEAF

ACT I

THE SIEGE

I

Cam

It is one hour before Camilla's life changes, though she doesn't yet know it.

All she knows, right now, as she cleans the high chair while Polly sits on her playmat after breakfast, is that her husband isn't here. He's gone somewhere, left her to deal with Polly's first day of nursery and her return to work by herself. Has he got a deadline? Has she forgotten some urgent project?

But Cam doesn't forget things. *Luke* forgets things. So . . . ?

Sunlight enters stage left in her kitchen in three distinct shafts. It's a perfect June day, and Cam woke a mixed bag of emotions: nervous but excited, sad, happy – her first day back at work after a long nine months' maternity leave. She sometimes longs for words in the English language that don't exist, and today is one such occasion. Trepidation, excitement; when she woke up, she thought: none of them cut it.

And Luke has chosen today to disappear.

He must have some work thing on. He's a ghostwriter, for MPs and celebrities, and has a co-working space he heads to when he needs to think. That'll be it. She won't think about it anymore. Won't ruminate on it – definitely not, absolutely no ruminating, Cam thinks, gripping the dishcloth too tightly.

She watches as Polly leans forward to grasp a toy that's

sitting just out of reach. She's so like Luke. Lean, blonde, a disposition as sunny as the weather outside. Cam watches as she picks up the toy and throws it, a wobbly, random, baby throw that could be deliberate, could be an accident. Funny, Cam's always liked people watching, but her baby is next level.

Her phone beeps and she reaches for it immediately, hoping Luke has replied to her, but it's her sister. *Morning*, it says, a selfie of Libby sitting on her sofa, dark hair mussed up in a pile on the top of her head. This kind of message is not unusual: Cam and Libby are engaged in a near-constant text conversation. It doesn't have a beginning or an end, just a regular back-and-forth, a tennis match that never finishes. They've been doing it for as long as they've had phones.

Morning, Cam replies, with a selfie of her in work clothes, anxious expression on her face that she didn't know she had until she took it.

OMG yes. The big day. Well – to bolster your confidence . . . look! Look who's 12 down in the Times *crossword!?* It's accompanied by a photograph of a clue, which reads *Author of bestselling recent novel about a hot air balloon ride romance (4, 5).*

It's her client, Maya Jones. Cam is her literary agent.

Cam types back: *Wow! I wonder if this is good press exposure? Do they print the answers next week?*

Libby sends a second photo of a very, very small set of answers for last week with a laughing emoji.

Cam: How many copies you reckon it'll sell?
Libby: . . . Four? What's your cut of four books?
Cam: £8 paperback × 0.1 royalty × 0.15 commission? What's that?
Libby: Drinks are on me, pal.

Cam forwards the crossword to Maya, then puts her phone away and yawns. Polly woke her and Luke last night at ten o'clock, one o'clock, and then some other time, three, four, Cam promised Luke she would stop looking at the time after he said it only upset her anyway. Polly – old enough now, in their opinion, to know much better – thought it was the middle of the day, was absolutely, categorically, not interested in sleeping. Luke had looked at Cam, Ewan the bloody dream sheep backlit red behind him, Polly actually chuckling with mirth, and said, 'Fancy a suicide pact?' And, God, they had laughed, the way they always have. The second Cam met Luke, he made her laugh, and, just like that, she was utterly beguiled despite everything: that he, a writer, was her client, and she his agent. As it turns out, nobody cared about that the way she thought they might.

Cam reluctantly gets Polly ready in the sling to walk to the nursery down the road, trying to accept that Luke, wherever he is, isn't going to see Polly before they leave. The house sits quietly behind them as she prepares to go, a loaded kind of silence which she tries to ignore: it's the day. The return to work.

Cam has had barely any time to process this change, spent the settling-in sessions stress-walking the streets outside, maternal guilt morphing the inside of the nursery into some awful Dickensian orphanage, staffed by ogres.

But now it's here, the day mother and daughter splinter into different existences. She said this to Luke only last night, who joked, 'Oh, bloody hell, are you not picking her up after?' She'd laughed at that. In every couple, Cam thinks, there is a calm one and an anxious wreck, and Cam is most definitely the latter to Luke's former.

Where *is* he?

She goes to grab her cardigan, and that's when she spots

it. On the table in the hallway is a piece of paper with her husband's handwriting on it. As she looks at it, a half-memory of a coffee-scented goodbye kiss from him drifts across her mind, another of him in the shower, the sound of the water running in the distance, both in the veil just beyond deep sleep. So vague she isn't sure that they happened at all.

Luke once said he would always kiss her goodbye. 'I'm never going to be one of those people who just forgets,' he once said. 'Or, worse, a dry peck on the cheek!'

But did he?

She picks up the note.

~~If anything~~ . . . is written on one side. Huh? *If anything*? Cam holds the piece of paper up to the light. She turns it over. *It's been so lovely with you both. Lx.*

Maybe the *If anything* . . . is old. The main note is this one, surely? An end-of-maternity-leave note. It's been so lovely. A kind of *Good luck*, maybe?

There's nothing else on it.

How weird. Luke – a writer, after all – is usually clear.

She finds their text thread. She's asked once where he is, called twice, but she'll text again.

As she stands there, overthinking, Polly strapped to her chest, she finds she doesn't know where to start. Everything's so loaded these days. Before the baby, time alone was just that. But now it's a currency. One person's me-time is the other's solo-parenting. They're not used to it. They've rowed about it . . .

All ok? Sorry to ask again. PS. It's about to happen! The big drop off!! I am to be a working woman once again.

She reads it over, used to proofreading for tone.

She touches the note, just once, sends the text, then leaves.

It is the twenty-first of June, the longest day of the year, and the hottest so far, too, even at eight o'clock in the morning. The sun is as sharp and yellow as lemon drops, and Cam turns her face to it, apricating in it. Huge flowers have bloomed in the street, big and open happy faces nodding as Cam walks by. She points them out to Polly (should Polly be understanding gestures yet?), thinking how much she takes the weather for granted lately. It's been balmy for six straight weeks. No breeze, no rain. The same high blue skies every day, pale at the edges, a deep cyan way up above, as if they're living inside sea glass.

Cam and Luke's lawn has turned yellow and beachy looking. Each night, once Polly is in bed, she takes a novel out there, sits in a deckchair, and just plunges deep into its pages, like diving into a pool containing other worlds. Luke deals with Polly if she wakes. And he knows better than to try and strike up a conversation with Cam, too, during what she calls her introvert hour.

They reach the nursery quickly. A three-storey Victorian building sandwiched between a bank and a laundrette, very London. Cam feels a dart of dread as it looms into view, that distinctly parental mix of guilt and approaching liberty. The thing about motherhood, it seems to Cam, is that most forms of freedom come with a price. But, today, she's just going to pay it, and try to relish it: the return to herself. To the job where she gets to read novels for a living.

Besides, Luke won't be fearing today, won't be imagining Polly not settling or sleeping or eating. Luke is happy-go-lucky, a man who never overthinks. If asked, he would say that the baby will be fine, he's got to work anyway, so what can you do? Sometimes, Luke tries to reassure Cam by telling her she cannot control situations, and there is nothing Cam finds less reassuring than this.

And, nevertheless, he clearly is not fearing today, is he? He's not even here. Gone to work, or wherever, without a second thought.

'Ah ha, Polly Deschamps,' the key worker says, greeting them at the door. Reflexively, Cam holds her daughter's warm body closer to her chest. 'We've been telling everyone about your first day,' the woman continues. 'We're going to have so much fun.'

'Hope so,' Cam says. She takes a breath, then lifts and passes Polly into the arms of the nursery worker – a woman whose name Cam doesn't even know, or has forgotten.

Polly swivels back and reaches for Cam, just once, their hands momentarily touching for the purest of seconds, before she is pulled away from her, and Cam is free, but, right now, she doesn't want to be.

She grabs her phone to tell Luke all of this, to say don't worry, I've done the nursery run, something perhaps slightly passive-aggressive, but that's when she looks at his Whats-App profile. His Last Seen: 05:10 a.m. Huh. She didn't notice it earlier when she was busy with Polly and cleaning up. 5:10 is so early, and not online at all since? Unlike him. So strange.

* * *

Cam walks into her agency's offices and, immediately, the aroma gets her: books. They're everywhere, and it smells like home. Proofs are strewn across the reception desk as she walks past. Foreign editions propping doors open. American copies forming makeshift end tables that people place their cups on.

In the kitchenette, having greeted a few colleagues, glad she used the Tube journey to apply too much make up, she makes a coffee and thumbs through a historical fiction debut someone else represents. She can feel the pull of the words immediately.

1

The streets are so dark they look sooty, lit only by a single oil lamp at its end.

And, just like that, she's in: Cam really could stay here, standing up in the kitchen, and read this whole thing, the way she has done her whole life: the back of cereal boxes in the mornings, *Sweet Valley High* books on the school bus.

She closes the cover and breathes out, thinking.

Look. This is fine. It's fine. Luke is doing something somewhere – she's forgotten what, her mind taken up with Polly, that's all. That's *all*. And Cam's here, with good coffee, books to delve into and to sell, *and* she's being paid for it. She's lucky. She's so lucky. She doesn't need to create problems.

But something is creeping up behind her. A kind of dread. That Last Seen. The note.

A beep.

Also.

A text from Libby. This is how she messages. Often one word at a time. This is how *they* message. Well, this or trading mutual insults, usually, anyway.

Libby: I'm baking a cake for this pissing client thing tonight.
    Is this unacceptable or okay?
    A video of a spinning cake, one side collapsed but repaired with icing.

391

Cam: Definitely acceptable.
Libby: Thanks for lying to me.
Cam: Always.

'Cam!' her boss, Stuart, says, rounding the corner to the kitchen. 'Welcome back.' Tanned, strawberry blond, mid-fifties. Ostensibly benign and somewhat dithery, he has a list full of bestselling writers that hints at his regular displays of brilliance. He is the sort of person you think isn't listening in a meeting, who then makes the best suggestion of anyone there.

'Baby well? Life feeling on an even keel yet?' he asks.

'Oh yes, better,' Cam says, thinking that the house is full of piles of laundry, of unopened bills. The baby doesn't sleep. This morning, Cam showered while shouting nursery rhymes to placate her. When Cam sits in the garden every night, she feels the tasks looming behind her, to-do list spectres that she doesn't have the time to deal with in the way she used to. 'All good here,' she adds brightly.

'Great stuff,' Stuart says. 'It all falls into place eventually.'

'Hmm.'

'Anyway,' he says. He raises his arms above his head – he has been, for the past couple of years, that most toxic of things: a gym convert – and starts stretching. Cam finds the best tactic is to ignore him when he does this, and so she pulls the sash window open, overlooking Pimlico below. Gardens out back, and here, out front, huge white Georgian buildings. She's missed it. The simplicities of a nice view and a hot cup of coffee that she can drink in peace.

'Did you send Adam's novel out?' he continues, two hands braced on the kitchen counter. Cam is worried he's going to start doing squats, but he stops and switches on the kettle instead.

She helps herself to a biscuit, replacing hours unslept with sugar. She discovered Adam's novel while on maternity leave. He'd sent her a query email. She had been checking her inbox, couldn't resist the premise, and asked for the full manuscript. Adam said he preferred to physically post the novel: that he felt like it was no longer his, that way. He'd sent it to her house, since she was off, and she'd offered him representation within three days. The thing is, this work – it doesn't feel like work to Cam. Nothing does that you'd do for free.

'I sent it out last night,' she answers Stuart. 'Couldn't help myself. I think it's going to go big.' She hopes her radar is accurate. Cam knows a good book when she sees one. That feeling you get as a reader, ten per cent in, where you just kind of *sink* into the novel and its world. This one is contemporary fiction about the son of two YouTubers who sues his parents for breach of privacy. She still remembers the moment she opened that padded envelope, read the first line, and thought: *yes*.

'I want to get a two-book deal, but he hasn't sent me a new idea yet,' she says.

'Hmm. You only need a one-line pitch, and it can change. Right, got a crisis meeting,' Stuart says, checking his watch, 'Author going nuts.'

Cam takes more biscuits to her desk and spies more texts from Libby, beginning with *The cake has betrayed me*.

She opens her laptop. She never shuts it down and it currently has twenty-five tabs open, almost all of them google searches.

Baby not finishing meals.
How to stop bickering with husband.
Should my pelvic floor be better by now?

She checks her email. No wild seven-figure pre-emptive offers for Adam's book yet. Next, her phone. Nothing from Luke. Should she ring him again, or . . . ?

Cam doesn't know where to begin. Her brain feels so full. Meetings, submissions, novels about to be published. There's a word for this that she recently learnt: *Fisselig*. A German word meaning, *flustered to the point of incompetence*.

She was mainlining Jaffa Cakes last night with Luke – who never gains an ounce – lying on top of their duvet. She had been moaning to him about, well, everything really. That Polly wasn't weaning or sleeping well. That she didn't know how she was going to work alongside it all. That she felt a failure most days. Things Cam would only admit in the middle of the night, and only to him, the person who never judges her. Luke had listened and offered her more Jaffa Cakes, not suggesting anything, but she didn't need suggestions, just needed him. 'Things feel – I don't know,' she had said. 'Just like they're not getting any easier.'

'I'm chatting to you and eating Jaffa Cakes,' he had said back, running a hand through his hair, past the small scar on his forehead that he got from falling off a bicycle as a child. 'Seems okay to me.'

'We're so unhealthy.'

'Junk food is our only defence,' Luke had said. 'Don't rob me of my pleasure in life. Look – when you go back, why don't you take an evening a week off Mum duty? I'll do bedtime. You go and do something. With Libby? Holly? A bar. The cinema.'

Cam had grimaced, though she'd appreciated the gesture. Going out would suit Luke, but not Cam. 'I like to go to bed with a book,' she'd said, sounding meek, but it was true. A paperback novel, pages rough under her fingertips. A candle.

Fresh pyjamas and sheets. Motherhood, for introverts, is a special kind of difficult, the usual escape routes not available, a thought Cam regularly feels guilty about, but is nevertheless true.

'You do that every night,' Luke had said, leaning over to touch her shoulder affectionately.

'I know that. I know I am lame.'

'Everyone needs a break. You need – space.' His expression became more serious. 'Cam – you ever drowning . . . you shout? And I'll rescue you. Okay?'

She'd nodded, so thankful she had married a man she could say anything to, but now, she thinks about that first statement.

Everyone needs a break. It contained a darkness within it, didn't it? Is *this* Luke getting *space*?

Has he actually been slightly huffy recently? Cam ponders it, trying not to spiral. Maybe. She heard him heave an irritated, lengthy sigh the other night when Polly woke; his footsteps as he got out of bed were heavy. When he'd returned, and she'd asked what she had wanted, he had ignored her, scrolled on his phone, his jaw tight. Uncharacteristic: Cam has remembered it for this reason.

No, but they went to a wedding last week, and he had been fine, then, hadn't he? They'd fallen into their old dynamic. He'd coaxed her onto the dance floor even though she categorically does not dance. 'You protest,' he'd said, waistcoat unbuttoned, 'but you dance so well with me.' She'd cajoled him back home at midnight; he had laughed when he'd seen she'd brought a pair of slippers in her handbag to wear in the taxi home.

God, she can't concentrate. The book on submission and Polly's first full day away from her and Luke's absence. They make Cam have that strange but familiar urge to check and check and check again. Emails, the nursery app. Anything.

Something comes in from Adam.

Adam@amazingadam.com
21 June
09:23
Subject (no subject)

No, no idea for a second novel yet. How urgent is it? I have a small-town whodunnit kind of thing on the back burner?

Cam hides a grimace and tells him to keep thinking, hoping he will read between the lines.

She grabs her phone and tries Luke again. *Welcome to the Vodafone messaging service.*

She sends another text: *I've had loads of office biscuits as well as those Jaffas! x*

Luke and Cam met when he walked into her office nine years ago. He was a journalist who had ghostwritten a memoir by a football manager about a Premier League team's rise to success: he'd been a jobbing journalist and had DMd the manager on social media (as a bet on a stag do, he'd later told her) who, to his surprise, had replied saying yes. Cam had enjoyed it a lot more than she expected to. Luke's prose was upfront, transparent, didn't purport to be anything other than what it was: pure entertainment.

Cam had offered him representation. He had replied with a single word: *Shit!* It had made Cam smile. She likes language in all its forms, and a well-timed swear word is the best.

She had sold the memoir to Penguin Random House. His next gig was an autobiography for a singer-songwriter her agency represented and, after that, he was up and running, established, and needing a little less agenting, which made it a lot easier for Cam to kiss him several months into their working relationship at a rainy London bus stop after too many glasses of wine. It was late summer, the mornings and evenings just beginning to smell as crisp and cold as apples. Luke had been in a T-shirt that got soaked in the downpour, and to this day, damp clothing reminds Cam of that night, that kiss, that illicit, shouldn't-be-doing-this kiss.

Anyway. Can't concentrate on a word, she continues to Luke. She waits eagerly for his response. *Just have an easy morning today!!* he will no doubt say, but she needs to hear it, needs to see his words to her. Cam makes Luke more sensible and Luke makes Cam have fun. That's how they work. That's the way they have always worked.

She sends a test WhatsApp, next. *Hello?* But . . . it doesn't deliver. She stares at it. A single grey tick. When . . . when do you begin to really worry?

No. He must actually be working hard. Phone off.

But the dread Cam felt in the kitchen rears its head again. She's kidding herself. Something is off.

She calls him again.

Nothing.

At what point is he – missing?

A text from Libby comes through, then a photo. She'll be running an outfit by Cam, as she often does. She catches one part of it – *It's for a party!! That's where people get together and have fun? Are you aware? LOL* – but she stops reading it, because that's when she hears it. Some sort of commotion outside. Is that sirens?

Fear runs its fingertip lightly up her spine, and Cam's imagination fires into action, fuelled by the books she reads

397

and works on. Things that only happen to other people could happen to me, she finds herself thinking. Ambulances, fire engines, warning sirens. Dead bodies and bad news and police hats held in hands and *we tried everything we could* said by kind doctors in green scrubs.

She rises from her desk. She'll just check outside, beyond the foyer. See what's going on.

Their receptionist is sitting in silence, the only noise the television on the wall cycling through news stories. Cam can't hear anything else.

It must be her imagination. Nothing more.

But then everything happens all at once, the way it sometimes does.

'We pause for a moment, here,' the news presenter on the television says, something unusual and grave in her tone, 'to bring you breaking news from central London.'

As Cam watches, the screen goes black and *BREAKING* flashes across it in white text. The voiceover switches to a male broadcaster. 'Police are trying to end a siege that began an hour ago in central London.' A grainy image appears on the screen. Cam stares at it, but she can't make it out. 'A man has taken three hostages in a warehouse in London. We have exclusive CCTV footage from a security guard on duty. Authorities are present at the scene and believe it to be a hostile act.'

Before Cam can digest this, she spots them outside: police.

Two officers, white shirts and black stab vests, no caps in hands but otherwise just the way she imagined, striding into her workplace. And Cam knows, somehow, in some deep dark place inside her, that they're here for her. She tells herself she is being stupid, highly-strung because of Luke's unread texts and absence, but that's the precise moment that she hears them say her name.

2

Cam's legs feel imaginary, too light. She walks across the foyer and could swear she's four inches from the ground, a ghost floating around a literary agency. It must be shock. Fear.

'That's me,' she finds herself saying loudly in the foyer. 'Camilla.'

'Are you the wife of Luke Deschamps?' One of the coppers turns from talking to the receptionist and looks directly at Cam.

'Yes,' she says quickly, thinking that at least it's not Polly. How strange it is the way the order of disasters inverts post-baby.

It's been so lovely with you both. What did he mean by that? Was that – a *goodbye*?

'DS Steven Lambert,' one of the coppers says. Late-thirties maybe. Pale, freckled. He's accompanied by a woman who introduces herself as PC Emma Smith. She has with her a notepad and biro, just holding them, standing there like a journalist from the eighties.

'Have you got time to have a quick chat?' Smith says, her tone gentle, but in the way somebody is when they've been told to do it.

'What's happened?'

'Is there somewhere we can . . .'

Cam indicates a meeting room off the foyer without thinking, wanting only information, and as quickly as possible.

'Is Luke okay?' she asks.

'Yes.'

Cam's shoulders drop six feet. In her relief, she bursts into an occupied room, apologizes, and heads to the one next door.

Steven Lambert meets her gaze and he looks tired. He might be almost forty, is a cliché of a workaholic. Dark circles, coffee on his breath. 'There is a hostage situation unfolding,' he says plainly.

'I saw it – on the news,' Cam says, blinking. Stunned that these two pieces have connected together: the police and the news story. Maybe she's dreaming. Maybe she's reading a novel.

'A siege. A man has taken three hostages in a warehouse in Bermondsey.'

Bermondsey. Luke's co-working space is in Bermondsey, and the word hits Cam with the strength of an anvil. She feels utterly disorientated, *Bermondsey* reverberating around her skull. Cartoon stars appear above her head. Her neck goes hot, a rising tide of blood working its way towards her face like a filling bath. She brings her hands to her chest and feels her pulse in both wrists.

'Oh my God,' Cam says. She brandishes her phone. 'That's why . . . is he okay?' And then she adds, to explain: 'I texted him – he . . . has someone got him?'

Lambert hesitates, and something about the gravity in his expression makes Cam stop speaking. He shifts in his seat, his shirt moving slightly up his arm, revealing a wrist tattoo. Cam can't quite make it out, some swirled symbol or other.

His eyes meet hers. 'Your husband hasn't been taken.'

'Oh! Good!'

'He is the person who has taken the hostages,' he finishes quietly.

3

Somewhere, in some previously inaccessible part of Cam's brain, a trapdoor opens, and she begins falling through it. 'What? No he isn't,' she says, the notion so absurd to her that Lambert merely needs to be corrected. As she looks at him, he shifts, and his tattoo disappears once more.

Cam's colleagues have begun clustering in the foyer. Because of the news, or the police, she isn't sure, and she becomes momentarily distracted by them. Instead of processing what's being said to her, she is trying to work out what her colleagues must be thinking, in that strange way people in crisis focus on the wrong thing sometimes.

'He's taken hostages?' she says to Lambert.

He wordlessly hands her a phone displaying a video on which he presses play. It's the same one the news had on.

In the centre of the frame are three hostages, sitting silently on three wooden chairs. They have their heads covered with black material, like something from a film. They're so motionless it looks like a freeze-frame, until she sees that they're breathing. The slightest rise and fall of their shoulders. Three sentient, terrified beings, taken.

It's grainy CCTV, hard to make out. For a few seconds, all is still, but then the hostage-taker steps into view.

Tall and slim, all in dark clothes, he moves in front of them, left to right, five, six, seven steps, then pauses, about to turn and move in the other direction. His walk, the shape of his arms . . . Cam sits very still, watching this eerily familiar man.

And then he turns and looks properly at the camera. It's just a glimpse, no more than a second.

But it is him.

It's him.

'I read it in a breathless day and a half - I loved every page, every character, every twist and turn'

LISA JEWELL

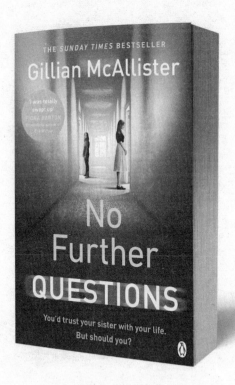

NURTURING WRITERS SINCE 1935

'A terrific premise, delivered
with panache'

CLARE MACKINTOSH

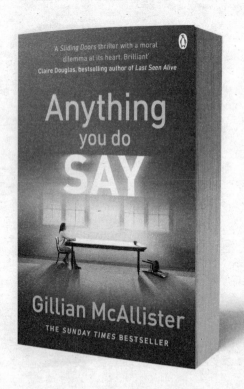

'A *Sliding Doors* thriller with a moral
dilemma at its heart. Brilliant'
Claire Douglas, bestselling author of *Last Seen Alive*

Anything
you do
SAY

Gillian McAllister

THE *SUNDAY TIMES* BESTSELLER

NURTURING WRITERS SINCE 1935

'A gripping, compelling page-turner that kept me up half the night'

LIZ NUGENT

Gillian McAllister

'Perfection. Intriguing and compelling.
An exceptional debut'
Clare Mackintosh, no.1 bestselling author of *I See You*

Everything

but the

TRUTH

We're all hiding something

NURTURING WRITERS SINCE 1935

'Brilliantly compelling... both grips and thrills'

LUCY CLARKE

NURTURING WRITERS SINCE 1935

You can run, you can hide...
But can you disappear for good?

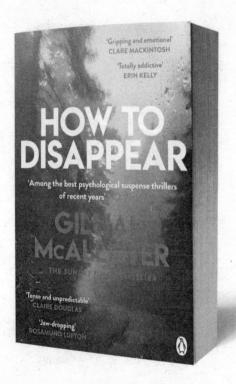

NURTURING WRITERS SINCE 1935

What would you do to protect your family?

THE INTERNATIONAL BESTSELLING PHENOMENON

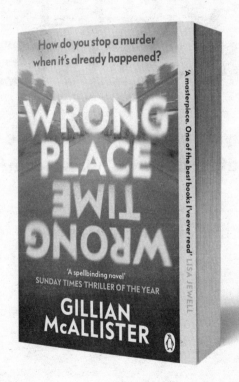

How do you stop a murder when it's already happened?

'A masterpiece. One of the best books I've ever read' LISA JEWELL

WRONG PLACE TIME WRONG

'A spellbinding novel'
SUNDAY TIMES THRILLER OF THE YEAR

GILLIAN McALLISTER

NURTURING WRITERS SINCE 1935

GILLIAN McALLISTER

Stay in touch with Gillian and get the latest news via her newsletter at

https://bit.ly/mcallister-newsletter

STAY IN TOUCH